Tomo

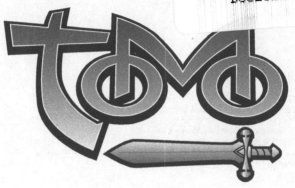

Betrayal of Trust

ZONDERVAN

Betrayal of Trust
Copyright © 2009 by Funnypages Productions, LLC

Requests for information should be addressed to:
Zondervan, *Grand Rapids, Michigan* 49530

Library of Congress Cataloging-in-Publication Data

Krueger, Jim.
  Betrayal of trust / story by Jim Krueger ; art by Ariel Padilla ; created by Tom
Bancroft and Rob Corley.
      p. cm. — (Tomo ; v. 7)
    "Published in conjunction with Funnypages Productions" — Verso t.p.
   Summary: Hana and Tomo rejoin Jou and the rebel forces in Argon Falls, and
Hana learns that the leader of the rebellion is her father.
   ISBN 978-0-310-71306-7 (softcover)
1. Graphic novels. [1. Graphic novels. 2. Fantasy. 3. Christian life—Fiction.] I.
Padilla, Ariel, 1968- ill. II. Bancroft, Tom. III. Corley, Rob. IV. Title.
   PZ7.7.K78Be 2009
   741.5'973—dc22

                                                        2009018217

Any Internet addresses (websites, blogs, etc.) and telephone numbers printed in
this book are offered as a resource. They are not intended in any way to be or
imply an endorsement by Zondervan, nor does Zondervan vouch for the content
of these sites and numbers for the life of this book.

This book published in conjunction with Funnypages Productions, LLC, 106
Mission Court, Suite 704, Franklin, TN 37067

Series Editor: Bud Rogers
Managing Art Director: Merit Kathan

Printed in the United States of America

09 10 11 12 13 /QG/ 5 4 3 2 1

BETRAYAL OF TRUST

SERIES EDITOR
BUD ROGERS

STORY BY
JIM KRUEGER

ART BY
ARIEL PADILLA
WITH **NOEL RODRIGUEZ** AND **DAN BORGOÑOS**

CREATED BY
TOM BANCROFT AND **ROB CORLEY**

funnypages
PRODUCTIONS

ZONDERVAN®

ZONDERVAN.com/
AUTHORTRACKER
follow your favorite authors

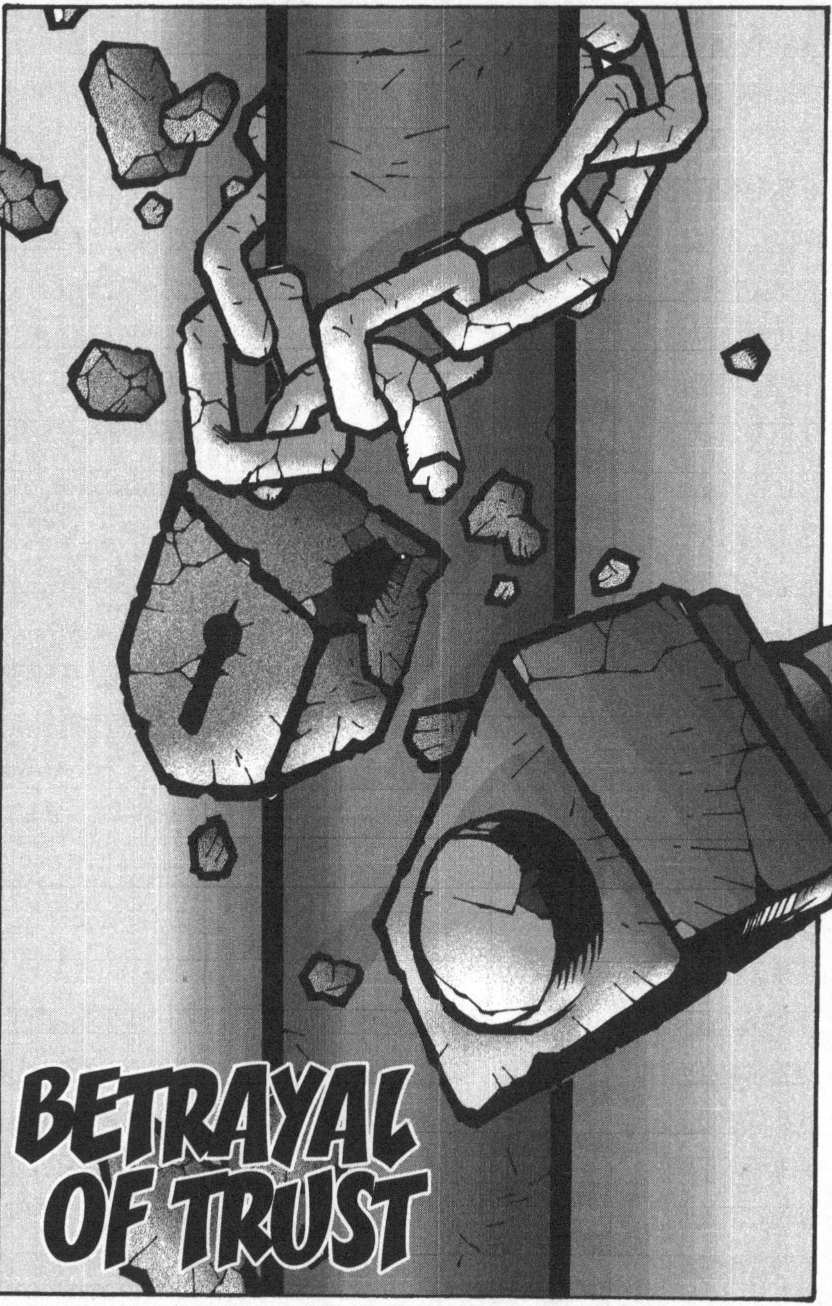
BETRAYAL
OF TRUST

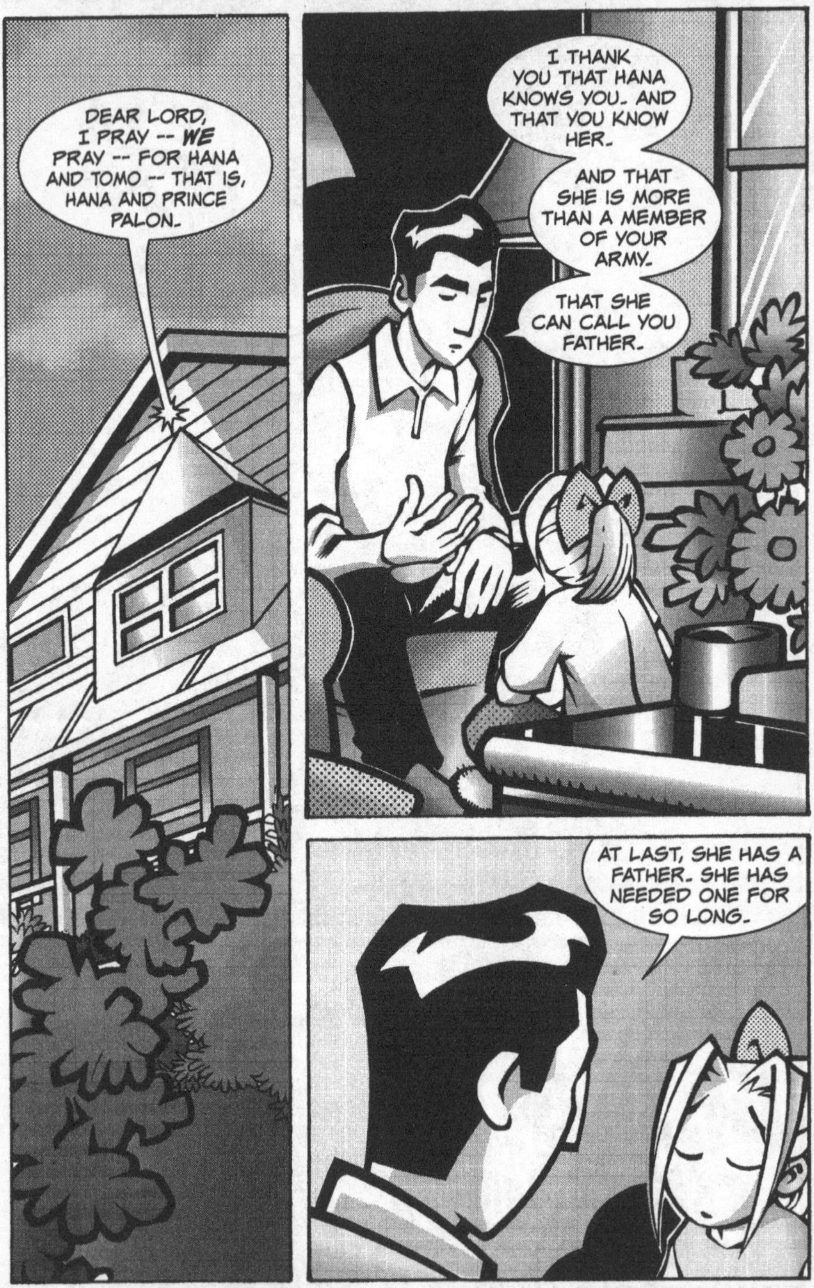
DEAR LORD, I PRAY -- WE PRAY -- FOR HANA AND TOMO -- THAT IS, HANA AND PRINCE PALON.
I THANK YOU THAT HANA KNOWS YOU. AND THAT YOU KNOW HER.
AND THAT SHE IS MORE THAN A MEMBER OF YOUR ARMY.
THAT SHE CAN CALL YOU FATHER.
AT LAST, SHE HAS A FATHER. SHE HAS NEEDED ONE FOR SO LONG.

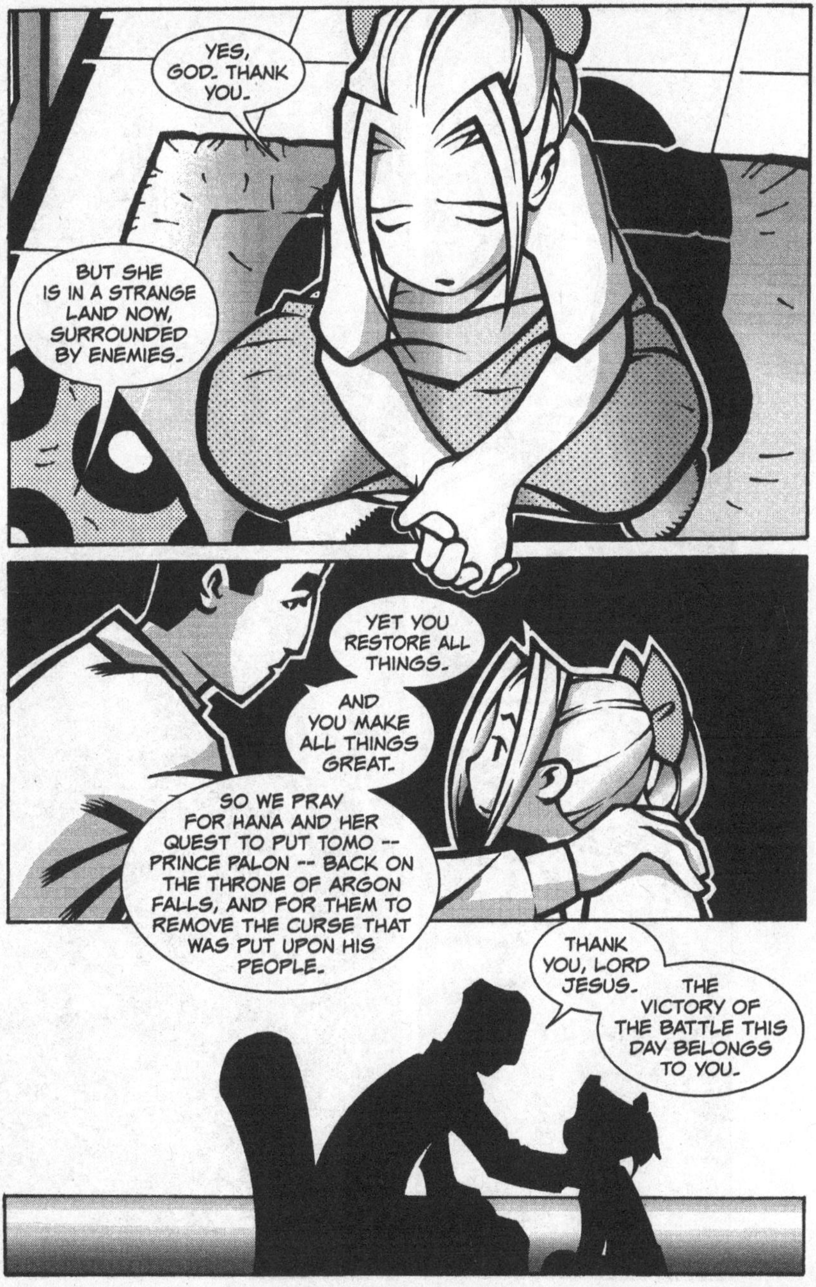
YES, GOD. THANK YOU.
BUT SHE IS IN A STRANGE LAND NOW, SURROUNDED BY ENEMIES.
YET YOU RESTORE ALL THINGS.
AND YOU MAKE ALL THINGS GREAT.
SO WE PRAY FOR HANA AND HER QUEST TO PUT TOMO -- PRINCE PALON -- BACK ON THE THRONE OF ARGON FALLS, AND FOR THEM TO REMOVE THE CURSE THAT WAS PUT UPON HIS PEOPLE.
THANK YOU, LORD JESUS.
THE VICTORY OF THE BATTLE THIS DAY BELONGS TO YOU.

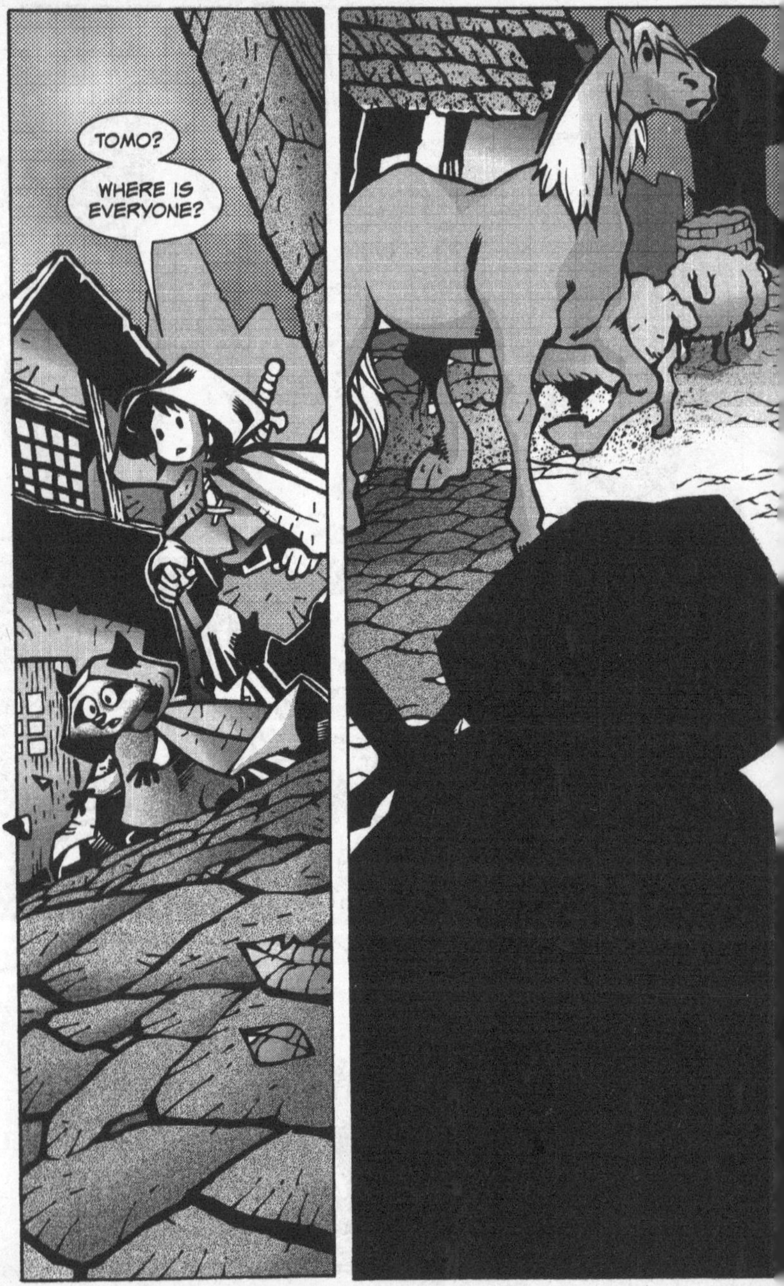
TOMO?
WHERE IS EVERYONE?

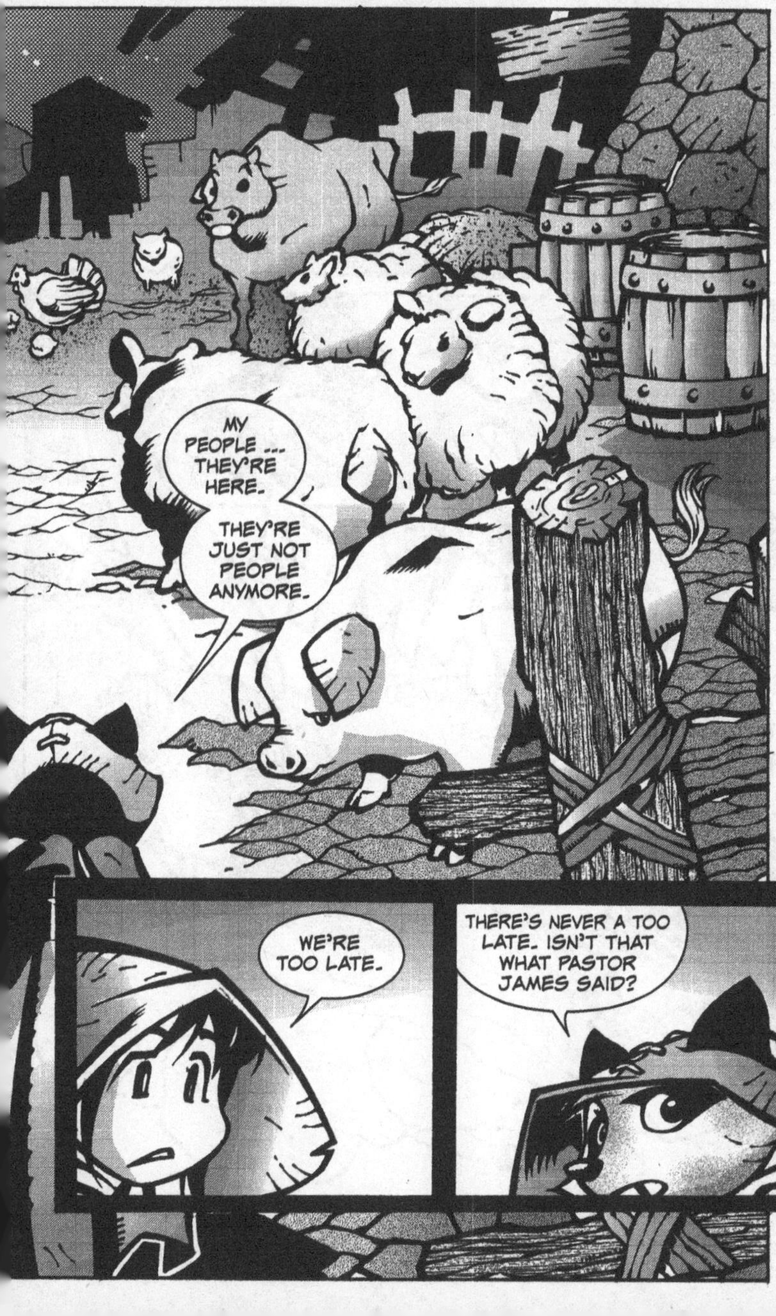
MY PEOPLE ... THEY'RE HERE.
THEY'RE JUST NOT PEOPLE ANYMORE.
WE'RE TOO LATE.
THERE'S NEVER A TOO LATE. ISN'T THAT WHAT PASTOR JAMES SAID?

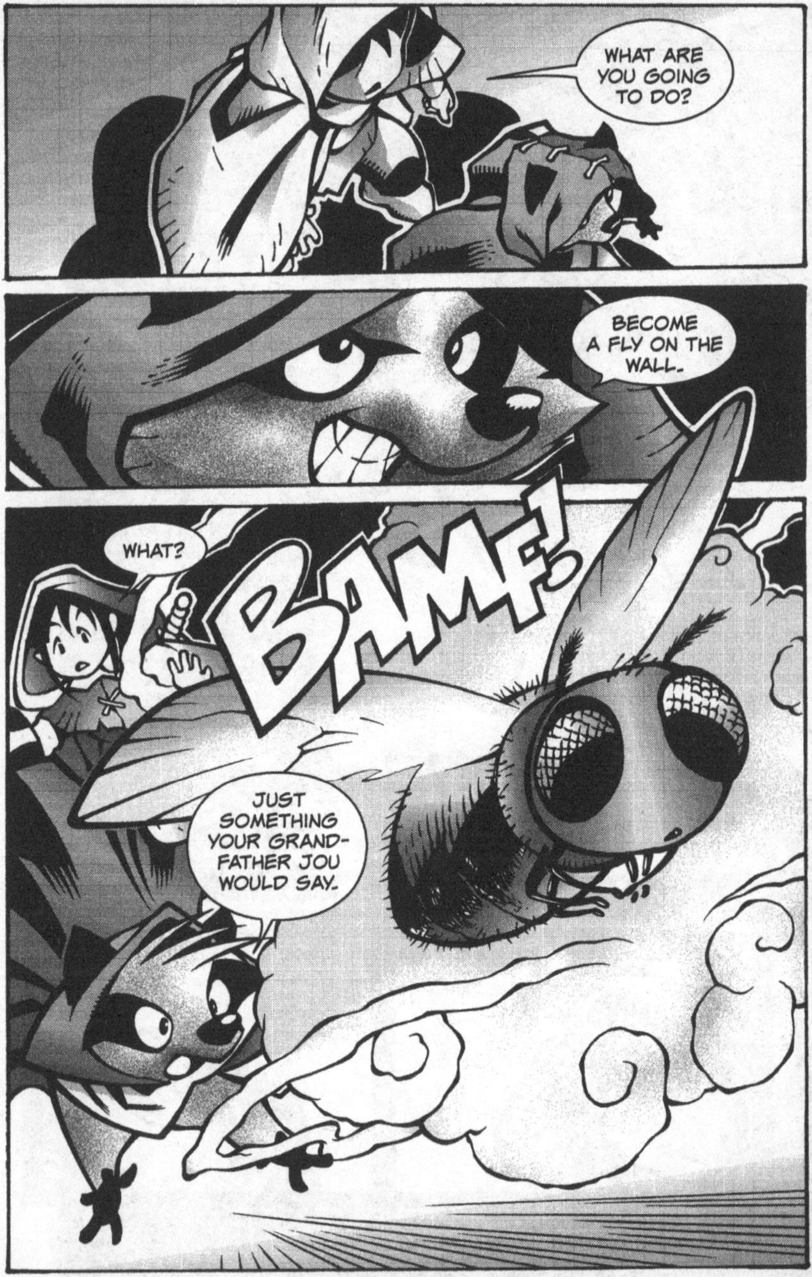

WHAT ARE YOU GOING TO DO?
BECOME A FLY ON THE WALL.
WHAT?
BAMF!
JUST SOMETHING YOUR GRAND-FATHER JOU WOULD SAY.

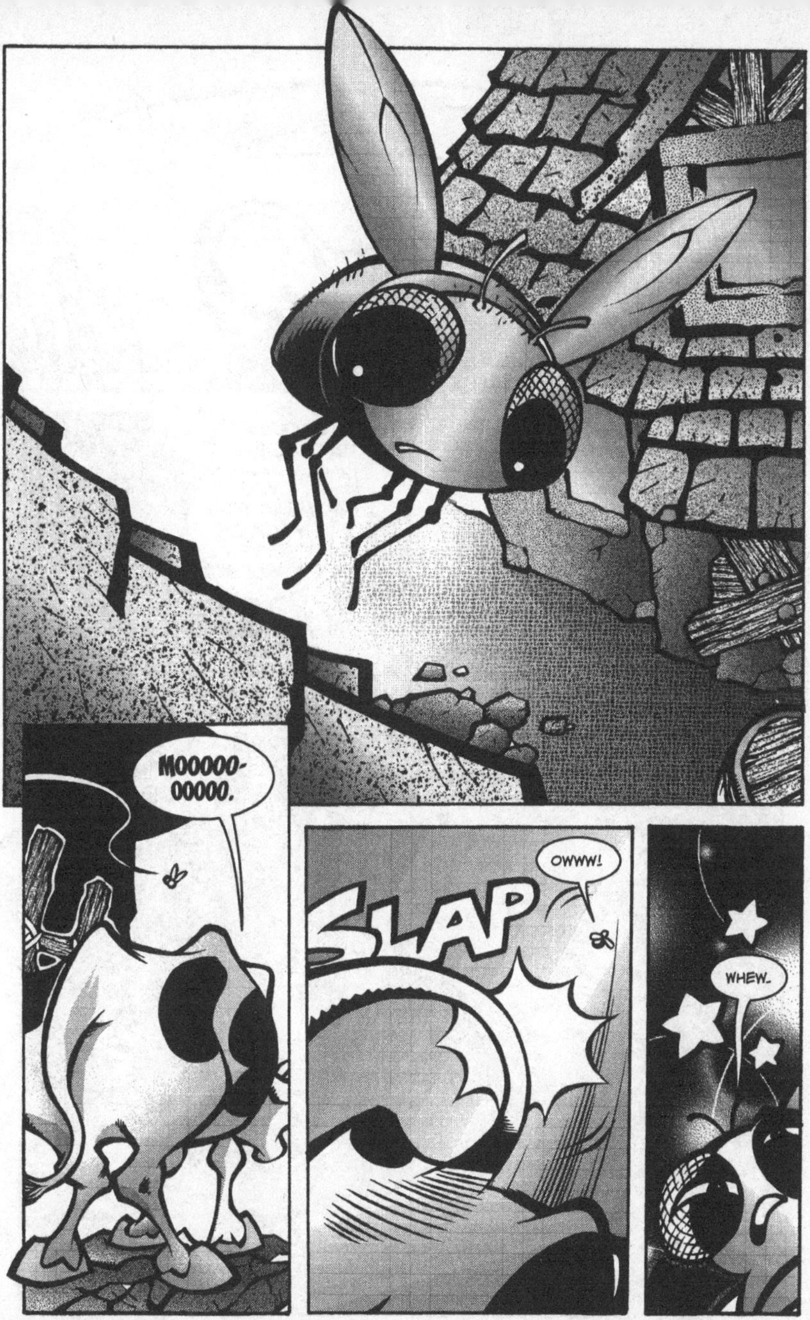
MOOOOO-
OOOOO.
SLAP
OWWW!
WHEW.

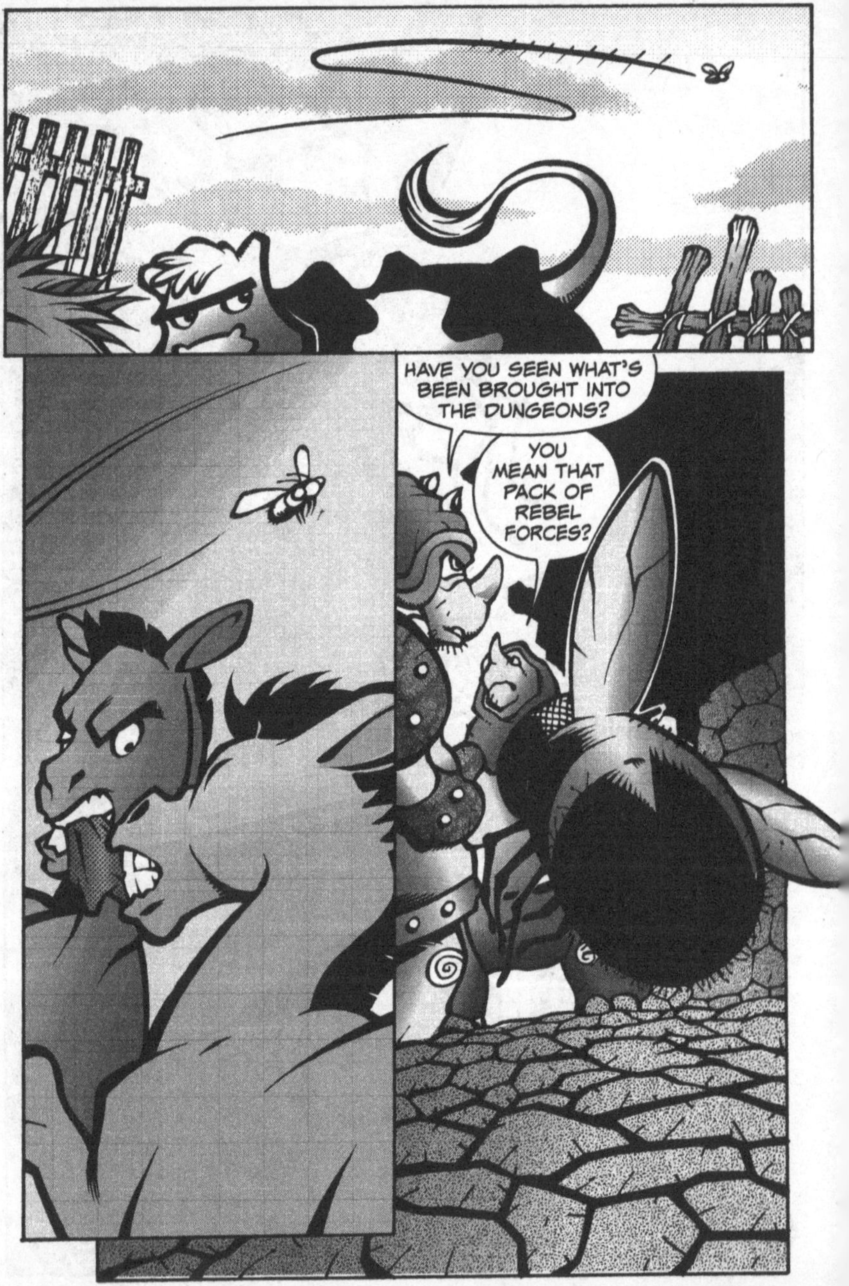
HAVE YOU SEEN WHAT'S BEEN BROUGHT INTO THE DUNGEONS?
YOU MEAN THAT PACK OF REBEL FORCES?

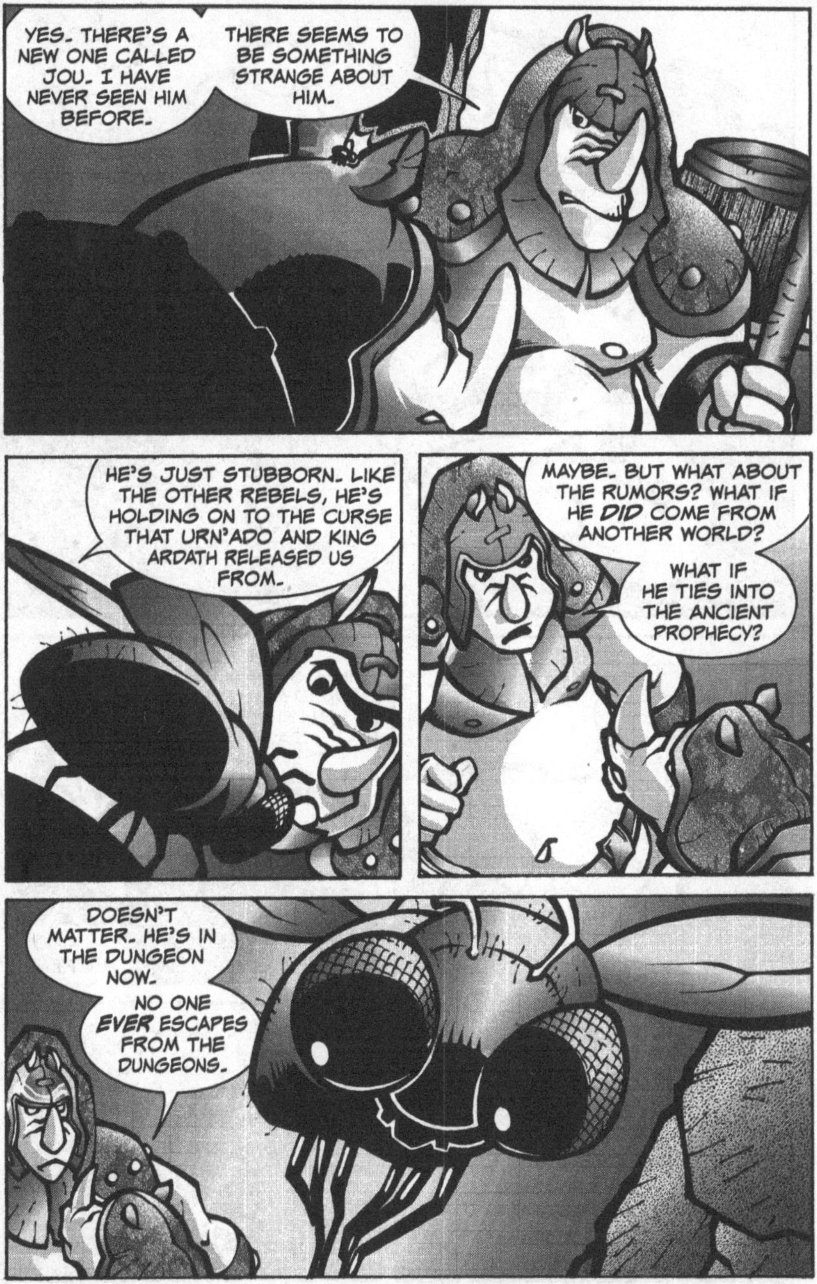
YES. THERE'S A NEW ONE CALLED JOU. I HAVE NEVER SEEN HIM BEFORE.
THERE SEEMS TO BE SOMETHING STRANGE ABOUT HIM.
HE'S JUST STUBBORN. LIKE THE OTHER REBELS, HE'S HOLDING ON TO THE CURSE THAT URN'ADO AND KING ARDATH RELEASED US FROM.
MAYBE. BUT WHAT ABOUT THE RUMORS? WHAT IF HE DID COME FROM ANOTHER WORLD?
WHAT IF HE TIES INTO THE ANCIENT PROPHECY?
DOESN'T MATTER. HE'S IN THE DUNGEON NOW.
NO ONE EVER ESCAPES FROM THE DUNGEONS.

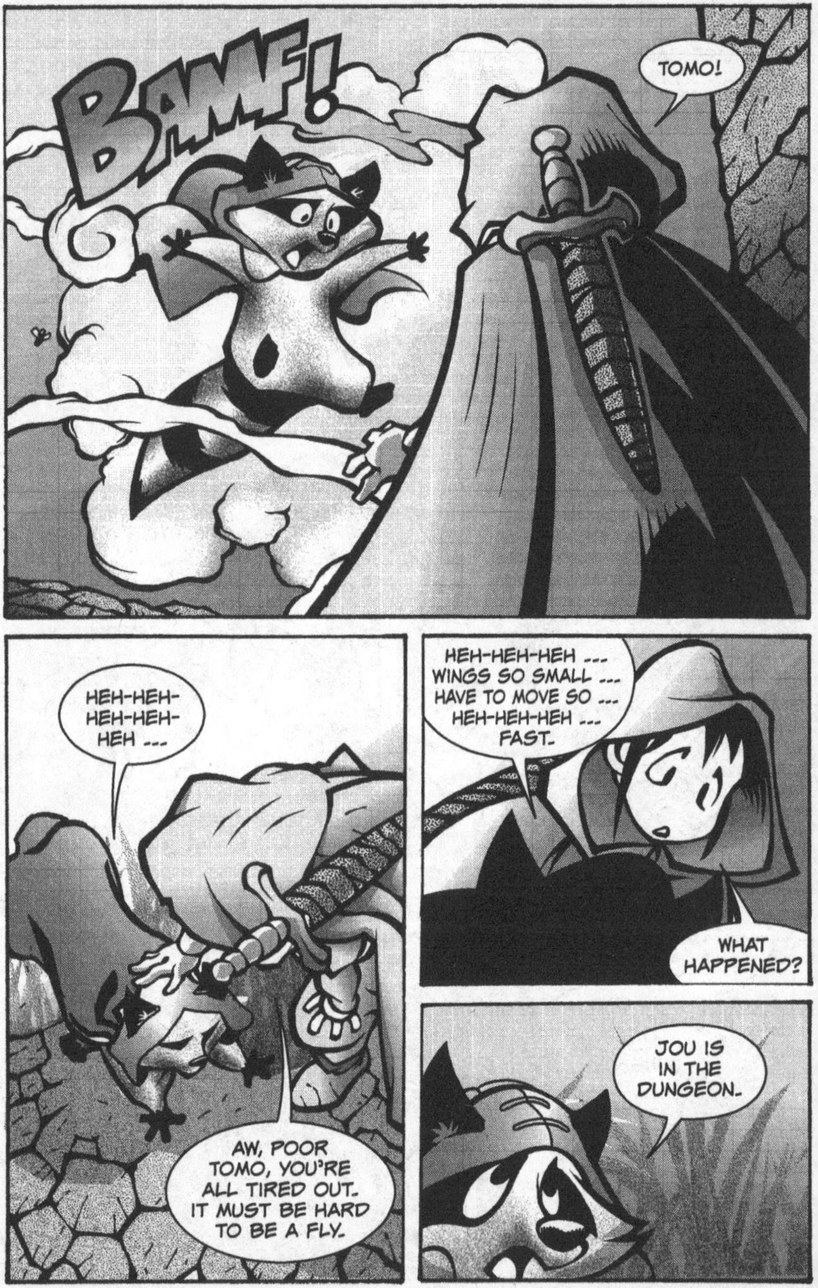
BAMF!
TOMO!
HEH-HEH-HEH-HEH-HEH ...
AW, POOR TOMO, YOU'RE ALL TIRED OUT. IT MUST BE HARD TO BE A FLY.
HEH-HEH-HEH ... WINGS SO SMALL ... HAVE TO MOVE SO ... HEH-HEH-HEH ... FAST.
WHAT HAPPENED?
JOU IS IN THE DUNGEON.

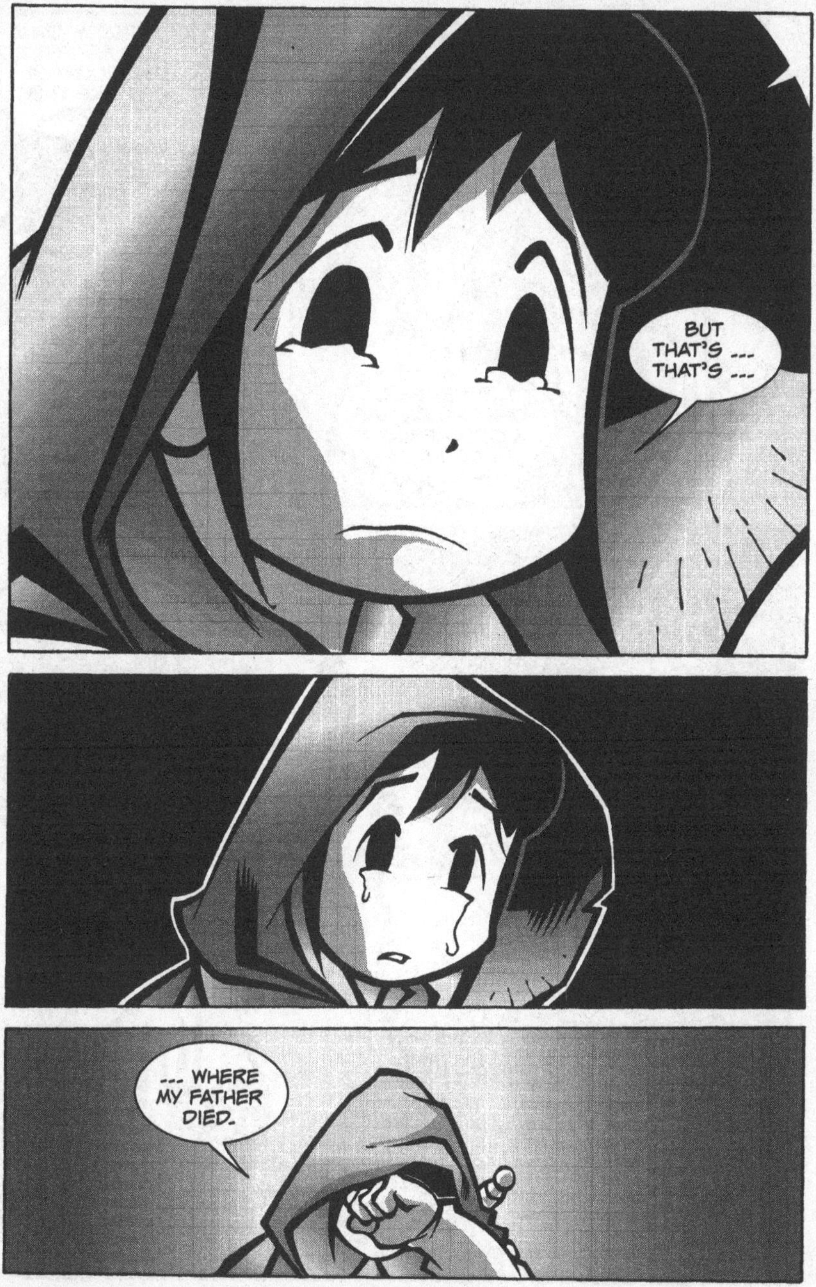
BUT THAT'S --- THAT'S ---
--- WHERE MY FATHER DIED.

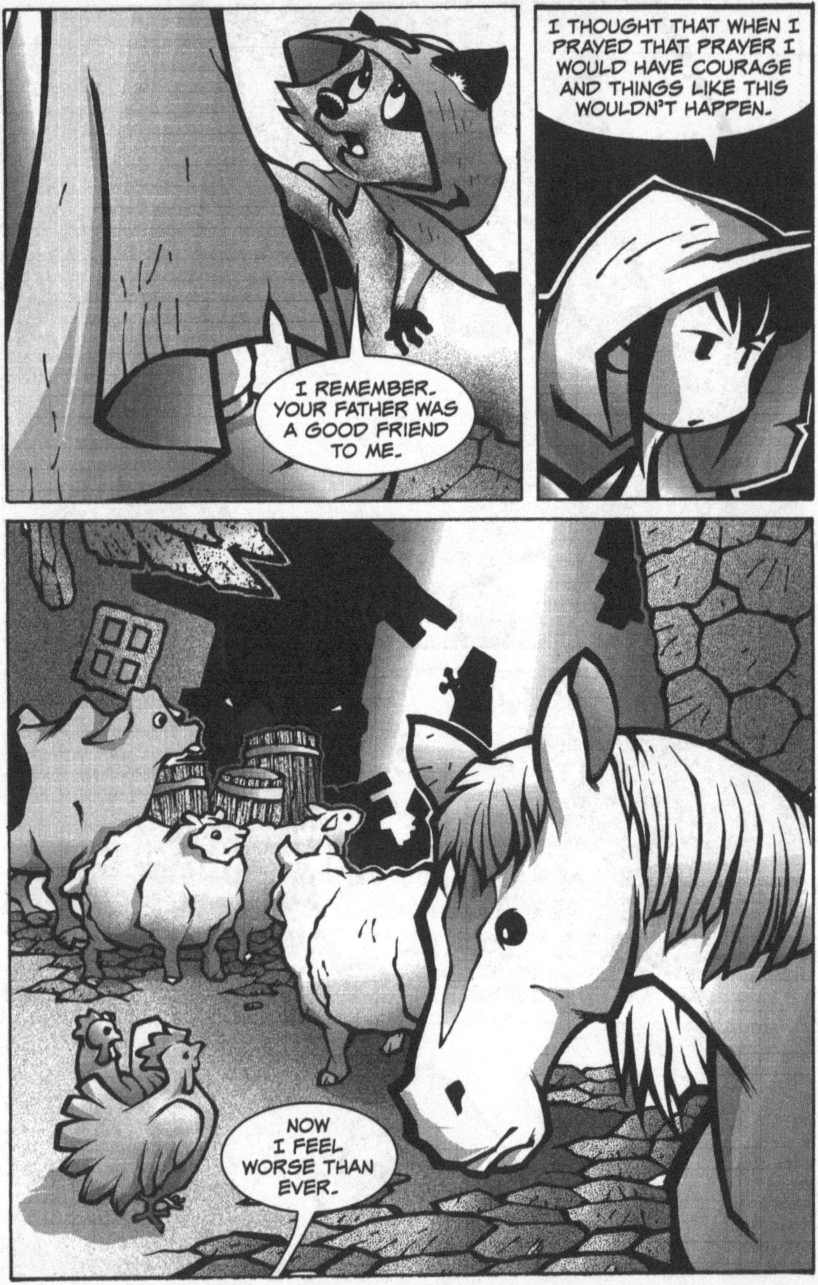
I REMEMBER. YOUR FATHER WAS A GOOD FRIEND TO ME.
I THOUGHT THAT WHEN I PRAYED THAT PRAYER I WOULD HAVE COURAGE AND THINGS LIKE THIS WOULDN'T HAPPEN.
NOW I FEEL WORSE THAN EVER.

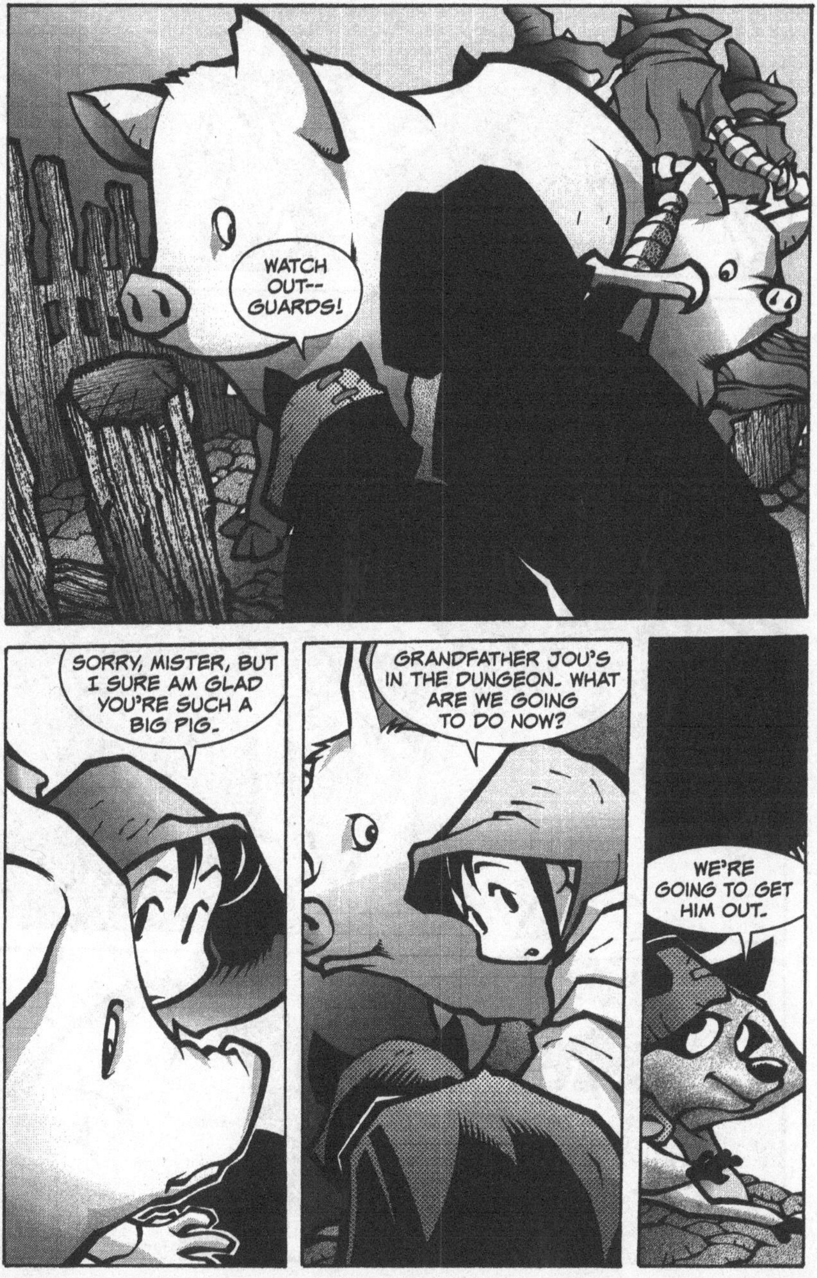
WATCH OUT-- GUARDS!
SORRY, MISTER, BUT I SURE AM GLAD YOU'RE SUCH A BIG PIG.
GRANDFATHER JOU'S IN THE DUNGEON. WHAT ARE WE GOING TO DO NOW?
WE'RE GOING TO GET HIM OUT.

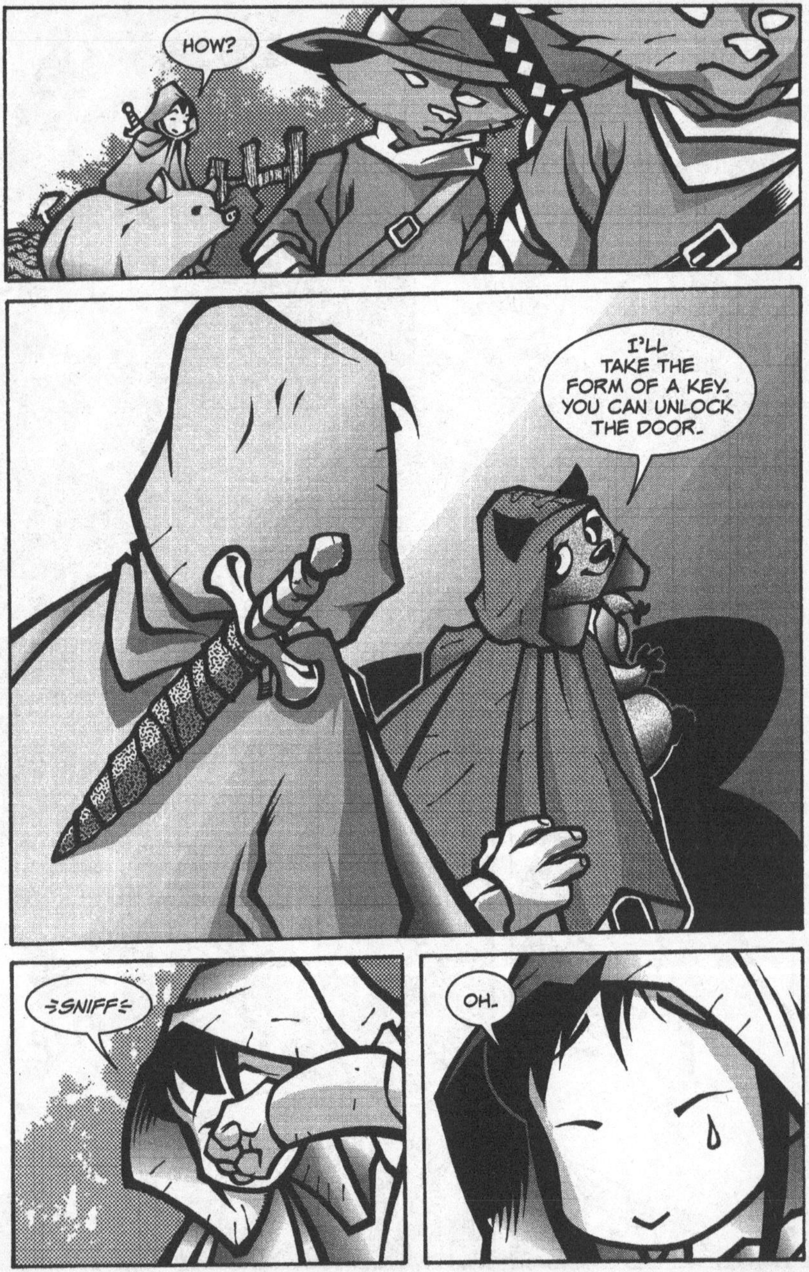
HOW?
I'LL TAKE THE FORM OF A KEY. YOU CAN UNLOCK THE DOOR.
=SNIFF=
OH.

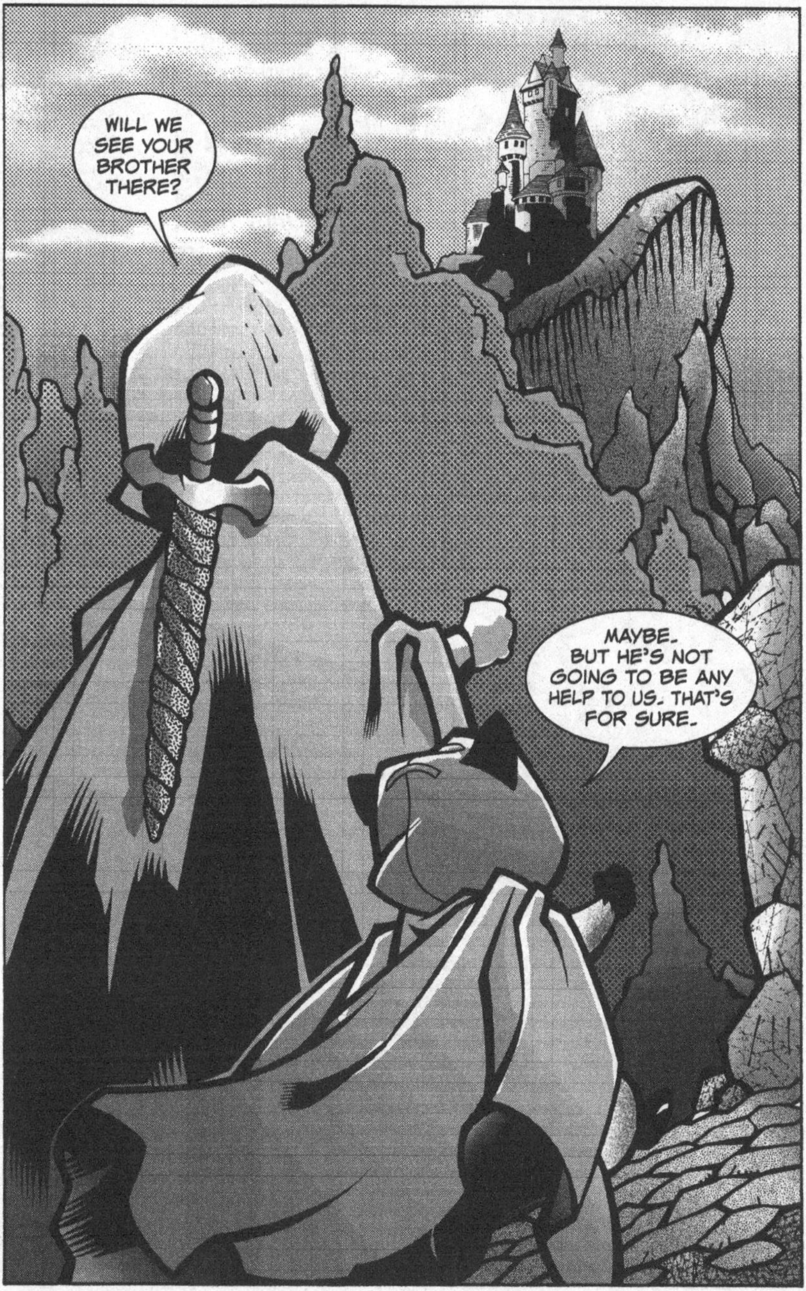
WILL WE SEE YOUR BROTHER THERE?
MAYBE. BUT HE'S NOT GOING TO BE ANY HELP TO US. THAT'S FOR SURE.

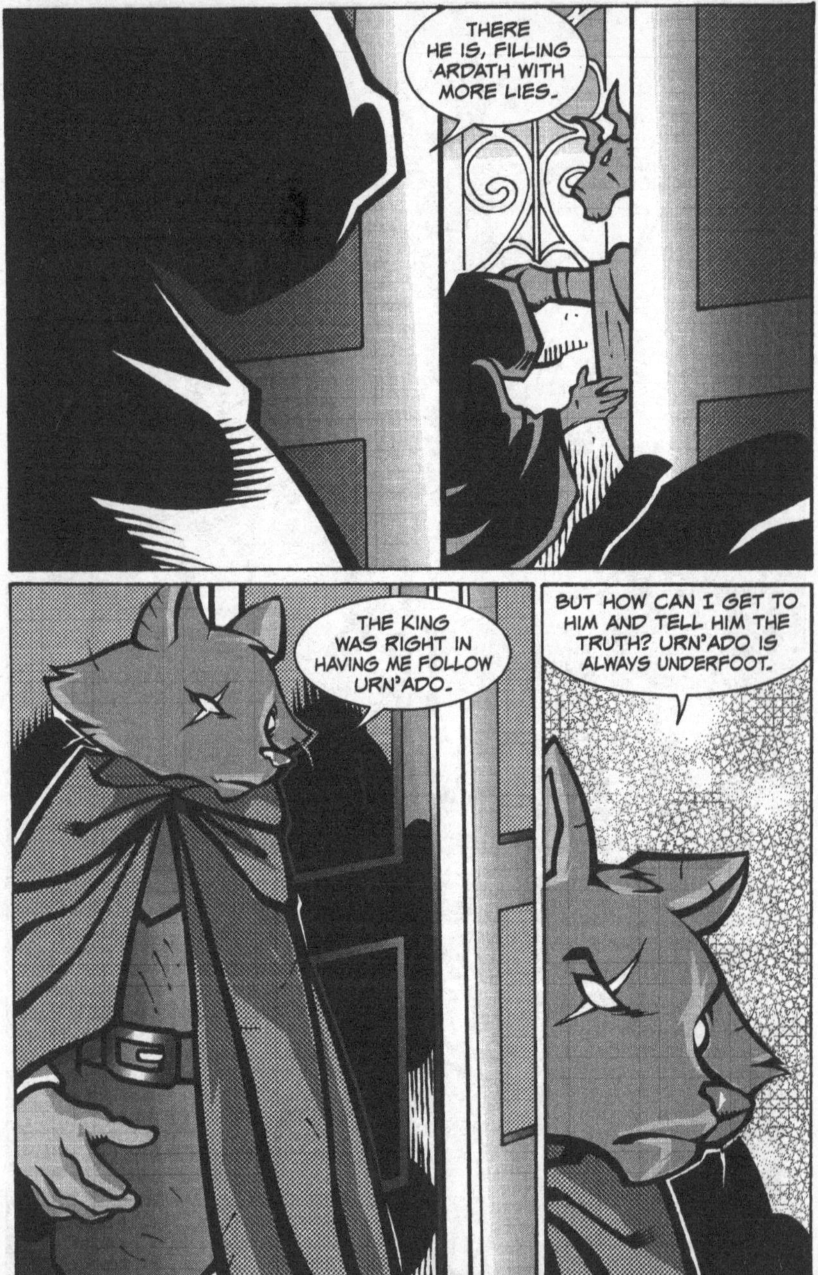
THERE HE IS, FILLING ARDATH WITH MORE LIES.
THE KING WAS RIGHT IN HAVING ME FOLLOW URN'ADO.
BUT HOW CAN I GET TO HIM AND TELL HIM THE TRUTH? URN'ADO IS ALWAYS UNDERFOOT.

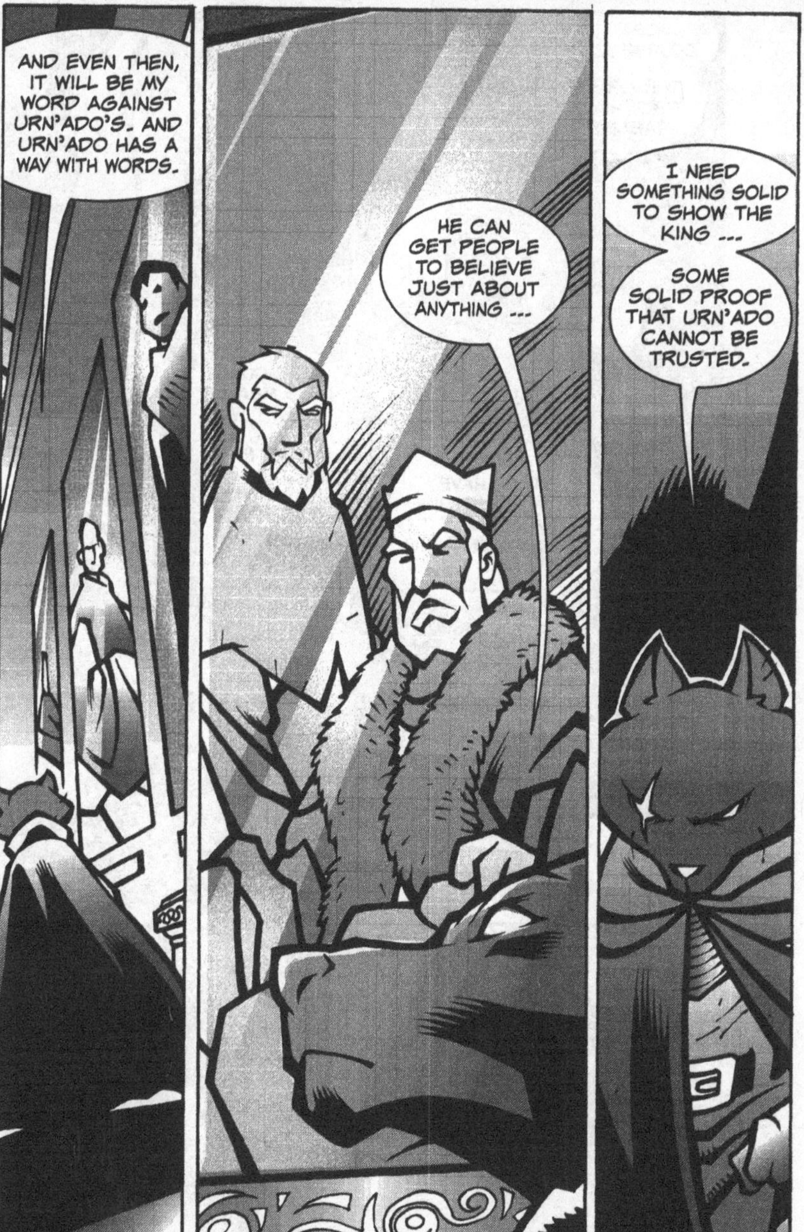
AND EVEN THEN, IT WILL BE MY WORD AGAINST URN'ADO'S. AND URN'ADO HAS A WAY WITH WORDS.
HE CAN GET PEOPLE TO BELIEVE JUST ABOUT ANYTHING ---
I NEED SOMETHING SOLID TO SHOW THE KING ---
SOME SOLID PROOF THAT URN'ADO CANNOT BE TRUSTED.

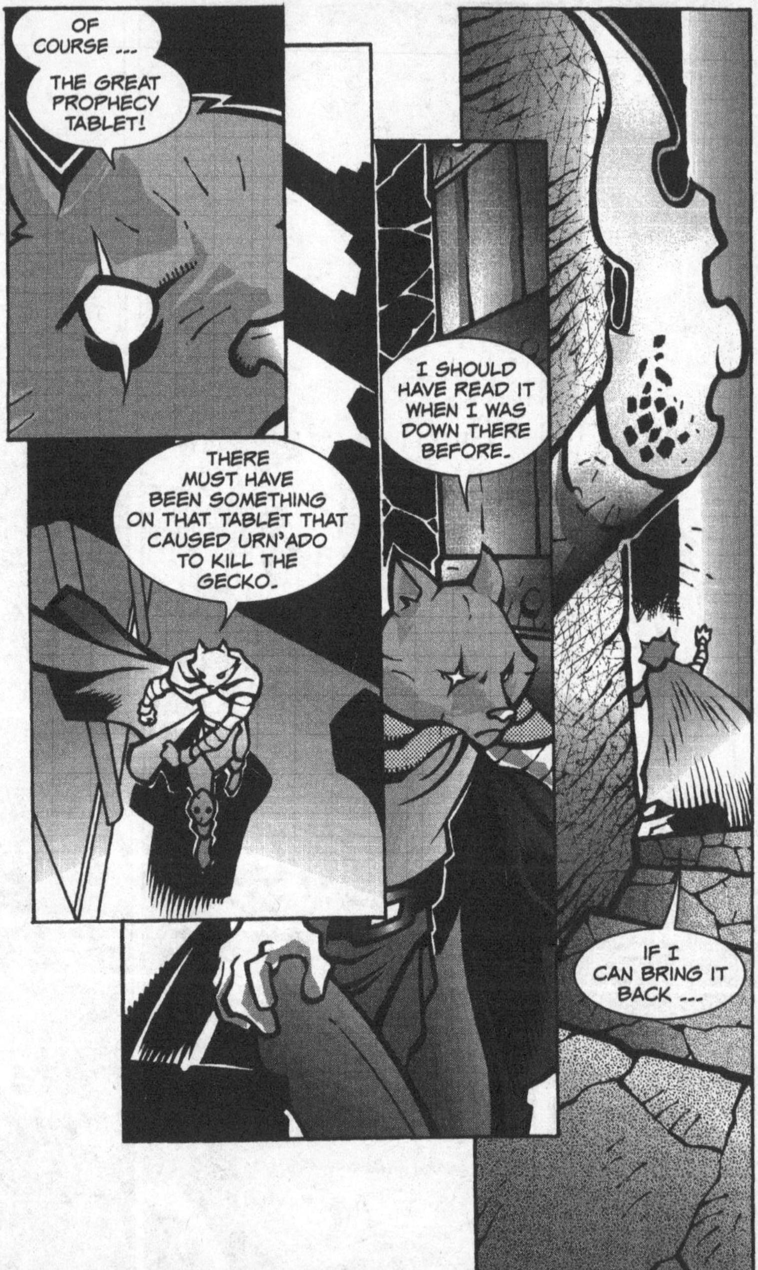
OF COURSE ...
THE GREAT PROPHECY TABLET!
THERE MUST HAVE BEEN SOMETHING ON THAT TABLET THAT CAUSED URN'ADO TO KILL THE GECKO.
I SHOULD HAVE READ IT WHEN I WAS DOWN THERE BEFORE.
IF I CAN BRING IT BACK ...

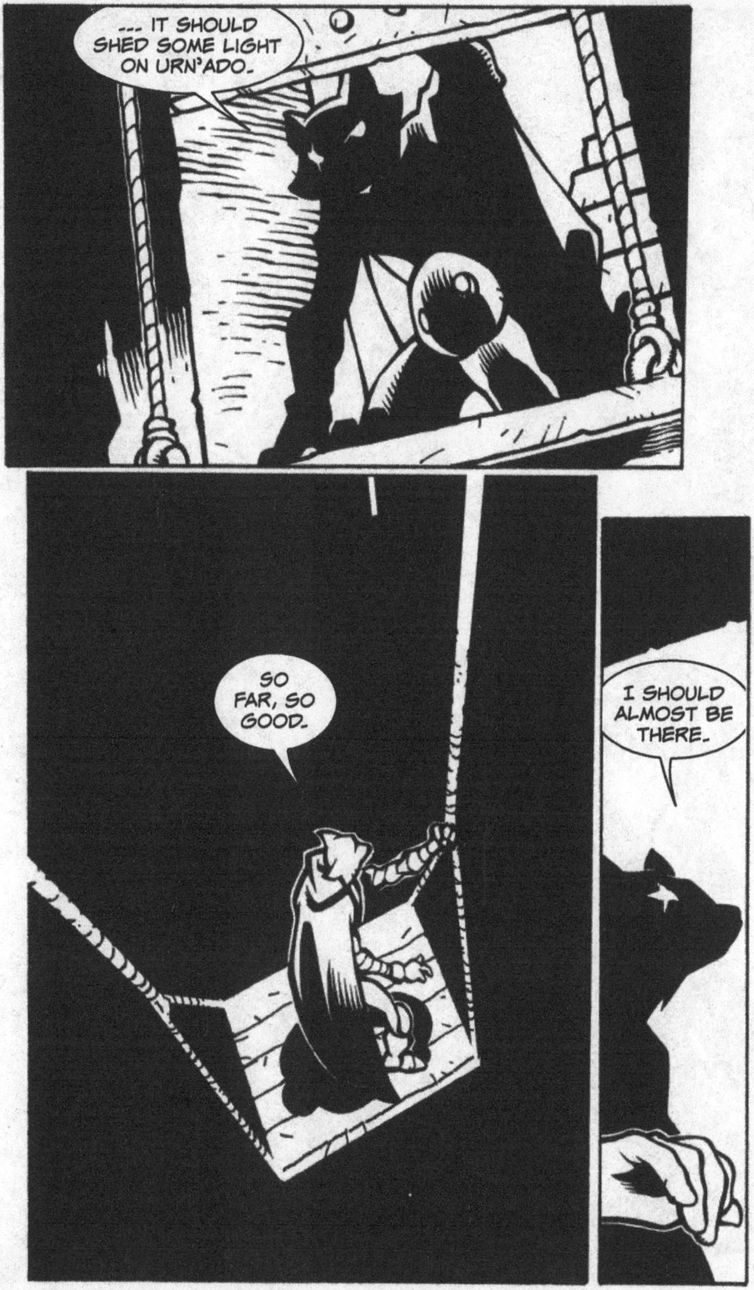
... IT SHOULD SHED SOME LIGHT ON URN'ADO.
SO FAR, SO GOOD.
I SHOULD ALMOST BE THERE.

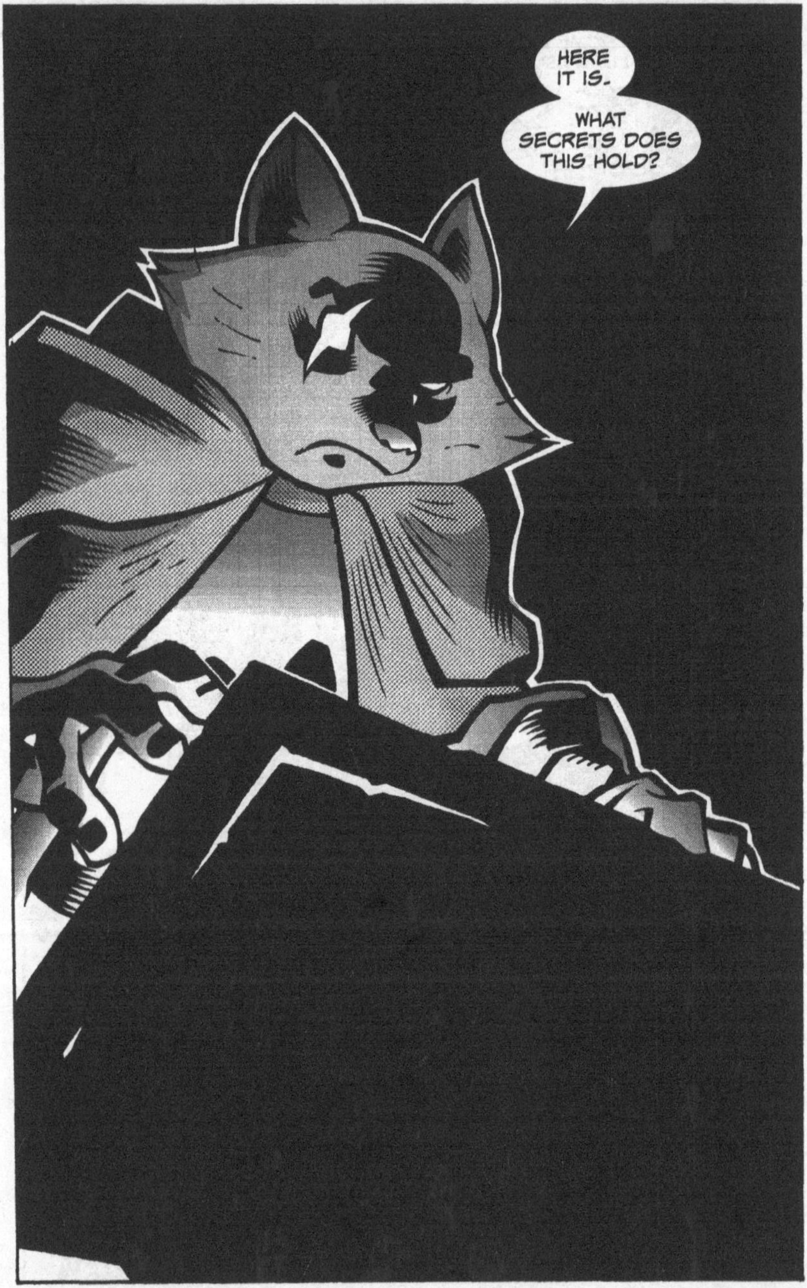
HERE IT IS.
WHAT SECRETS DOES THIS HOLD?

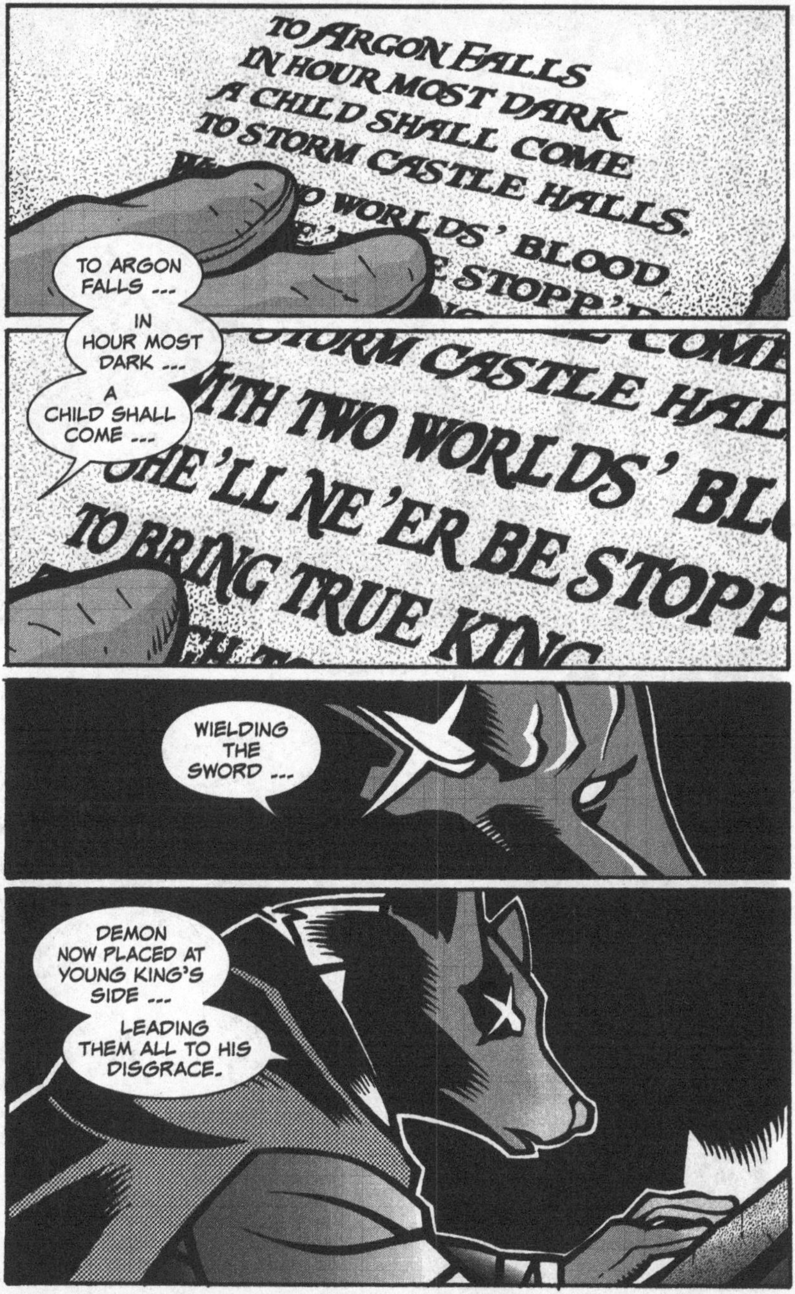
TO ARGON FALLS
IN HOUR MOST DARK
A CHILD SHALL COME
TO STORM CASTLE HALLS.
TO ARGON FALLS ---
IN HOUR MOST DARK ---
A CHILD SHALL COME ---
WIELDING THE SWORD ---
DEMON NOW PLACED AT YOUNG KING'S SIDE ---
LEADING THEM ALL TO HIS DISGRACE.

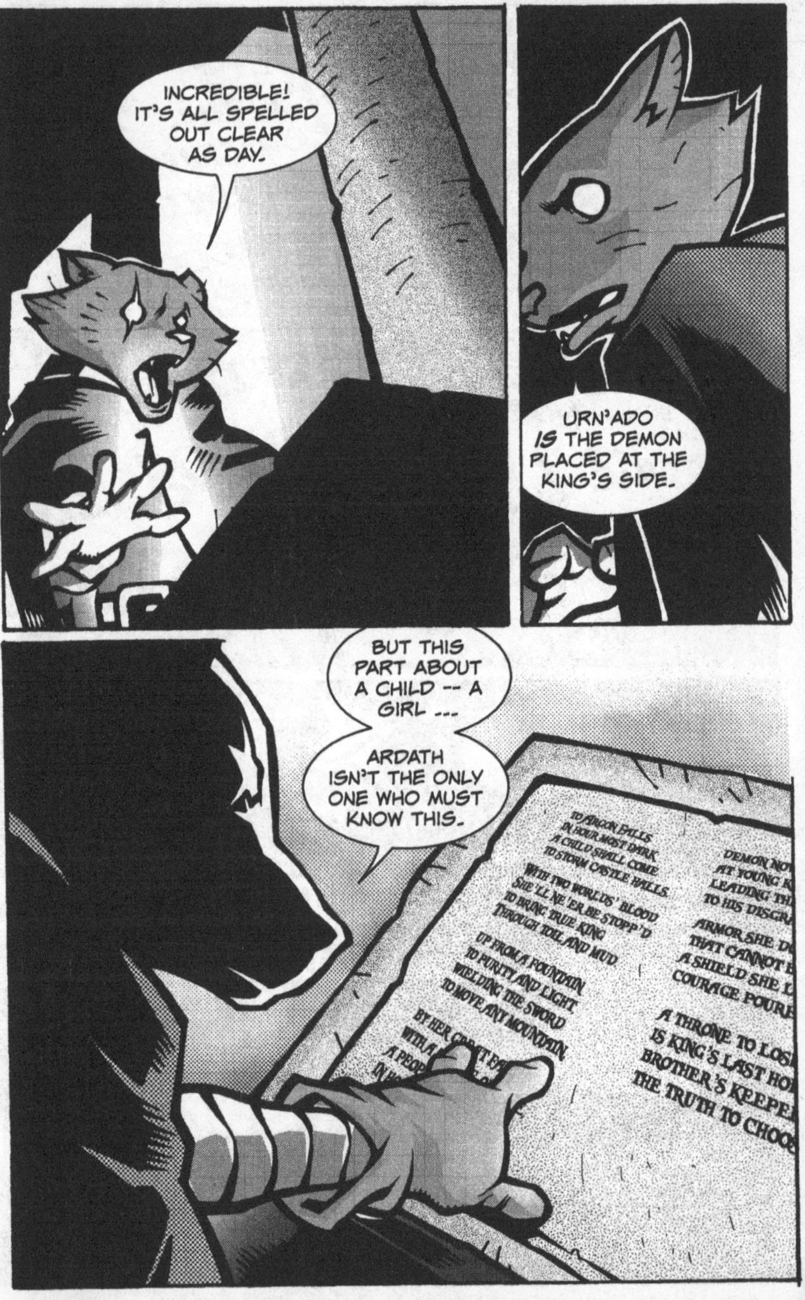
INCREDIBLE! IT'S ALL SPELLED OUT CLEAR AS DAY.
URN'ADO *IS* THE DEMON PLACED AT THE KING'S SIDE.
BUT THIS PART ABOUT A CHILD -- A GIRL ...
ARDATH ISN'T THE ONLY ONE WHO MUST KNOW THIS.
TO ARGON FALLS
IN HOUR MOST DARK
A CHILD SHALL COME
TO STORM CASTLE HALLS.
WITH TWO WORLDS' BLOOD
SHE'LL NE'ER BE STOPP'D
TO BRING TRUE KING
THROUGH TOIL AND MUD
UP FROM A FOUNTAIN
TO PURITY AND LIGHT
WIELDING THE SWORD
TO MOVE ANY MOUNTAIN

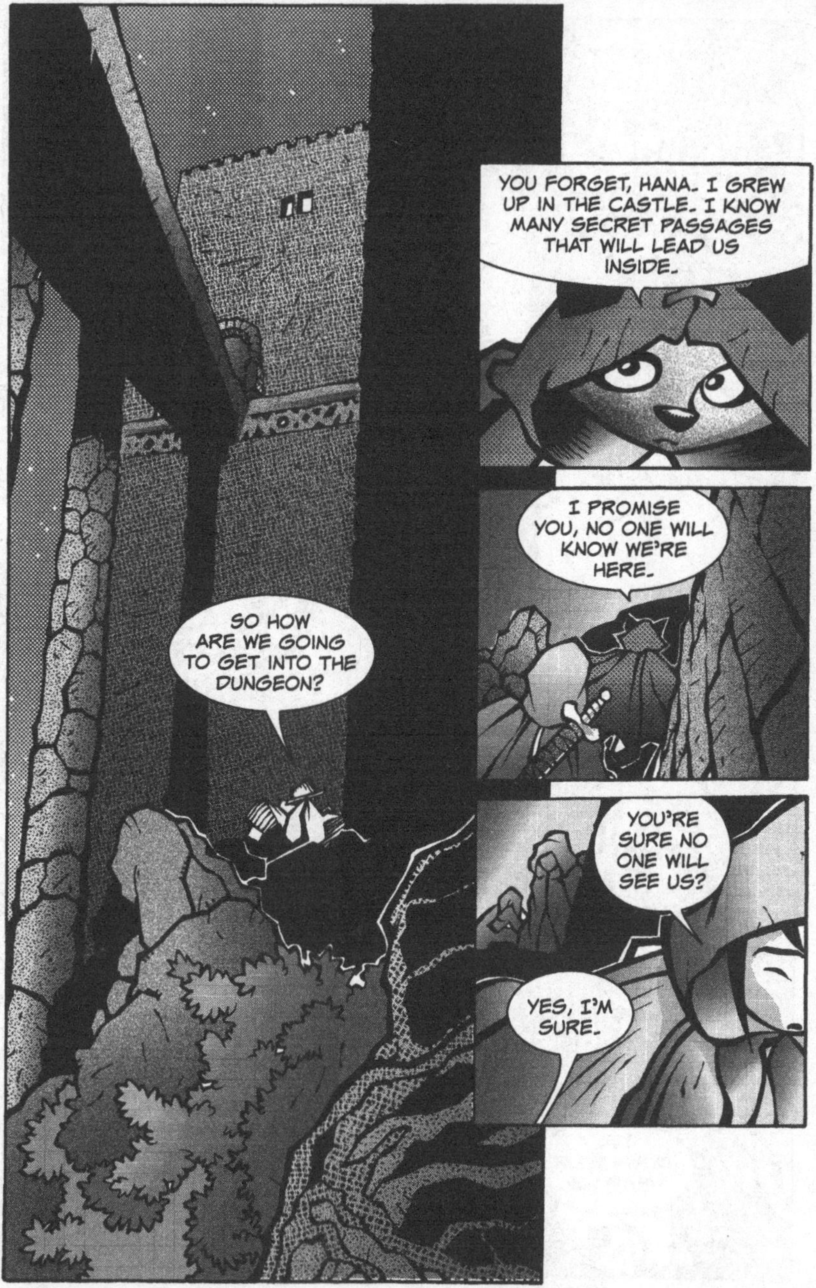
SO HOW ARE WE GOING TO GET INTO THE DUNGEON?
YOU FORGET, HANA. I GREW UP IN THE CASTLE. I KNOW MANY SECRET PASSAGES THAT WILL LEAD US INSIDE.
I PROMISE YOU, NO ONE WILL KNOW WE'RE HERE.
YOU'RE SURE NO ONE WILL SEE US?
YES, I'M SURE.

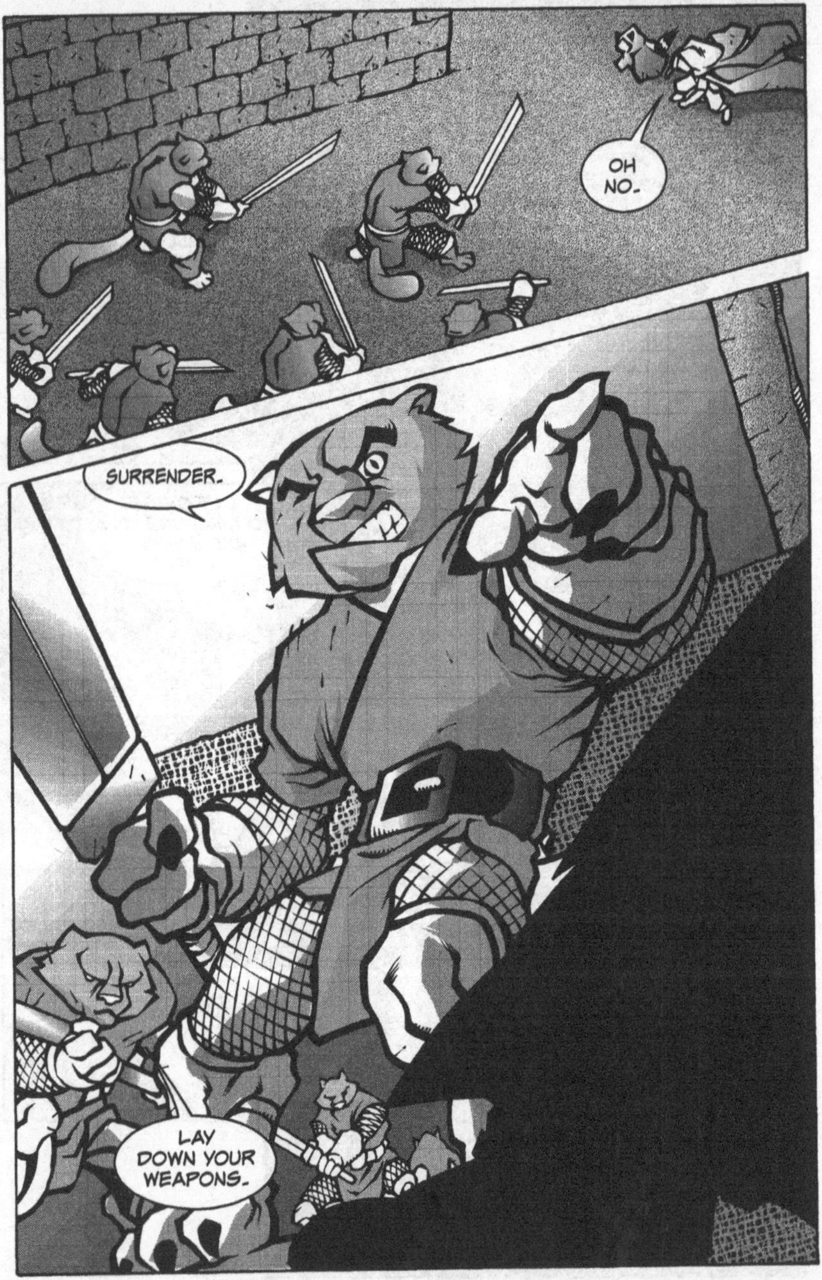
OH NO.
SURRENDER.
LAY DOWN YOUR WEAPONS.

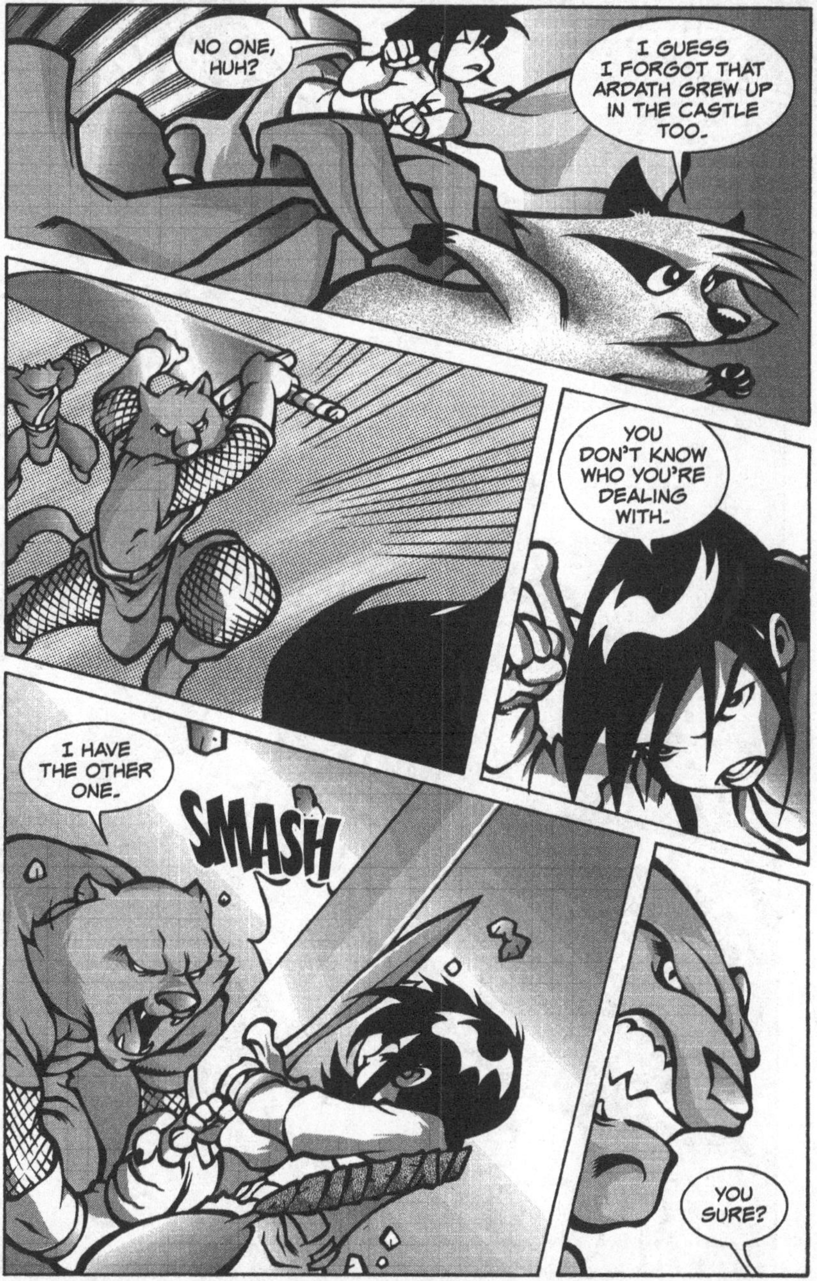

NO ONE, HUH?
I GUESS I FORGOT THAT ARDATH GREW UP IN THE CASTLE TOO.
YOU DON'T KNOW WHO YOU'RE DEALING WITH.
I HAVE THE OTHER ONE.
SMASH
YOU SURE?

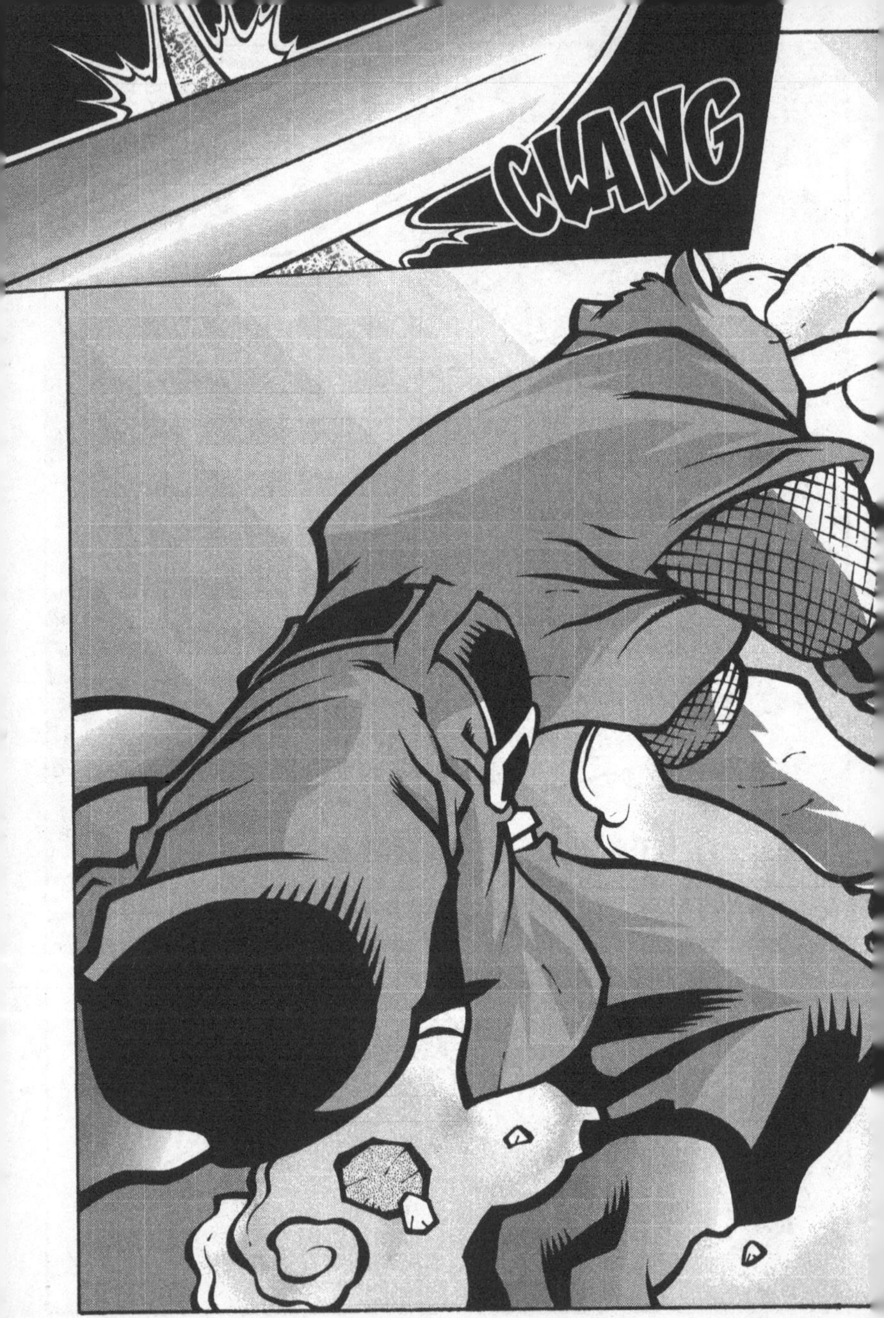
CLANG

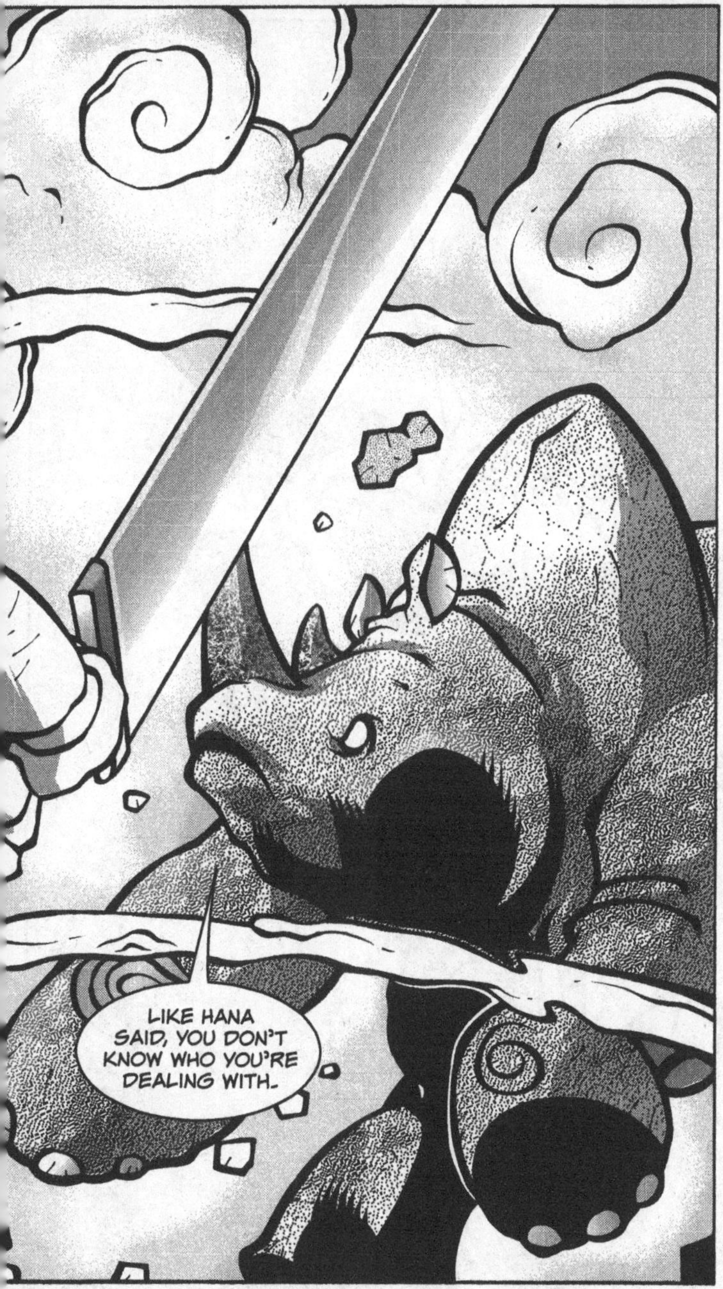
LIKE HANA SAID, YOU DON'T KNOW WHO YOU'RE DEALING WITH.

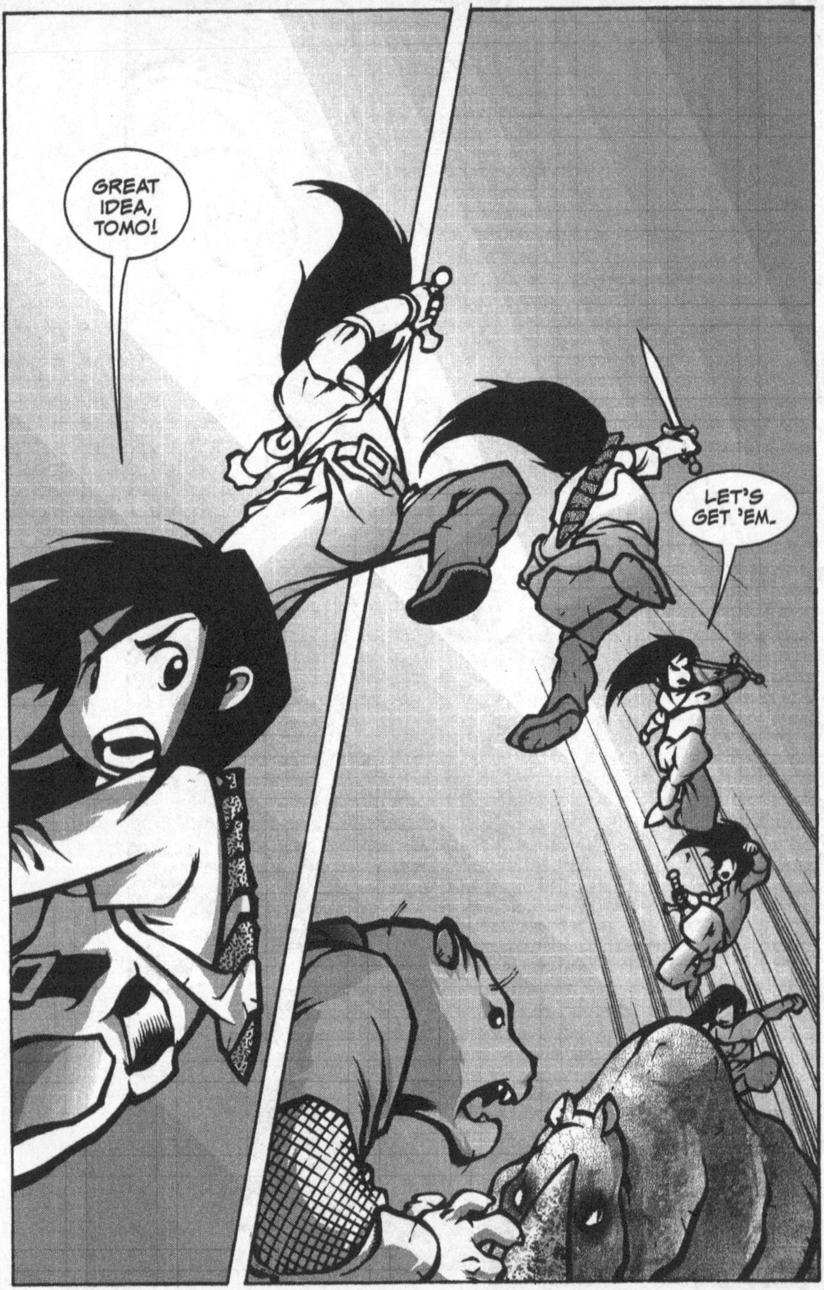
GREAT IDEA, TOMO!
LET'S GET 'EM.

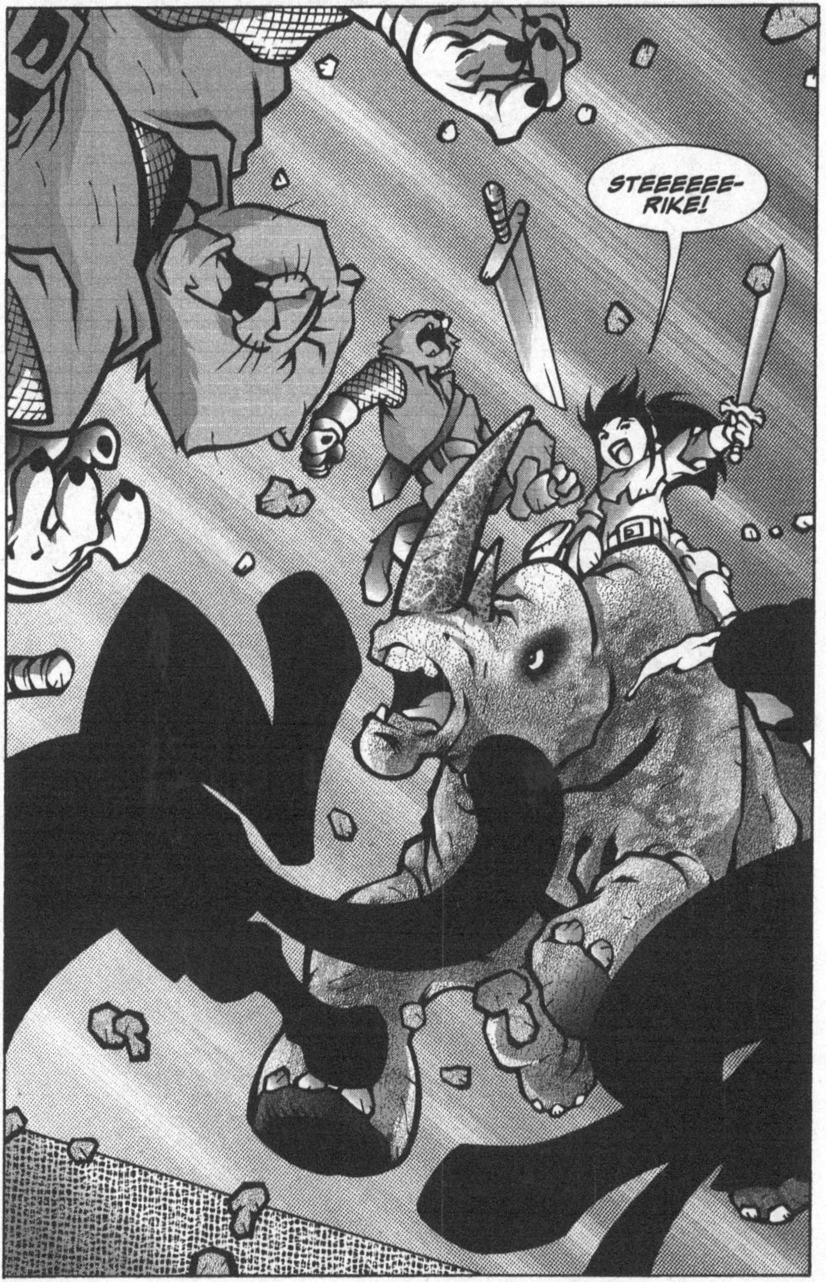
STEEEEEEE-
RIKE!

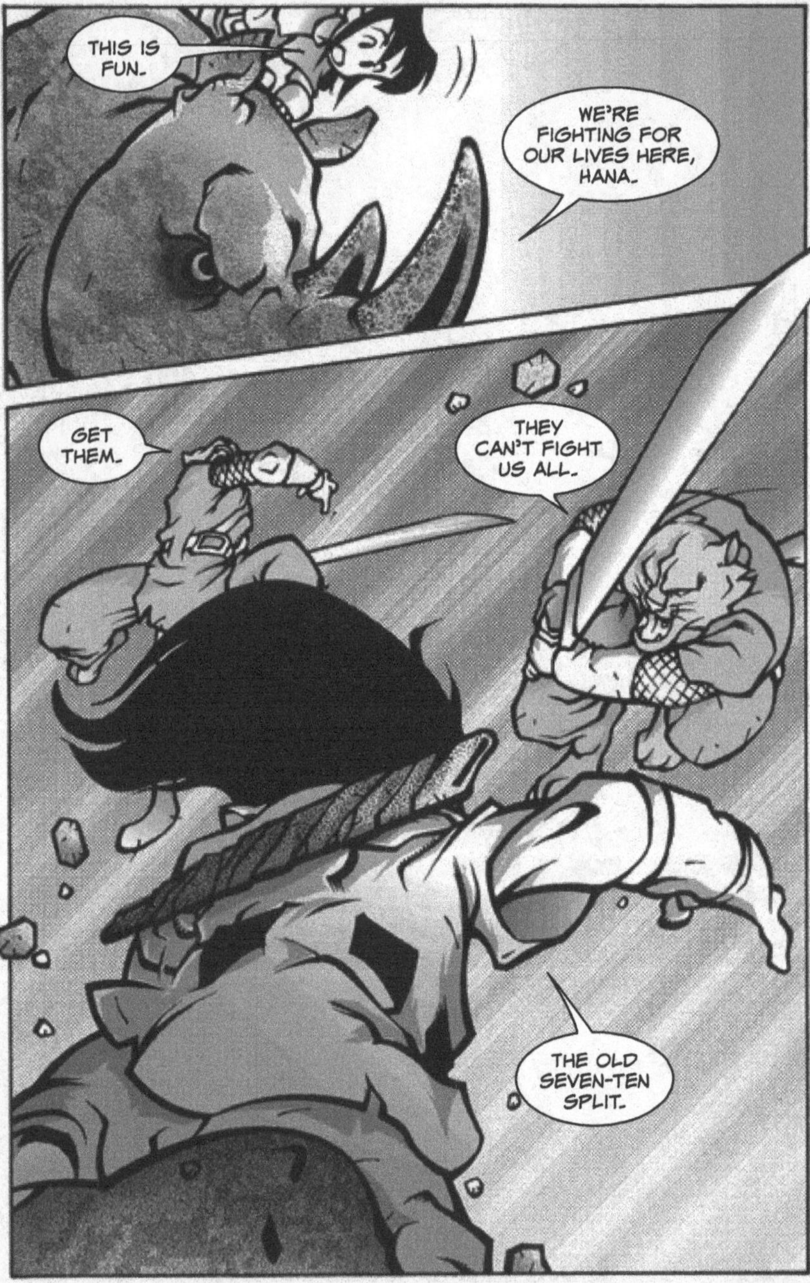
THIS IS FUN.
WE'RE FIGHTING FOR OUR LIVES HERE, HANA.
GET THEM.
THEY CAN'T FIGHT US ALL.
THE OLD SEVEN-TEN SPLIT.

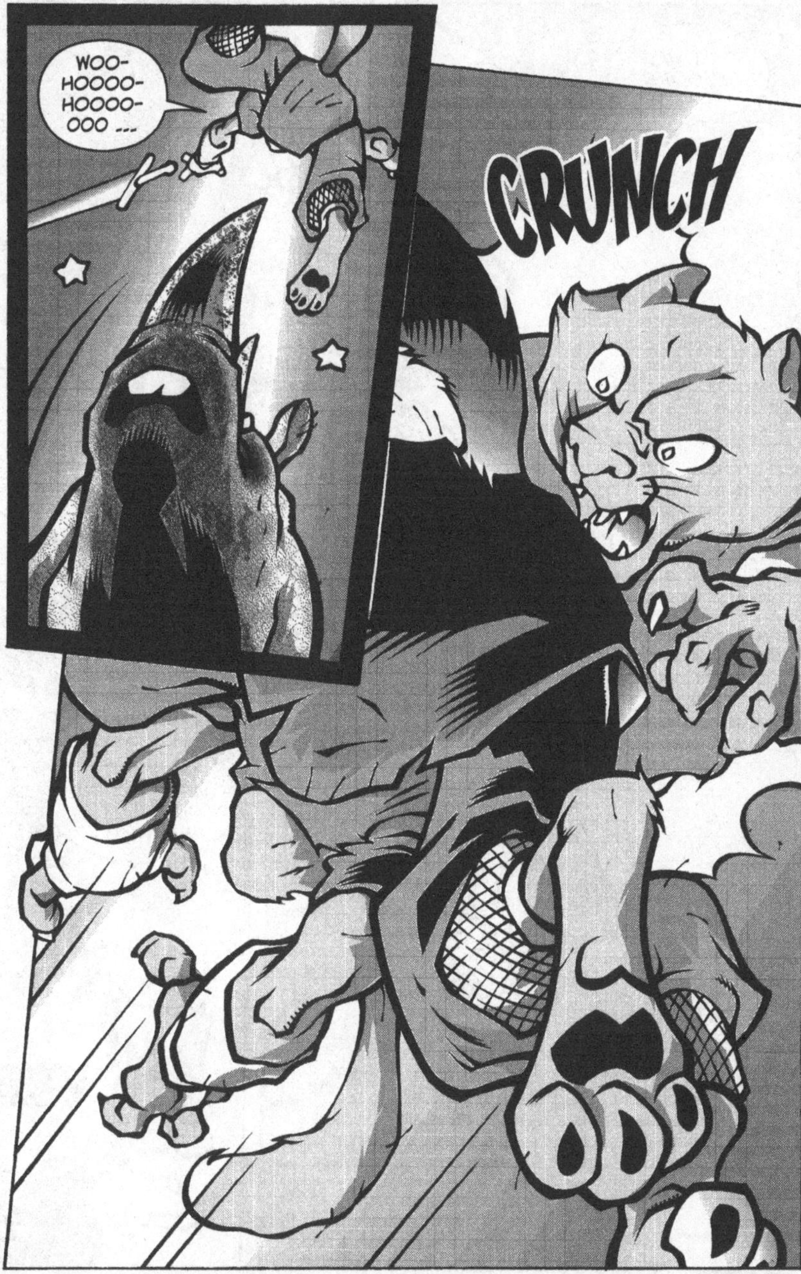
WOO-
HOOOO-
HOOOO-
OOO ...
CRUNCH

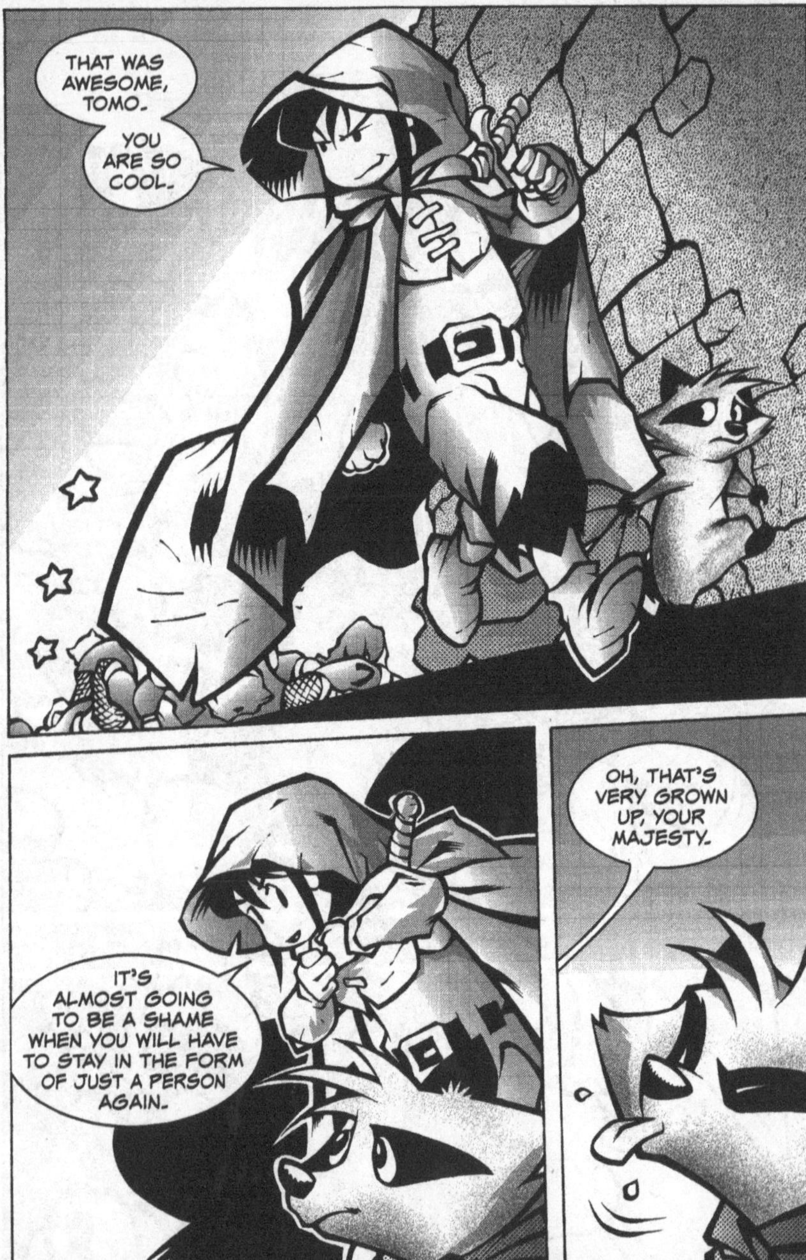
THAT WAS AWESOME, TOMO.
YOU ARE SO COOL.
IT'S ALMOST GOING TO BE A SHAME WHEN YOU WILL HAVE TO STAY IN THE FORM OF JUST A PERSON AGAIN.
OH, THAT'S VERY GROWN UP, YOUR MAJESTY.

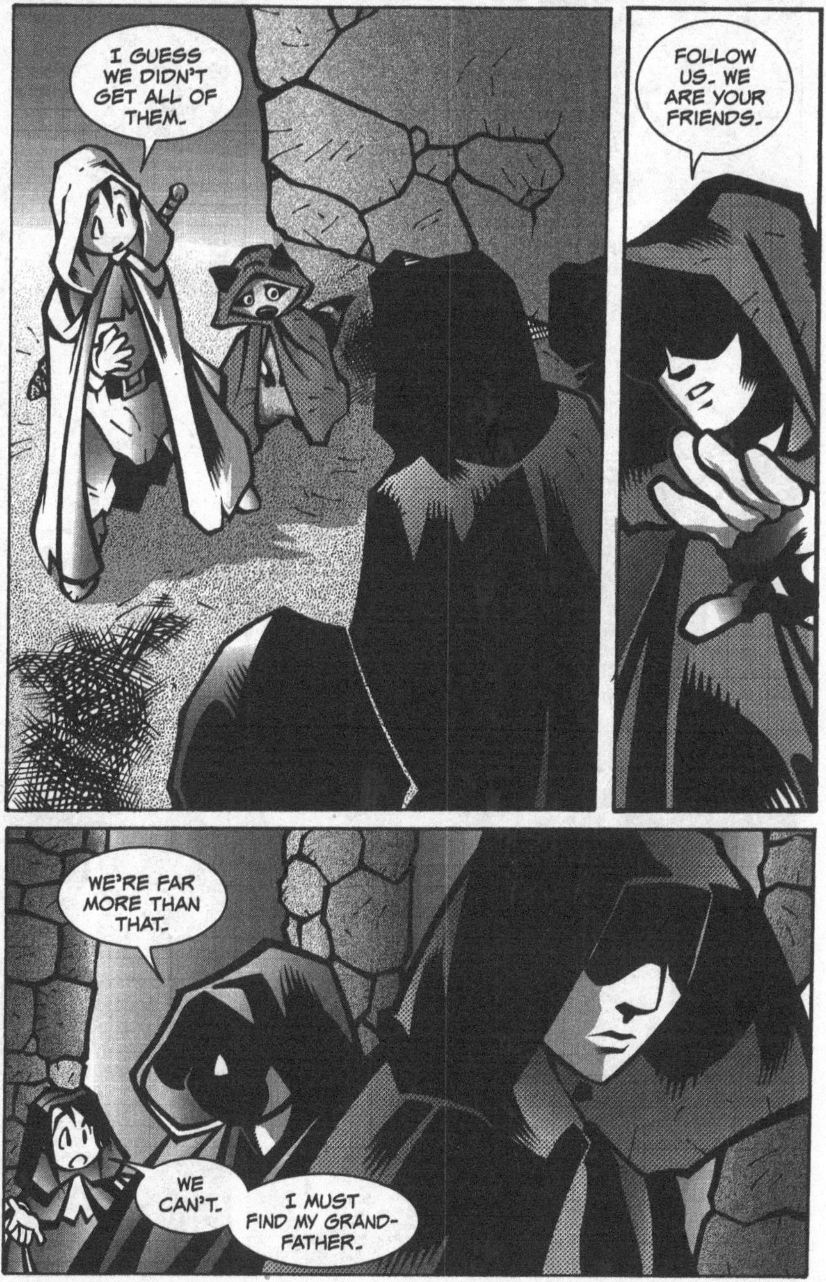
I GUESS WE DIDN'T GET ALL OF THEM.
FOLLOW US. WE ARE YOUR FRIENDS.
WE'RE FAR MORE THAN THAT.
WE CAN'T.
I MUST FIND MY GRAND-FATHER.

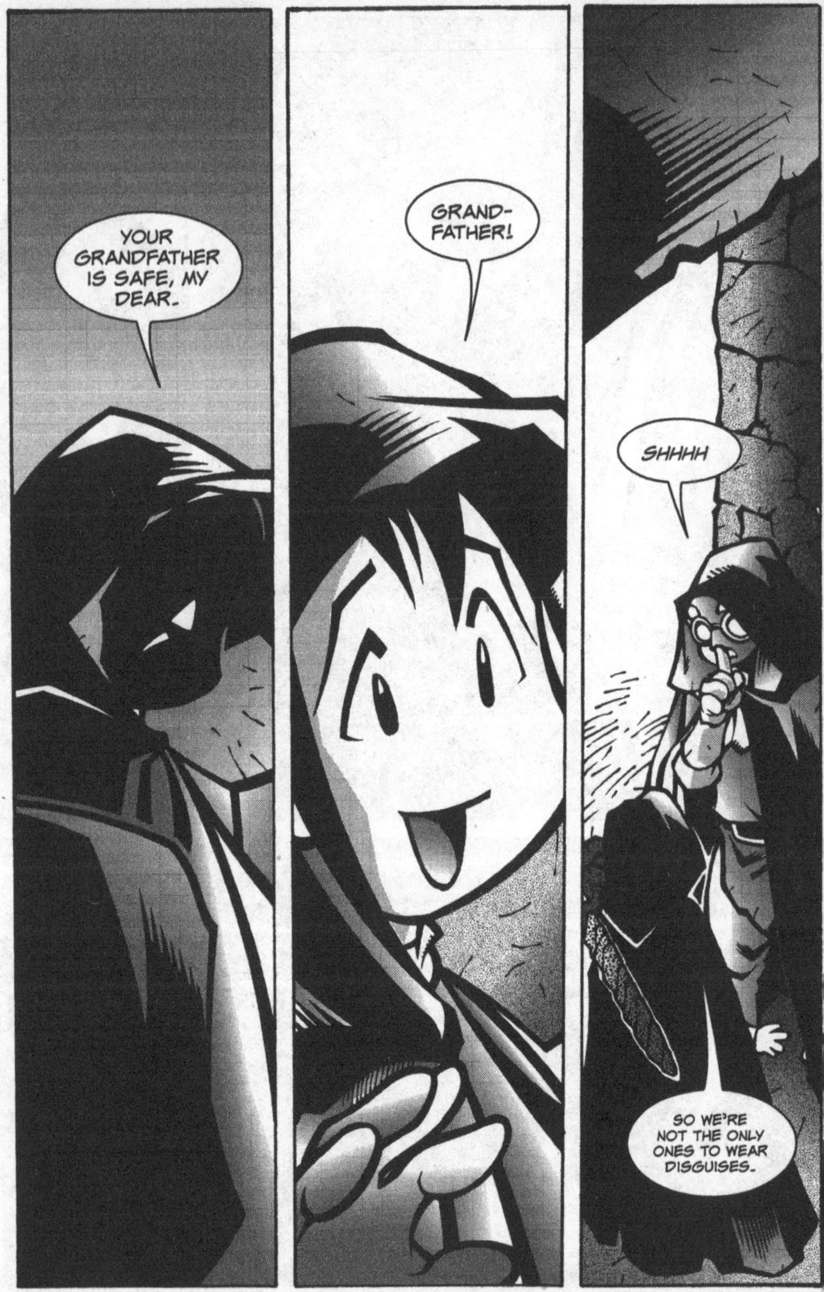
YOUR GRANDFATHER IS SAFE, MY DEAR.
GRAND-FATHER!
SHHHH
SO WE'RE NOT THE ONLY ONES TO WEAR DISGUISES.

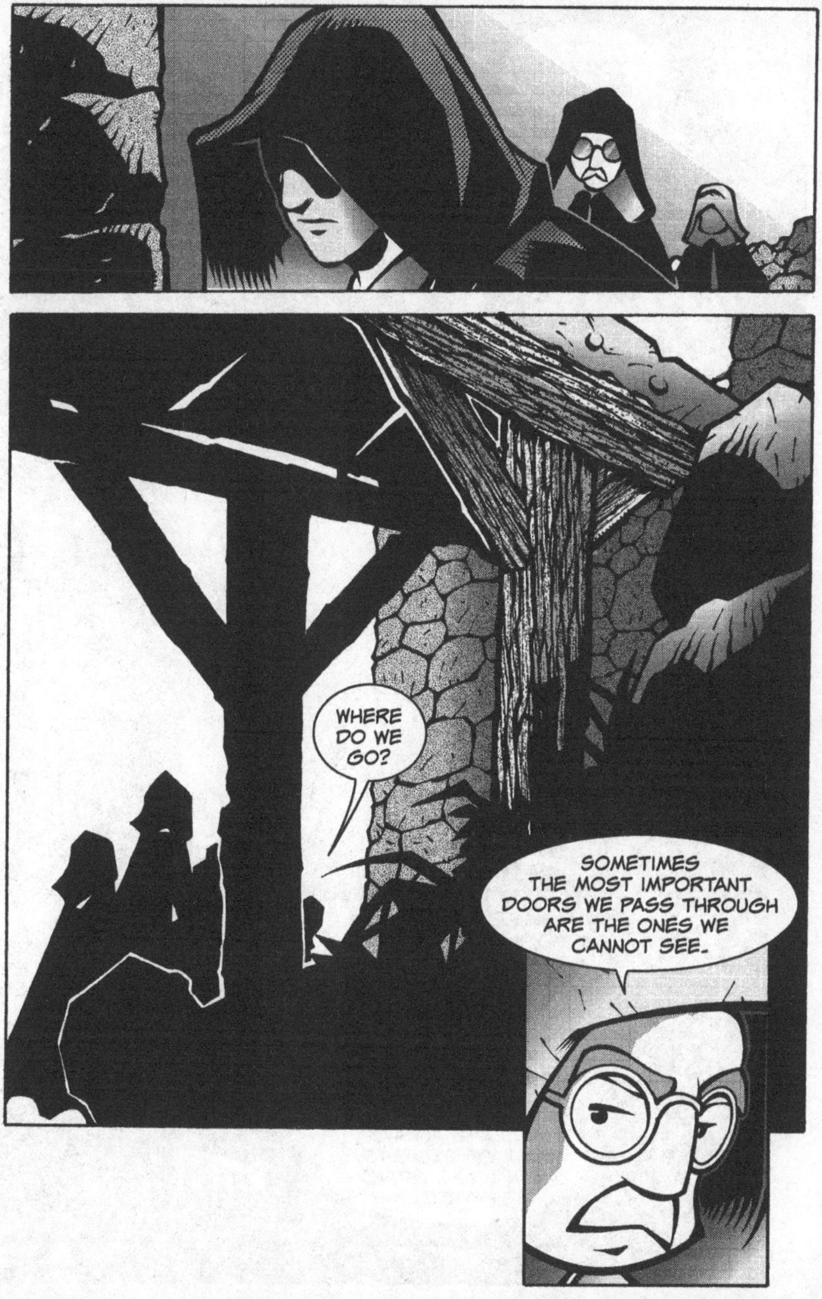
WHERE DO WE GO?
SOMETIMES THE MOST IMPORTANT DOORS WE PASS THROUGH ARE THE ONES WE CANNOT SEE.

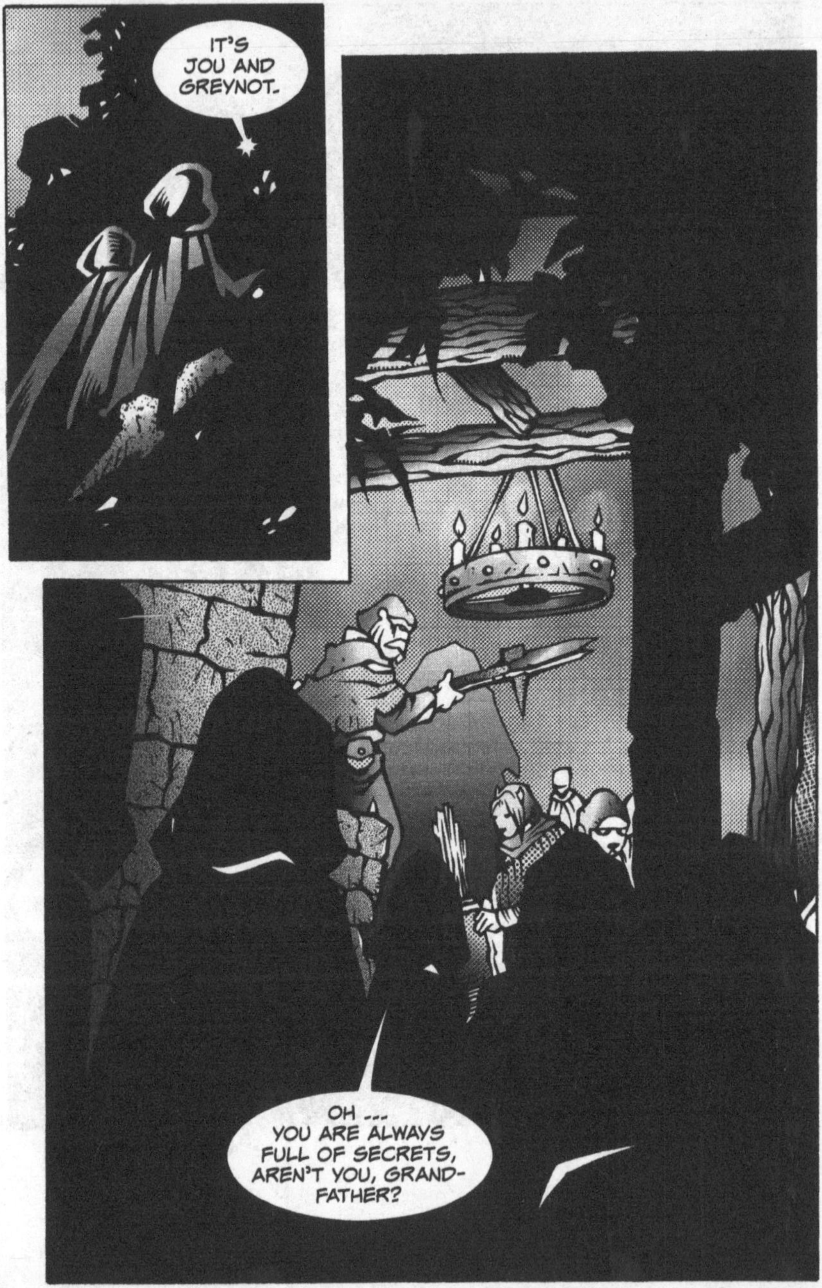
IT'S JOU AND GREYNOT.
OH ... YOU ARE ALWAYS FULL OF SECRETS, AREN'T YOU, GRAND-FATHER?

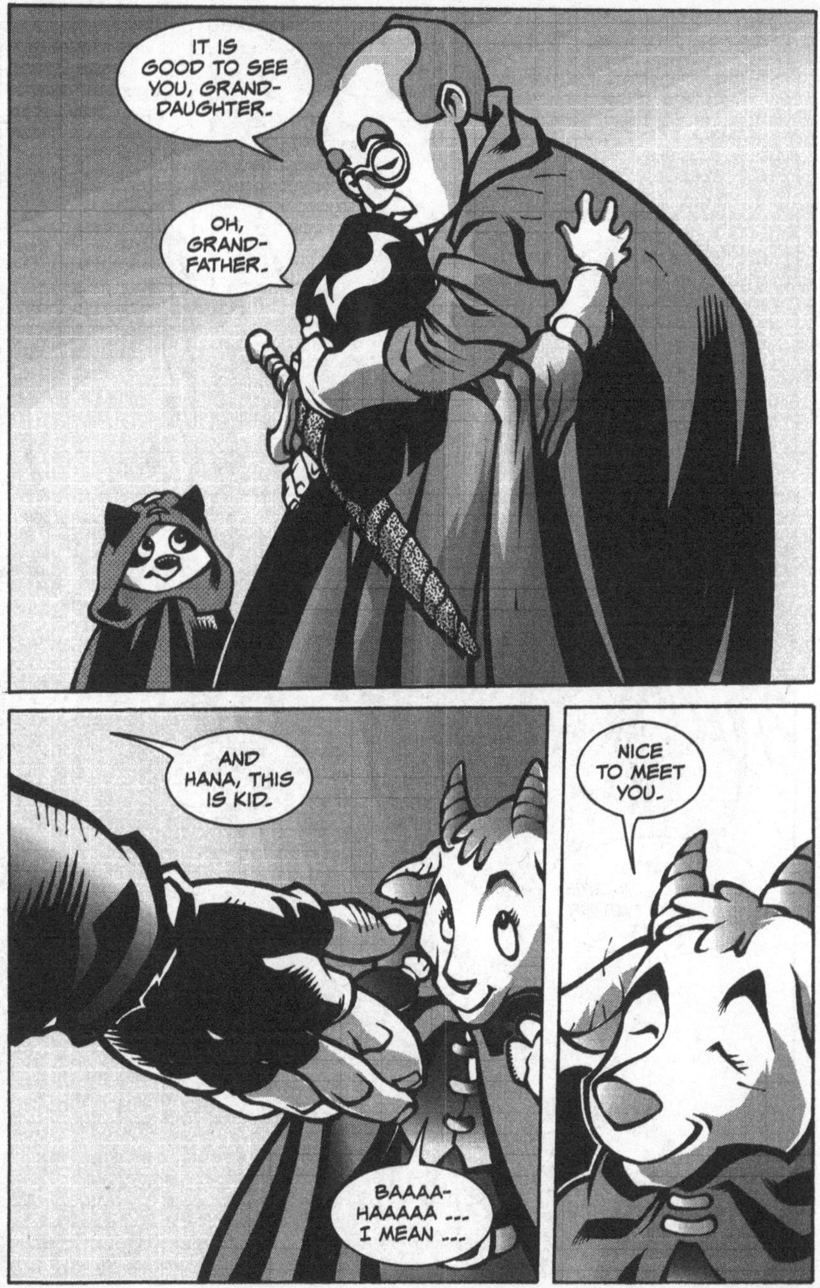
IT IS GOOD TO SEE YOU, GRAND-DAUGHTER.
OH, GRAND-FATHER.
AND HANA, THIS IS KID.
BAAAA-HAAAAA ... I MEAN ...
NICE TO MEET YOU.

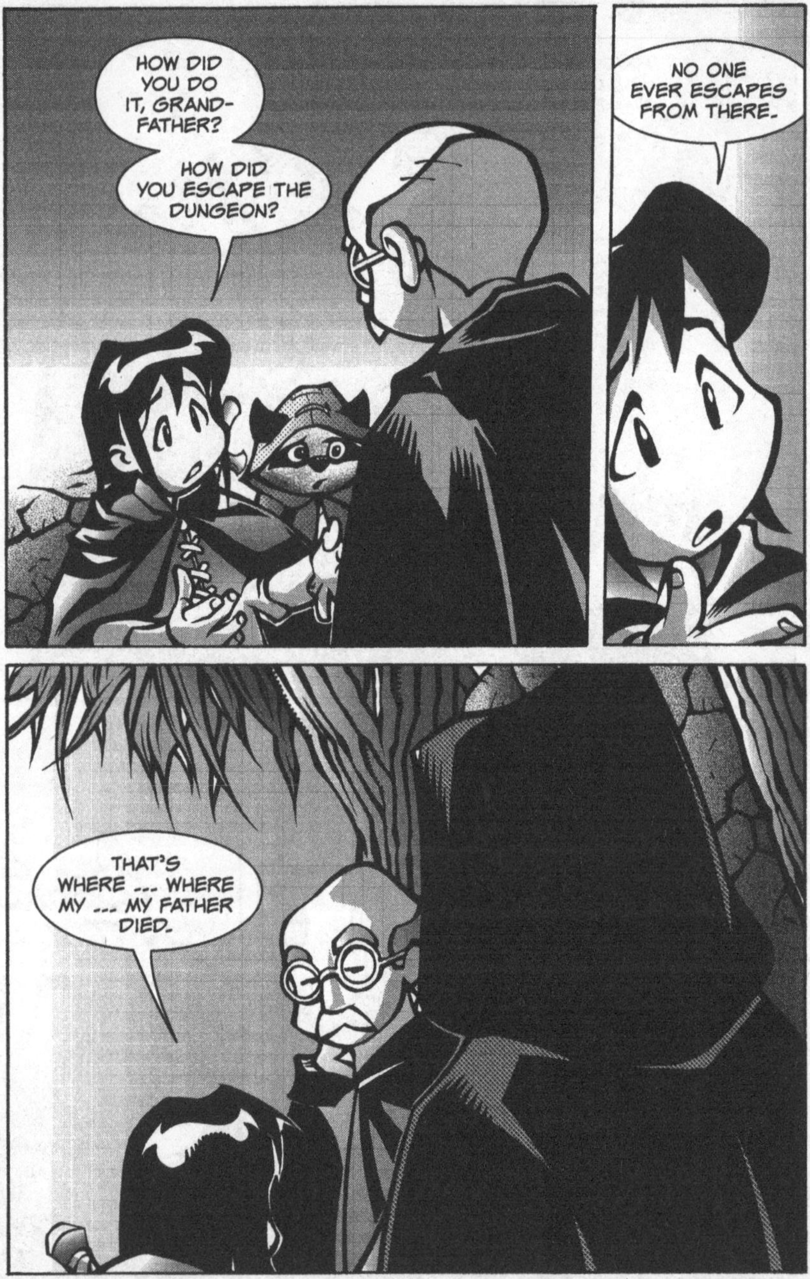
HOW DID YOU DO IT, GRAND-FATHER?
HOW DID YOU ESCAPE THE DUNGEON?
NO ONE EVER ESCAPES FROM THERE.
THAT'S WHERE ... WHERE MY ... MY FATHER DIED.

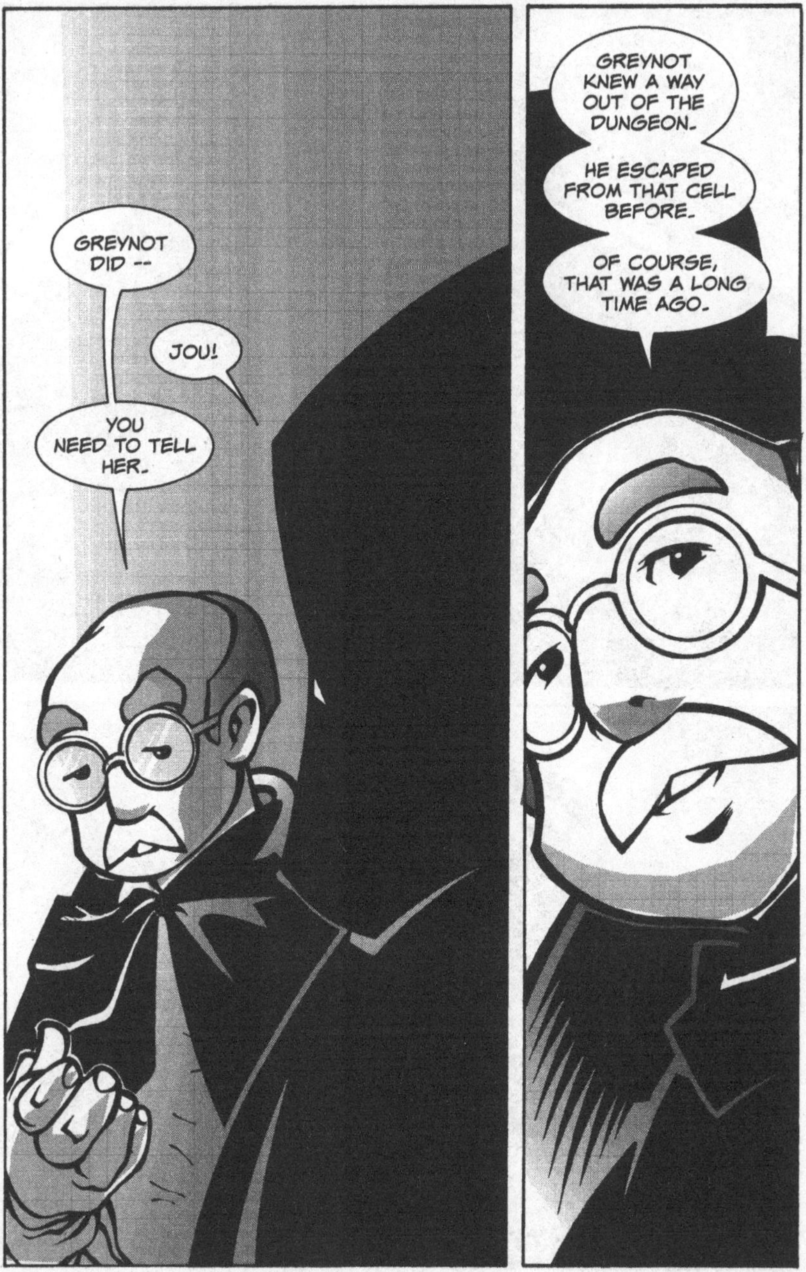
GREYNOT DID --
JOU!
YOU NEED TO TELL HER.
GREYNOT KNEW A WAY OUT OF THE DUNGEON.
HE ESCAPED FROM THAT CELL BEFORE.
OF COURSE, THAT WAS A LONG TIME AGO.

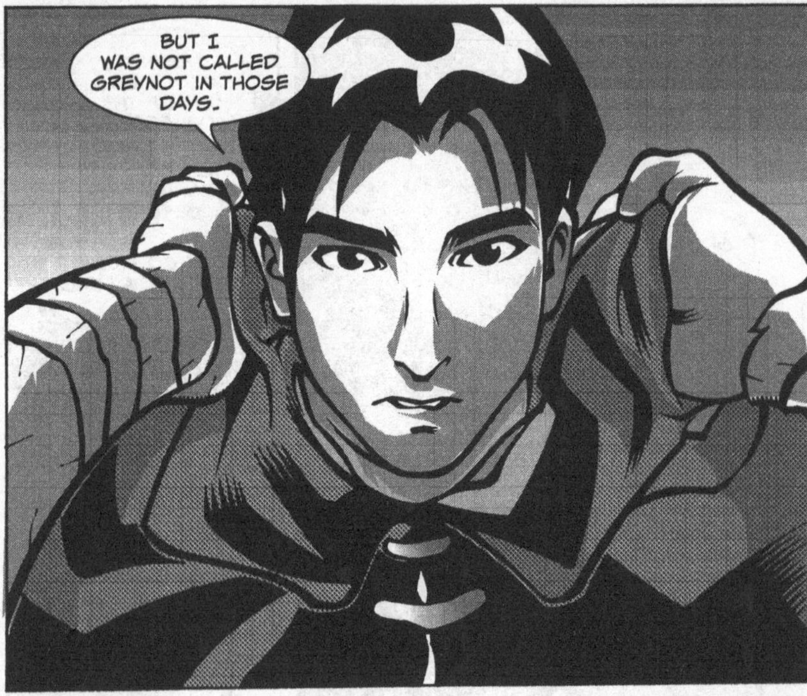
BUT I WAS NOT CALLED GREYNOT IN THOSE DAYS.

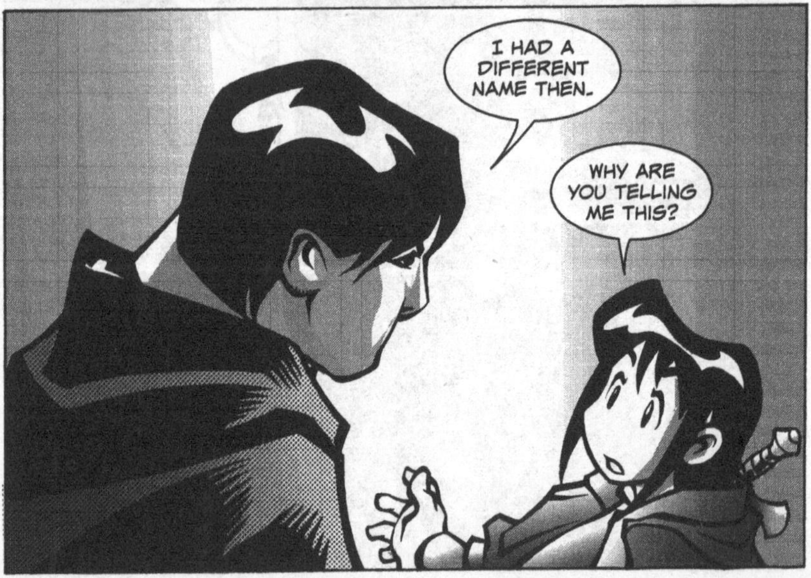
I HAD A DIFFERENT NAME THEN.
WHY ARE YOU TELLING ME THIS?

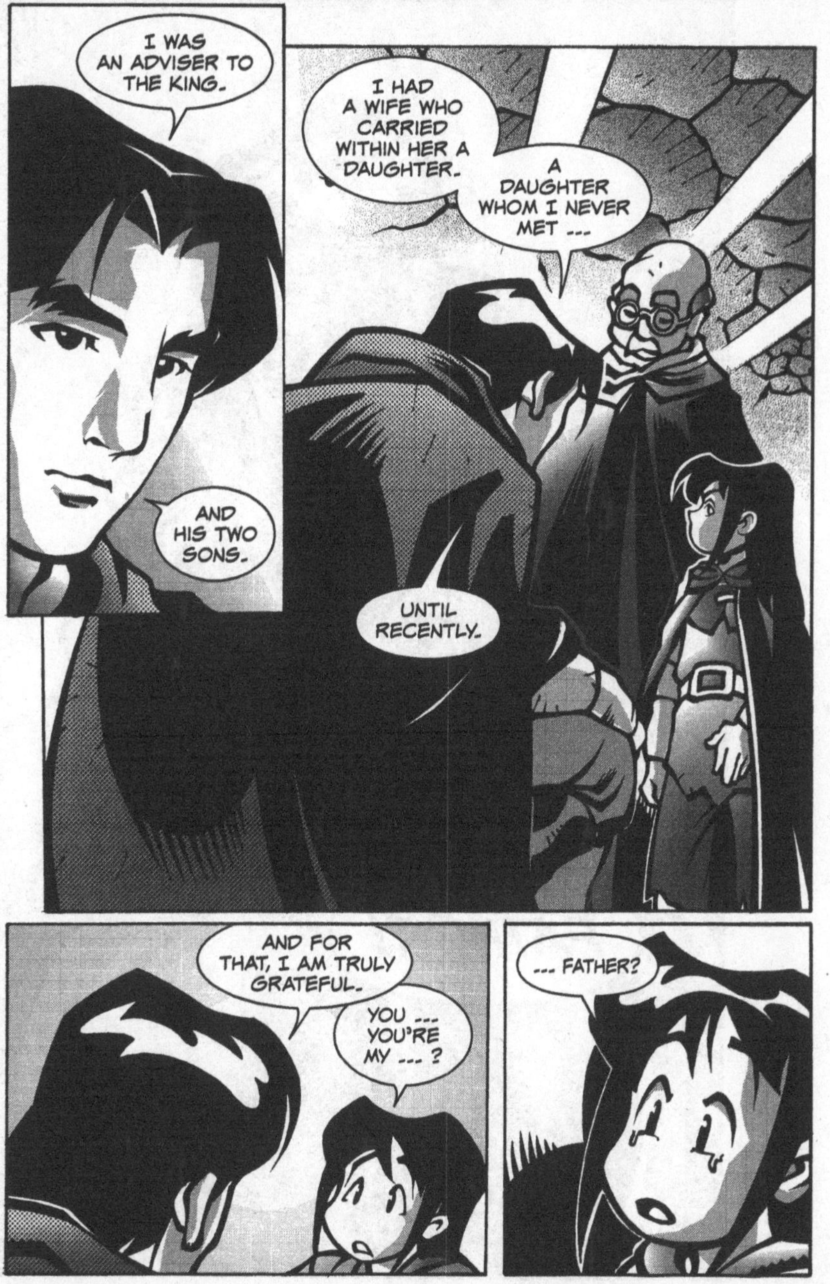
I WAS AN ADVISER TO THE KING.
AND HIS TWO SONS.
I HAD A WIFE WHO CARRIED WITHIN HER A DAUGHTER.
A DAUGHTER WHOM I NEVER MET ...
UNTIL RECENTLY.
AND FOR THAT, I AM TRULY GRATEFUL.
YOU ... YOU'RE MY ... ?
... FATHER?

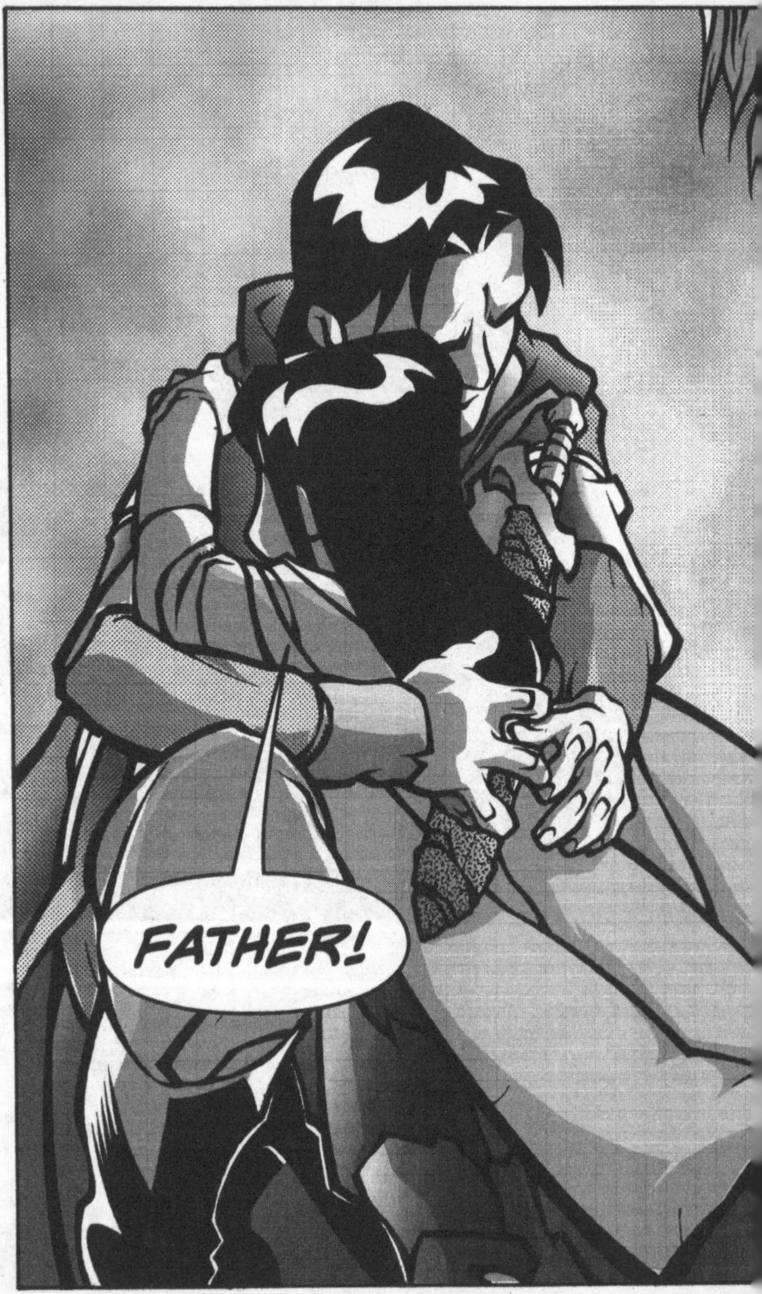
FATHER!

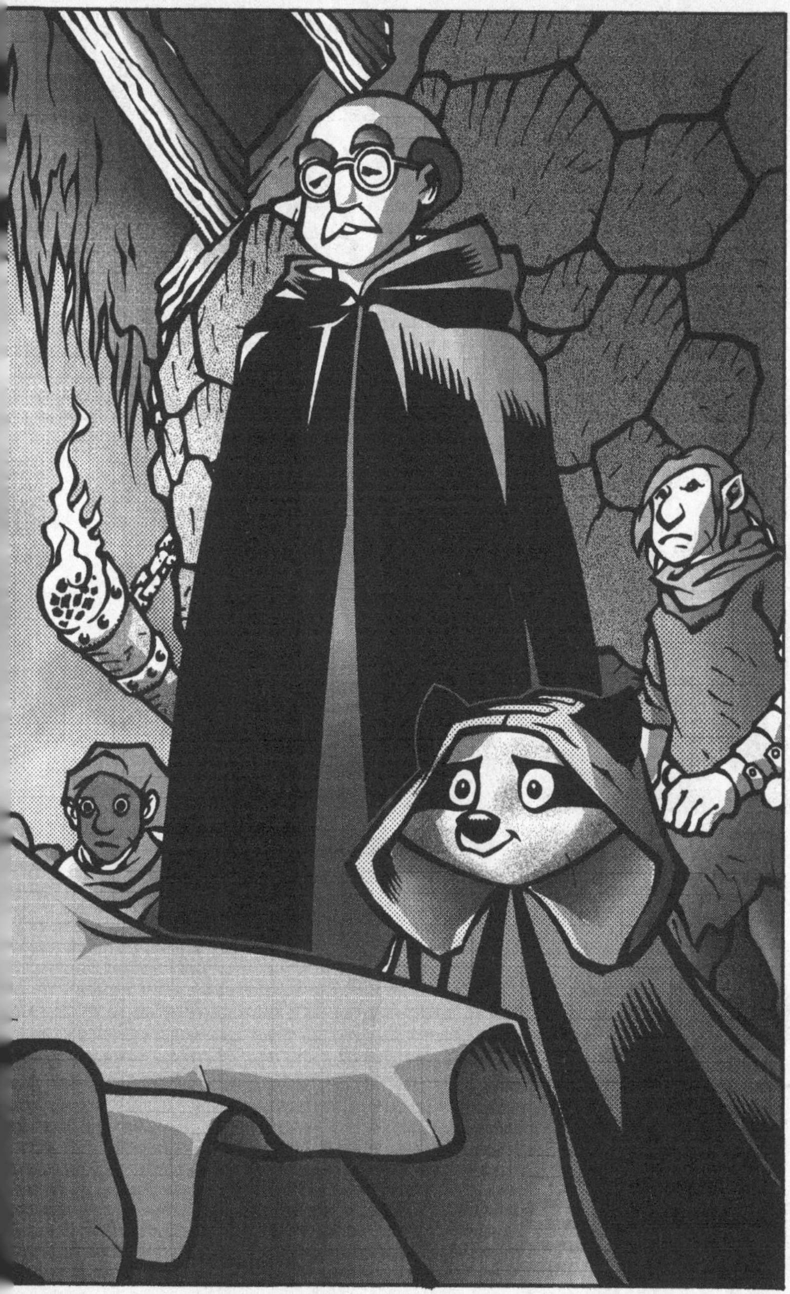

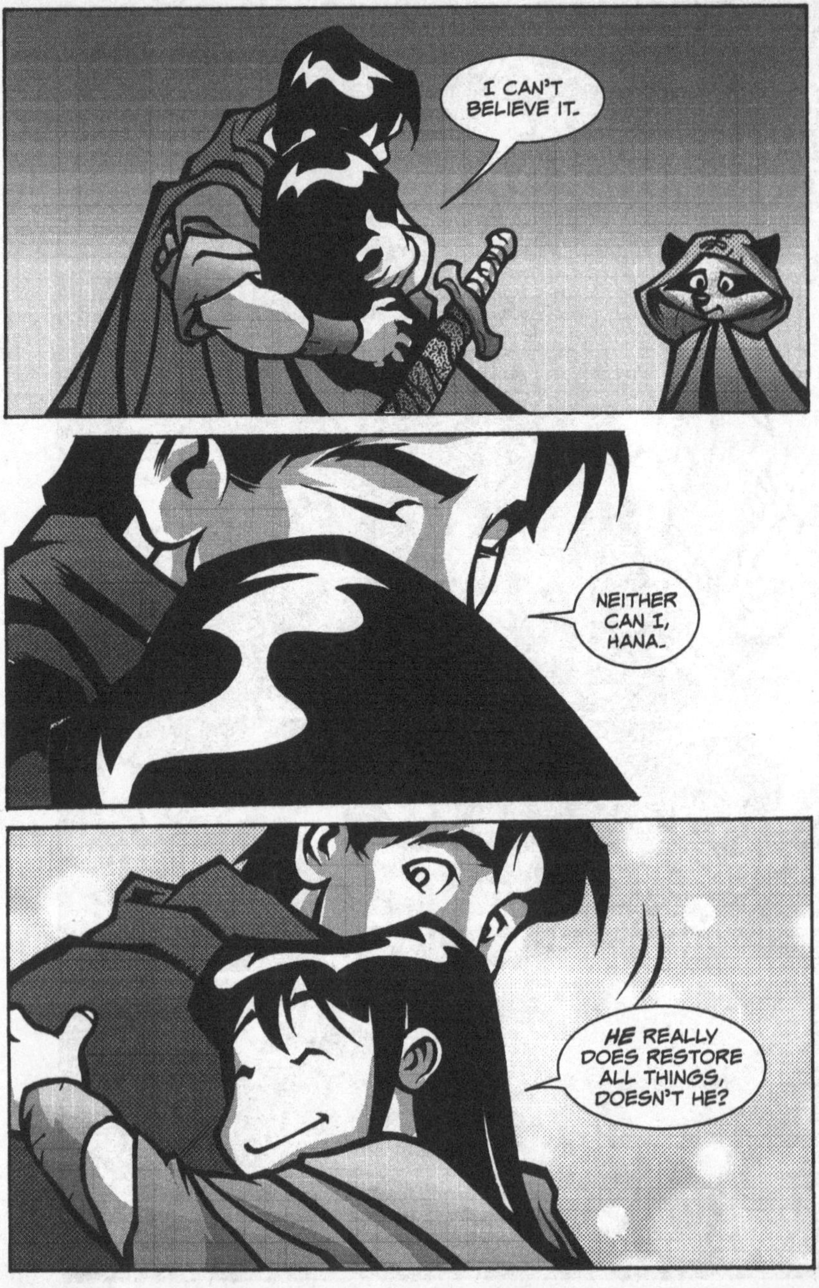
I CAN'T BELIEVE IT.
NEITHER CAN I, HANA.
HE REALLY DOES RESTORE ALL THINGS, DOESN'T HE?

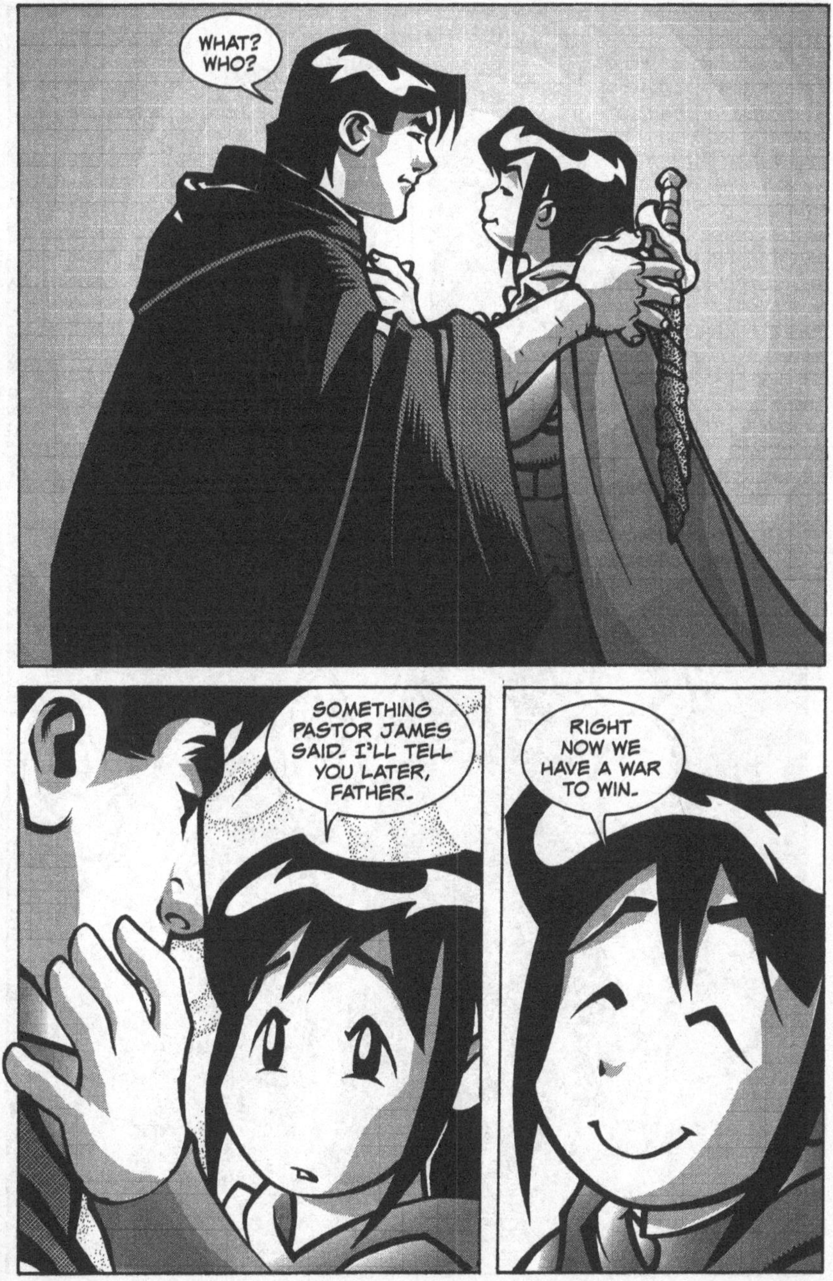
WHAT? WHO?
SOMETHING PASTOR JAMES SAID. I'LL TELL YOU LATER, FATHER.
RIGHT NOW WE HAVE A WAR TO WIN.

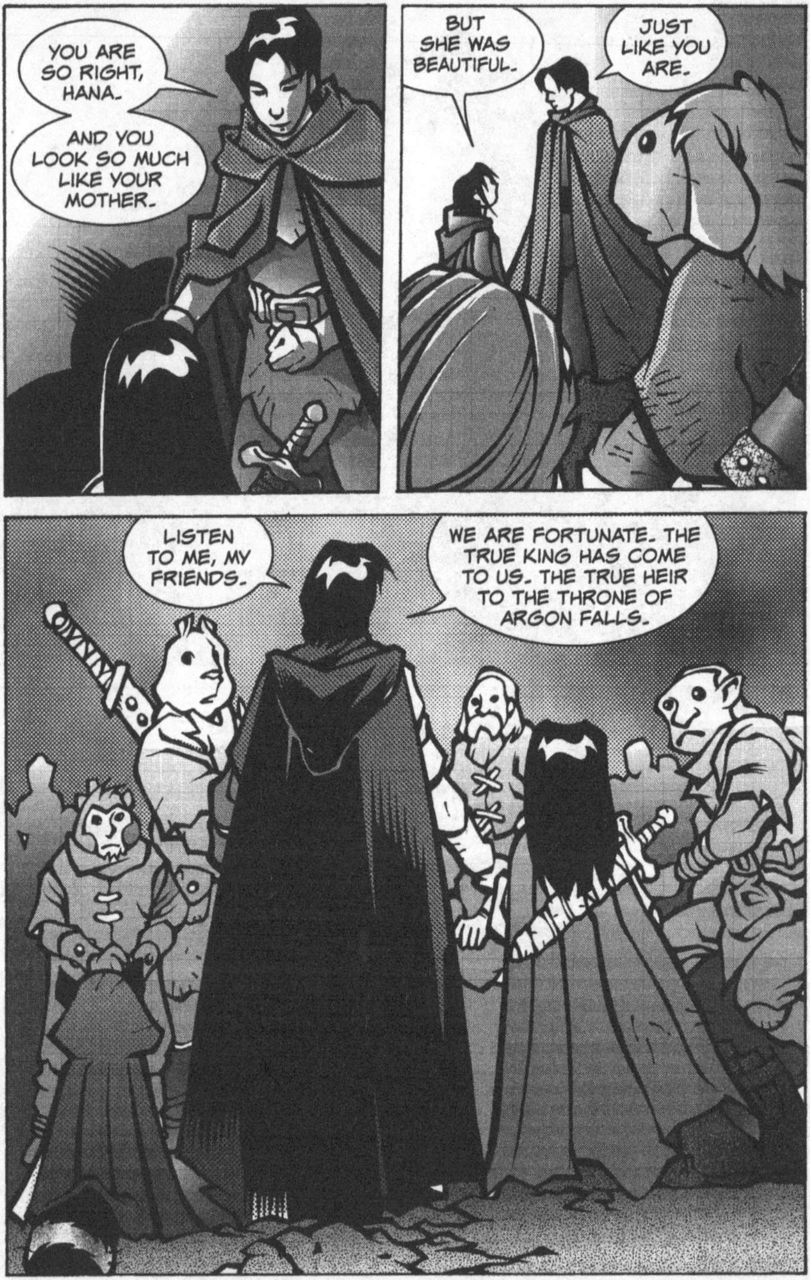
YOU ARE SO RIGHT, HANA.
AND YOU LOOK SO MUCH LIKE YOUR MOTHER.
BUT SHE WAS BEAUTIFUL.
JUST LIKE YOU ARE.
LISTEN TO ME, MY FRIENDS.
WE ARE FORTUNATE. THE TRUE KING HAS COME TO US. THE TRUE HEIR TO THE THRONE OF ARGON FALLS.

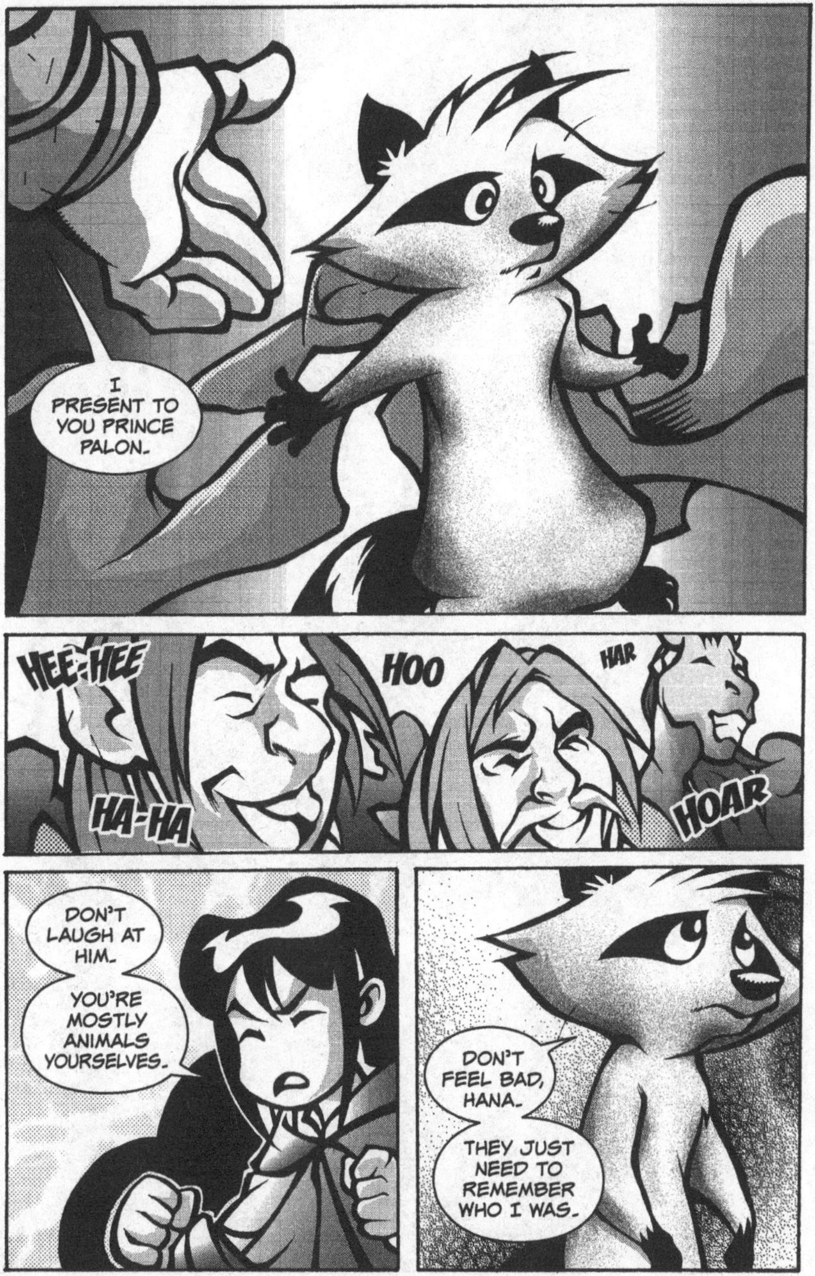
I PRESENT TO YOU PRINCE PALON.
HEE-HEE
HA-HA
HOO
HAR
HOAR
DON'T LAUGH AT HIM.
YOU'RE MOSTLY ANIMALS YOURSELVES.
DON'T FEEL BAD, HANA.
THEY JUST NEED TO REMEMBER WHO I WAS.

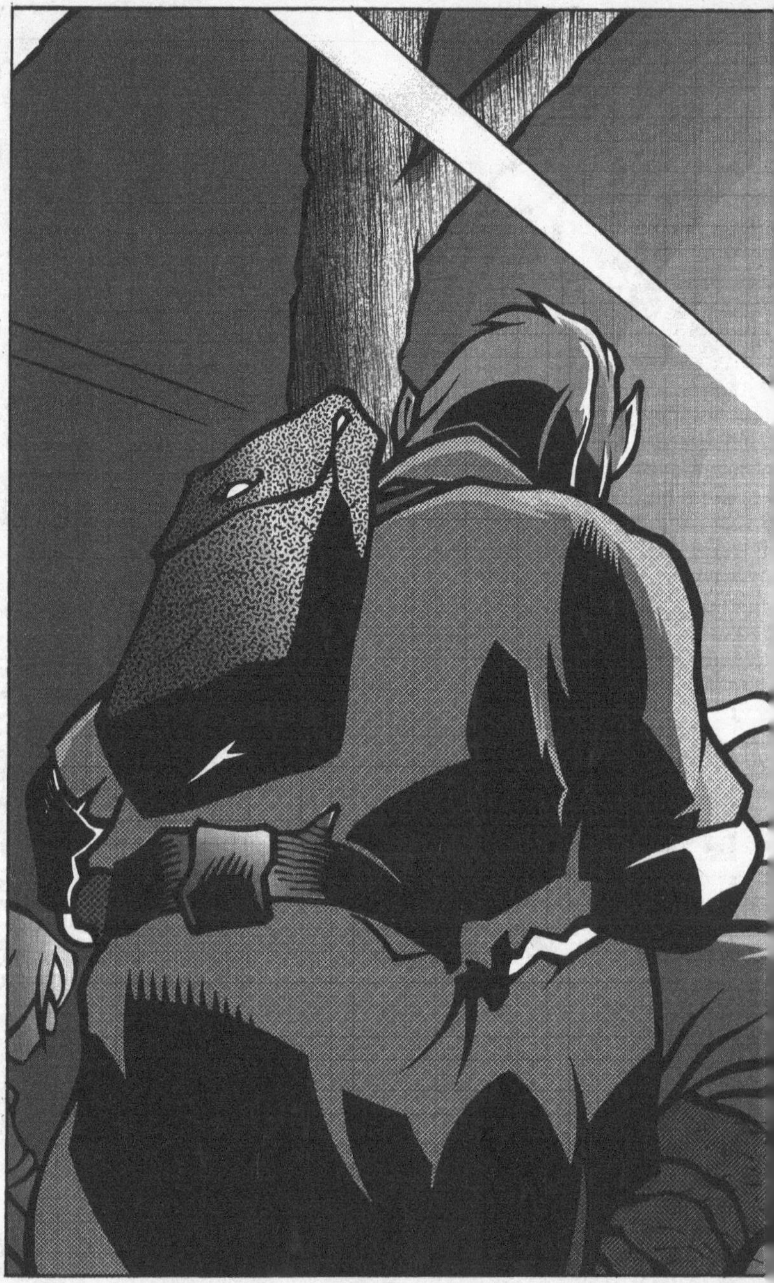

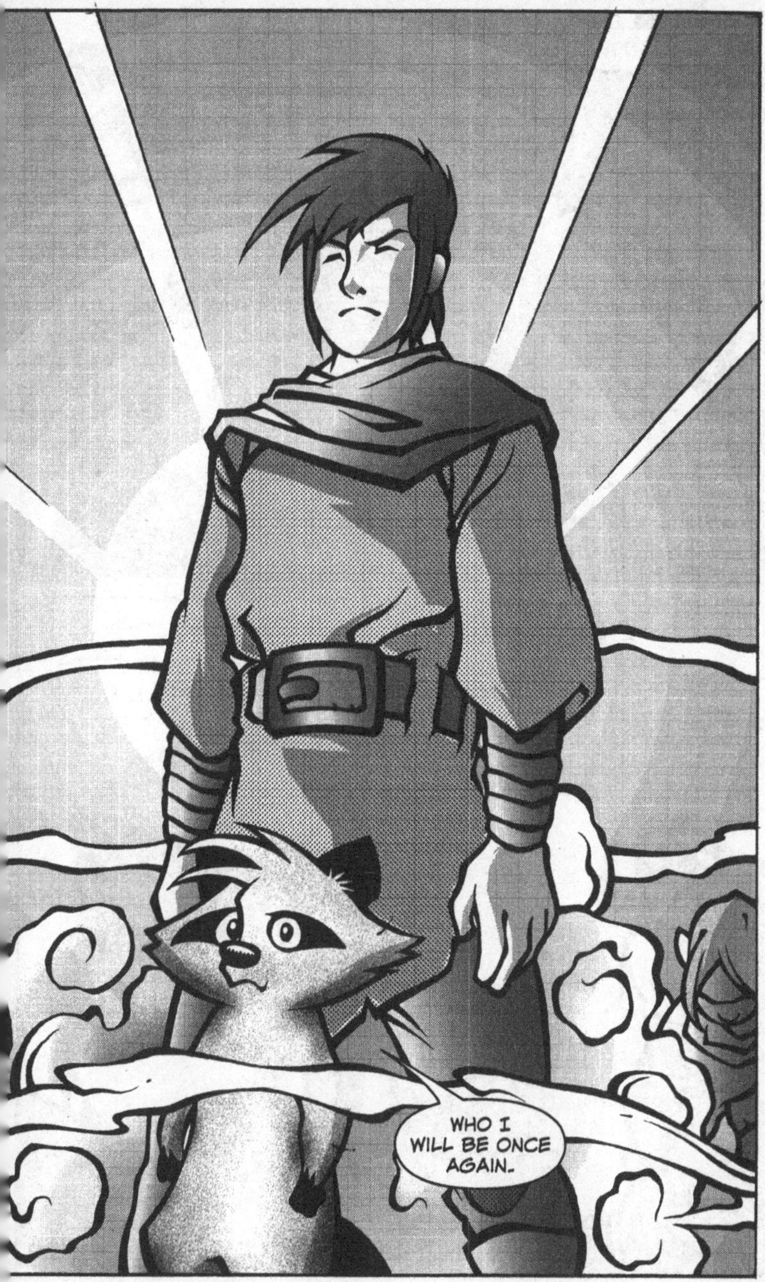
WHO I
WILL BE ONCE
AGAIN.

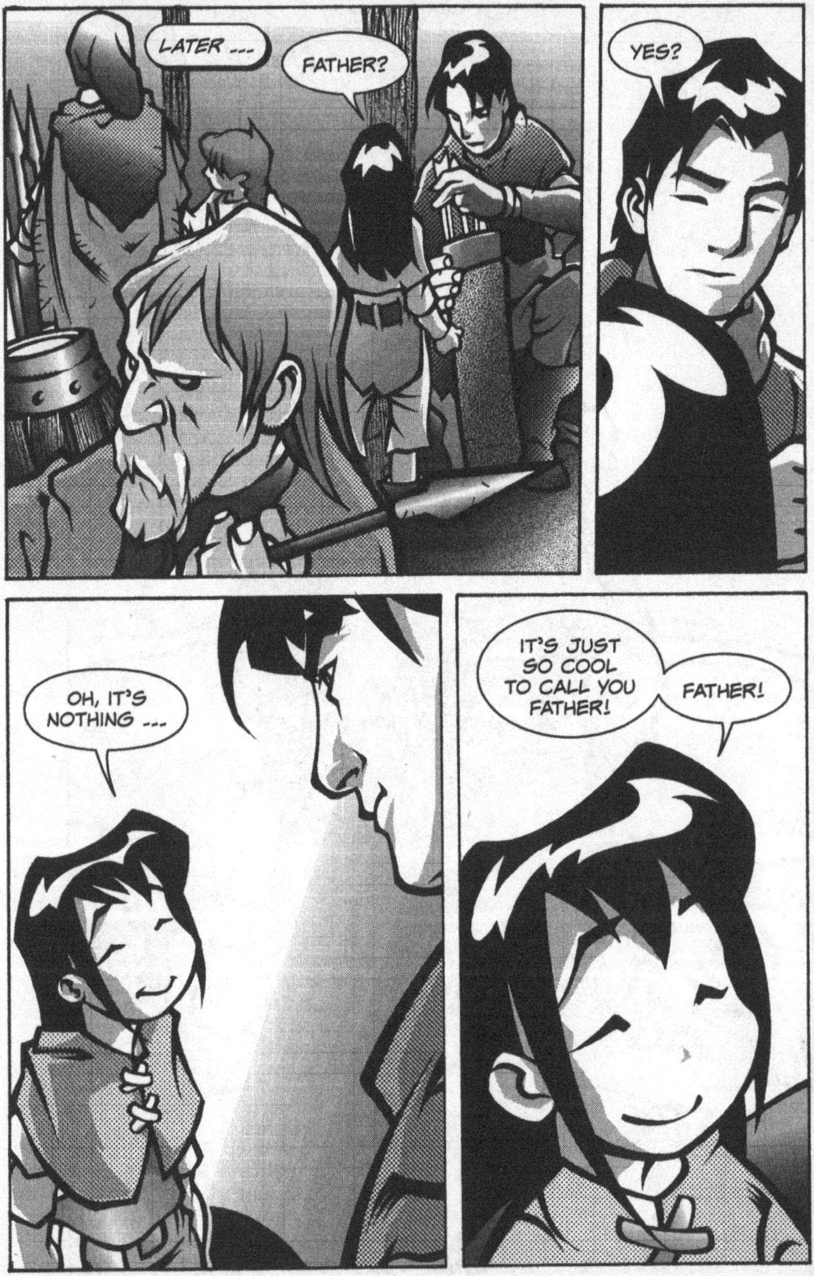
LATER ---
FATHER?
YES?
OH, IT'S NOTHING ---
IT'S JUST SO COOL TO CALL YOU FATHER!
FATHER!

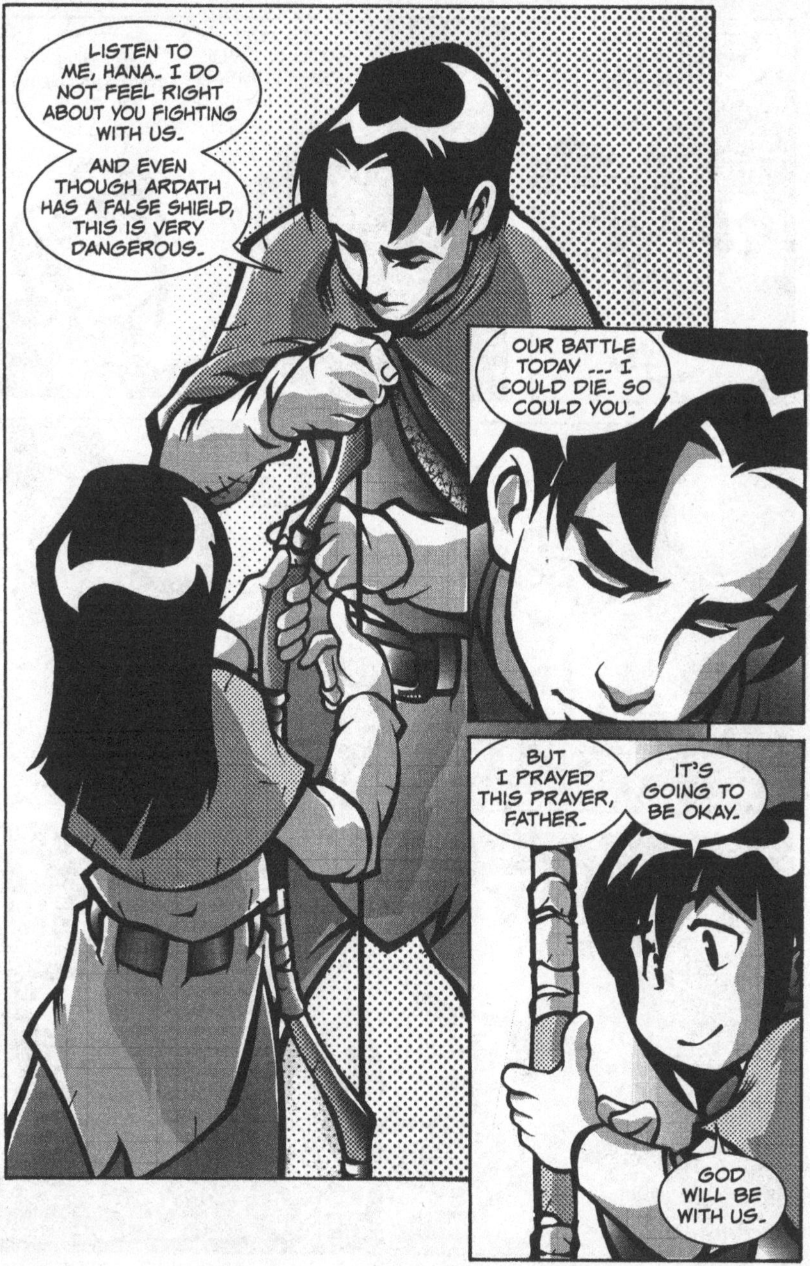
LISTEN TO ME, HANA. I DO NOT FEEL RIGHT ABOUT YOU FIGHTING WITH US.
AND EVEN THOUGH ARDATH HAS A FALSE SHIELD, THIS IS VERY DANGEROUS.
OUR BATTLE TODAY ... I COULD DIE. SO COULD YOU.
BUT I PRAYED THIS PRAYER, FATHER.
IT'S GOING TO BE OKAY.
GOD WILL BE WITH US.

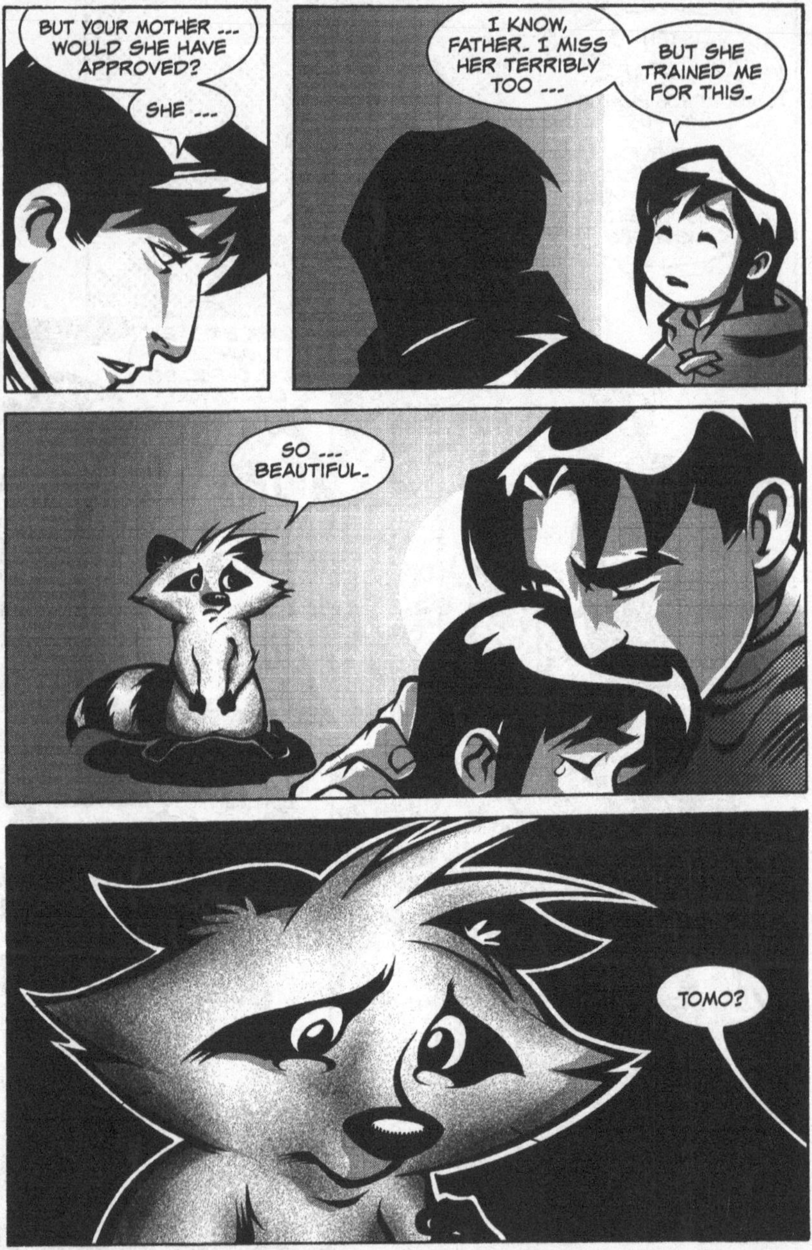
BUT YOUR MOTHER ... WOULD SHE HAVE APPROVED?
SHE ...
I KNOW, FATHER. I MISS HER TERRIBLY TOO ...
BUT SHE TRAINED ME FOR THIS.
SO ... BEAUTIFUL.
TOMO?

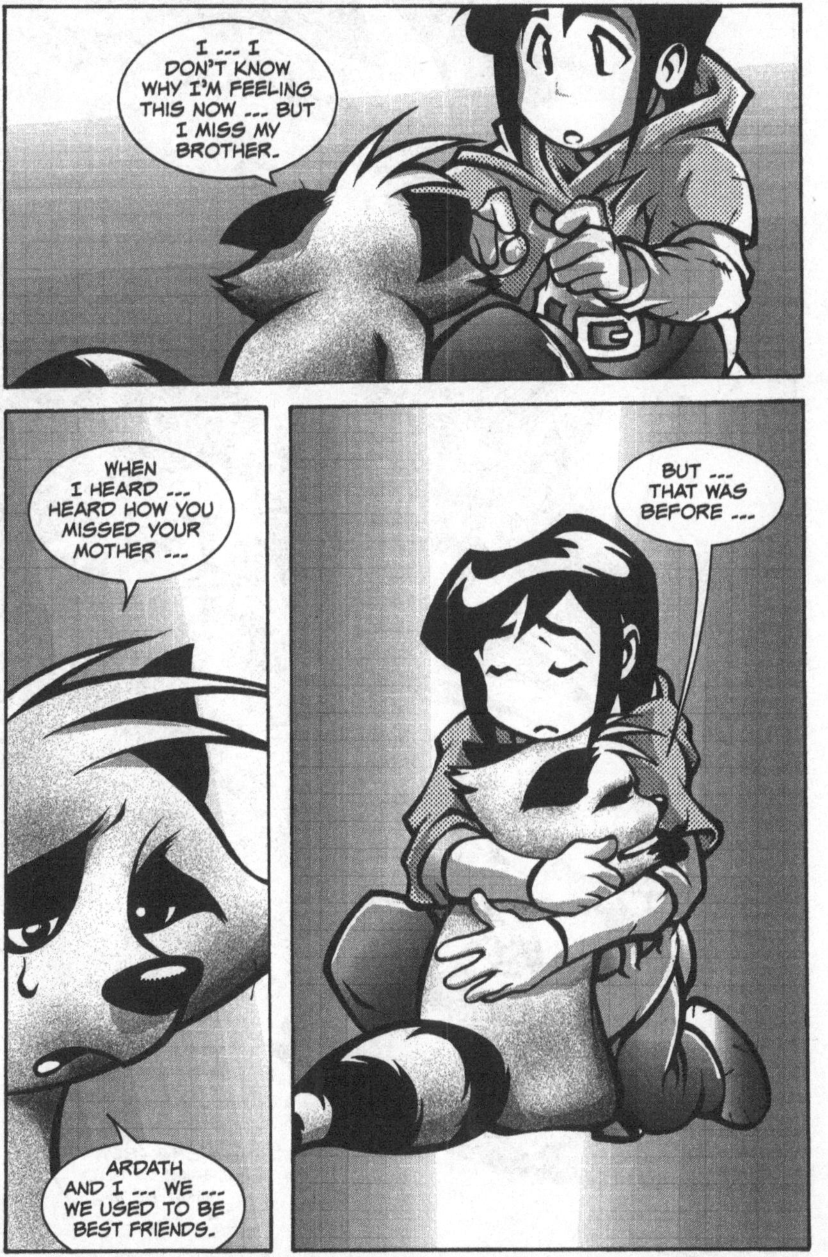
I ... I DON'T KNOW WHY I'M FEELING THIS NOW ... BUT I MISS MY BROTHER.
WHEN I HEARD ... HEARD HOW YOU MISSED YOUR MOTHER ...
ARDATH AND I ... WE ... WE USED TO BE BEST FRIENDS.
BUT ... THAT WAS BEFORE ...

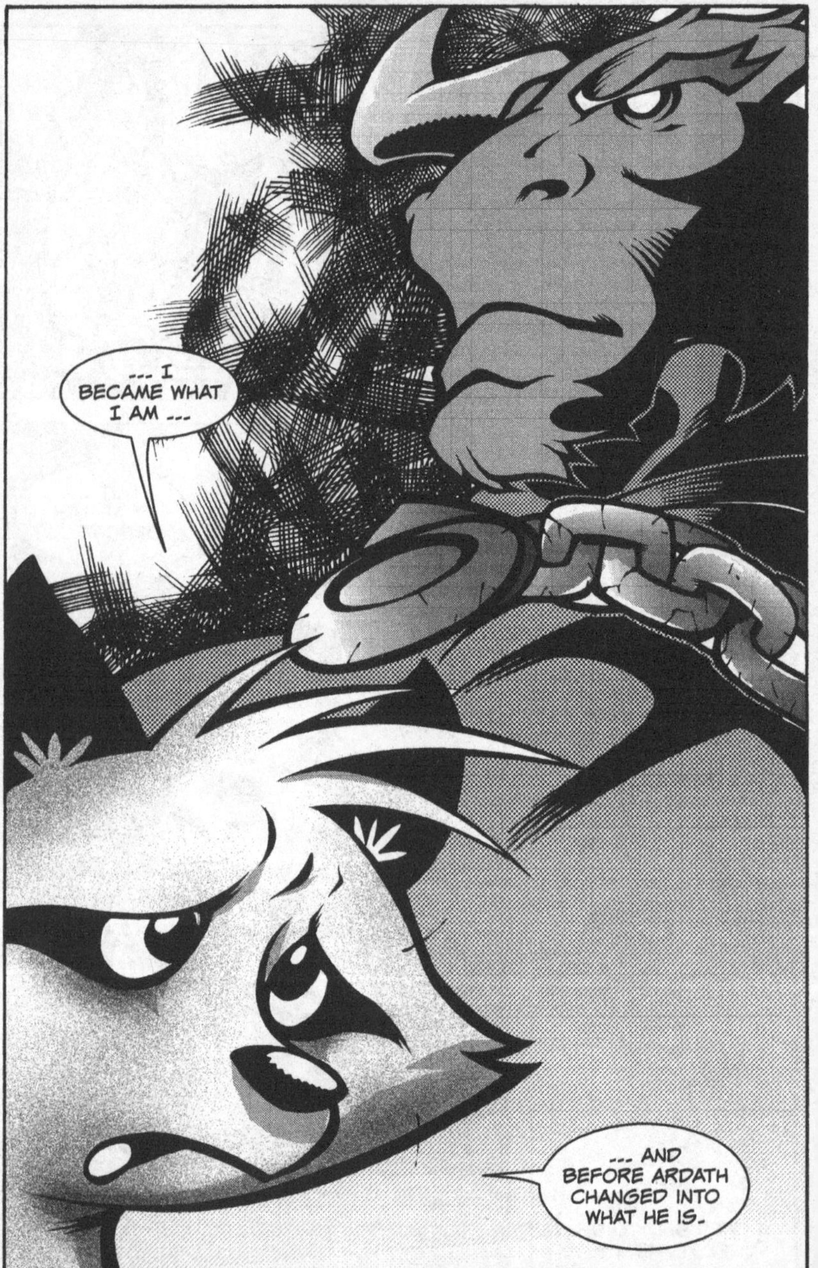
--- I BECAME WHAT I AM ---
--- AND BEFORE ARDATH CHANGED INTO WHAT HE IS.

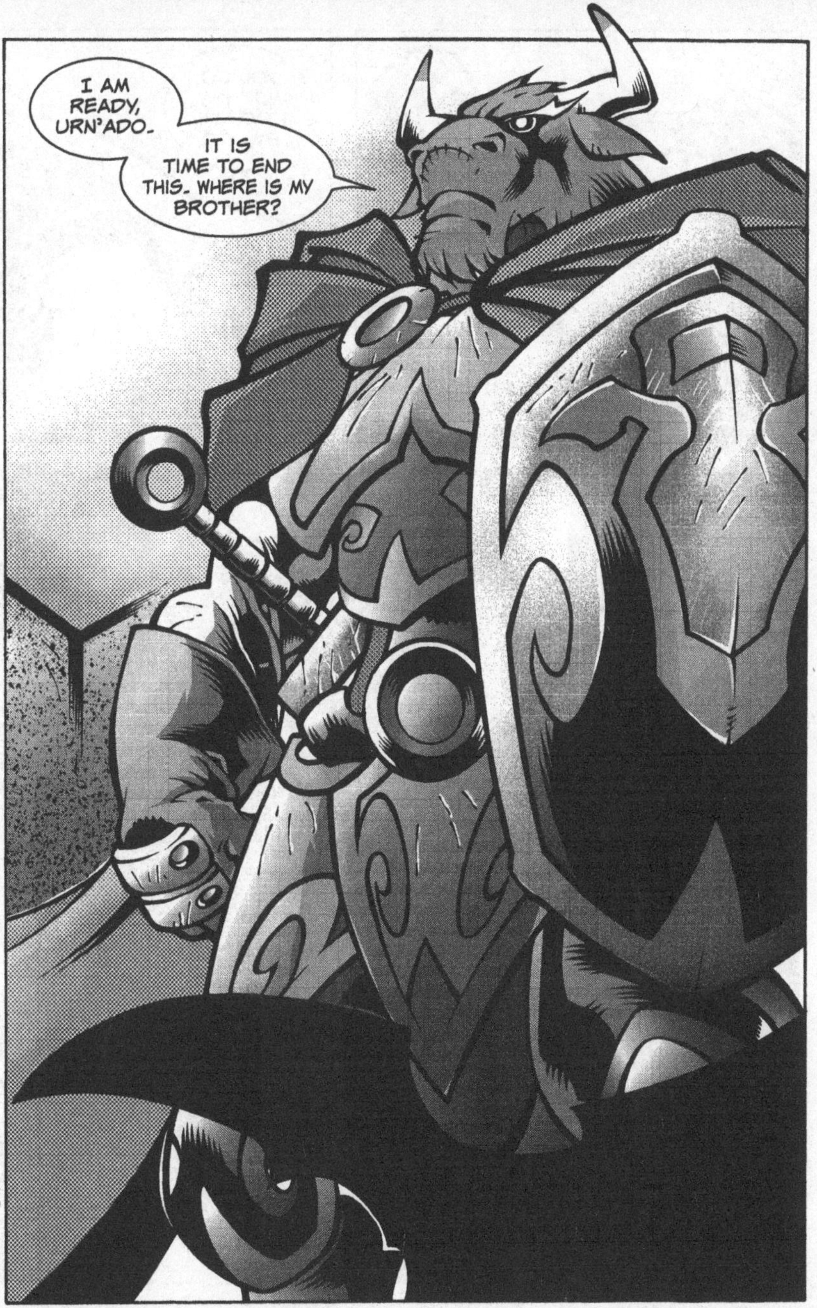
I AM READY, URN'ADO.
IT IS TIME TO END THIS. WHERE IS MY BROTHER?

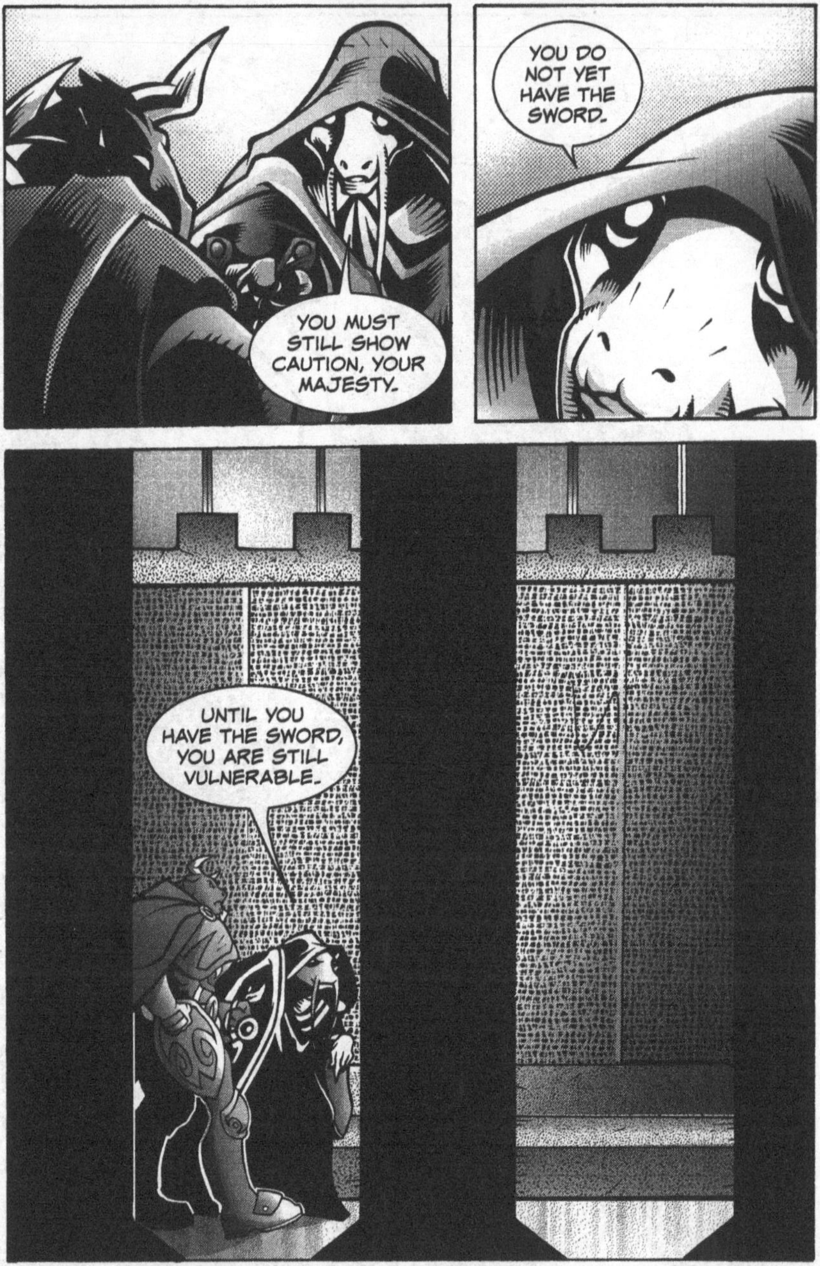
YOU MUST STILL SHOW CAUTION, YOUR MAJESTY.
YOU DO NOT YET HAVE THE SWORD.
UNTIL YOU HAVE THE SWORD, YOU ARE STILL VULNERABLE.

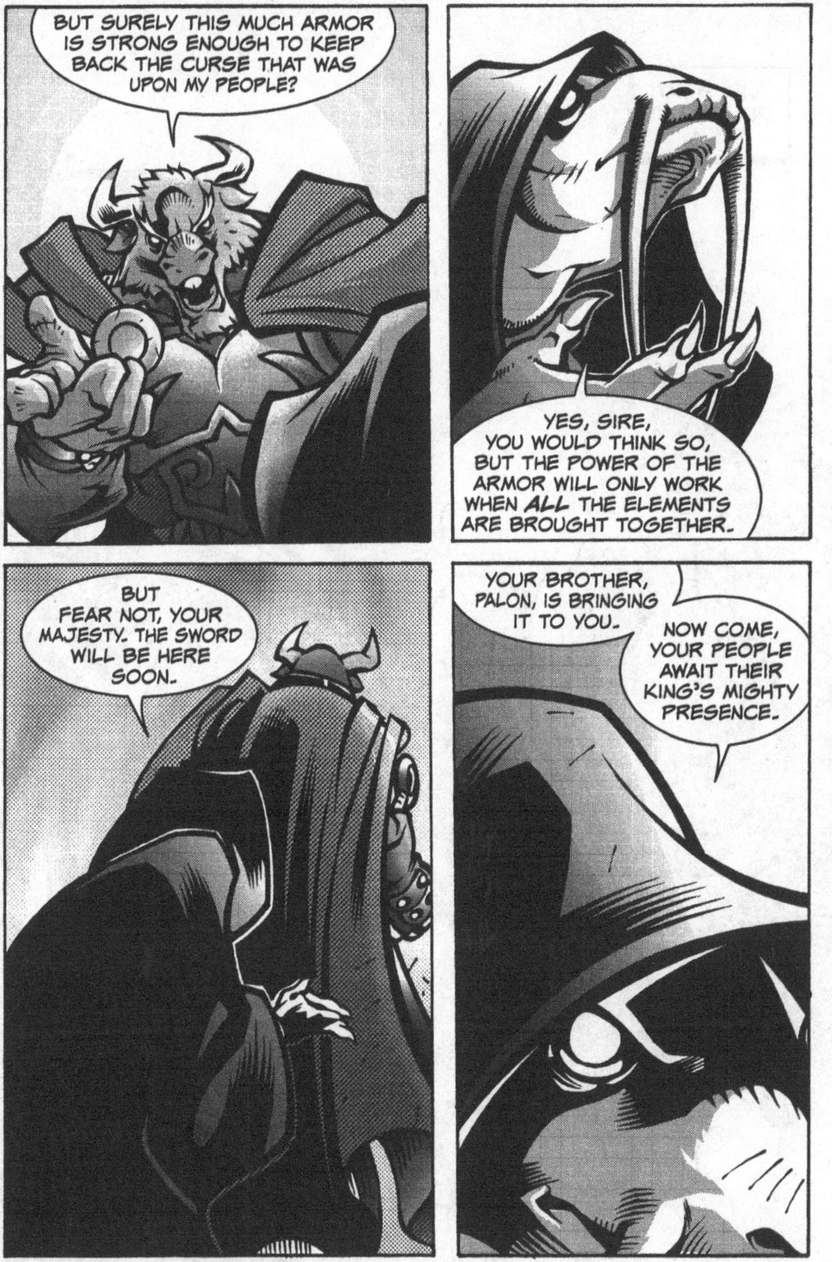
BUT SURELY THIS MUCH ARMOR IS STRONG ENOUGH TO KEEP BACK THE CURSE THAT WAS UPON MY PEOPLE?
YES, SIRE, YOU WOULD THINK SO, BUT THE POWER OF THE ARMOR WILL ONLY WORK WHEN ALL THE ELEMENTS ARE BROUGHT TOGETHER.
BUT FEAR NOT, YOUR MAJESTY. THE SWORD WILL BE HERE SOON.
YOUR BROTHER, PALON, IS BRINGING IT TO YOU.
NOW COME, YOUR PEOPLE AWAIT THEIR KING'S MIGHTY PRESENCE.

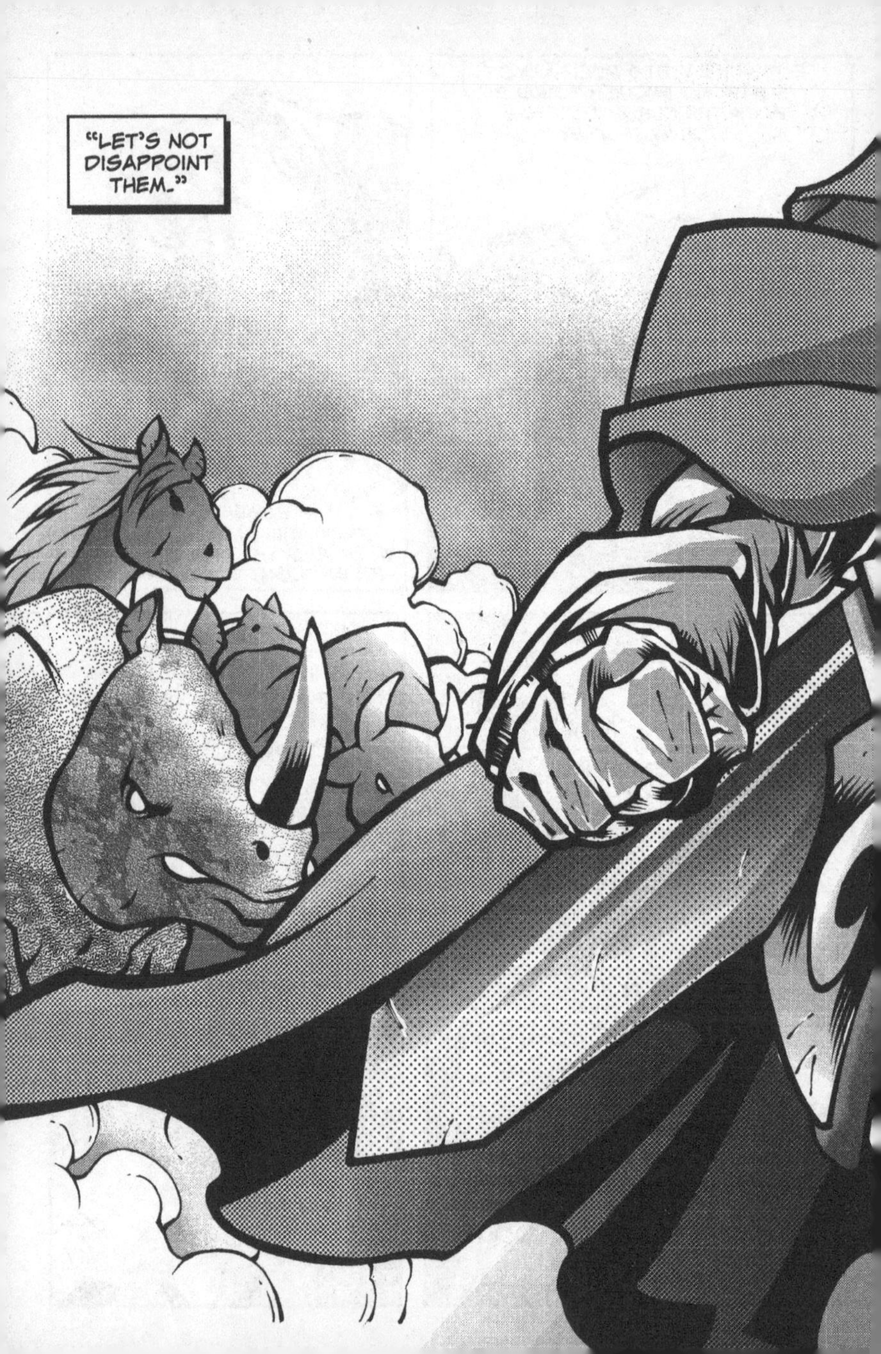
"LET'S NOT DISAPPOINT THEM."

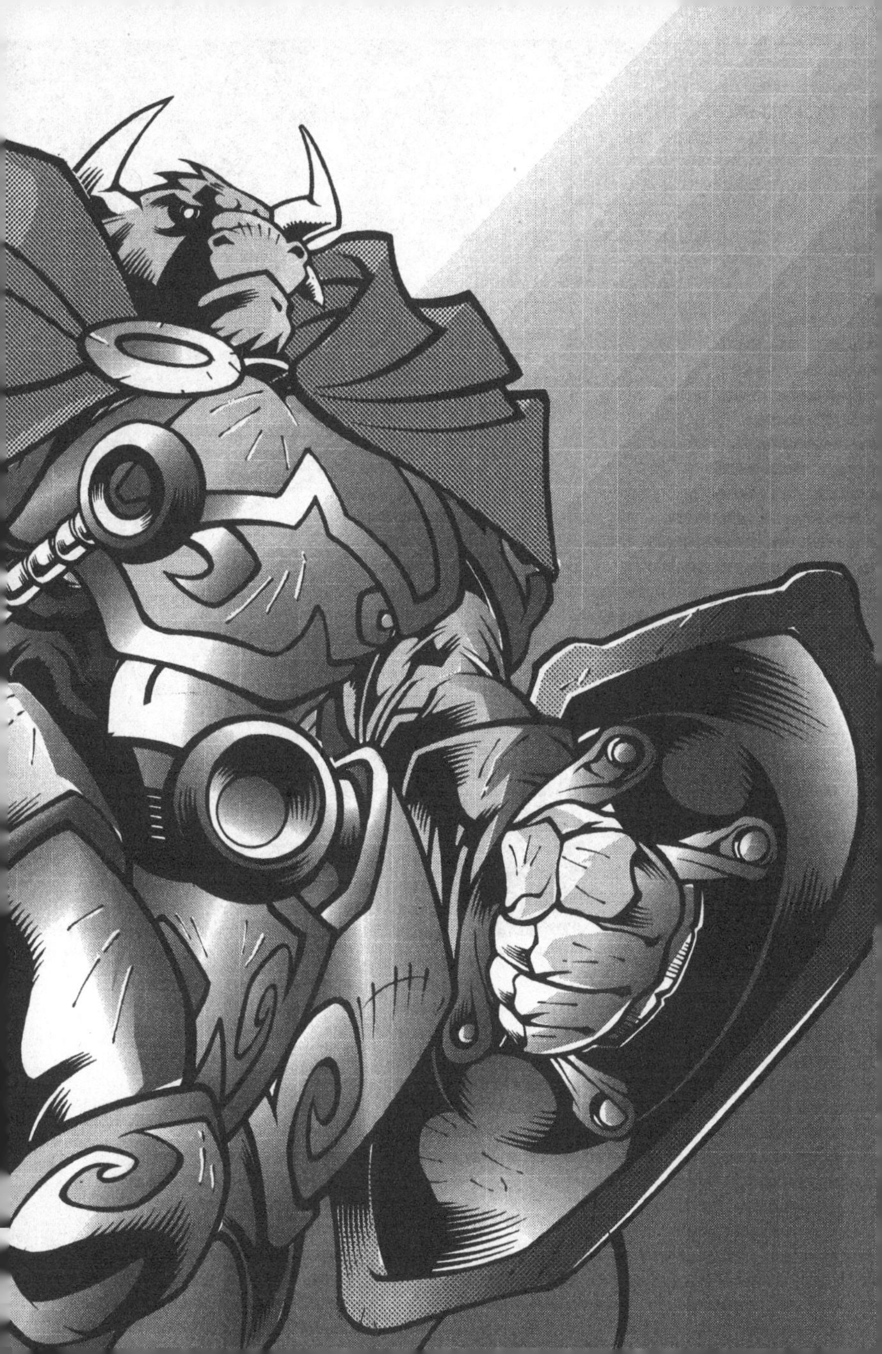

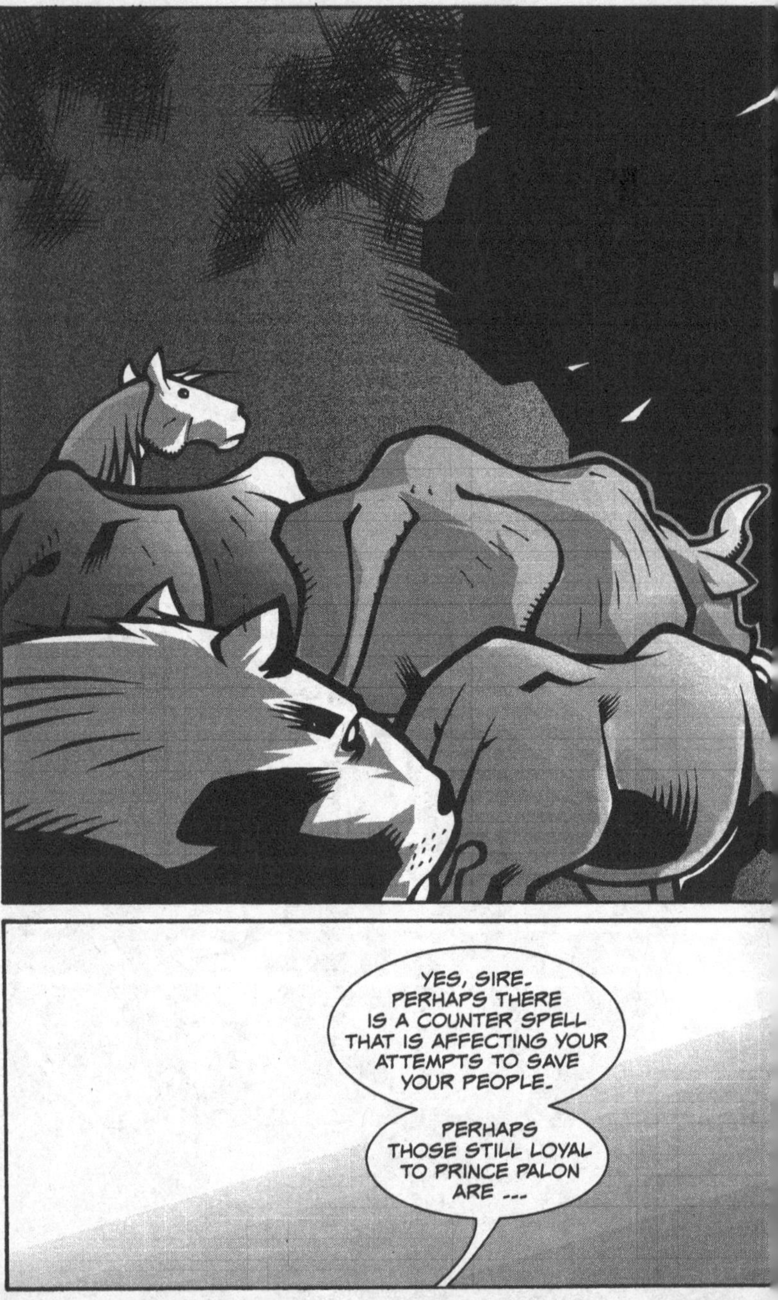
YES, SIRE. PERHAPS THERE IS A COUNTER SPELL THAT IS AFFECTING YOUR ATTEMPTS TO SAVE YOUR PEOPLE.
PERHAPS THOSE STILL LOYAL TO PRINCE PALON ARE ...

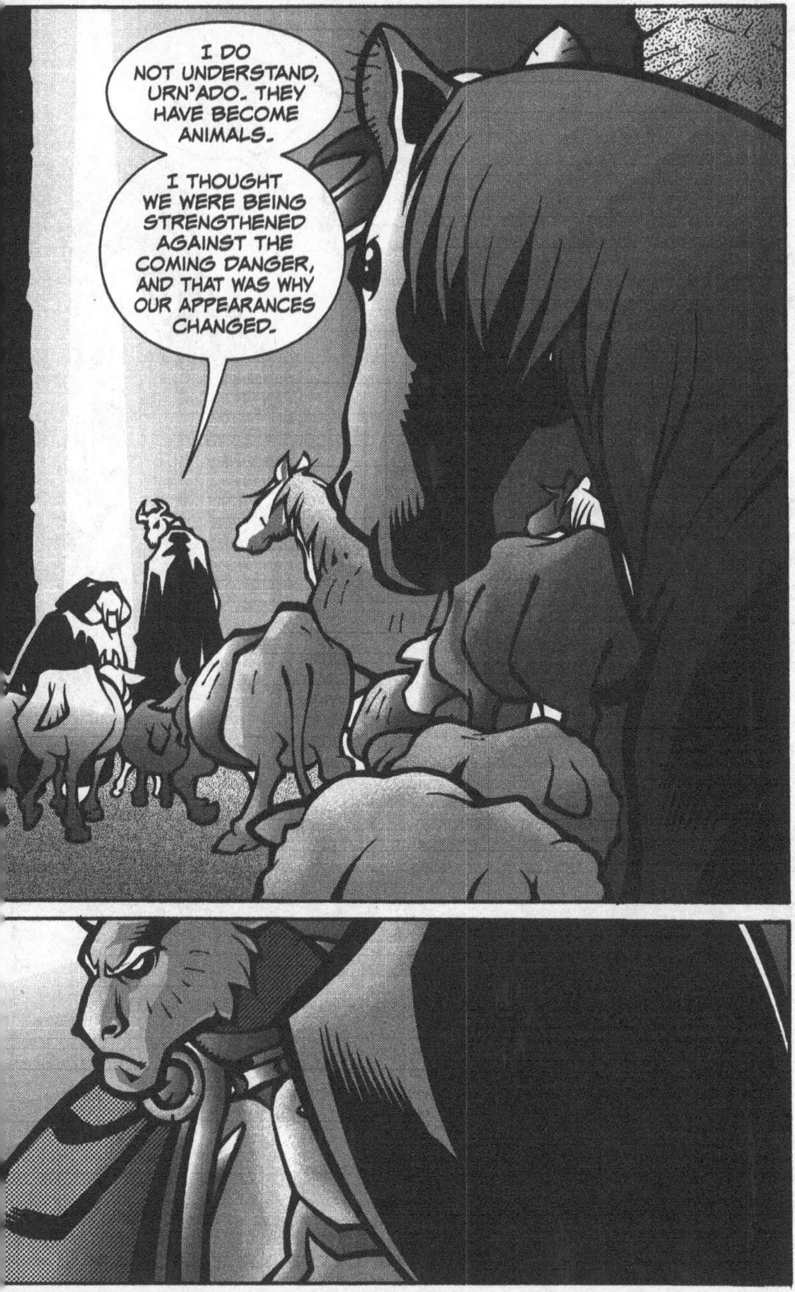
I DO NOT UNDERSTAND, URN'ADO. THEY HAVE BECOME ANIMALS.
I THOUGHT WE WERE BEING STRENGTHENED AGAINST THE COMING DANGER, AND THAT WAS WHY OUR APPEARANCES CHANGED.

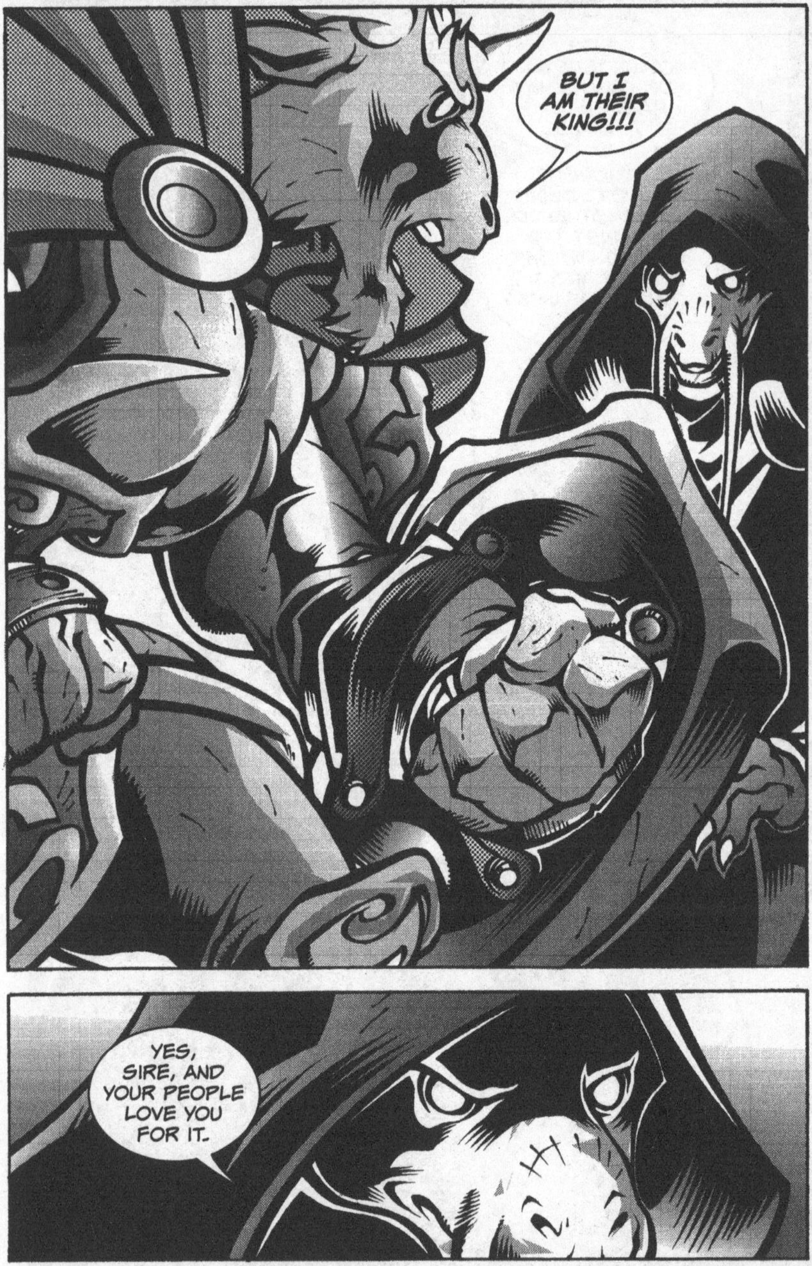
BUT I AM THEIR KING!!!
YES, SIRE, AND YOUR PEOPLE LOVE YOU FOR IT.

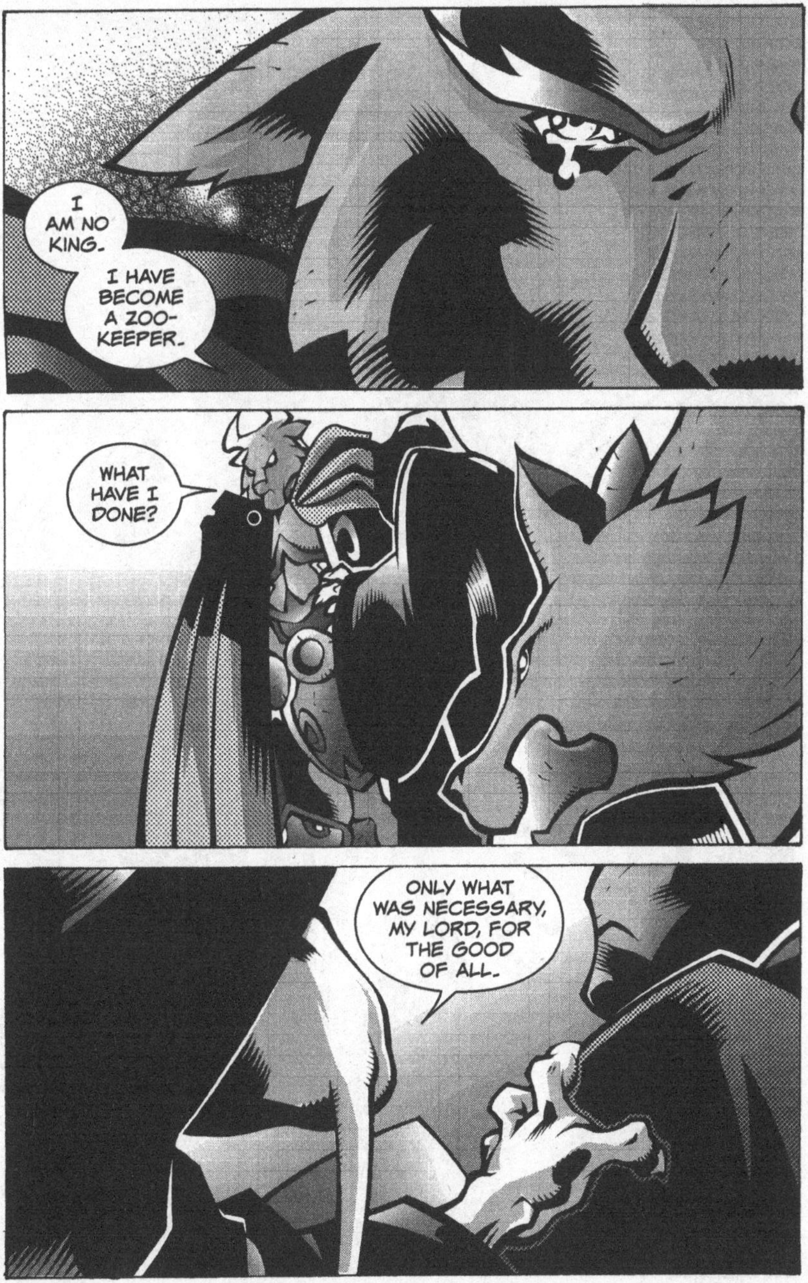
I AM NO KING.
I HAVE BECOME A ZOO-KEEPER.
WHAT HAVE I DONE?
ONLY WHAT WAS NECESSARY, MY LORD, FOR THE GOOD OF ALL.

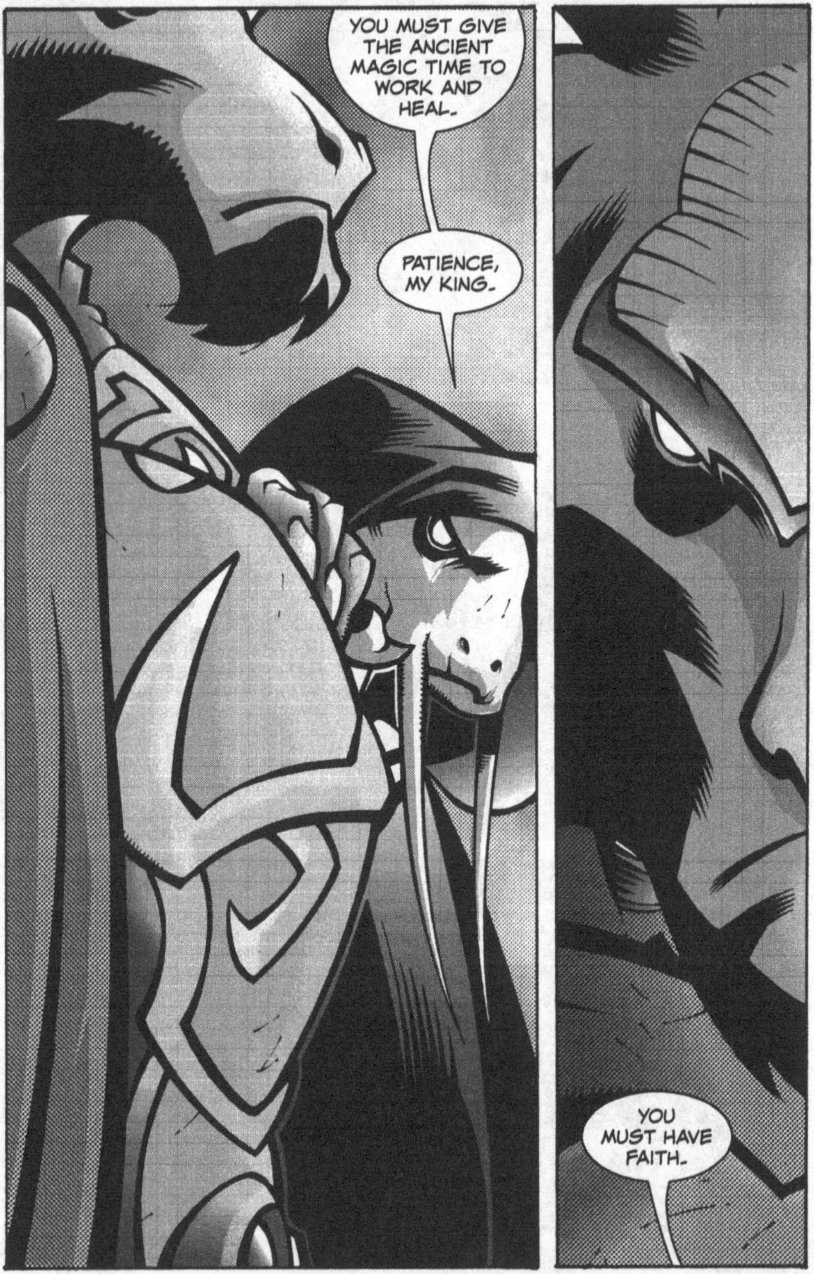
YOU MUST GIVE THE ANCIENT MAGIC TIME TO WORK AND HEAL.
PATIENCE, MY KING.
YOU MUST HAVE FAITH.

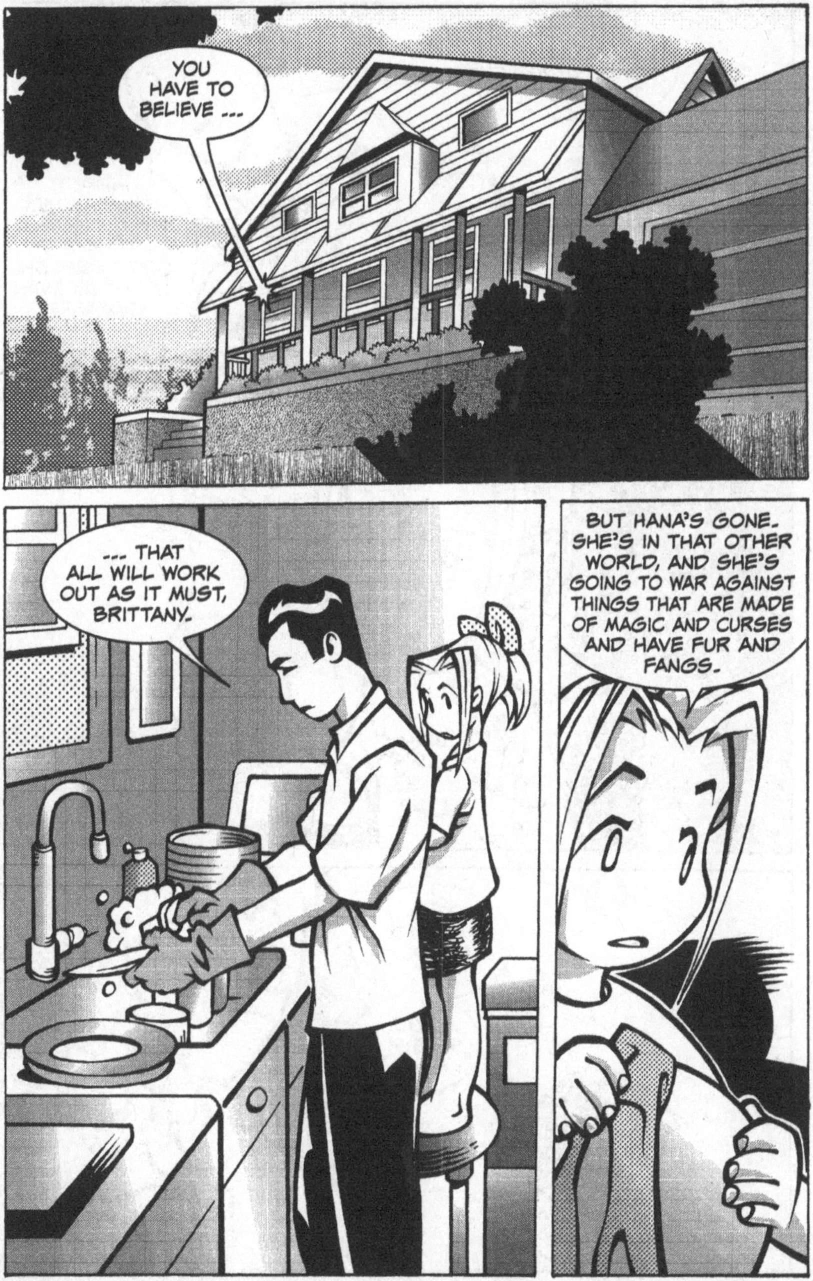
YOU HAVE TO BELIEVE ...
... THAT ALL WILL WORK OUT AS IT MUST, BRITTANY.
BUT HANA'S GONE. SHE'S IN THAT OTHER WORLD, AND SHE'S GOING TO WAR AGAINST THINGS THAT ARE MADE OF MAGIC AND CURSES AND HAVE FUR AND FANGS.

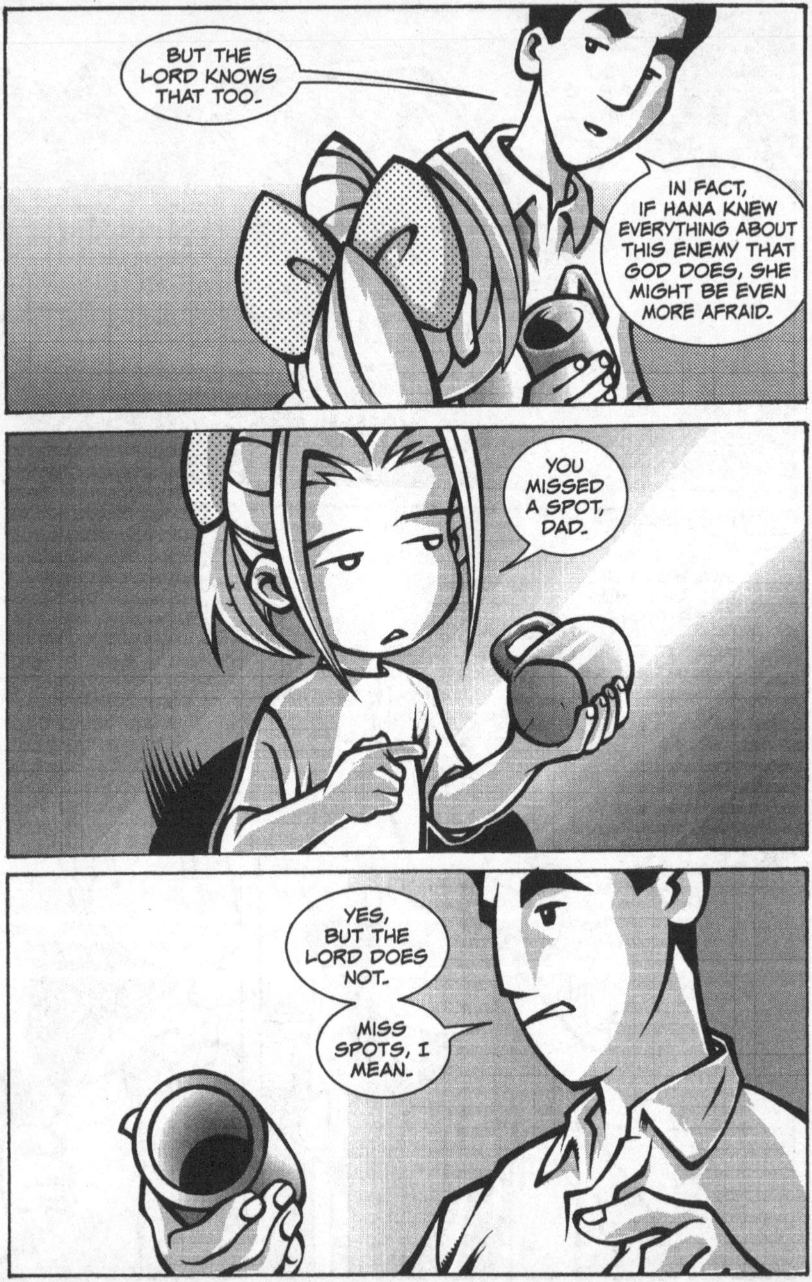
BUT THE LORD KNOWS THAT TOO.
IN FACT, IF HANA KNEW EVERYTHING ABOUT THIS ENEMY THAT GOD DOES, SHE MIGHT BE EVEN MORE AFRAID.
YOU MISSED A SPOT, DAD.
YES, BUT THE LORD DOES NOT.
MISS SPOTS, I MEAN.

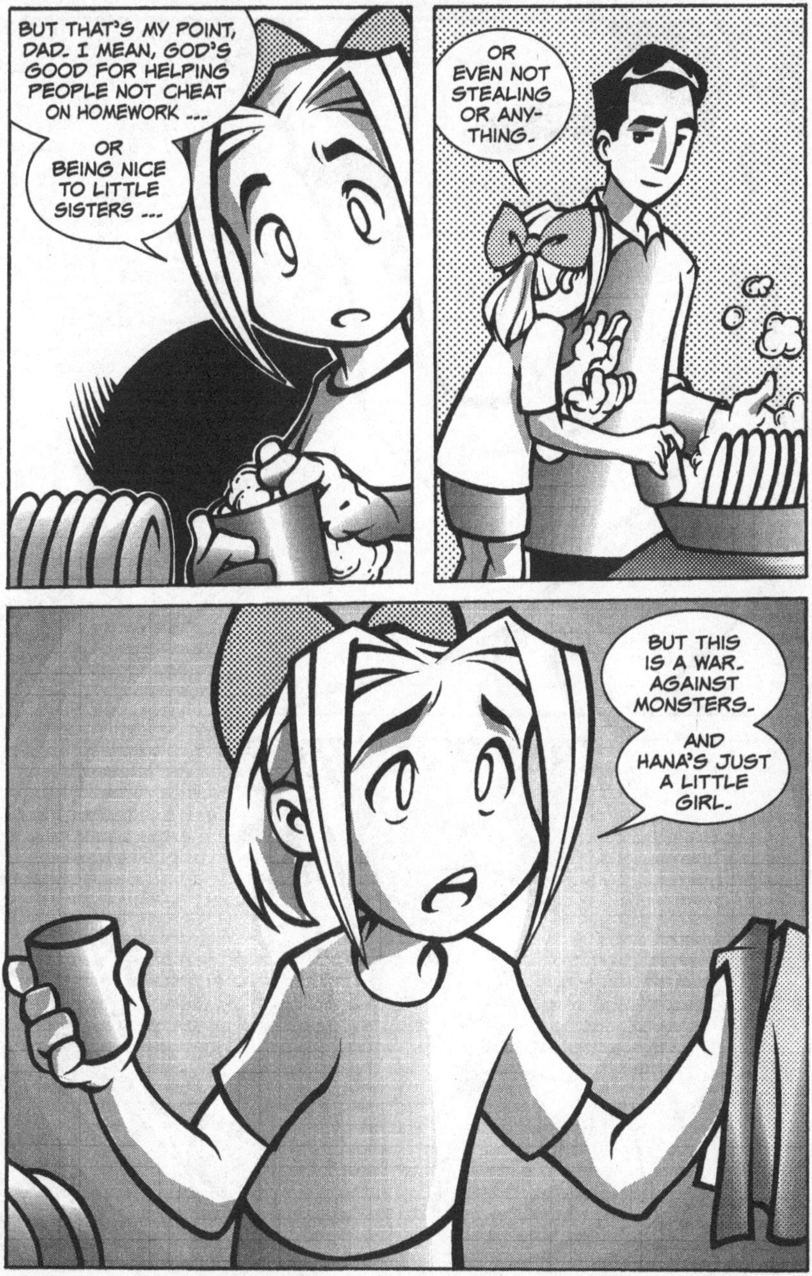
BUT THAT'S MY POINT, DAD. I MEAN, GOD'S GOOD FOR HELPING PEOPLE NOT CHEAT ON HOMEWORK ...
OR BEING NICE TO LITTLE SISTERS ...
OR EVEN NOT STEALING OR ANY-THING.
BUT THIS IS A WAR. AGAINST MONSTERS.
AND HANA'S JUST A LITTLE GIRL.

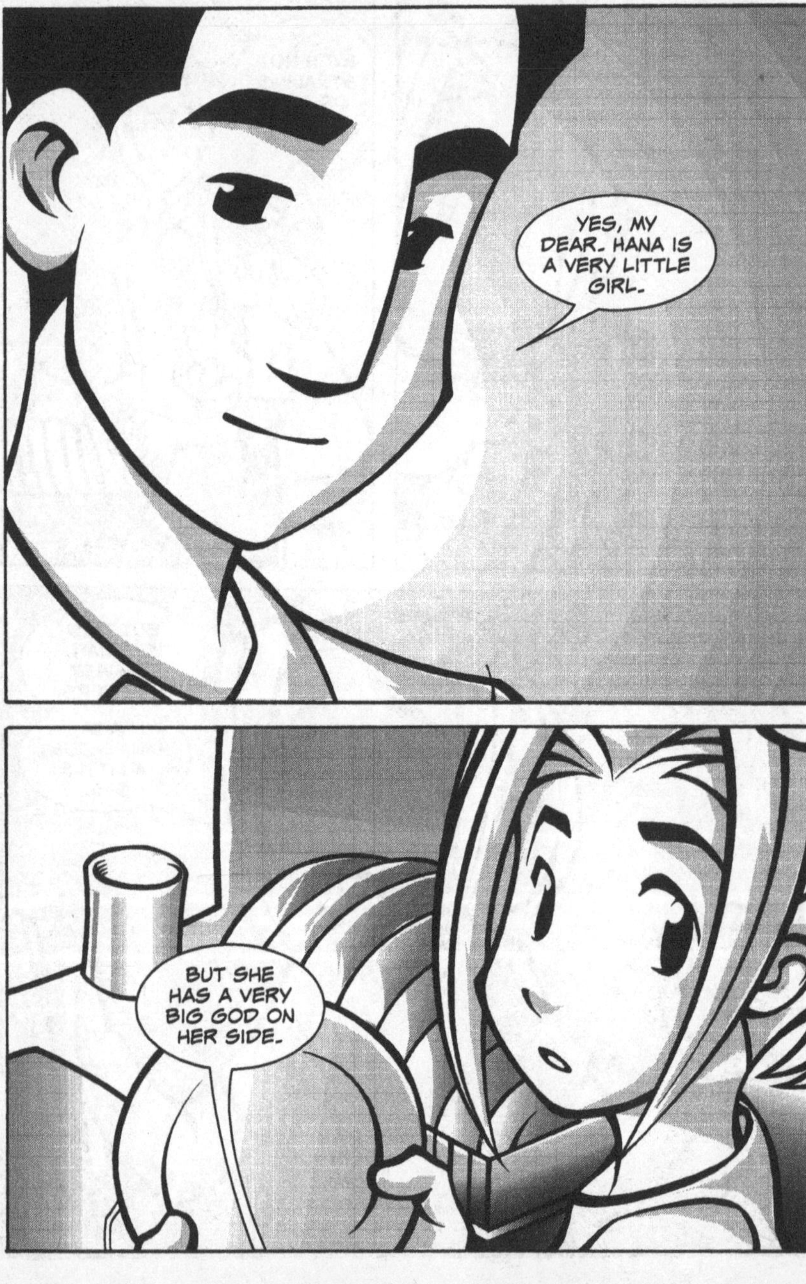
YES, MY DEAR. HANA IS A VERY LITTLE GIRL.
BUT SHE HAS A VERY BIG GOD ON HER SIDE.

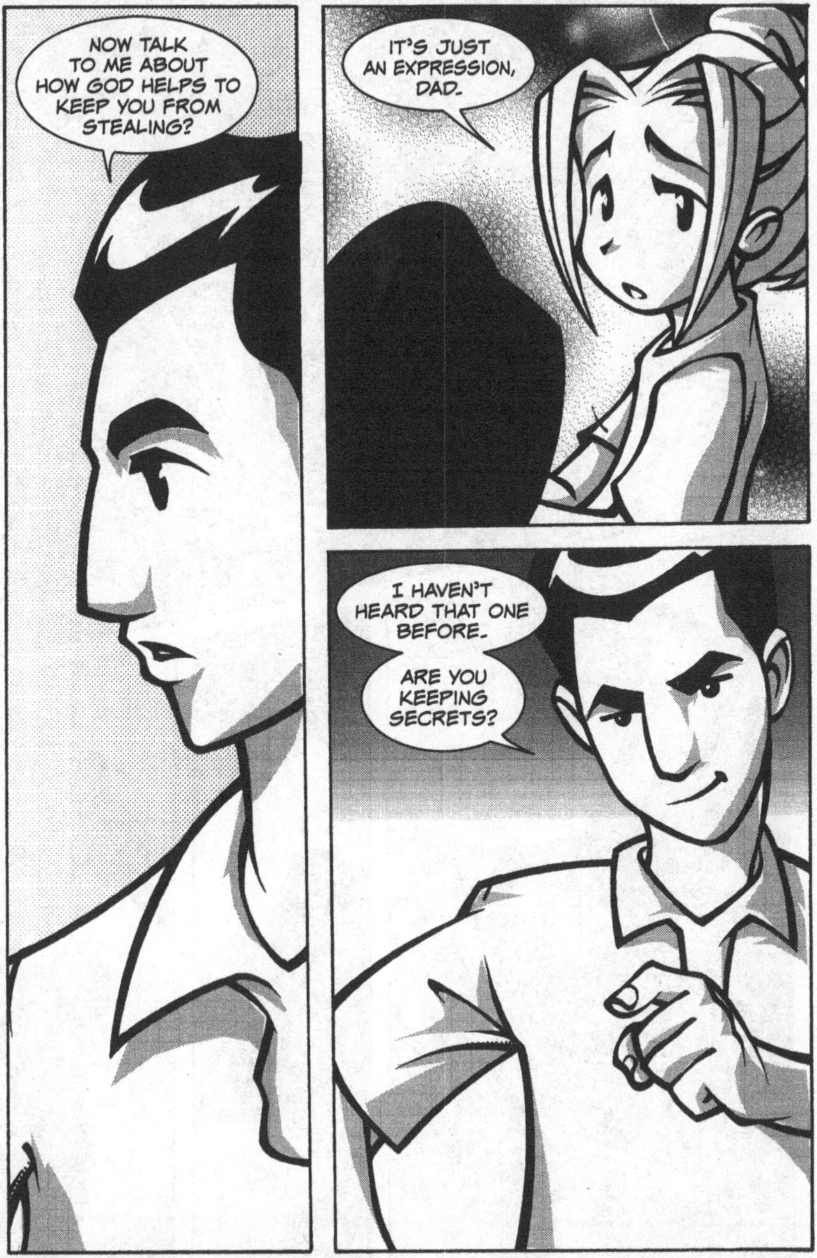
NOW TALK TO ME ABOUT HOW GOD HELPS TO KEEP YOU FROM STEALING?
IT'S JUST AN EXPRESSION, DAD.
I HAVEN'T HEARD THAT ONE BEFORE.
ARE YOU KEEPING SECRETS?

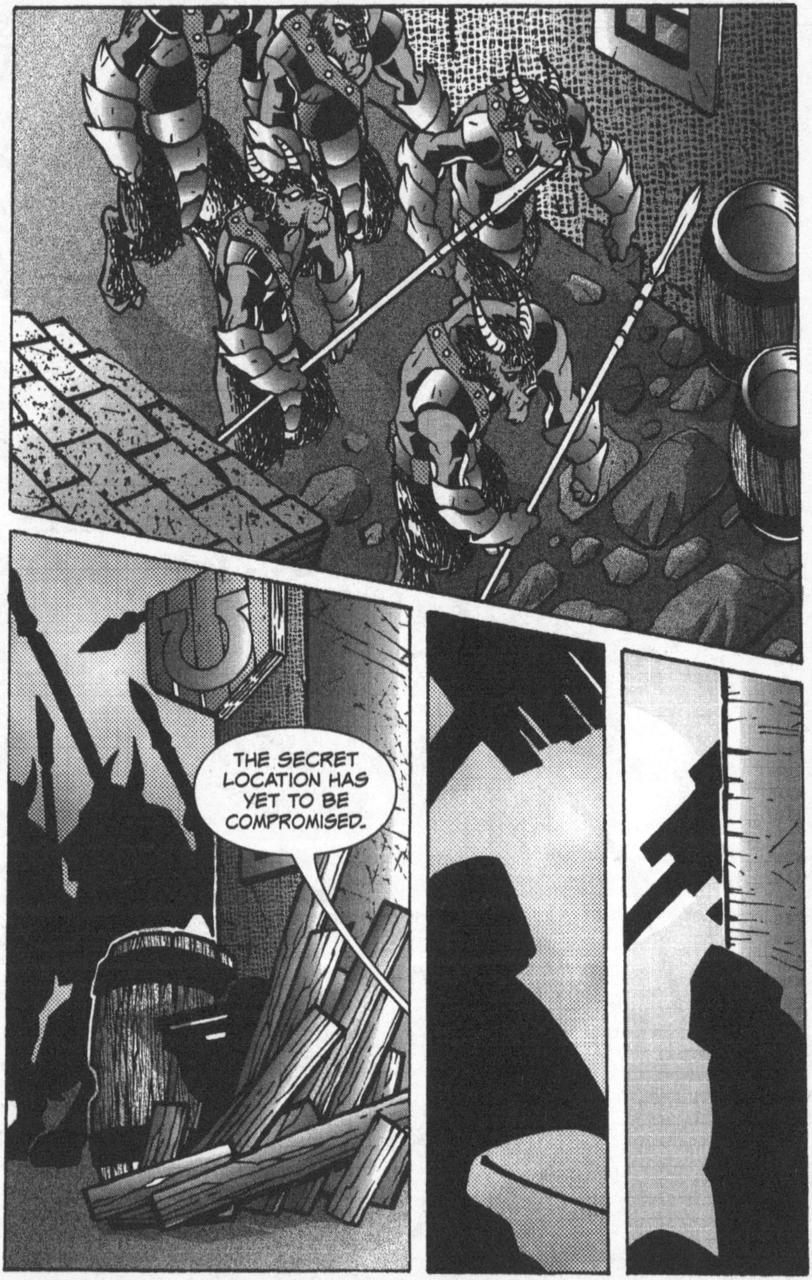
THE SECRET LOCATION HAS YET TO BE COMPROMISED.

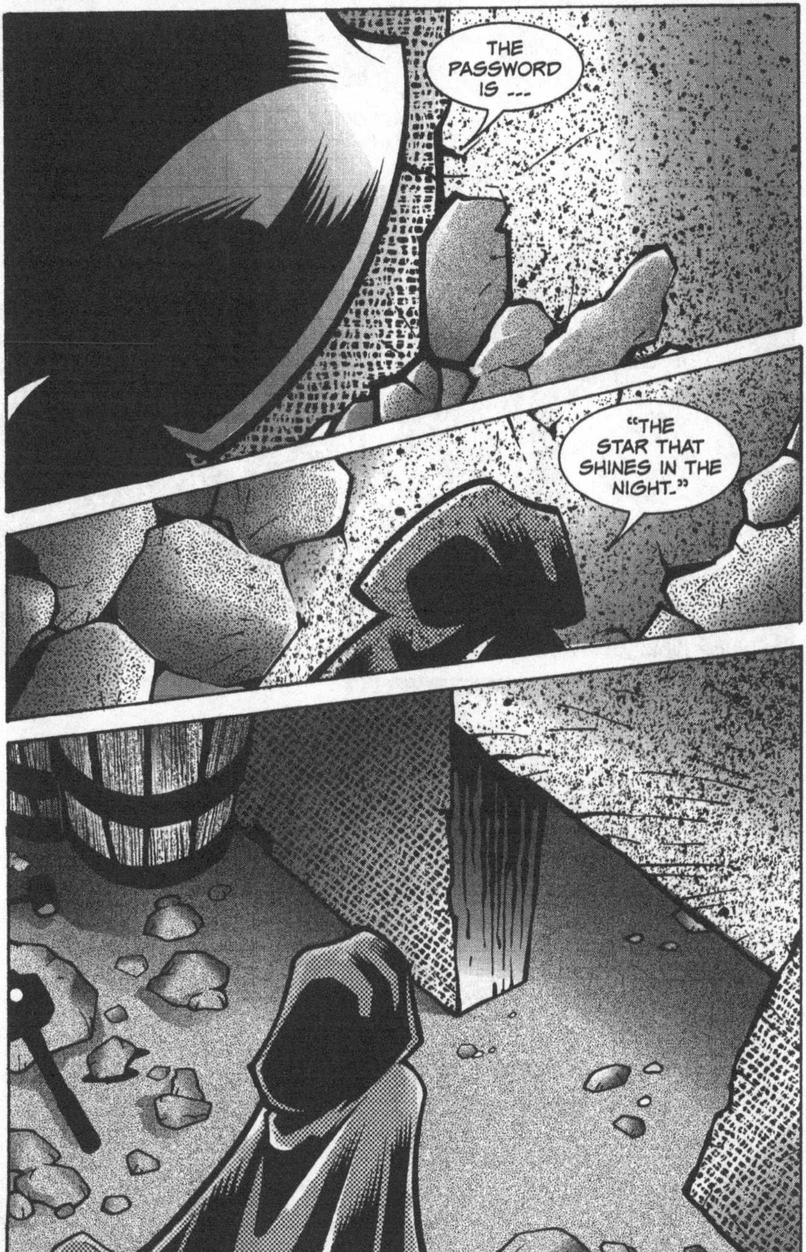
THE PASSWORD IS ---
"THE STAR THAT SHINES IN THE NIGHT."

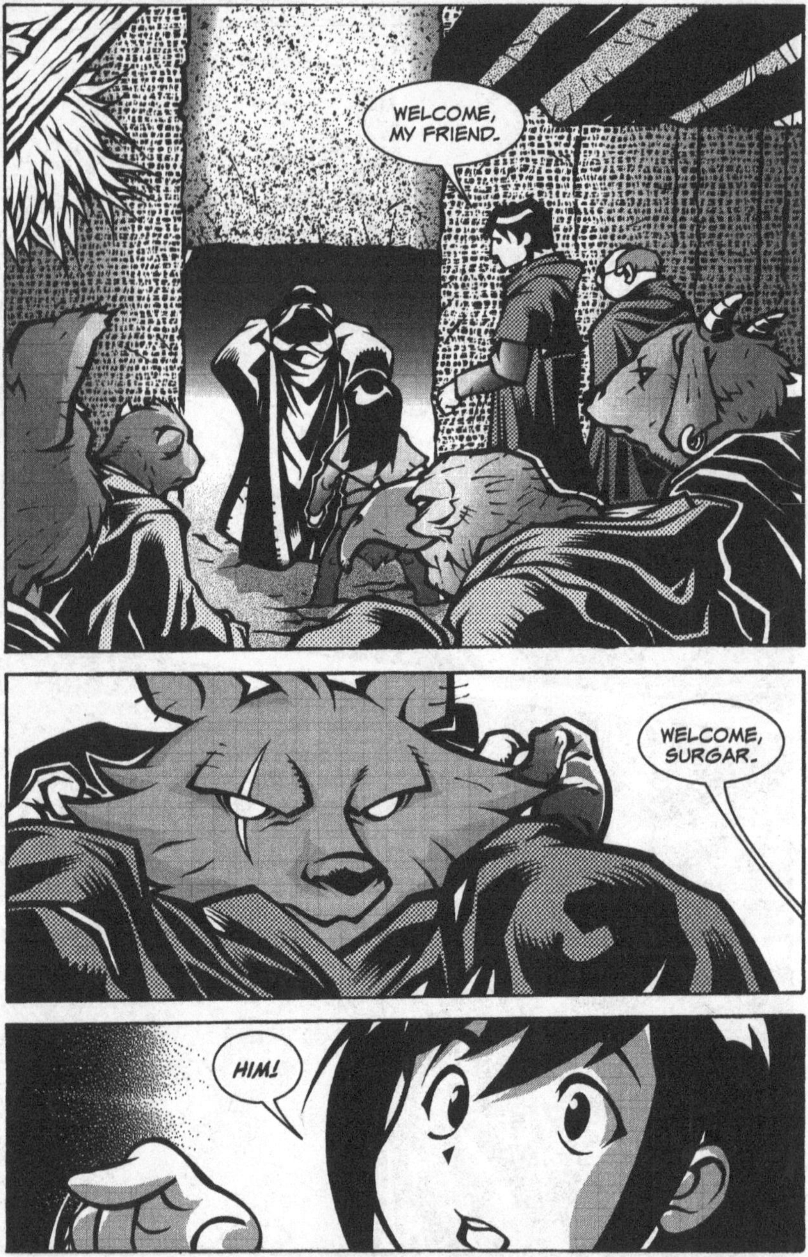
WELCOME, MY FRIEND.
WELCOME, SURGAR.
HIM!

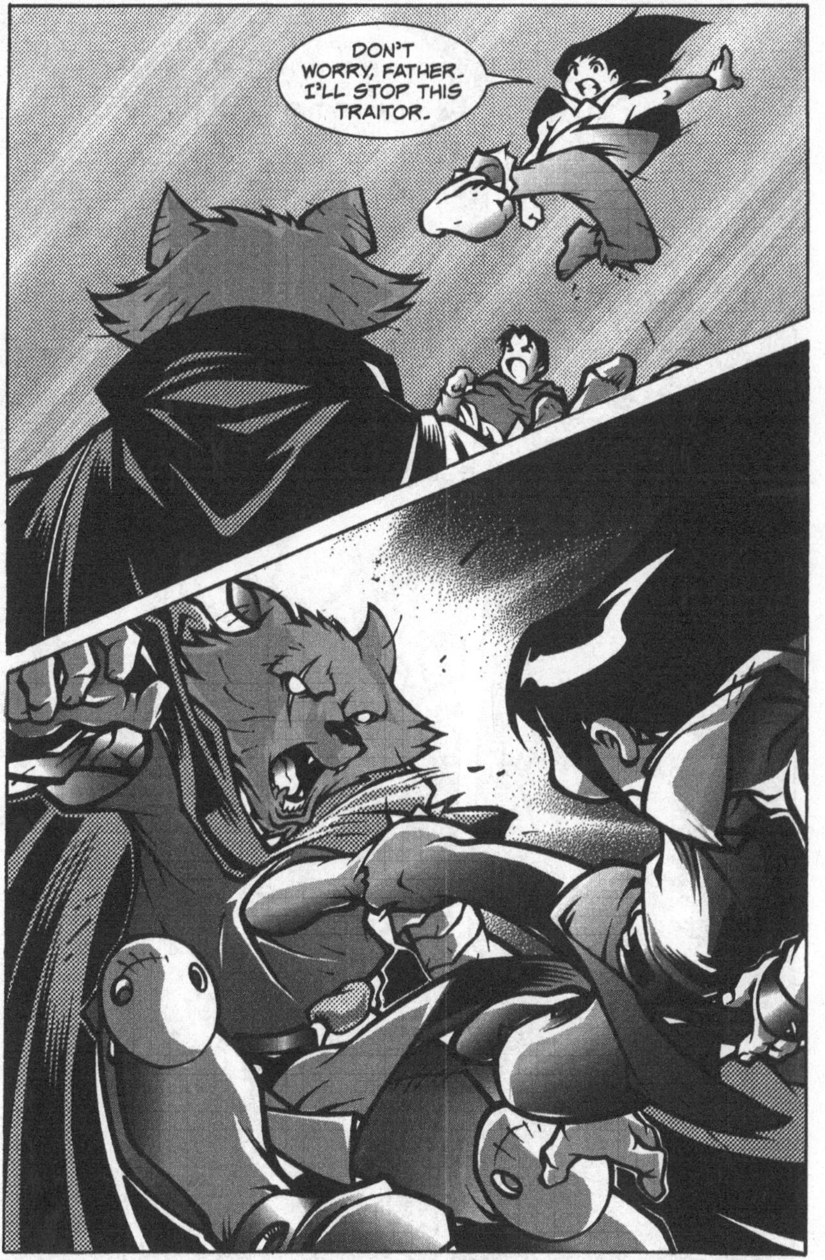
DON'T WORRY, FATHER. I'LL STOP THIS TRAITOR.

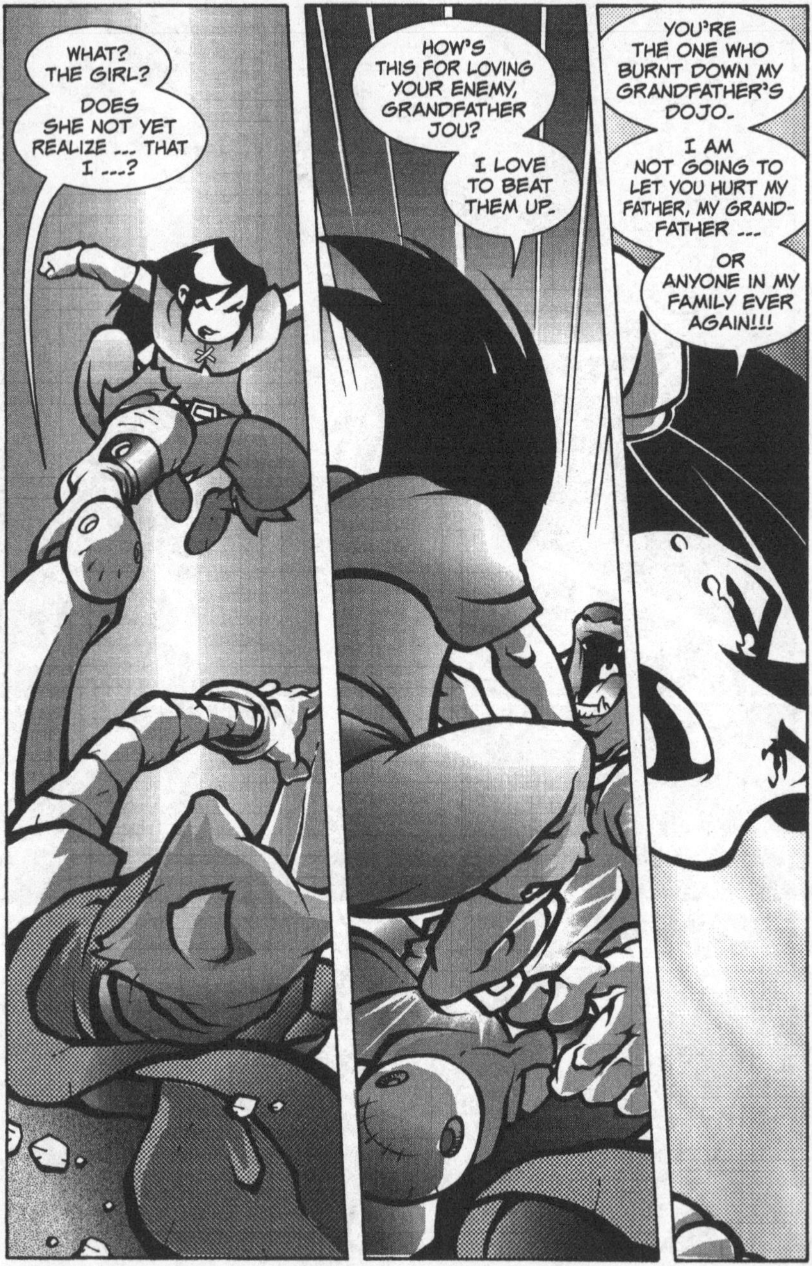
WHAT? THE GIRL?
DOES SHE NOT YET REALIZE ... THAT I ...?
HOW'S THIS FOR LOVING YOUR ENEMY, GRANDFATHER JOU?
I LOVE TO BEAT THEM UP.
YOU'RE THE ONE WHO BURNT DOWN MY GRANDFATHER'S DOJO.
I AM NOT GOING TO LET YOU HURT MY FATHER, MY GRAND-FATHER ...
OR ANYONE IN MY FAMILY EVER AGAIN!!!

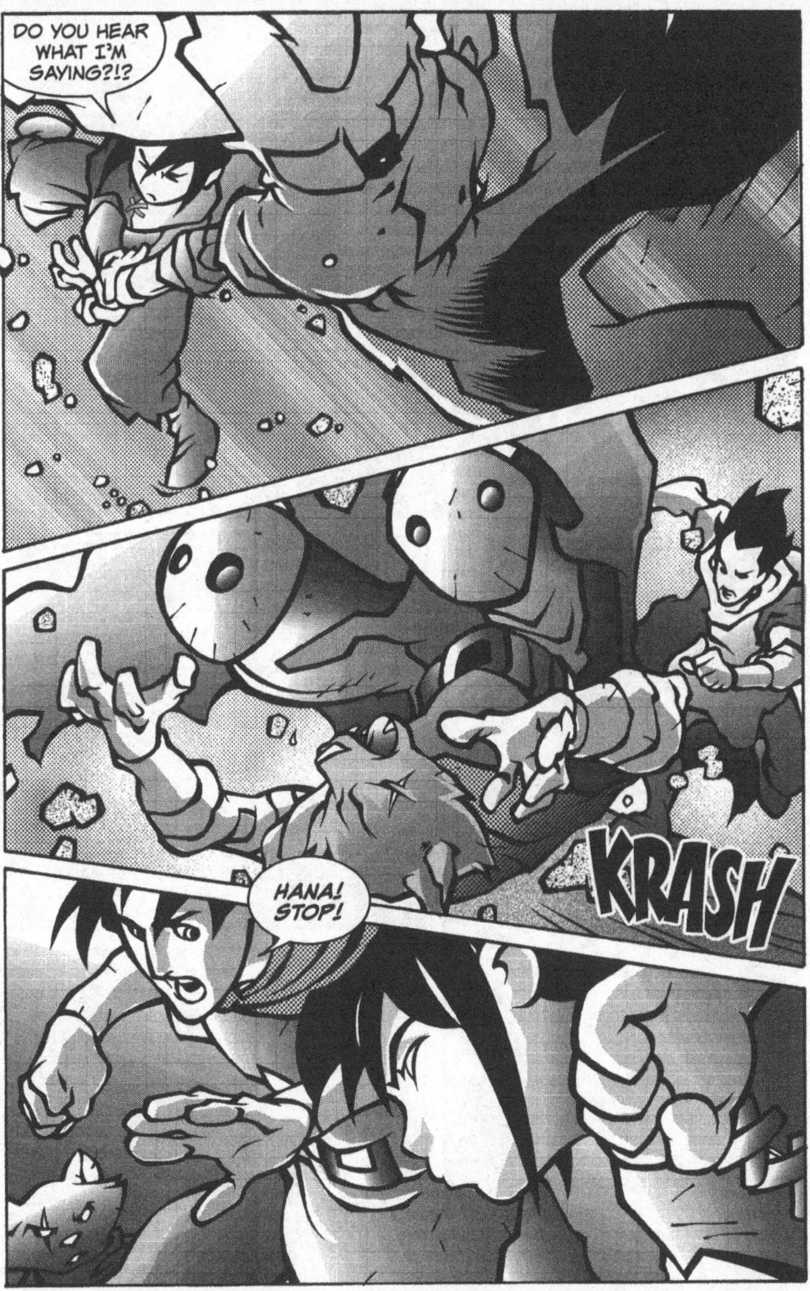
DO YOU HEAR WHAT I'M SAYING?!?
KRASH
HANA! STOP!

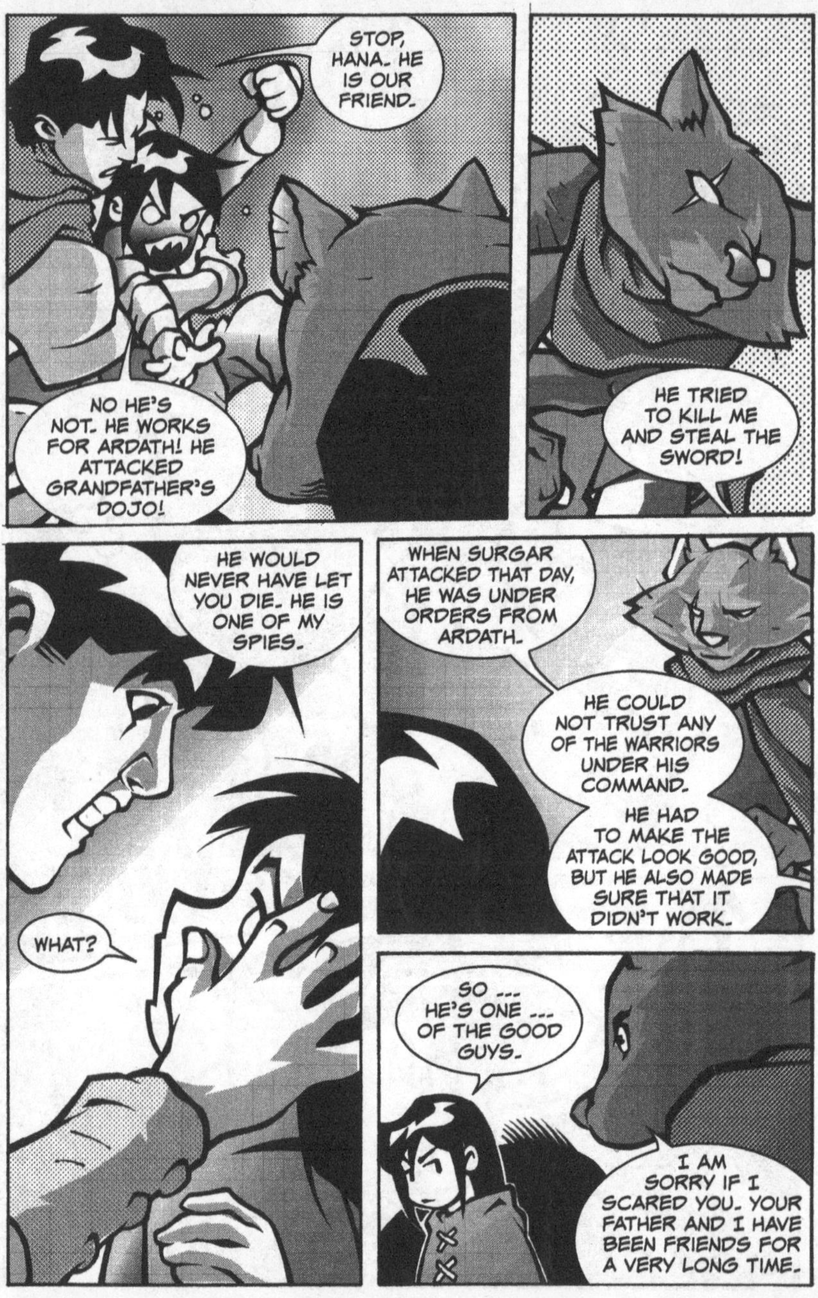

STOP, HANA. HE IS OUR FRIEND.
NO HE'S NOT. HE WORKS FOR ARDATH! HE ATTACKED GRANDFATHER'S DOJO!
HE TRIED TO KILL ME AND STEAL THE SWORD!
HE WOULD NEVER HAVE LET YOU DIE. HE IS ONE OF MY SPIES.
WHAT?
WHEN SURGAR ATTACKED THAT DAY, HE WAS UNDER ORDERS FROM ARDATH.
HE COULD NOT TRUST ANY OF THE WARRIORS UNDER HIS COMMAND.
HE HAD TO MAKE THE ATTACK LOOK GOOD, BUT HE ALSO MADE SURE THAT IT DIDN'T WORK.
SO ... HE'S ONE ... OF THE GOOD GUYS.
I AM SORRY IF I SCARED YOU. YOUR FATHER AND I HAVE BEEN FRIENDS FOR A VERY LONG TIME.

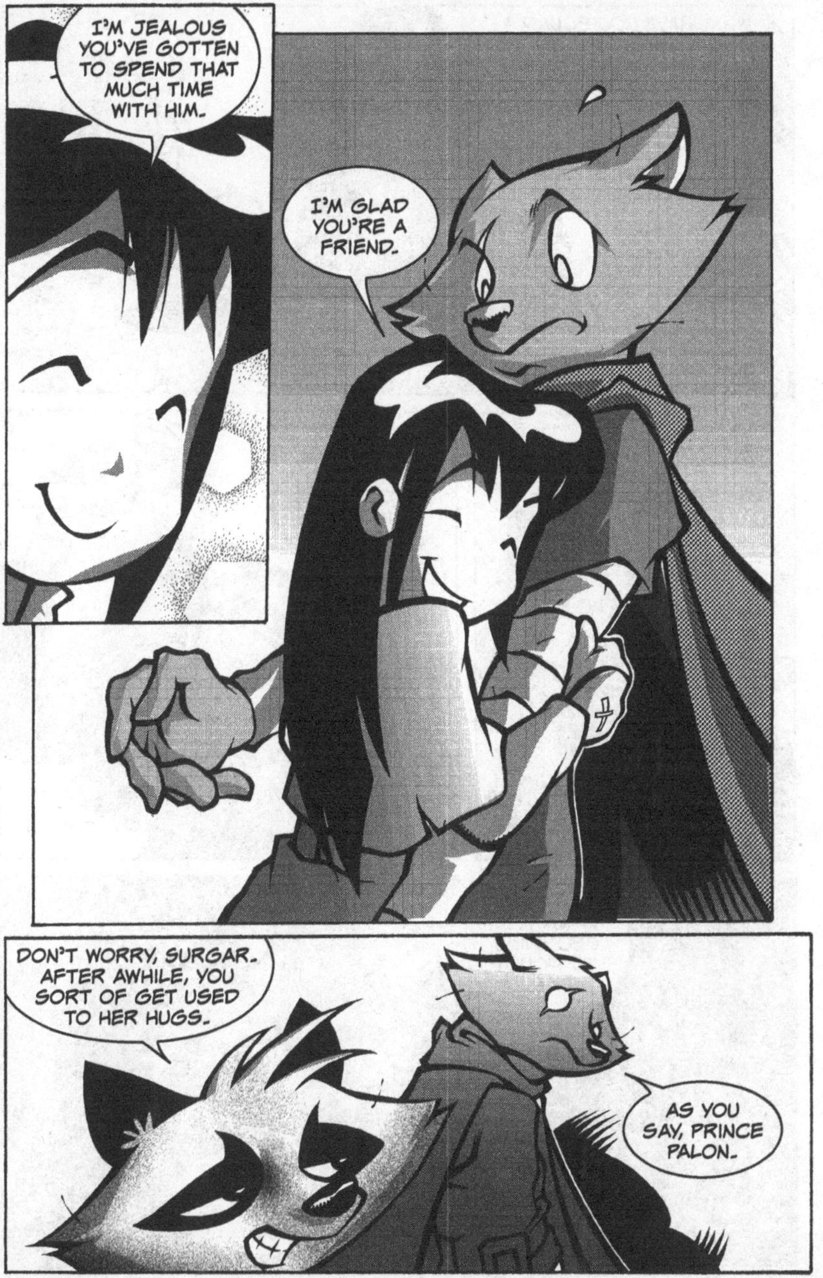
I'M JEALOUS YOU'VE GOTTEN TO SPEND THAT MUCH TIME WITH HIM.
I'M GLAD YOU'RE A FRIEND.
DON'T WORRY, SURGAR. AFTER AWHILE, YOU SORT OF GET USED TO HER HUGS.
AS YOU SAY, PRINCE PALON.

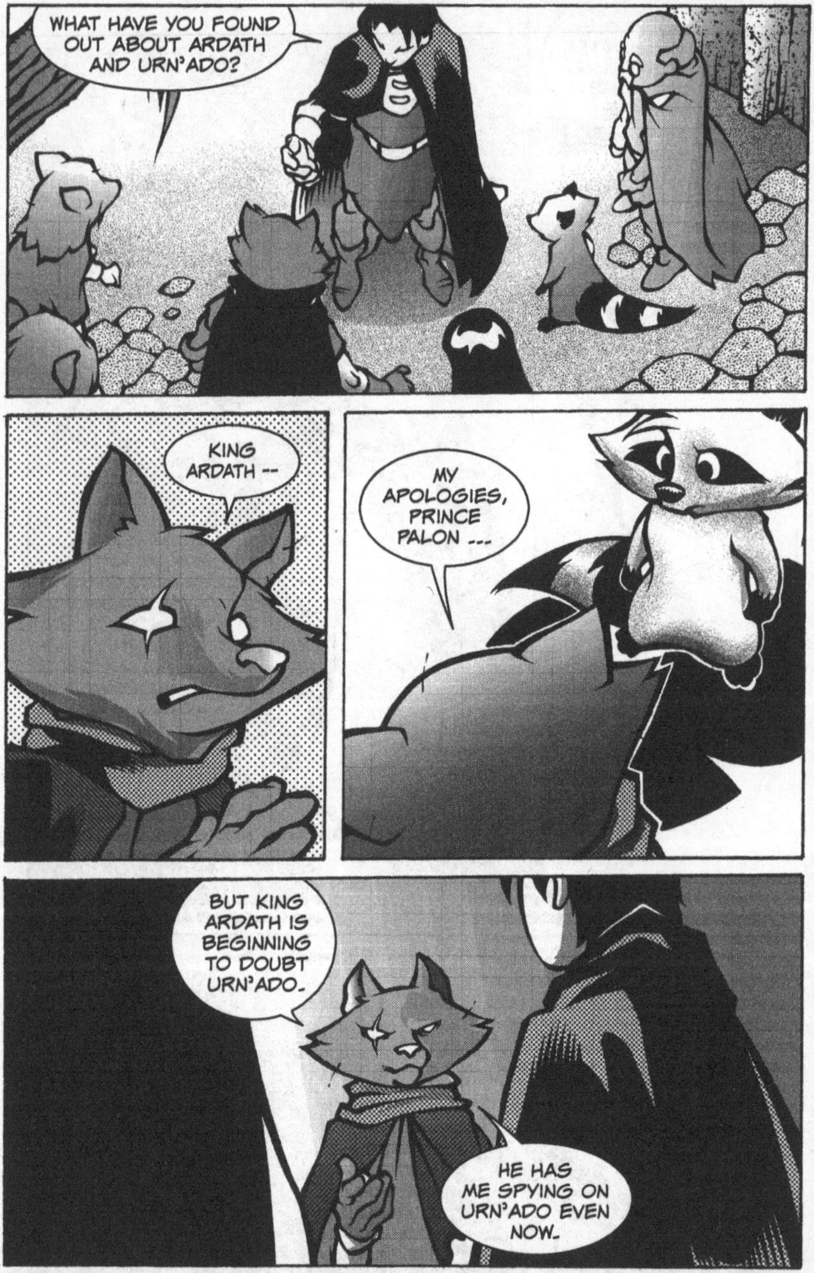
WHAT HAVE YOU FOUND OUT ABOUT ARDATH AND URN'ADO?
KING ARDATH --
MY APOLOGIES, PRINCE PALON ---
BUT KING ARDATH IS BEGINNING TO DOUBT URN'ADO.
HE HAS ME SPYING ON URN'ADO EVEN NOW.

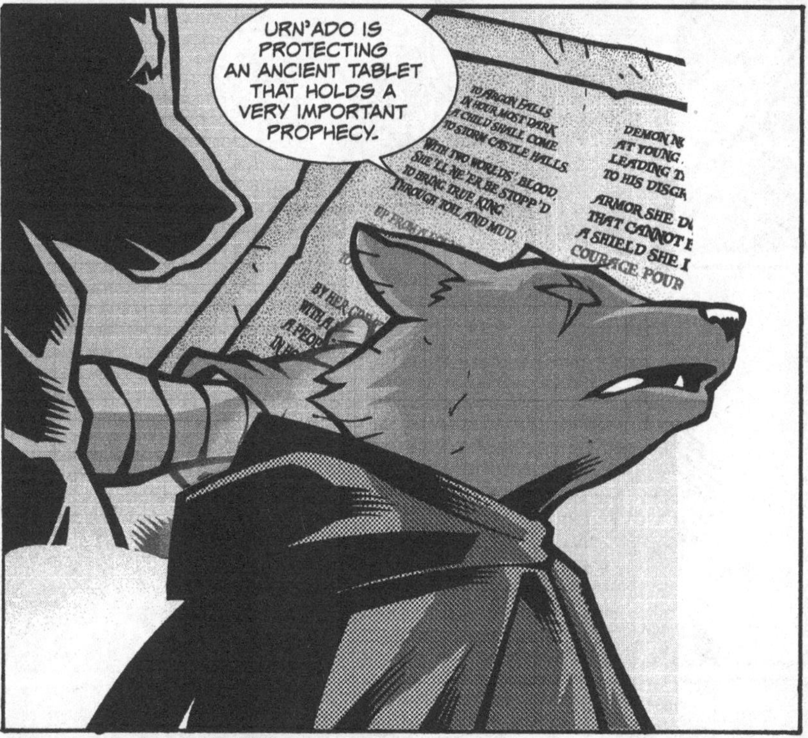
URN'ADO IS PROTECTING AN ANCIENT TABLET THAT HOLDS A VERY IMPORTANT PROPHECY.
TO ARGON FALLS
IN YOUR MOST DARK
A CHILD SHALL COME
TO STORM CASTLE HALLS.
WITH TWO WORLDS' BLOOD,
SHE'LL NE'ER BE STOPP'D
TO BRING TRUE KING
THROUGH TOIL AND MUD.

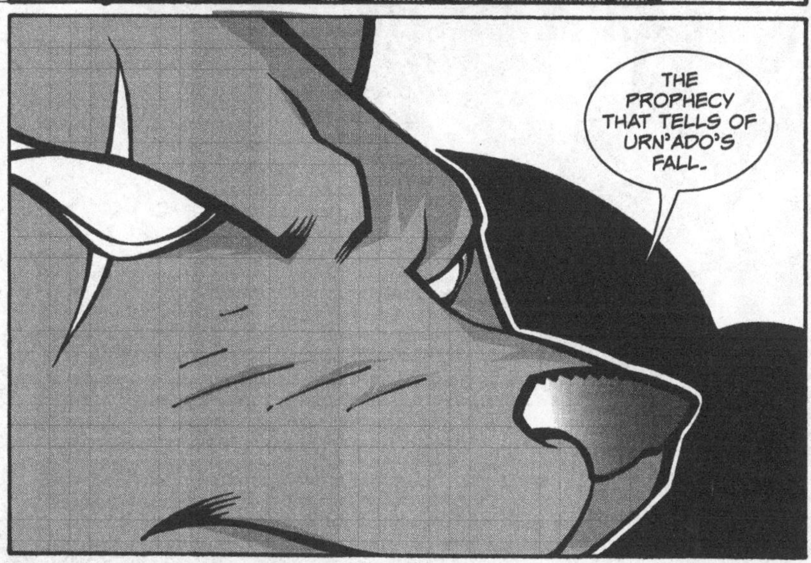
THE PROPHECY THAT TELLS OF URN'ADO'S FALL.

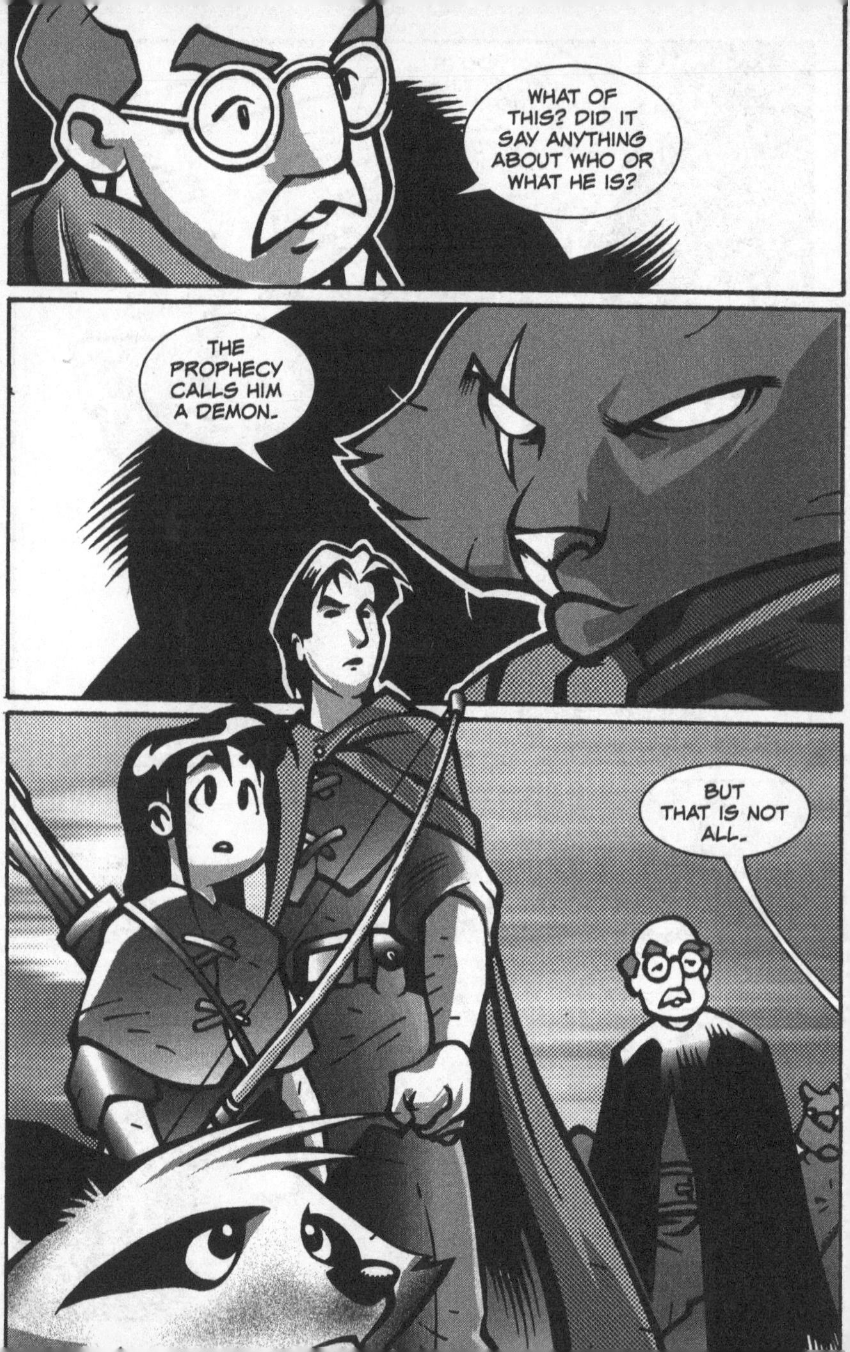
WHAT OF THIS? DID IT SAY ANYTHING ABOUT WHO OR WHAT HE IS?
THE PROPHECY CALLS HIM A DEMON.
BUT THAT IS NOT ALL.

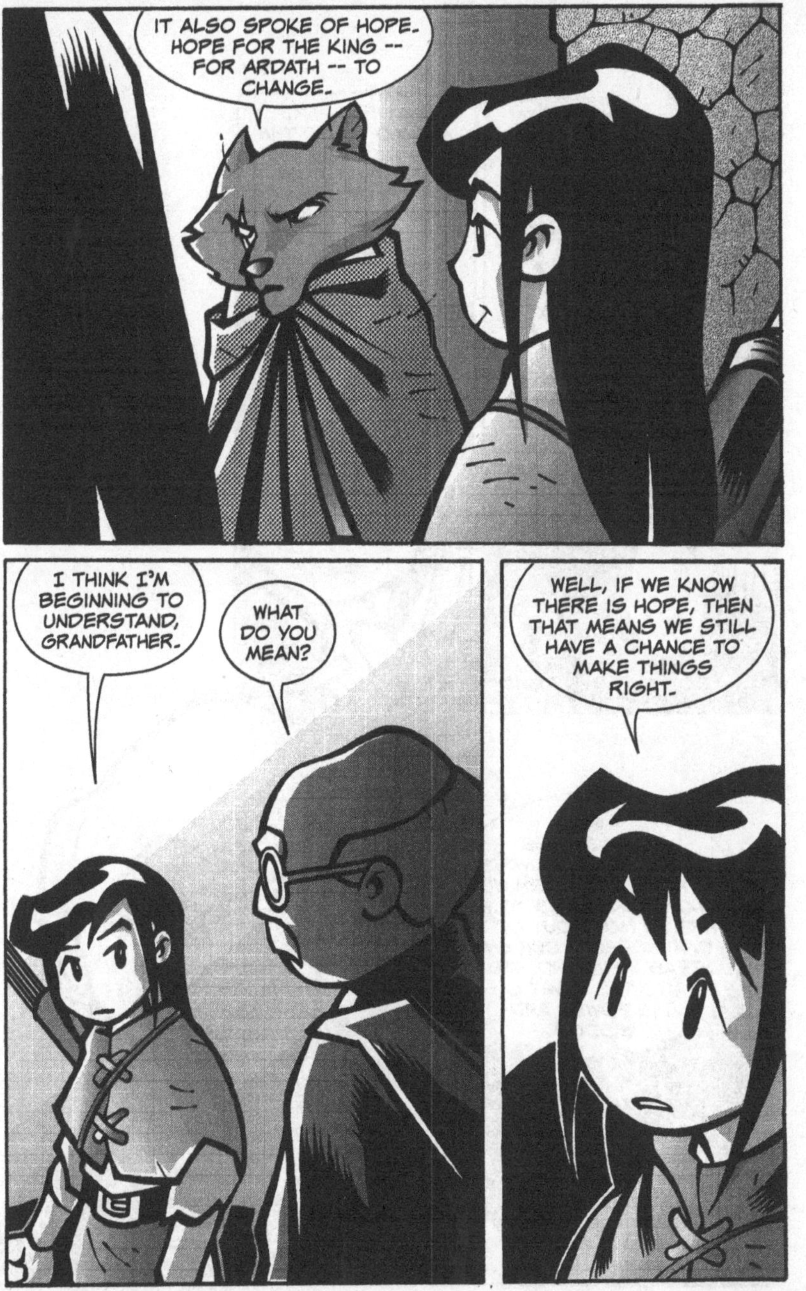
IT ALSO SPOKE OF HOPE. HOPE FOR THE KING -- FOR ARDATH -- TO CHANGE.
I THINK I'M BEGINNING TO UNDERSTAND, GRANDFATHER.
WHAT DO YOU MEAN?
WELL, IF WE KNOW THERE IS HOPE, THEN THAT MEANS WE STILL HAVE A CHANCE TO MAKE THINGS RIGHT.

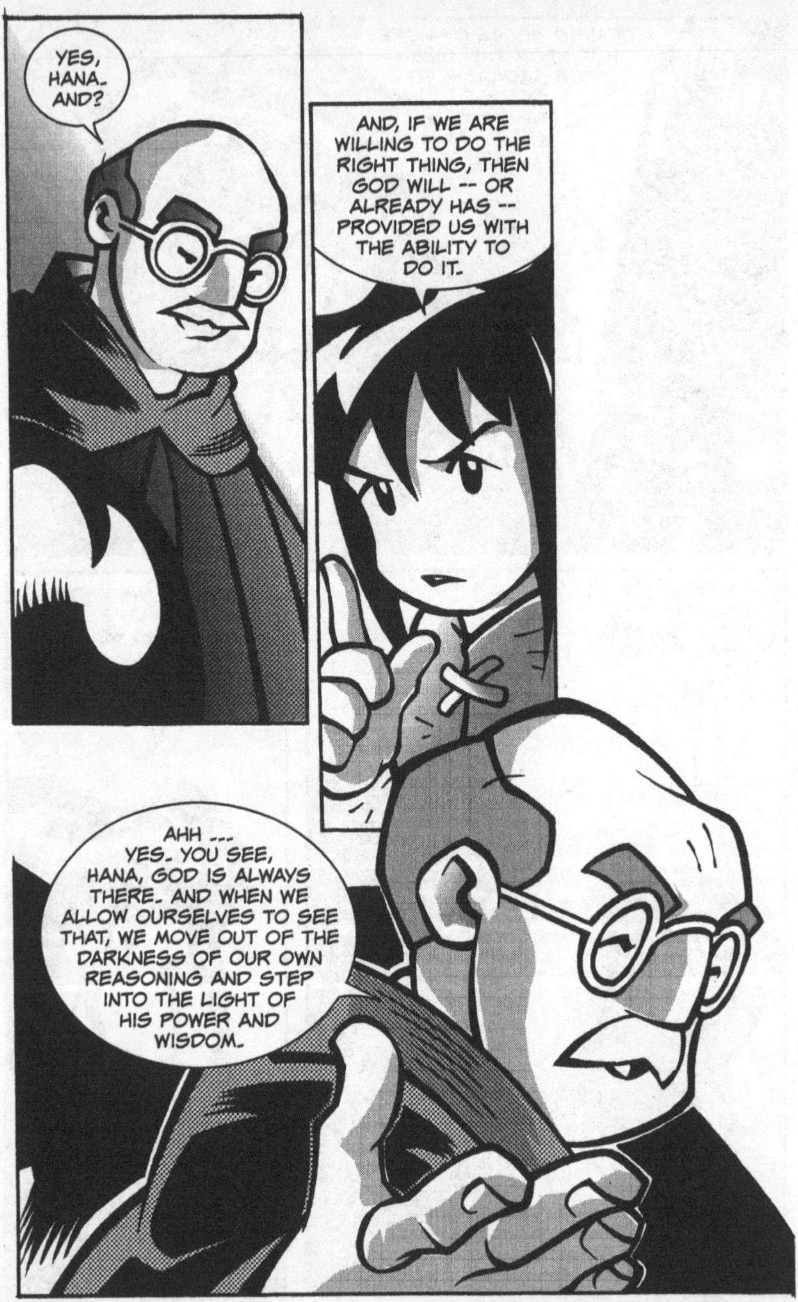
YES, HANA. AND?
AND, IF WE ARE WILLING TO DO THE RIGHT THING, THEN GOD WILL -- OR ALREADY HAS -- PROVIDED US WITH THE ABILITY TO DO IT.
AHH ... YES. YOU SEE, HANA, GOD IS ALWAYS THERE. AND WHEN WE ALLOW OURSELVES TO SEE THAT, WE MOVE OUT OF THE DARKNESS OF OUR OWN REASONING AND STEP INTO THE LIGHT OF HIS POWER AND WISDOM.

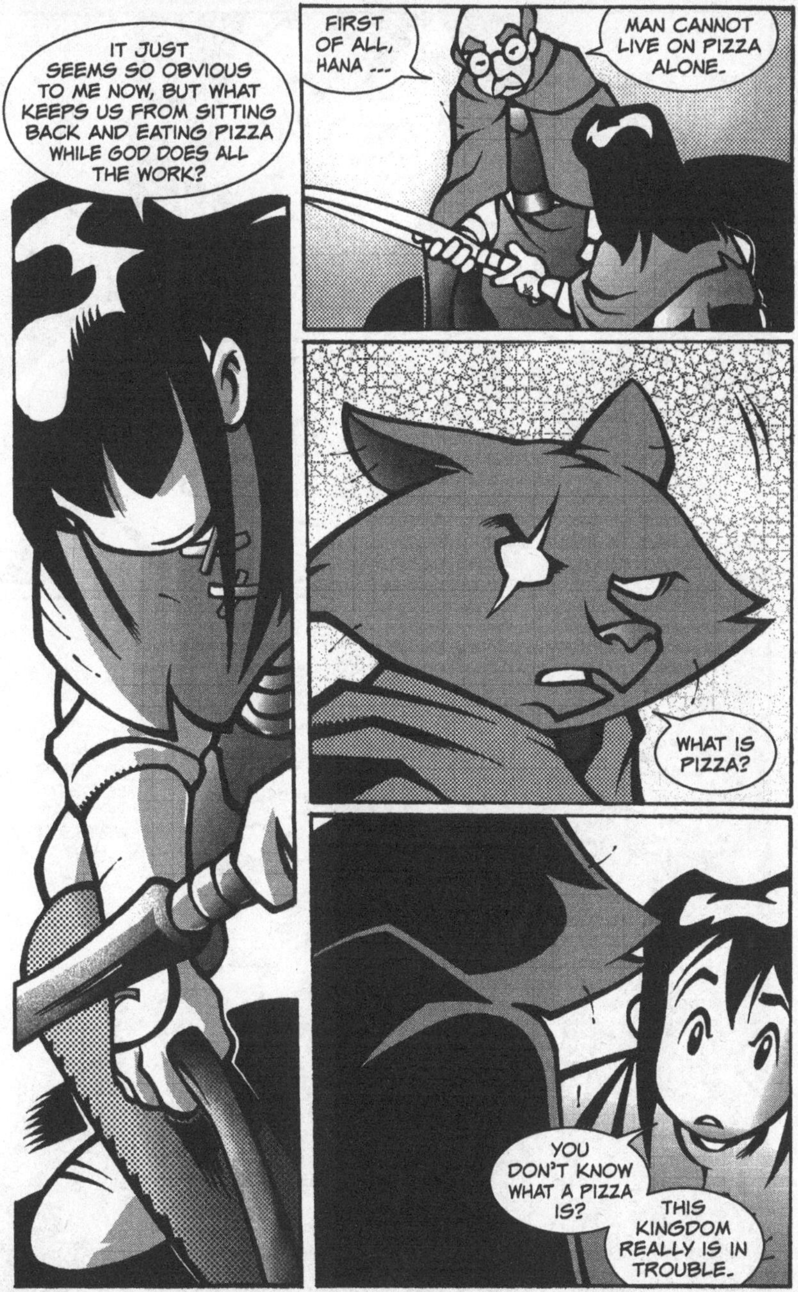
IT JUST SEEMS SO OBVIOUS TO ME NOW, BUT WHAT KEEPS US FROM SITTING BACK AND EATING PIZZA WHILE GOD DOES ALL THE WORK?
FIRST OF ALL, HANA ...
MAN CANNOT LIVE ON PIZZA ALONE.
WHAT IS PIZZA?
YOU DON'T KNOW WHAT A PIZZA IS?
THIS KINGDOM REALLY IS IN TROUBLE.

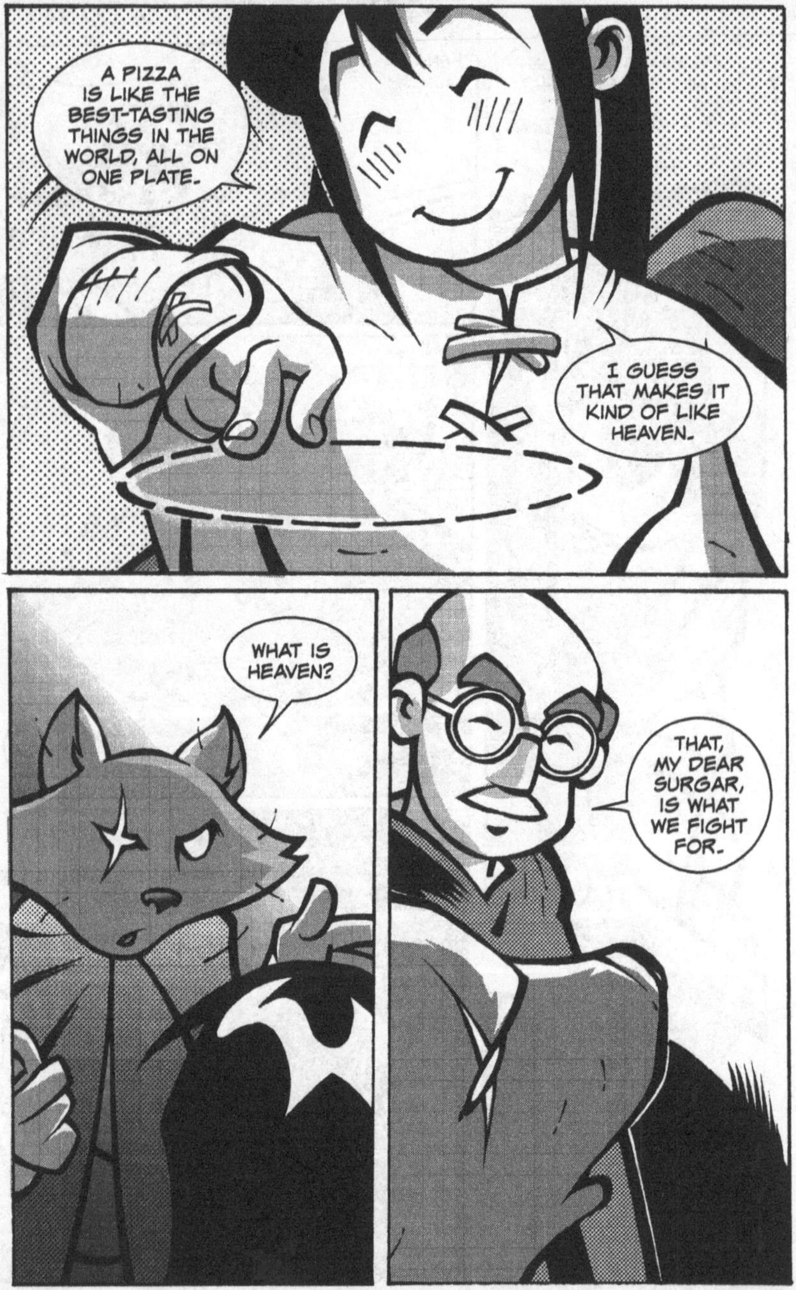
A PIZZA IS LIKE THE BEST-TASTING THINGS IN THE WORLD, ALL ON ONE PLATE.
I GUESS THAT MAKES IT KIND OF LIKE HEAVEN.
WHAT IS HEAVEN?
THAT, MY DEAR SURGAR, IS WHAT WE FIGHT FOR.

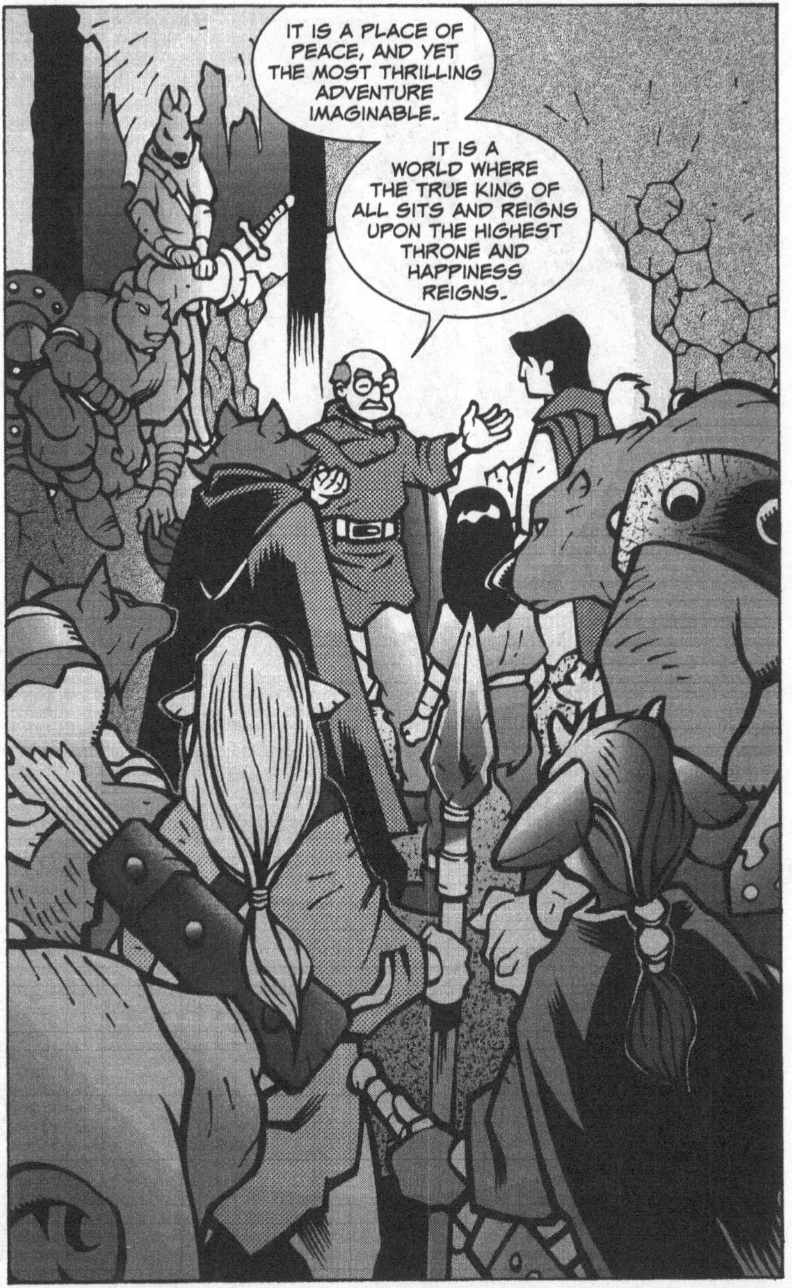
IT IS A PLACE OF PEACE, AND YET THE MOST THRILLING ADVENTURE IMAGINABLE.
IT IS A WORLD WHERE THE TRUE KING OF ALL SITS AND REIGNS UPON THE HIGHEST THRONE AND HAPPINESS REIGNS.

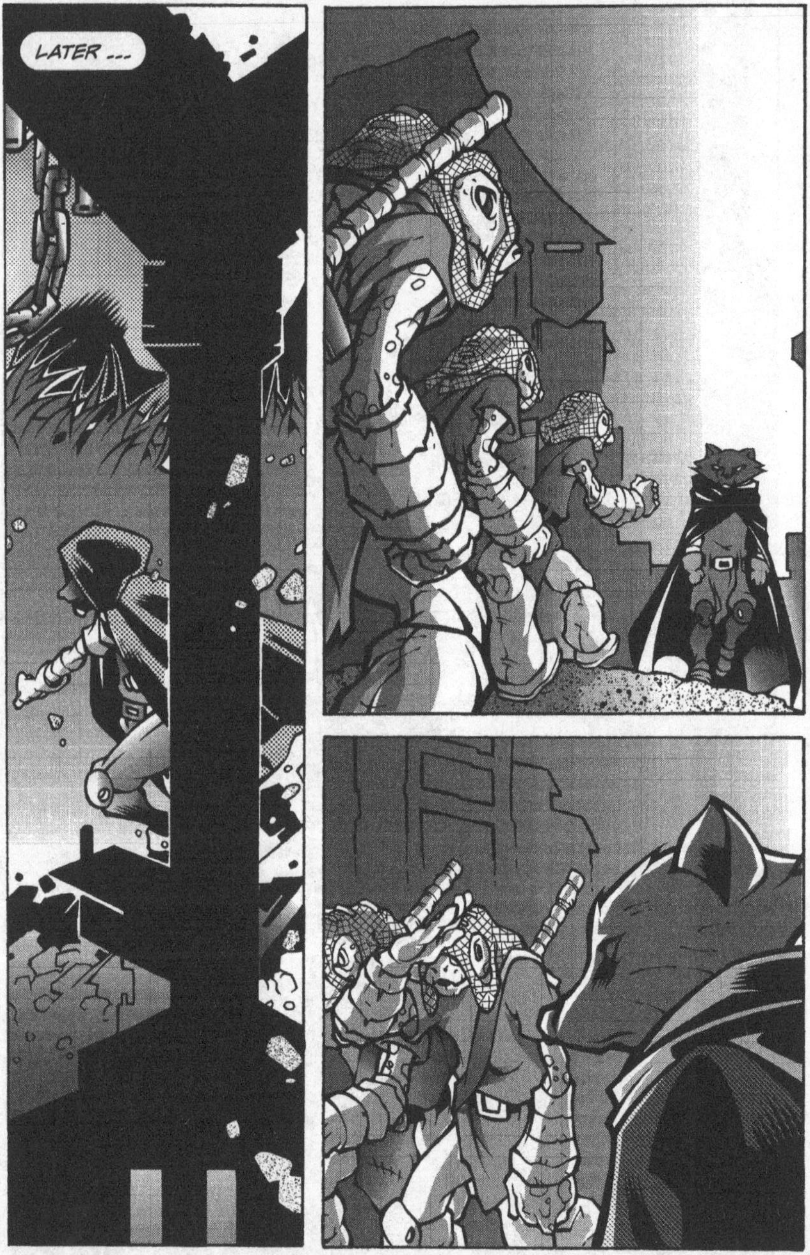
LATER ---

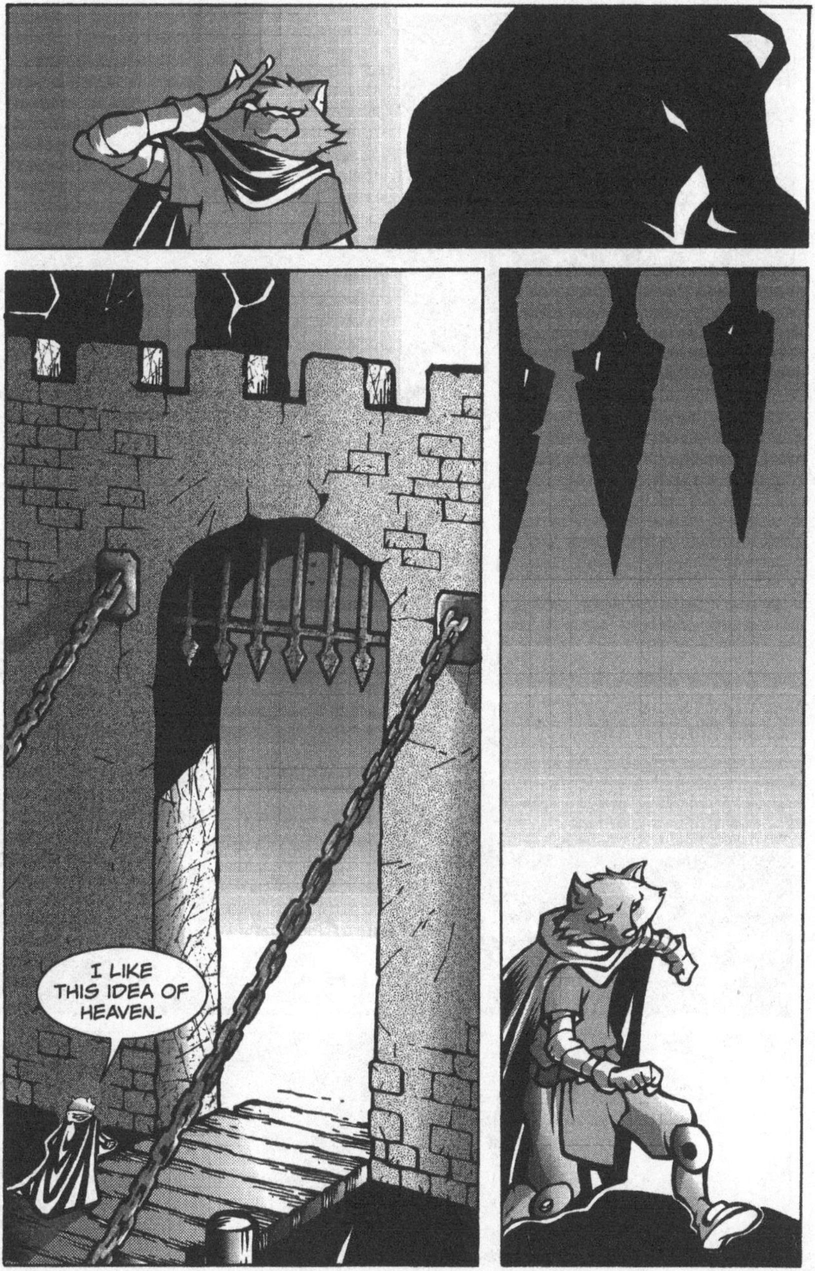
I LIKE THIS IDEA OF HEAVEN.

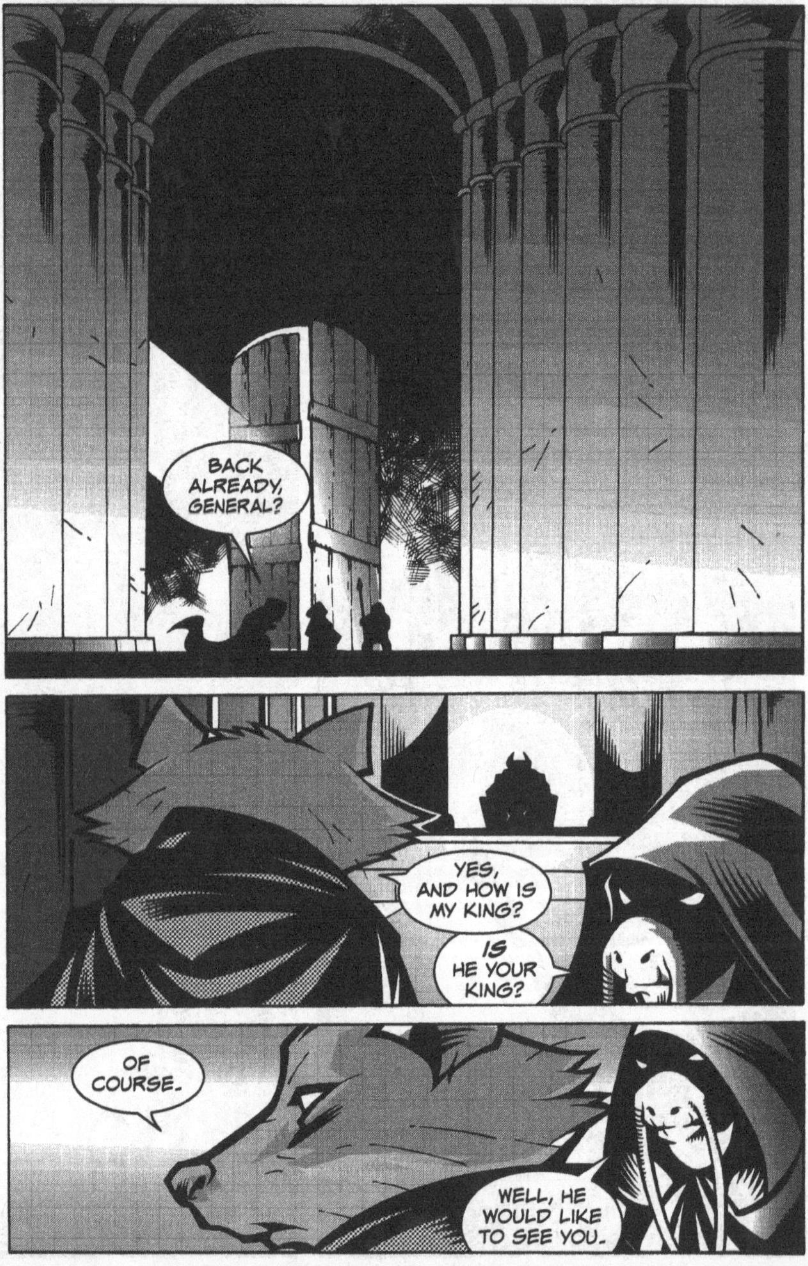
BACK ALREADY, GENERAL?
YES, AND HOW IS MY KING?
IS HE YOUR KING?
OF COURSE.
WELL, HE WOULD LIKE TO SEE YOU.

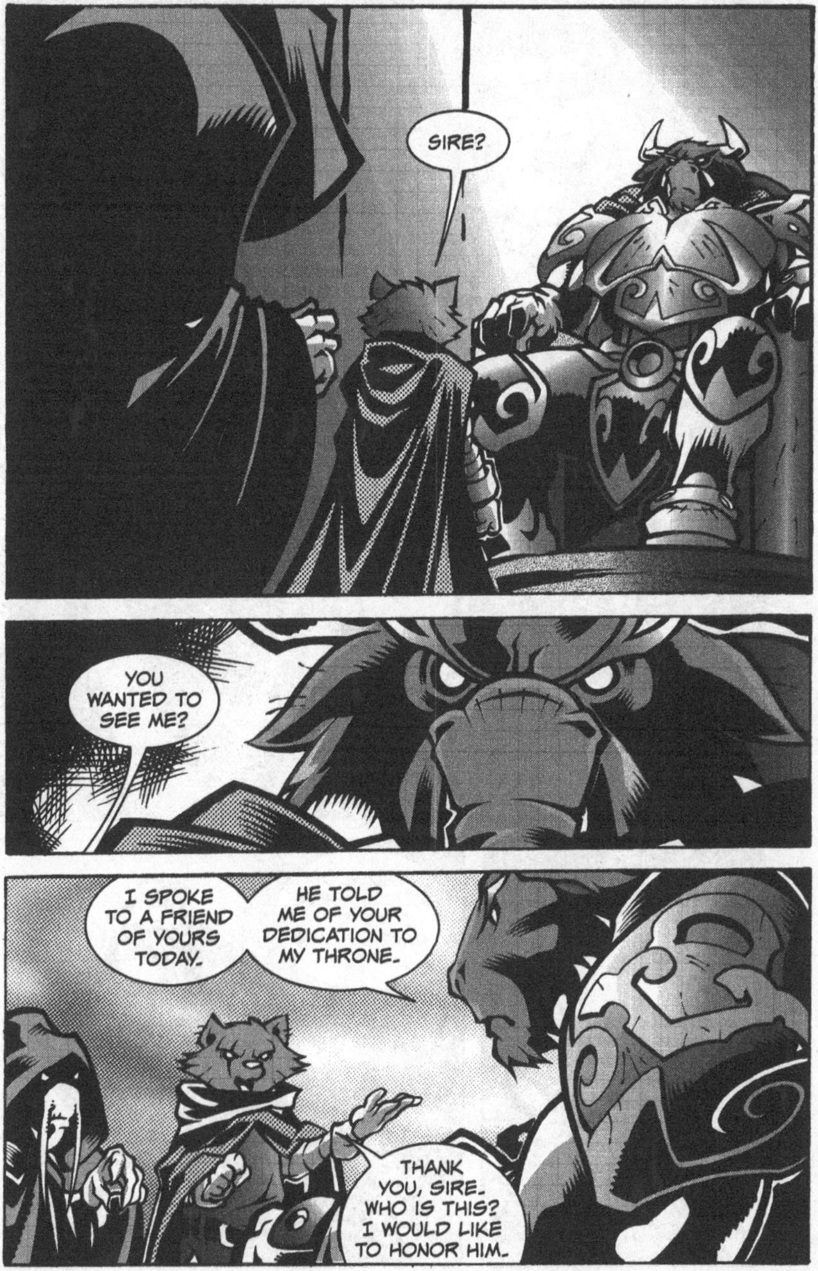
SIRE?
YOU WANTED TO SEE ME?
I SPOKE TO A FRIEND OF YOURS TODAY.
HE TOLD ME OF YOUR DEDICATION TO MY THRONE.
THANK YOU, SIRE. WHO IS THIS? I WOULD LIKE TO HONOR HIM.

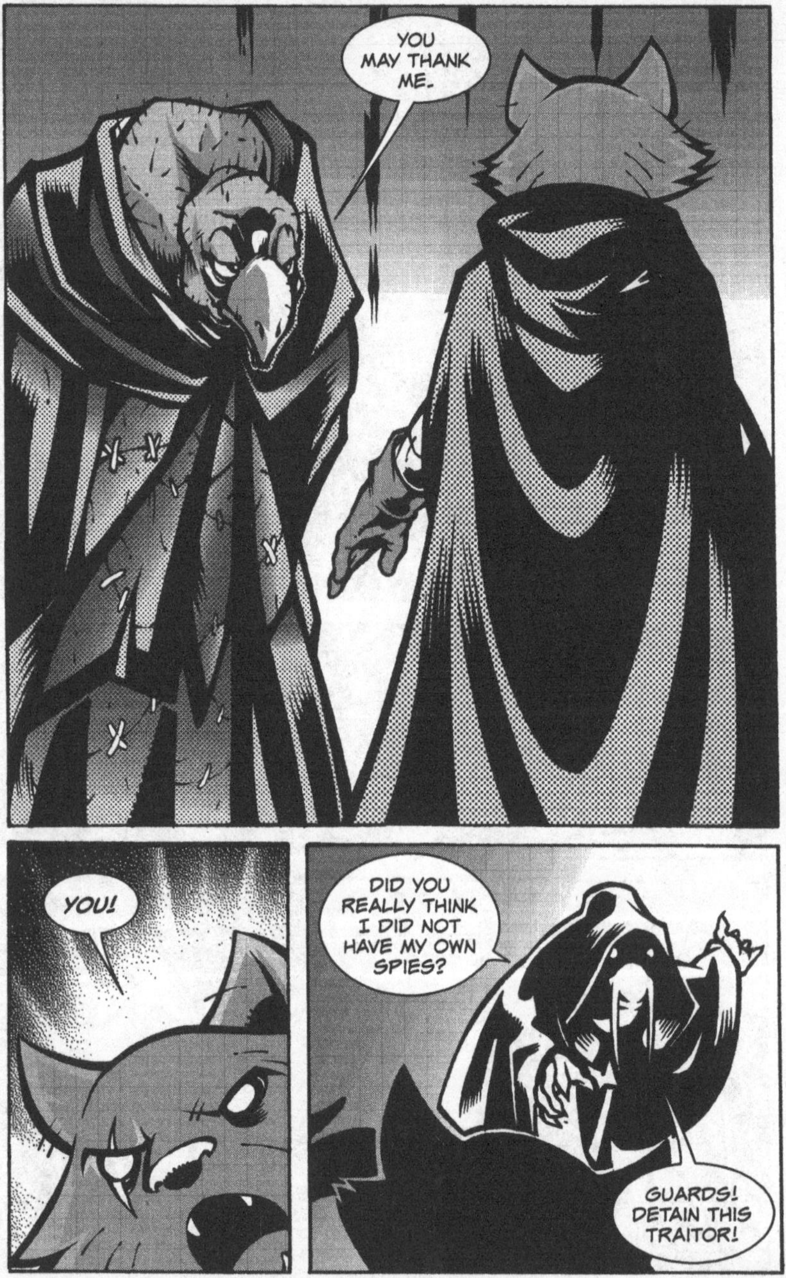
YOU MAY THANK ME.
YOU!
DID YOU REALLY THINK I DID NOT HAVE MY OWN SPIES?
GUARDS! DETAIN THIS TRAITOR!

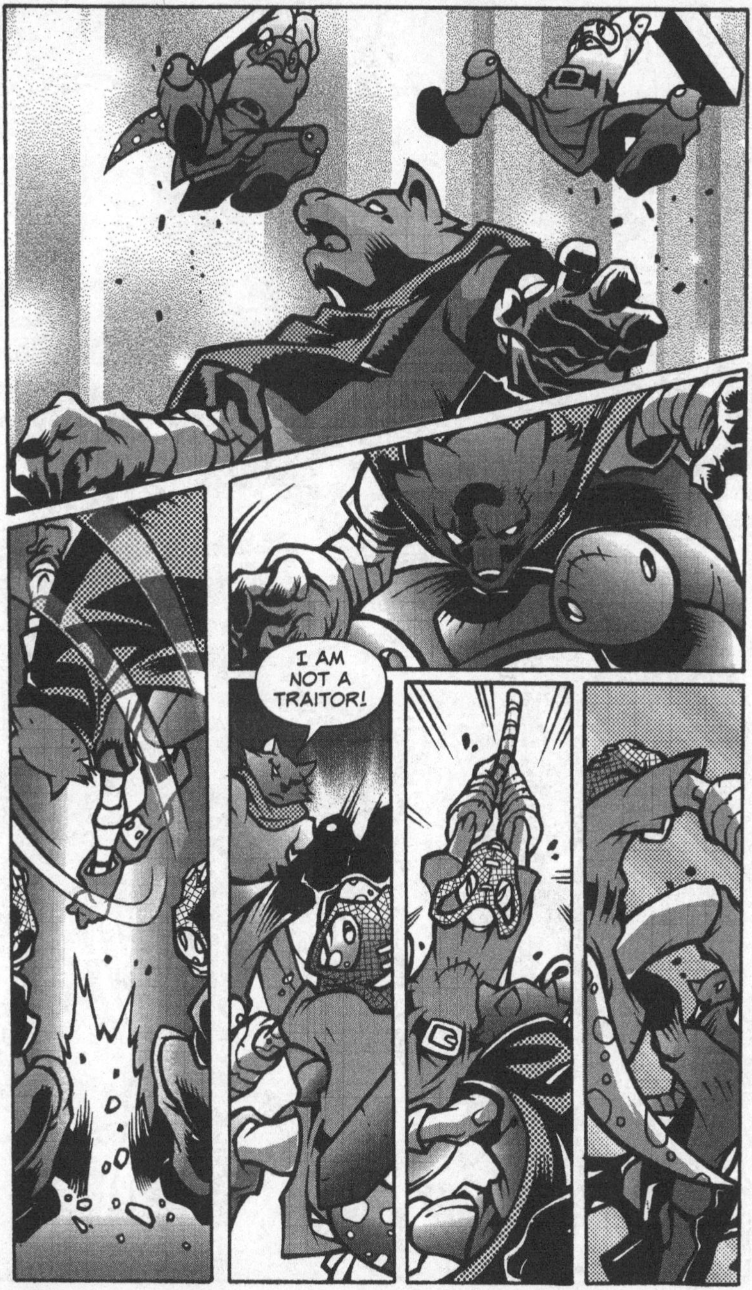
I AM NOT A TRAITOR!

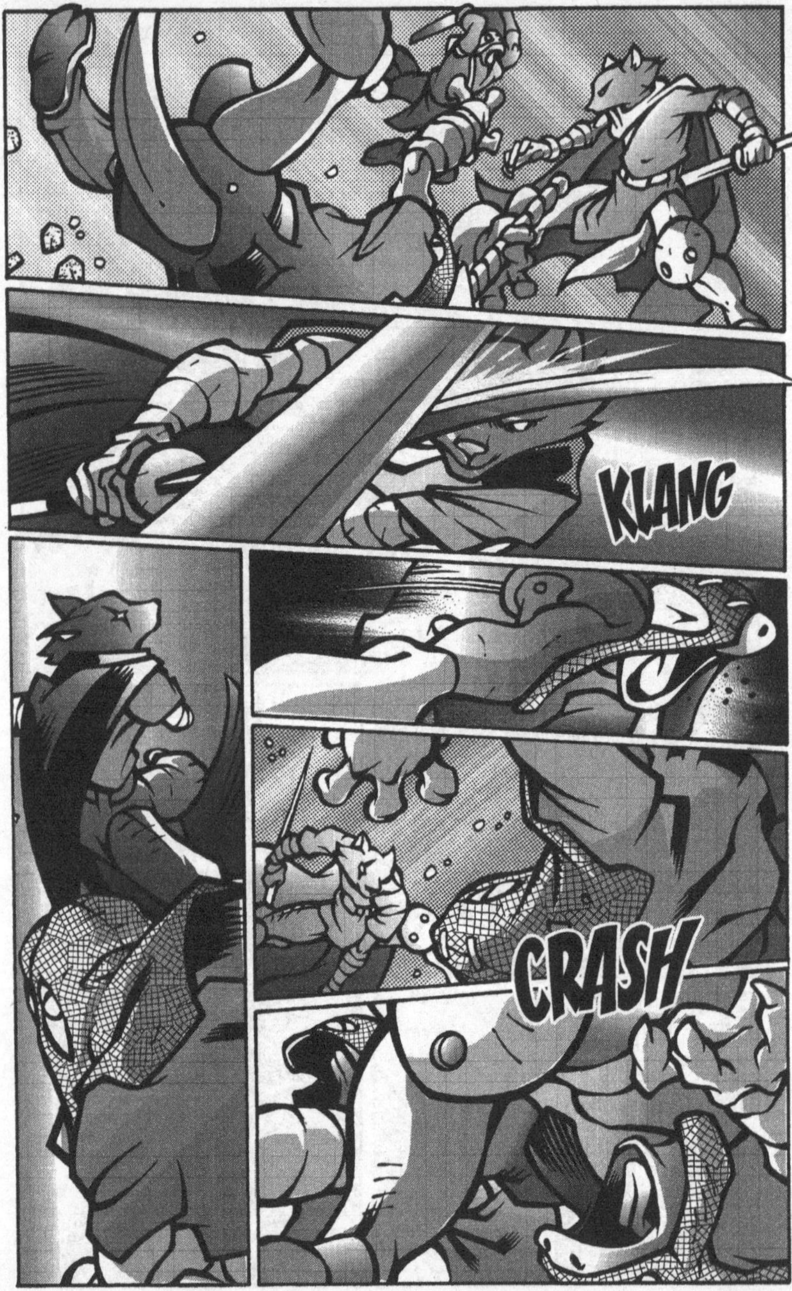
KLANG
CRASH

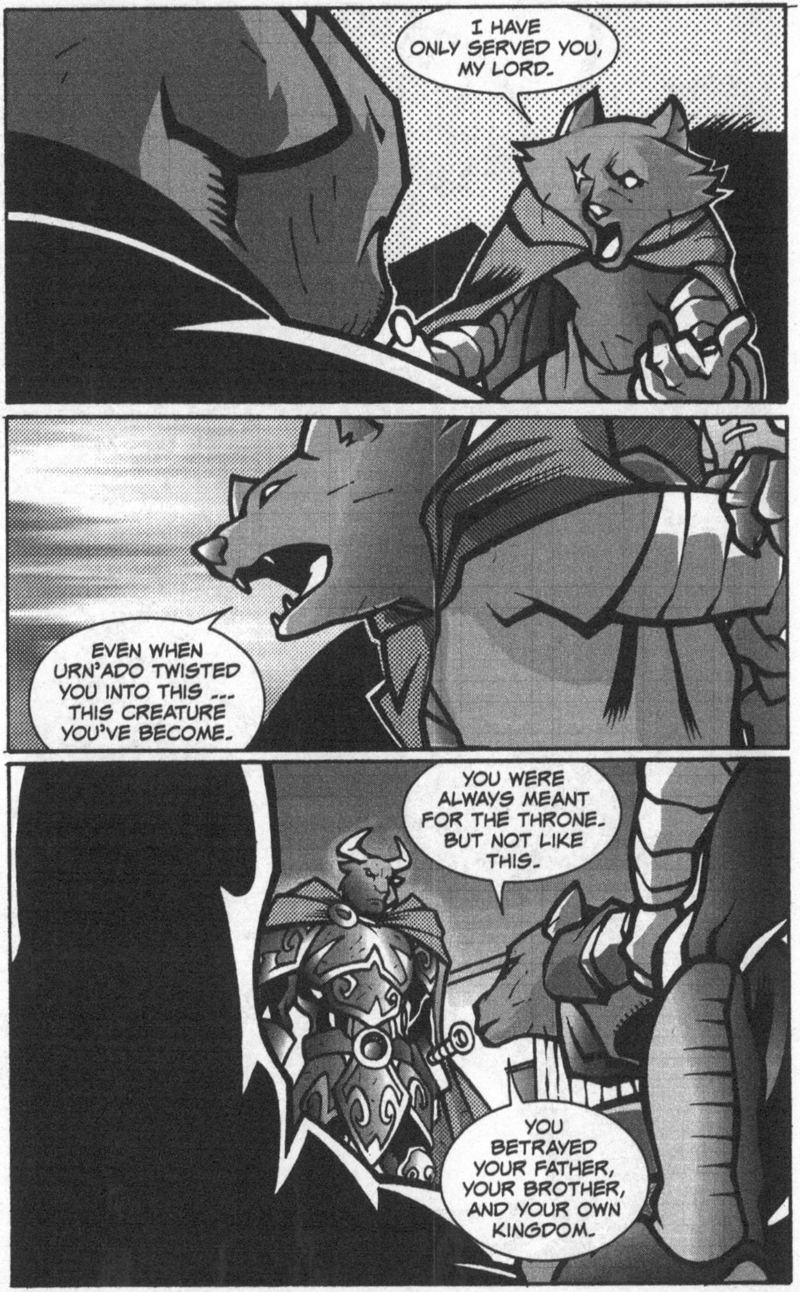

I HAVE ONLY SERVED YOU, MY LORD.
EVEN WHEN URN'ADO TWISTED YOU INTO THIS ... THIS CREATURE YOU'VE BECOME.
YOU WERE ALWAYS MEANT FOR THE THRONE. BUT NOT LIKE THIS.
YOU BETRAYED YOUR FATHER, YOUR BROTHER, AND YOUR OWN KINGDOM.

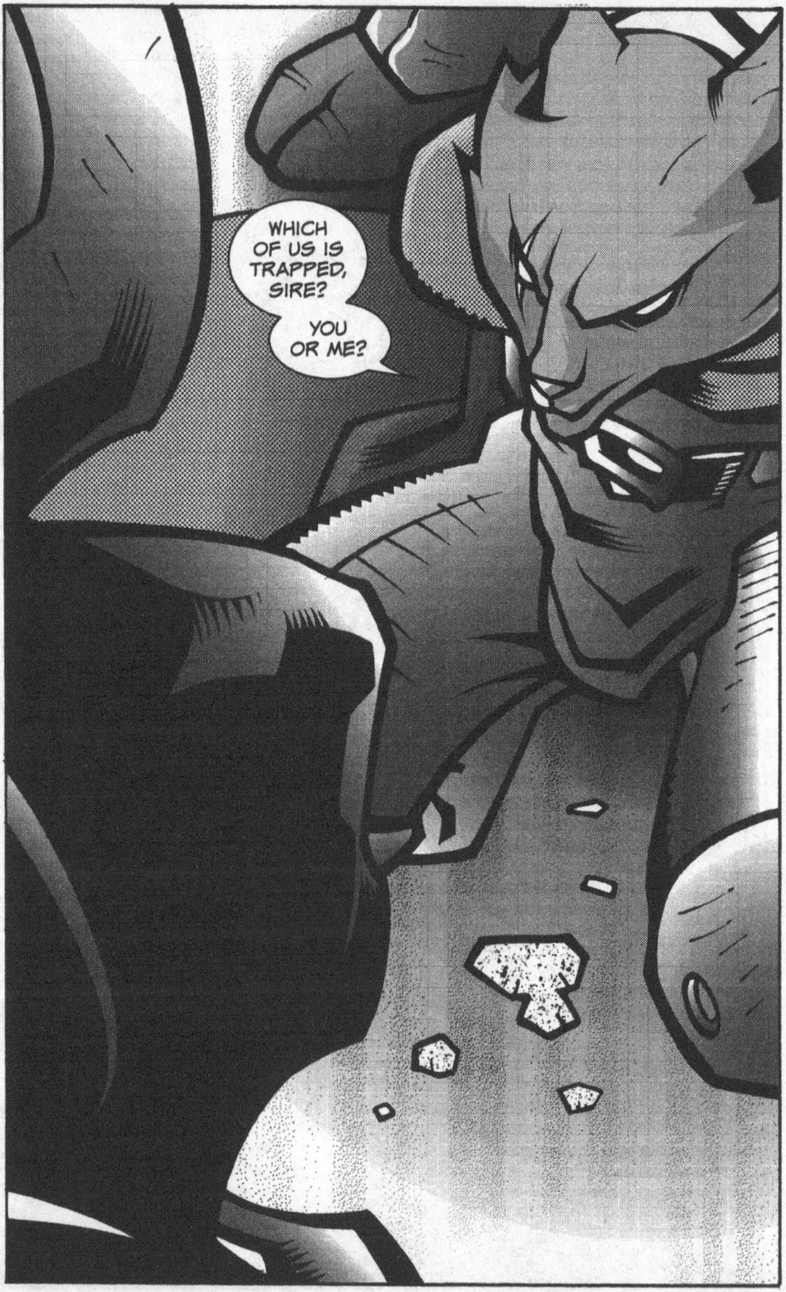
WHICH OF US IS TRAPPED, SIRE?
YOU OR ME?

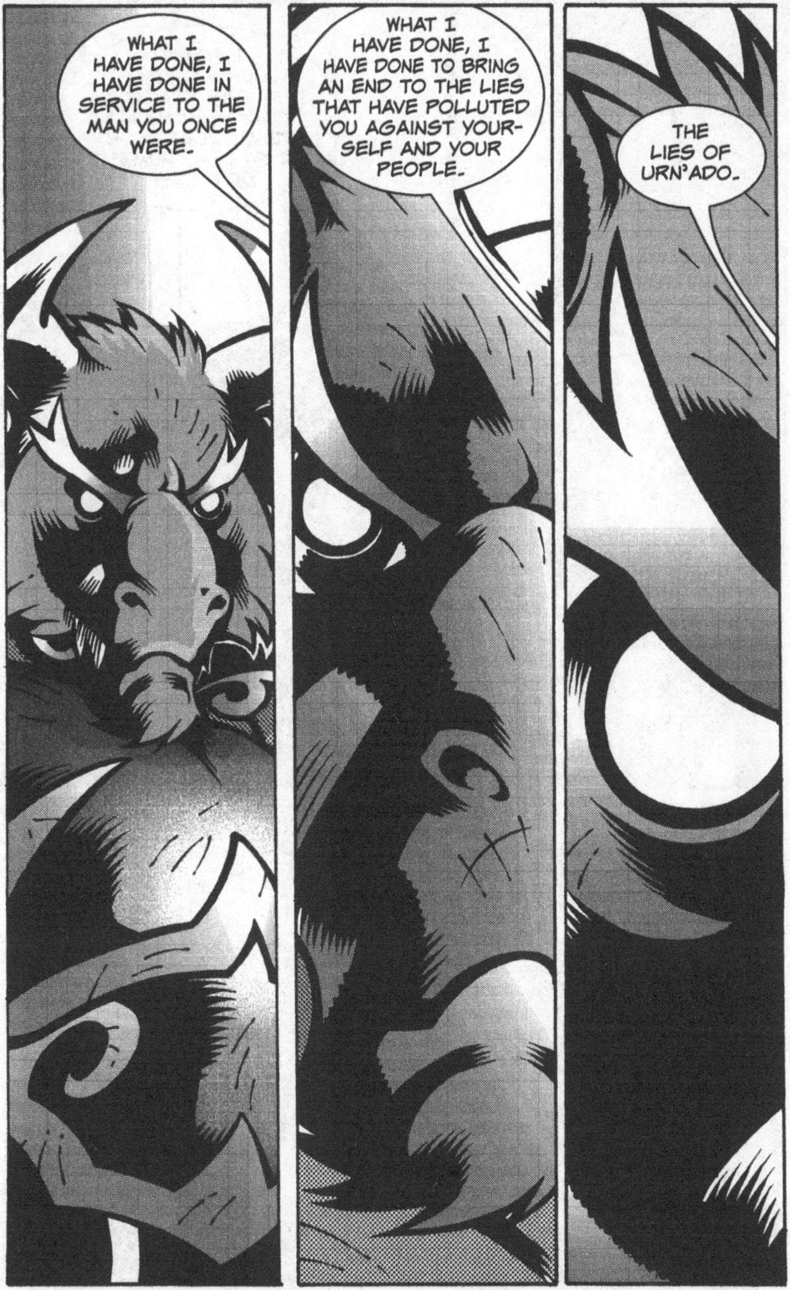
WHAT I HAVE DONE, I HAVE DONE IN SERVICE TO THE MAN YOU ONCE WERE.
WHAT I HAVE DONE, I HAVE DONE TO BRING AN END TO THE LIES THAT HAVE POLLUTED YOU AGAINST YOUR-SELF AND YOUR PEOPLE.
THE LIES OF URN'ADO.

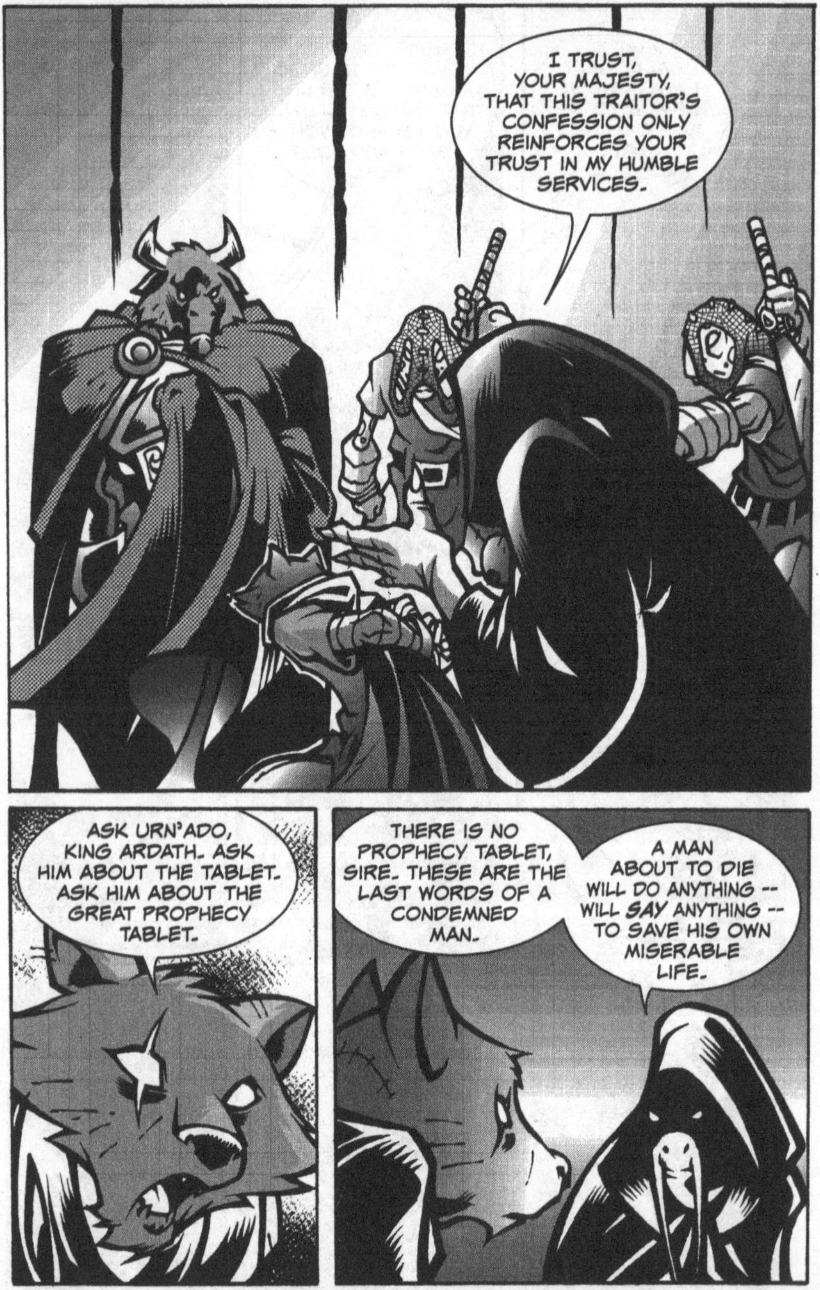
I TRUST, YOUR MAJESTY, THAT THIS TRAITOR'S CONFESSION ONLY REINFORCES YOUR TRUST IN MY HUMBLE SERVICES.
ASK URN'ADO, KING ARDATH. ASK HIM ABOUT THE TABLET. ASK HIM ABOUT THE GREAT PROPHECY TABLET.
THERE IS NO PROPHECY TABLET, SIRE. THESE ARE THE LAST WORDS OF A CONDEMNED MAN.
A MAN ABOUT TO DIE WILL DO ANYTHING -- WILL *SAY* ANYTHING -- TO SAVE HIS OWN MISERABLE LIFE.

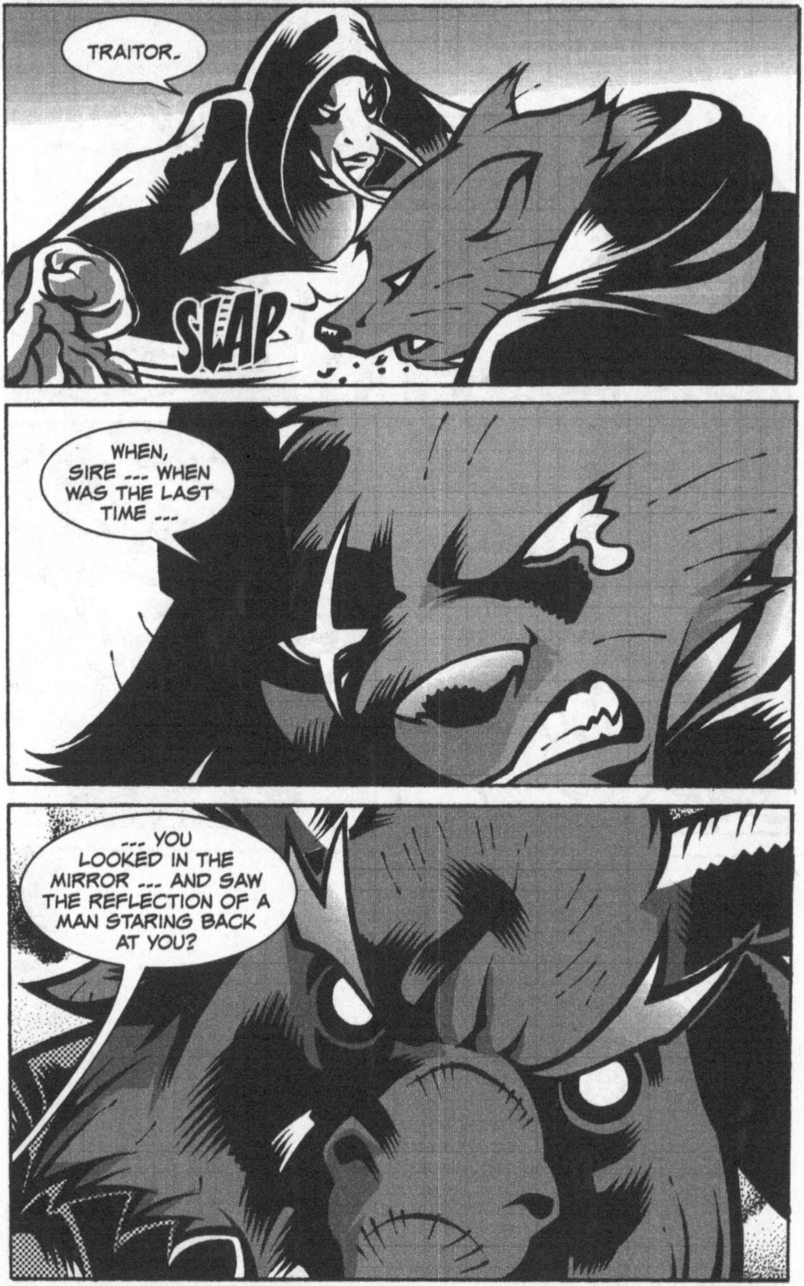
TRAITOR.
SLAP
WHEN, SIRE ... WHEN WAS THE LAST TIME ...
... YOU LOOKED IN THE MIRROR ... AND SAW THE REFLECTION OF A MAN STARING BACK AT YOU?

CLICK

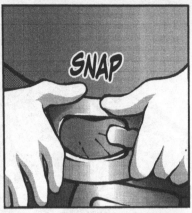

SNAP

TIWNG

SHKKK

GRPD

SO HOW DO I LOOK?

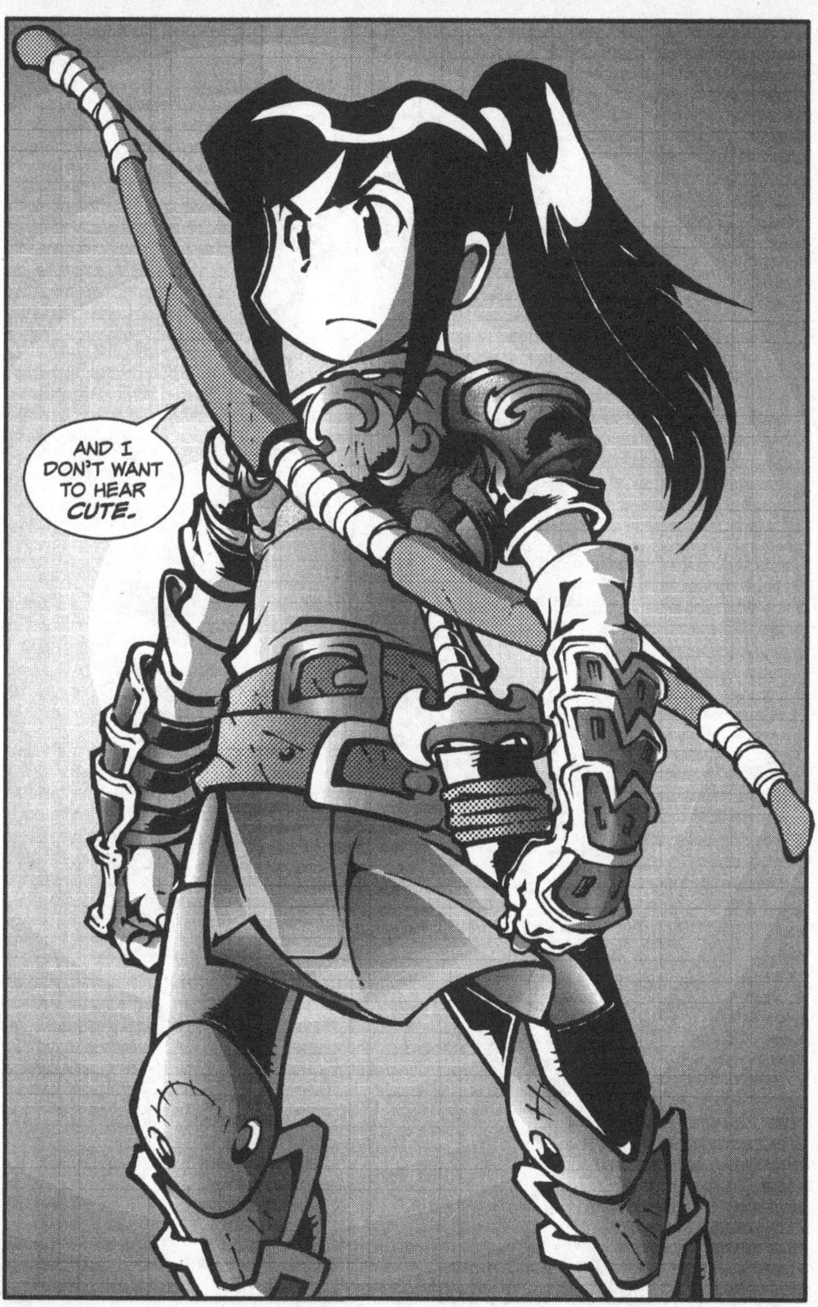
AND I DON'T WANT TO HEAR CUTE.

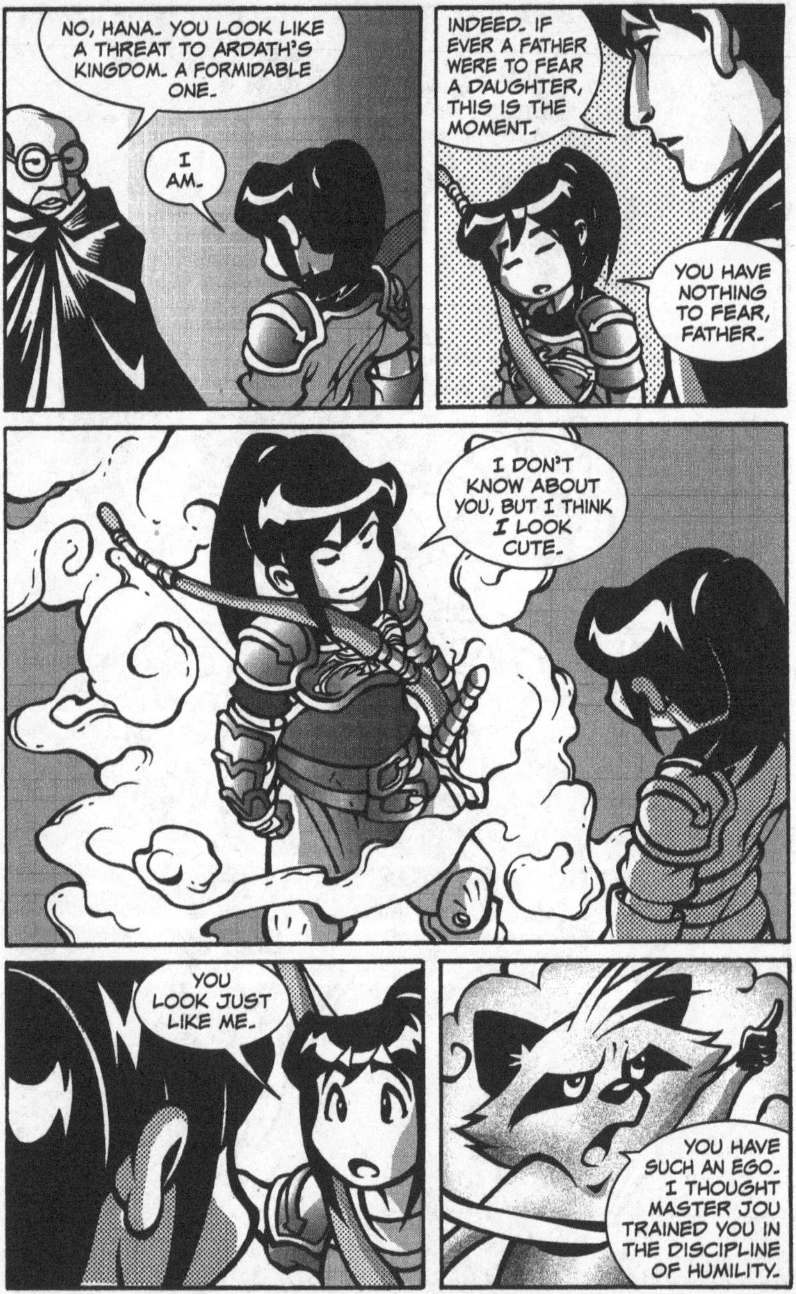
NO, HANA. YOU LOOK LIKE A THREAT TO ARDATH'S KINGDOM. A FORMIDABLE ONE.
I AM.
INDEED. IF EVER A FATHER WERE TO FEAR A DAUGHTER, THIS IS THE MOMENT.
YOU HAVE NOTHING TO FEAR, FATHER.
I DON'T KNOW ABOUT YOU, BUT I THINK *I* LOOK CUTE.
YOU LOOK JUST LIKE ME.
YOU HAVE SUCH AN EGO. I THOUGHT MASTER JOU TRAINED YOU IN THE DISCIPLINE OF HUMILITY.

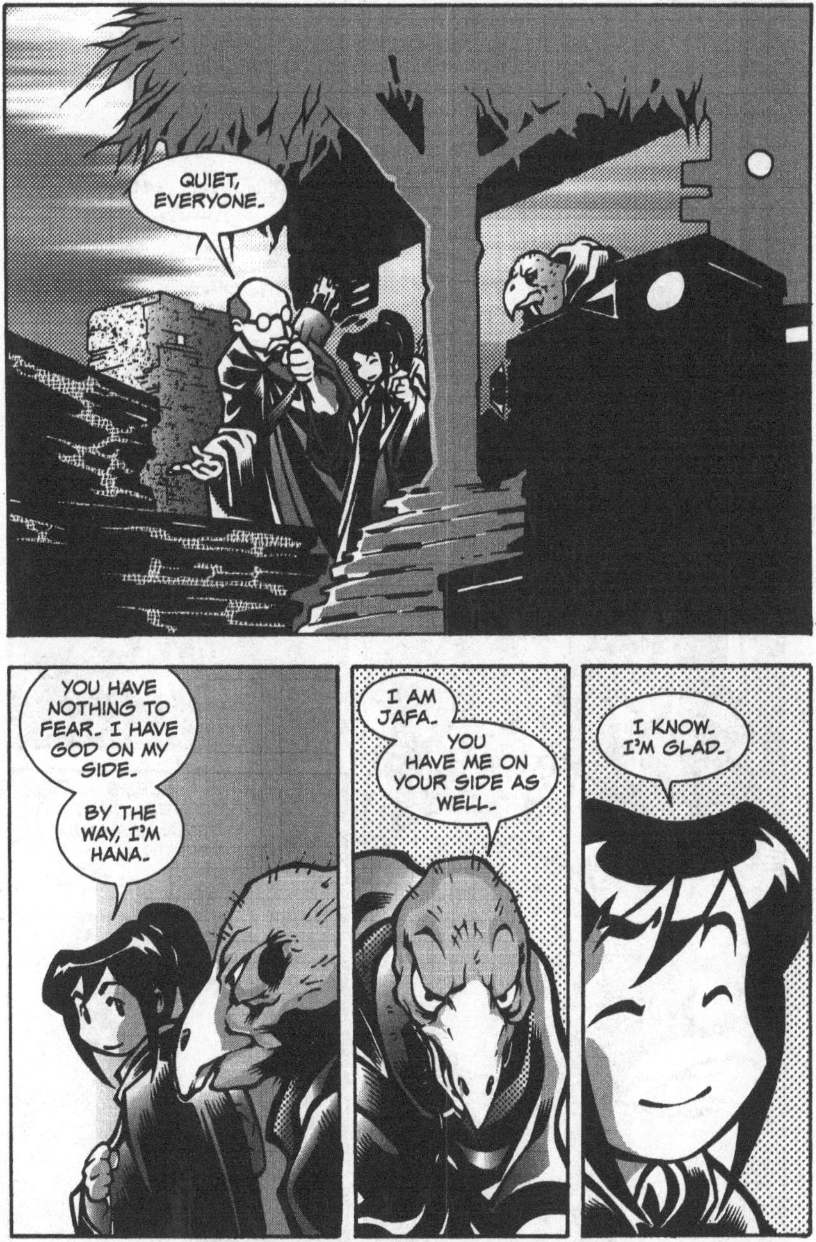
QUIET, EVERYONE.
YOU HAVE NOTHING TO FEAR. I HAVE GOD ON MY SIDE.
BY THE WAY, I'M HANA.
I AM JAFA.
YOU HAVE ME ON YOUR SIDE AS WELL.
I KNOW. I'M GLAD.

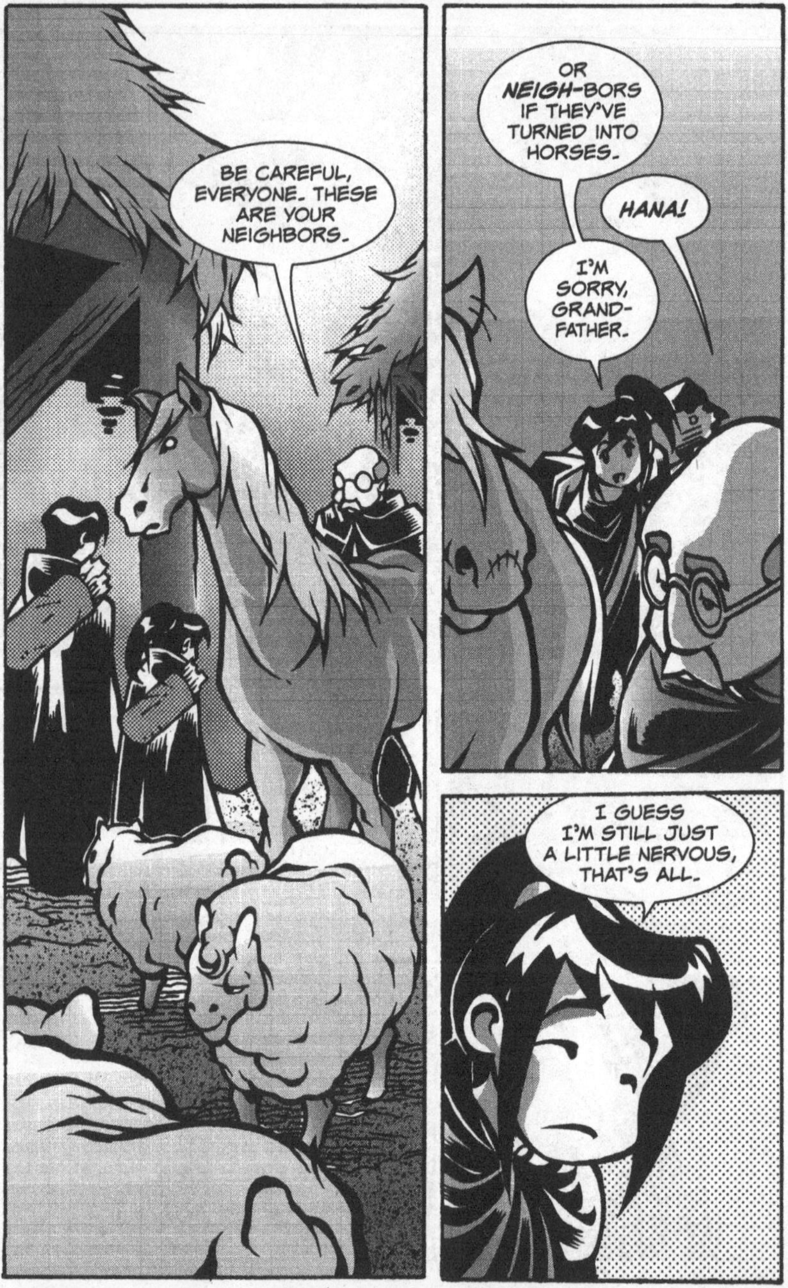
BE CAREFUL, EVERYONE. THESE ARE YOUR NEIGHBORS.
OR *NEIGH*-BORS IF THEY'VE TURNED INTO HORSES.
I'M SORRY, GRANDFATHER.
HANA!
I GUESS I'M STILL JUST A LITTLE NERVOUS, THAT'S ALL.

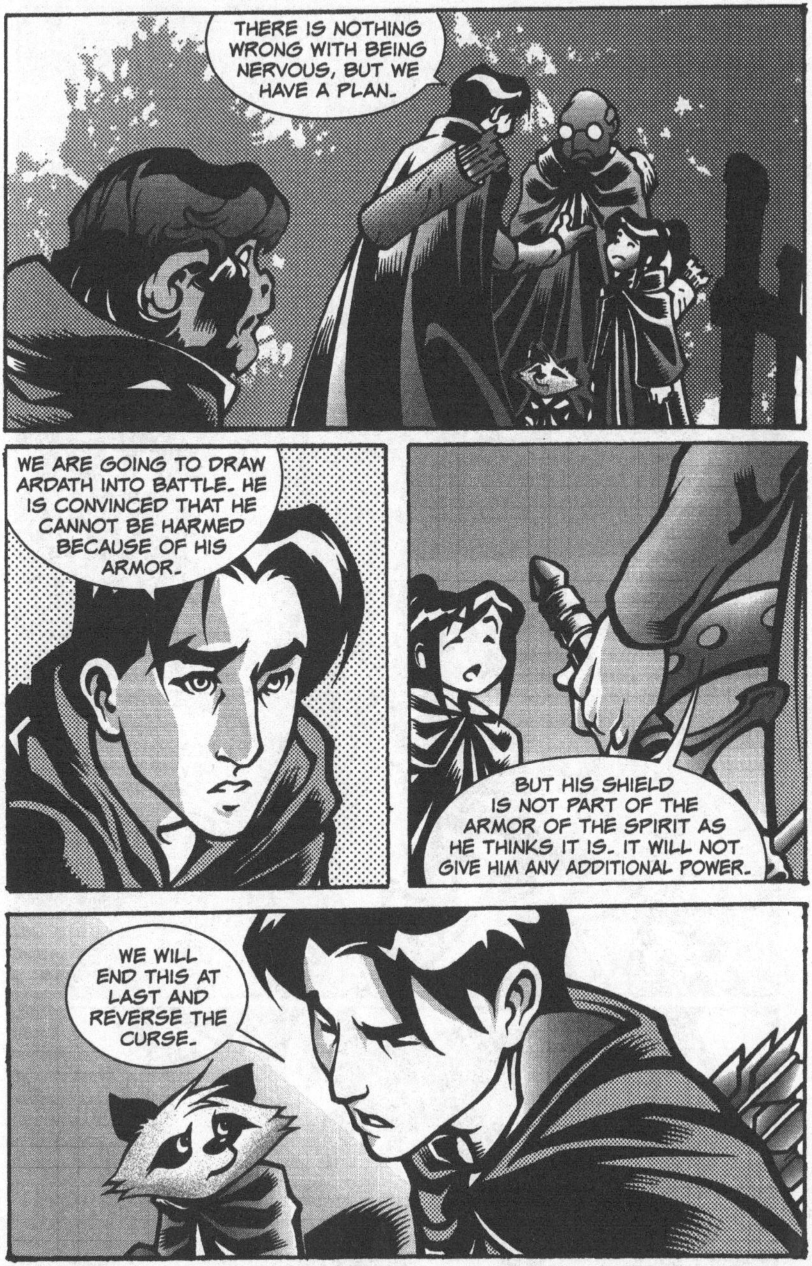
THERE IS NOTHING WRONG WITH BEING NERVOUS, BUT WE HAVE A PLAN.
WE ARE GOING TO DRAW ARDATH INTO BATTLE. HE IS CONVINCED THAT HE CANNOT BE HARMED BECAUSE OF HIS ARMOR.
BUT HIS SHIELD IS NOT PART OF THE ARMOR OF THE SPIRIT AS HE THINKS IT IS. IT WILL NOT GIVE HIM ANY ADDITIONAL POWER.
WE WILL END THIS AT LAST AND REVERSE THE CURSE.

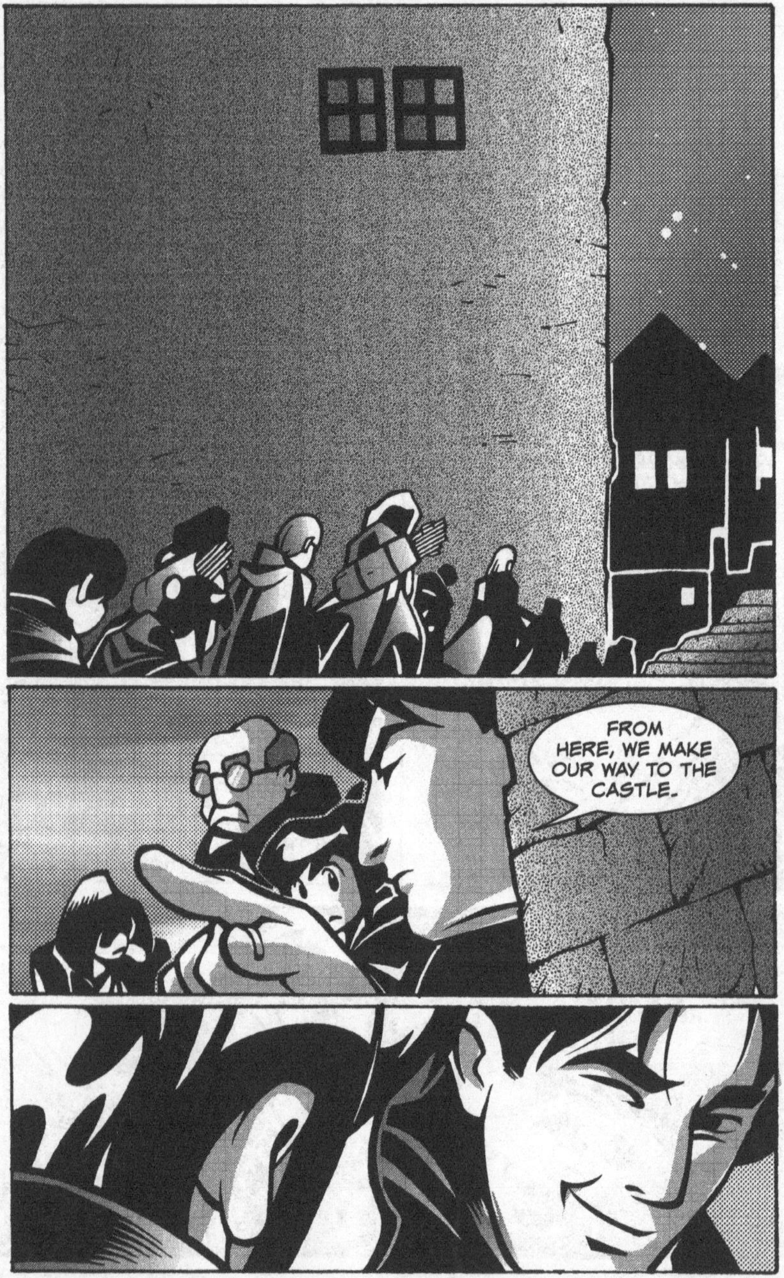
FROM HERE, WE MAKE OUR WAY TO THE CASTLE.

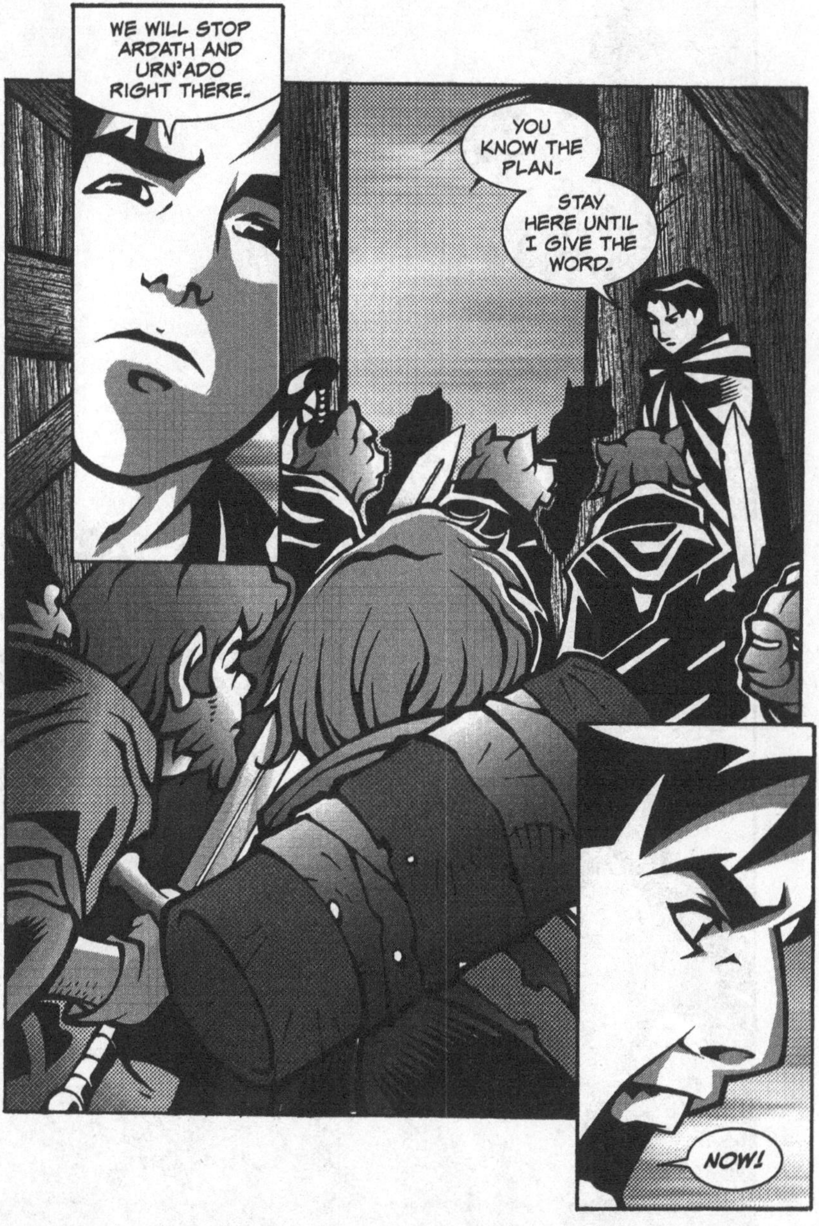
WE WILL STOP ARDATH AND URN'ADO RIGHT THERE.
YOU KNOW THE PLAN.
STAY HERE UNTIL I GIVE THE WORD.
NOW!

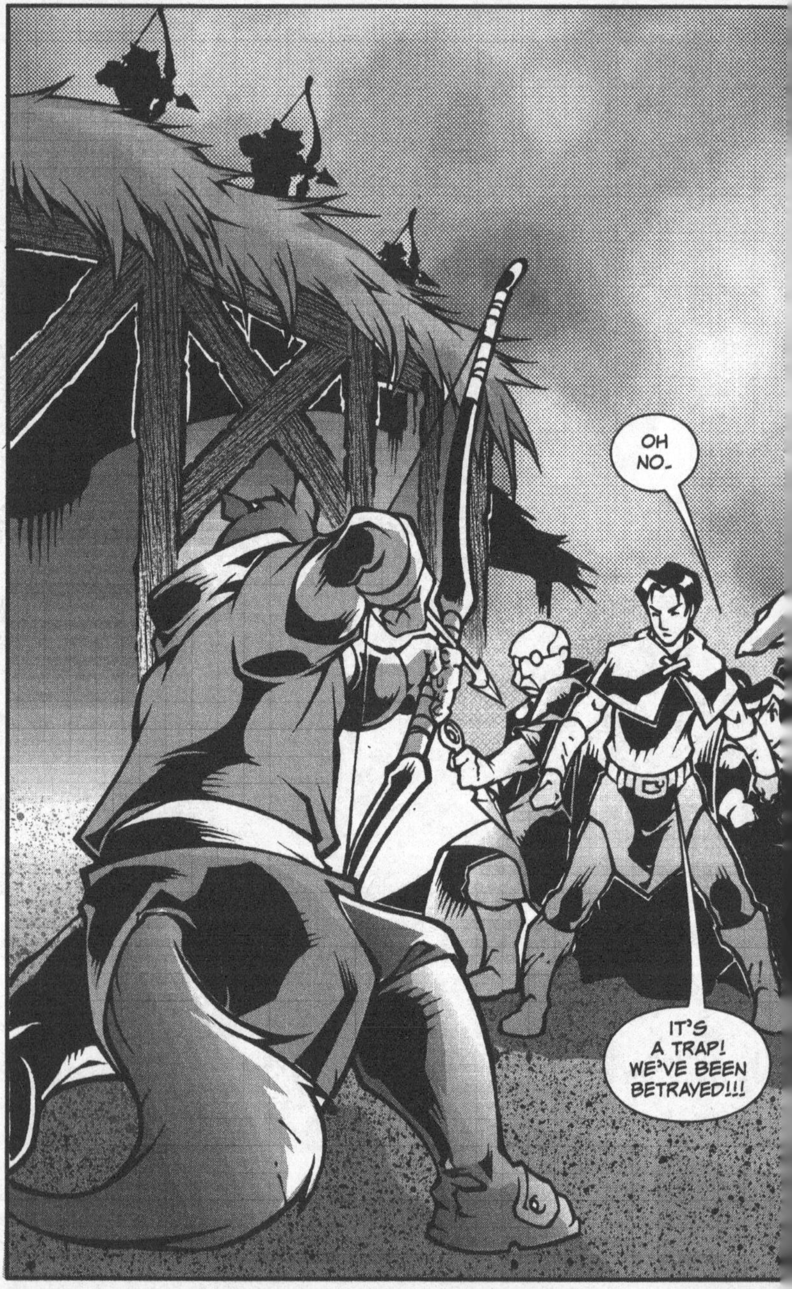
OH NO-
IT'S A TRAP! WE'VE BEEN BETRAYED!!!

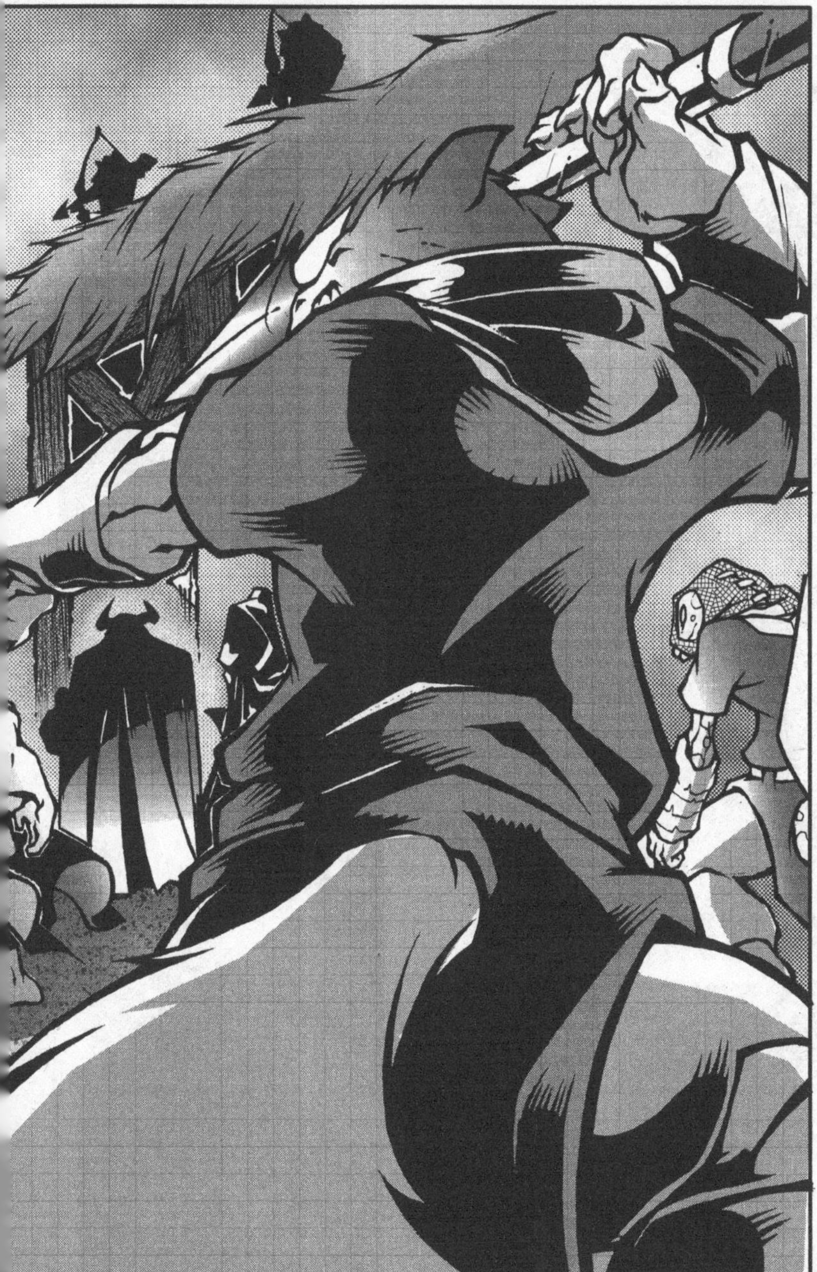

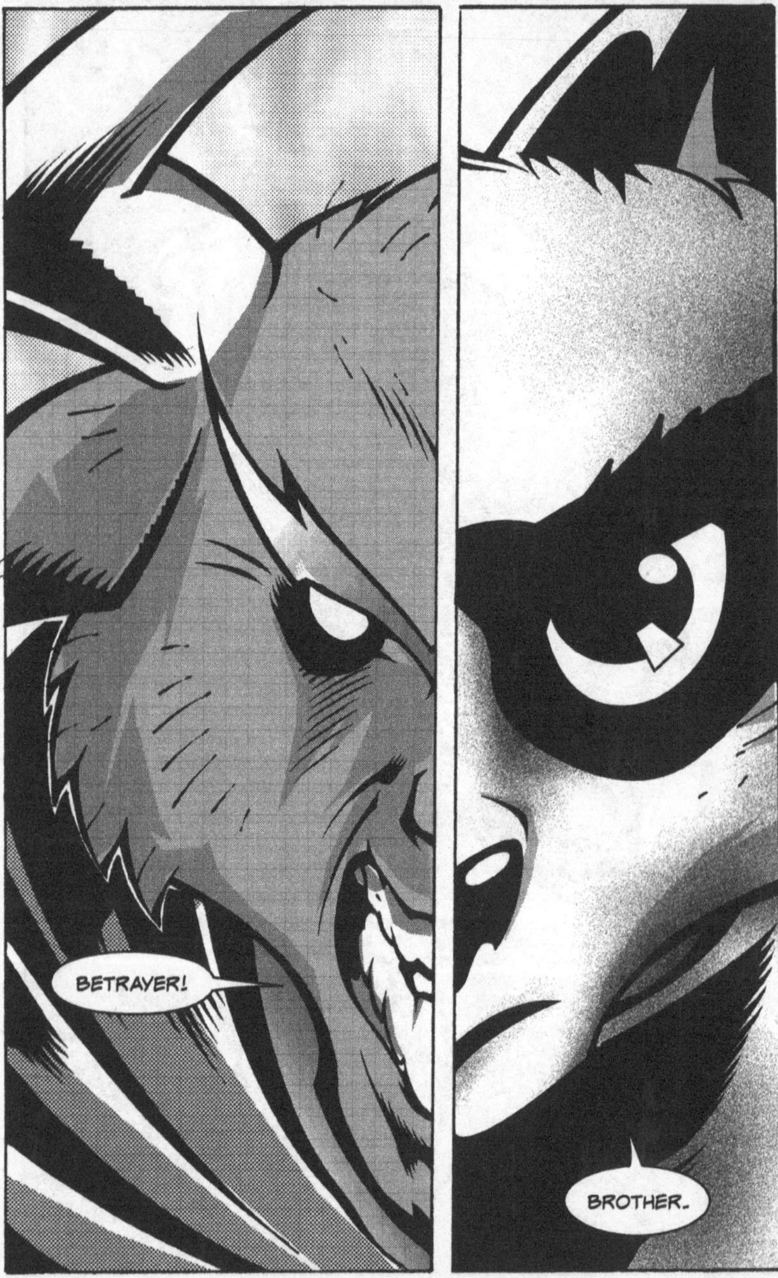
BETRAYER!
BROTHER.

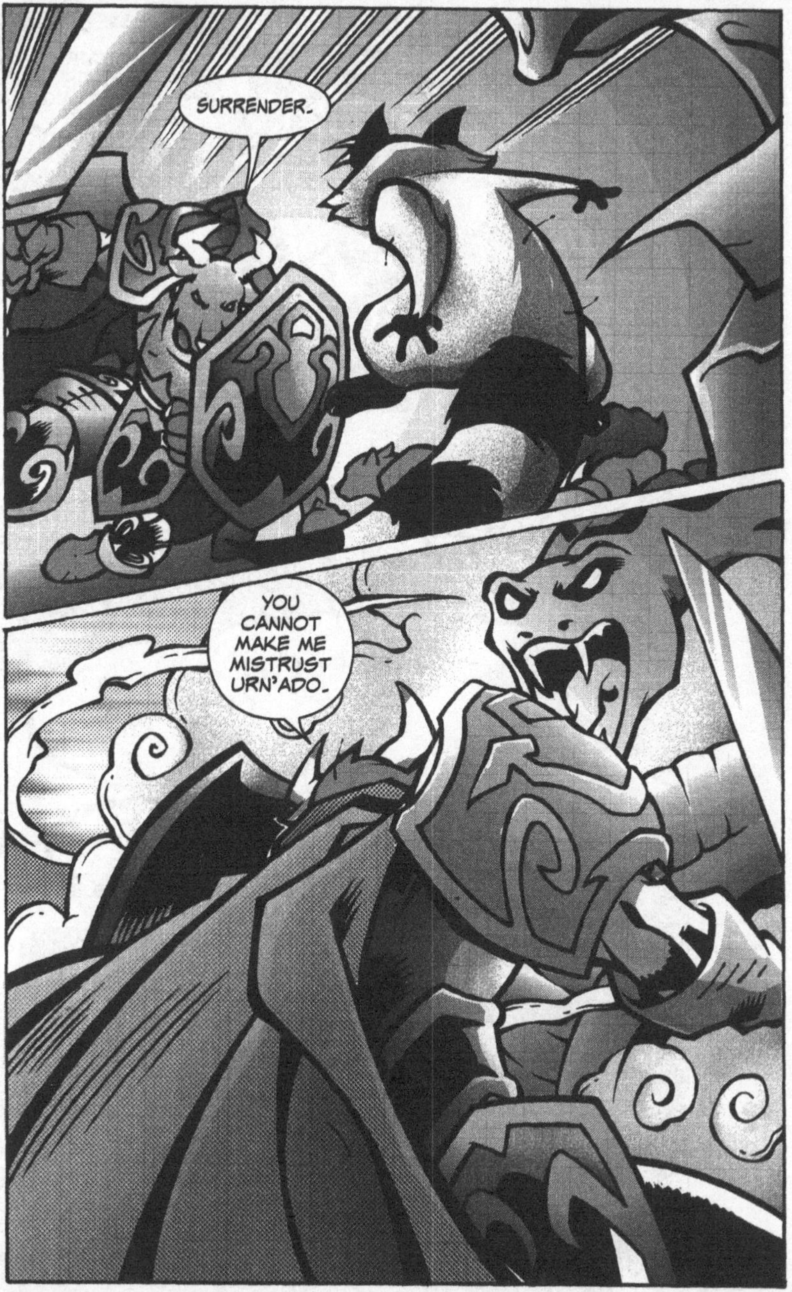
SURRENDER.
YOU CANNOT MAKE ME MISTRUST URN'ADO.

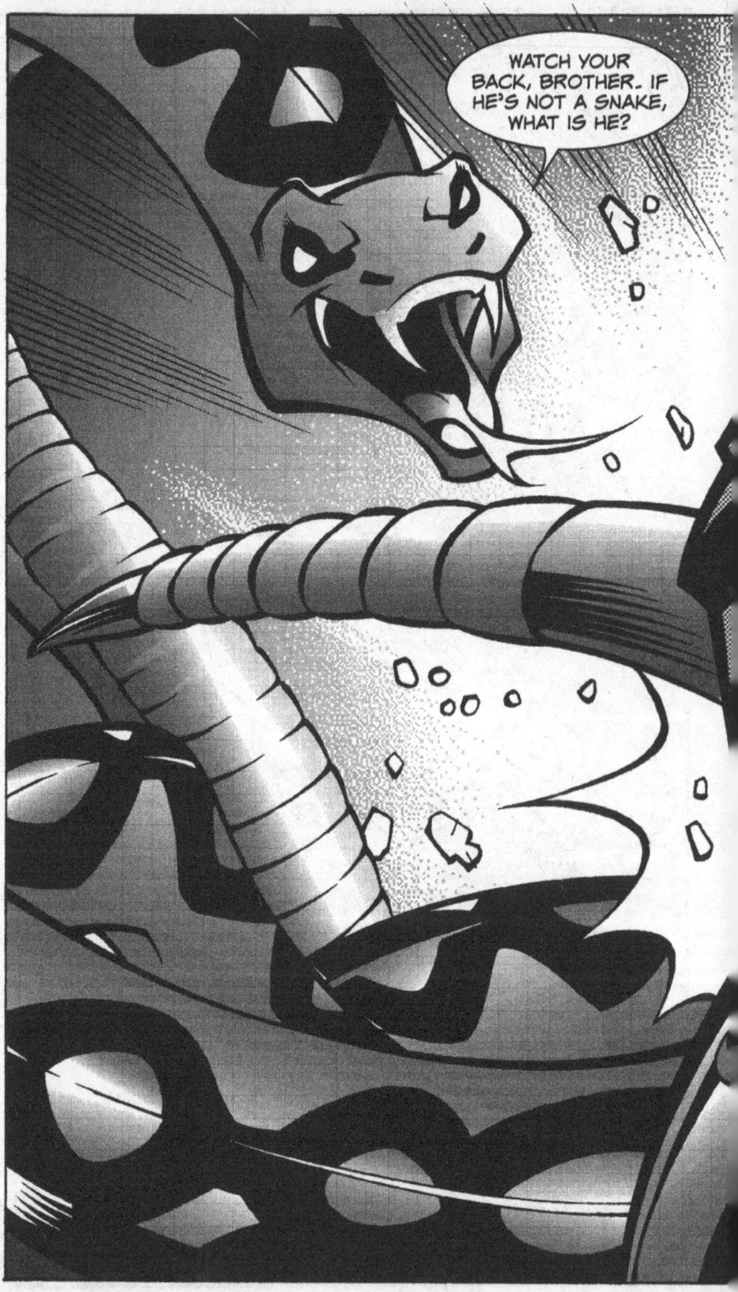
WATCH YOUR BACK, BROTHER. IF HE'S NOT A SNAKE, WHAT IS HE?

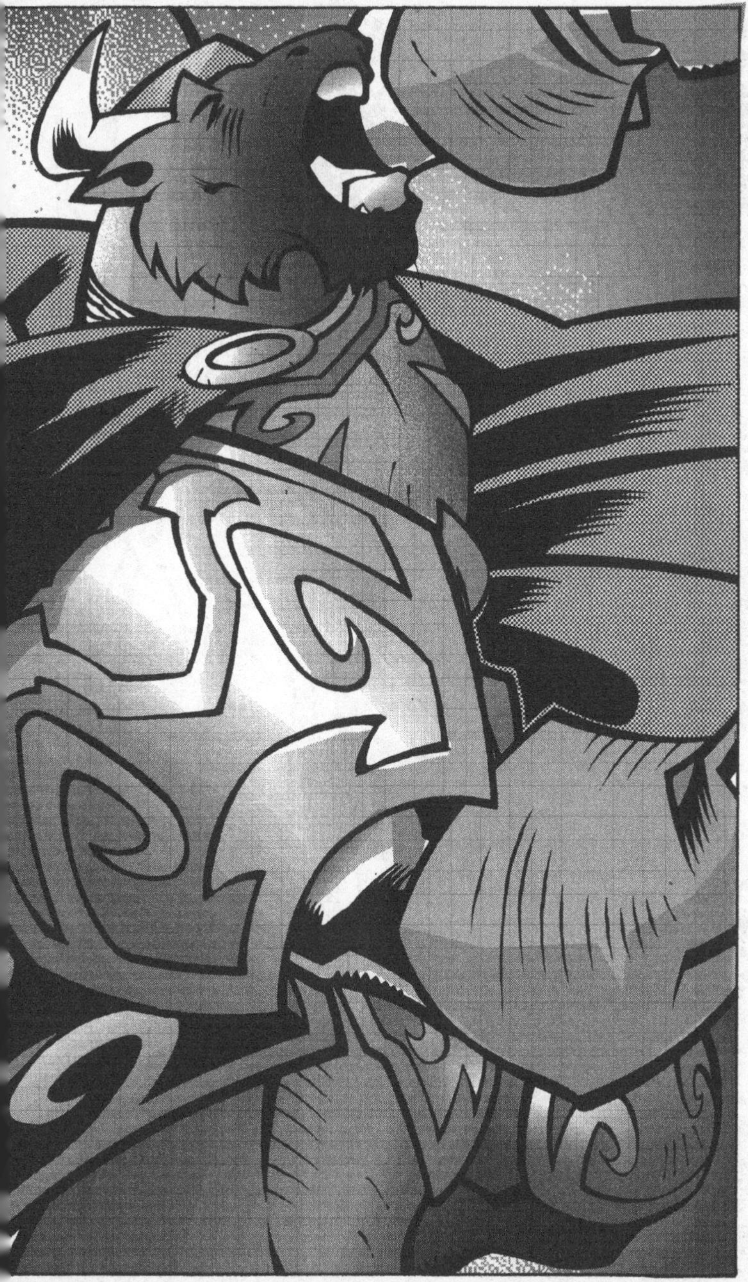

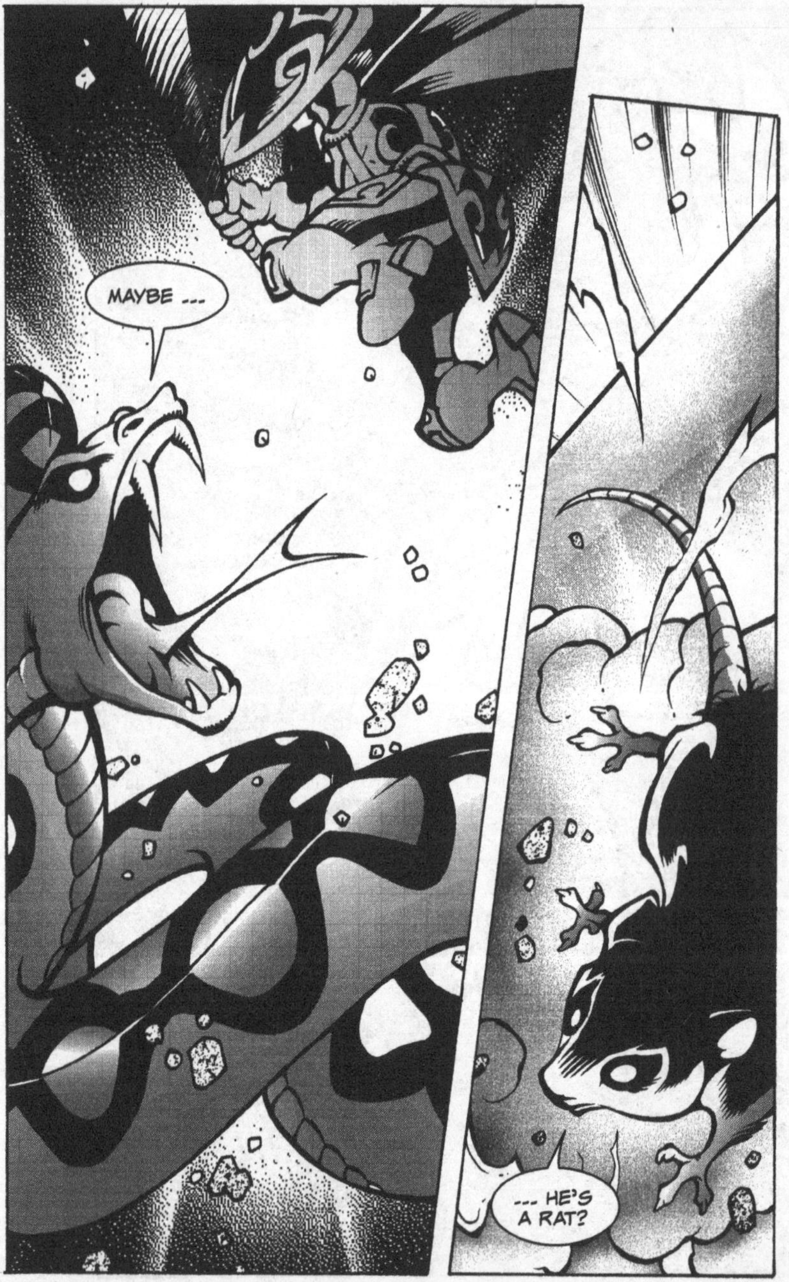
MAYBE ---
--- HE'S A RAT?

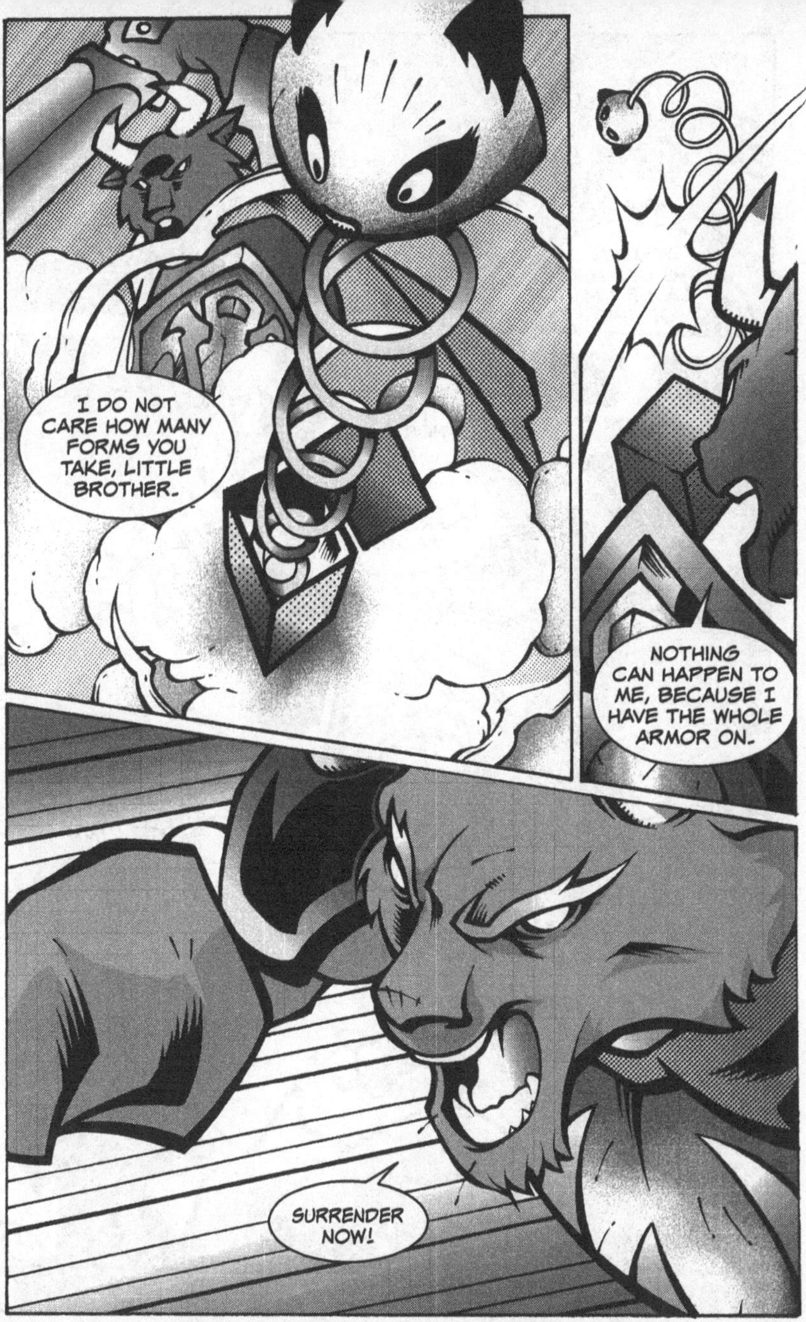
I DO NOT CARE HOW MANY FORMS YOU TAKE, LITTLE BROTHER.
NOTHING CAN HAPPEN TO ME, BECAUSE I HAVE THE WHOLE ARMOR ON.
SURRENDER NOW!

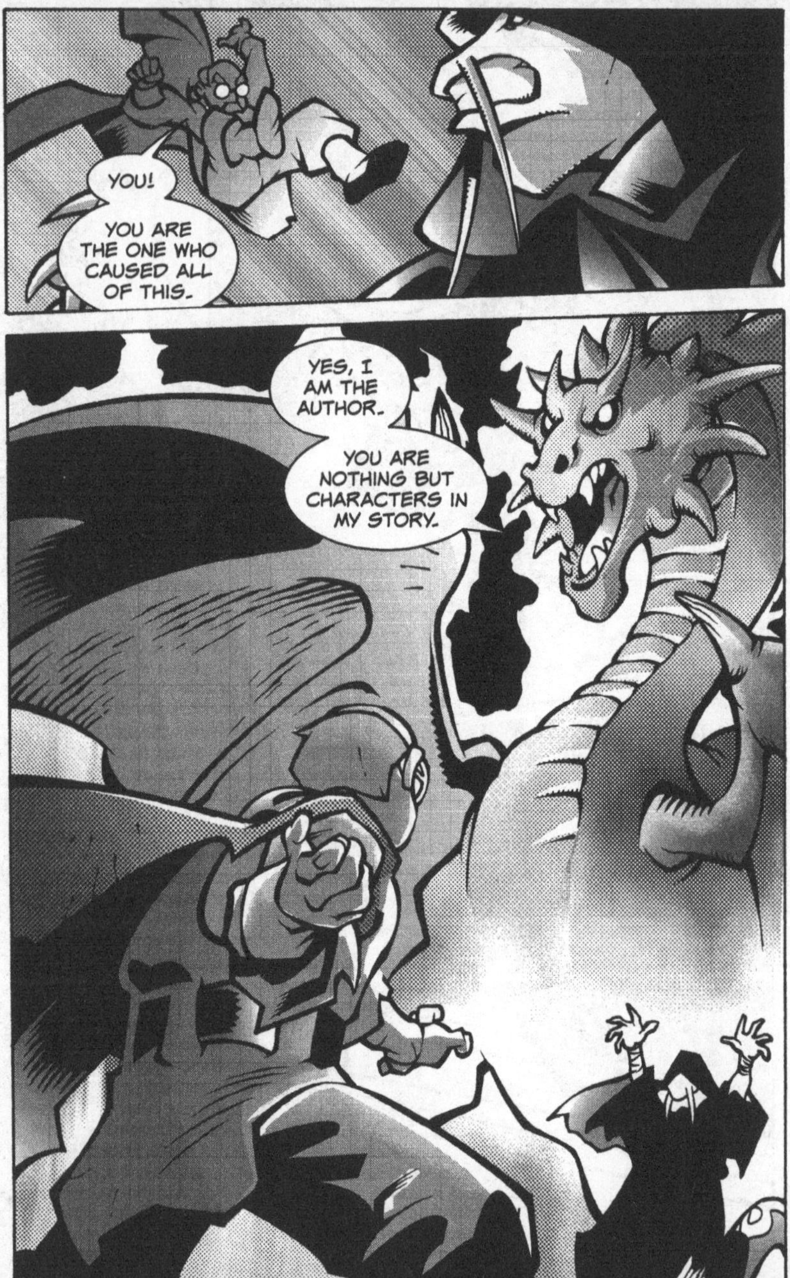
YOU!
YOU ARE THE ONE WHO CAUSED ALL OF THIS.
YES, I AM THE AUTHOR.
YOU ARE NOTHING BUT CHARACTERS IN MY STORY.

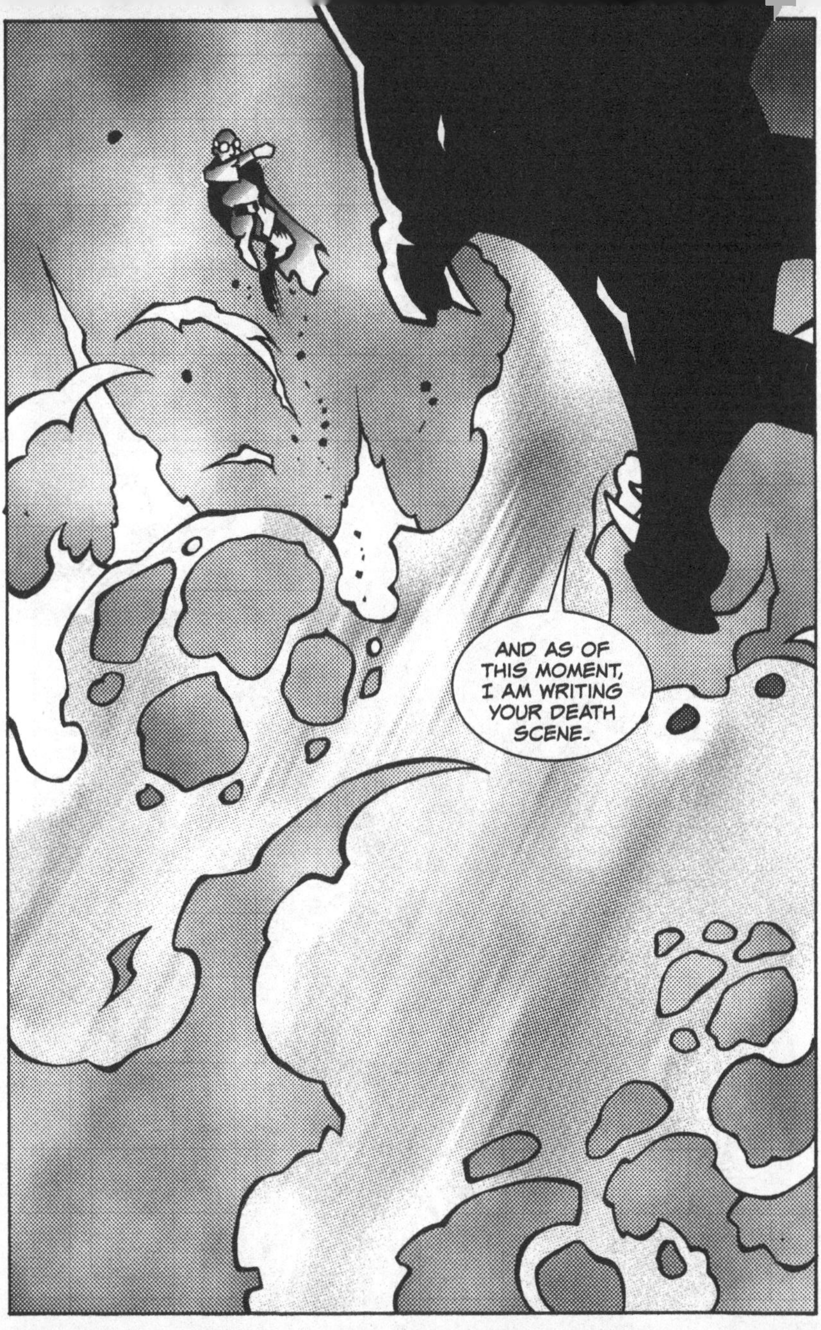
AND AS OF THIS MOMENT, I AM WRITING YOUR DEATH SCENE.

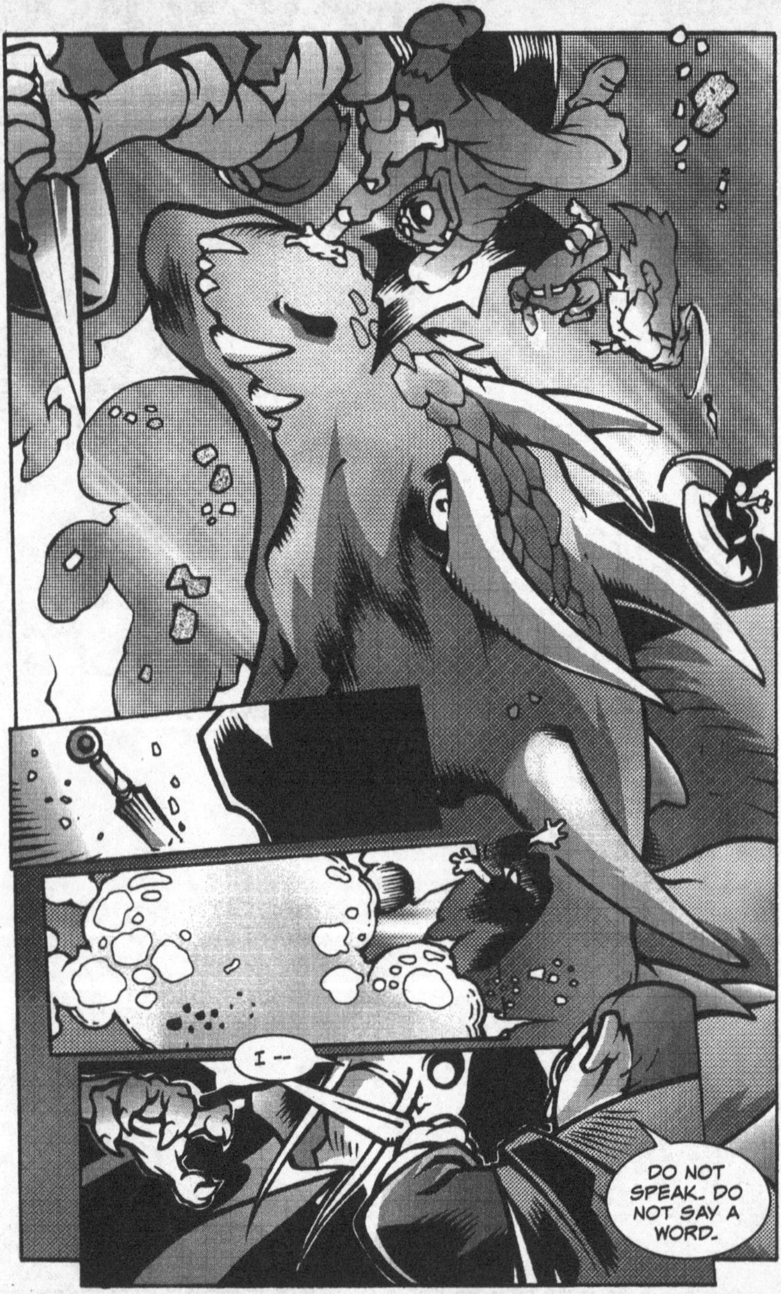
I --
DO NOT SPEAK. DO NOT SAY A WORD.

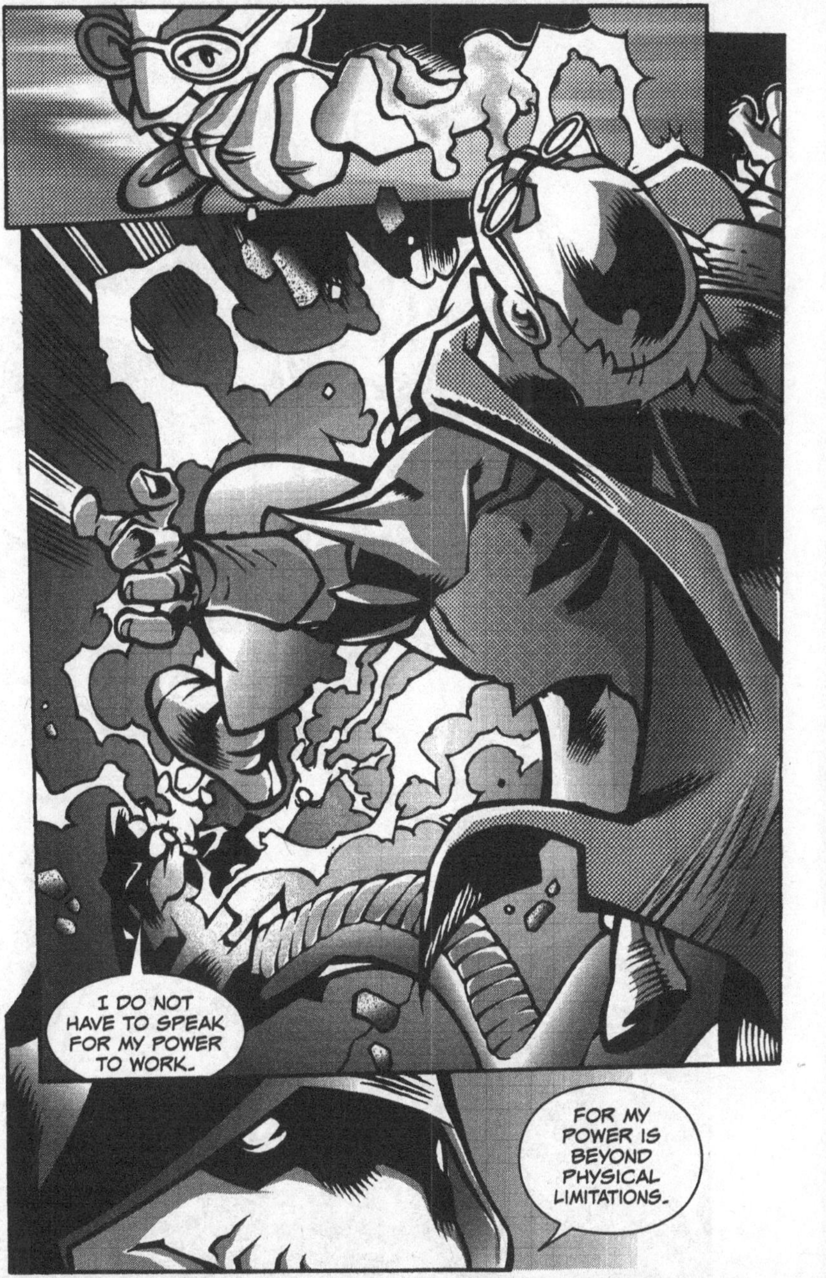
I DO NOT HAVE TO SPEAK FOR MY POWER TO WORK.
FOR MY POWER IS BEYOND PHYSICAL LIMITATIONS.

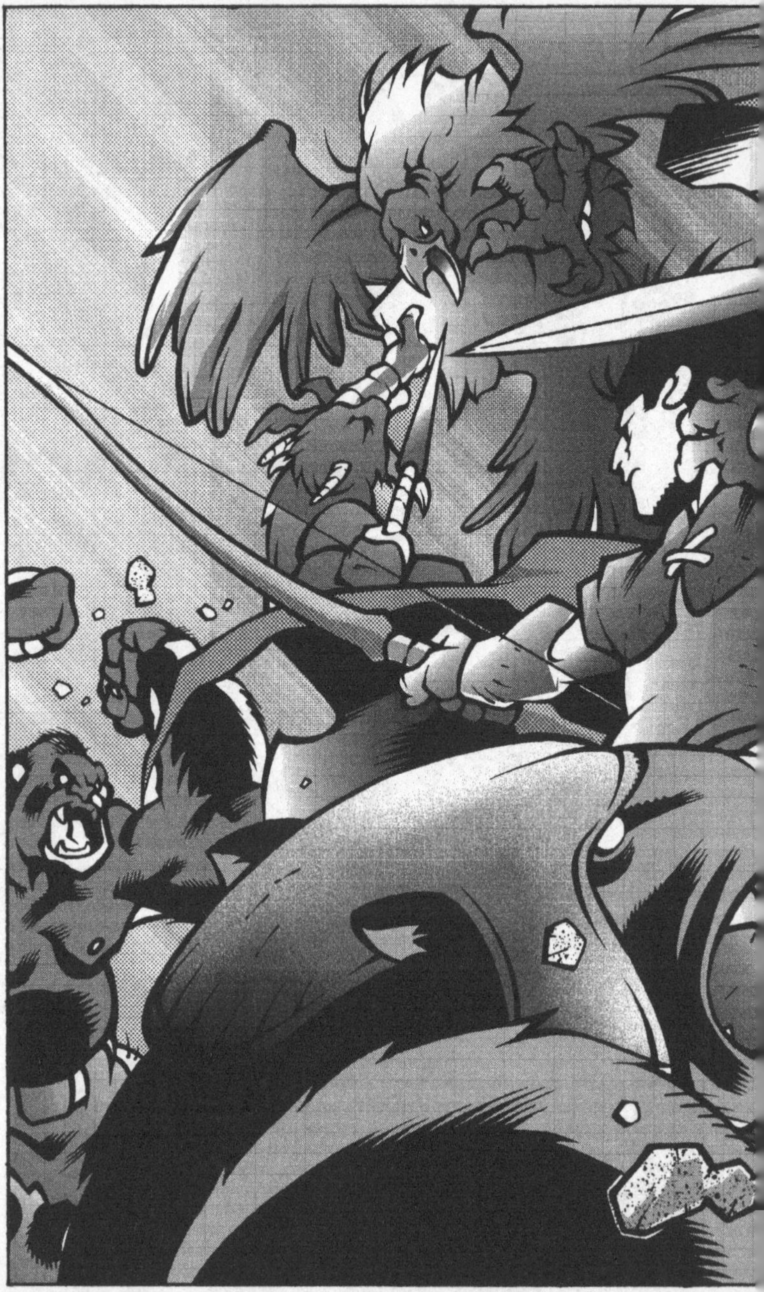

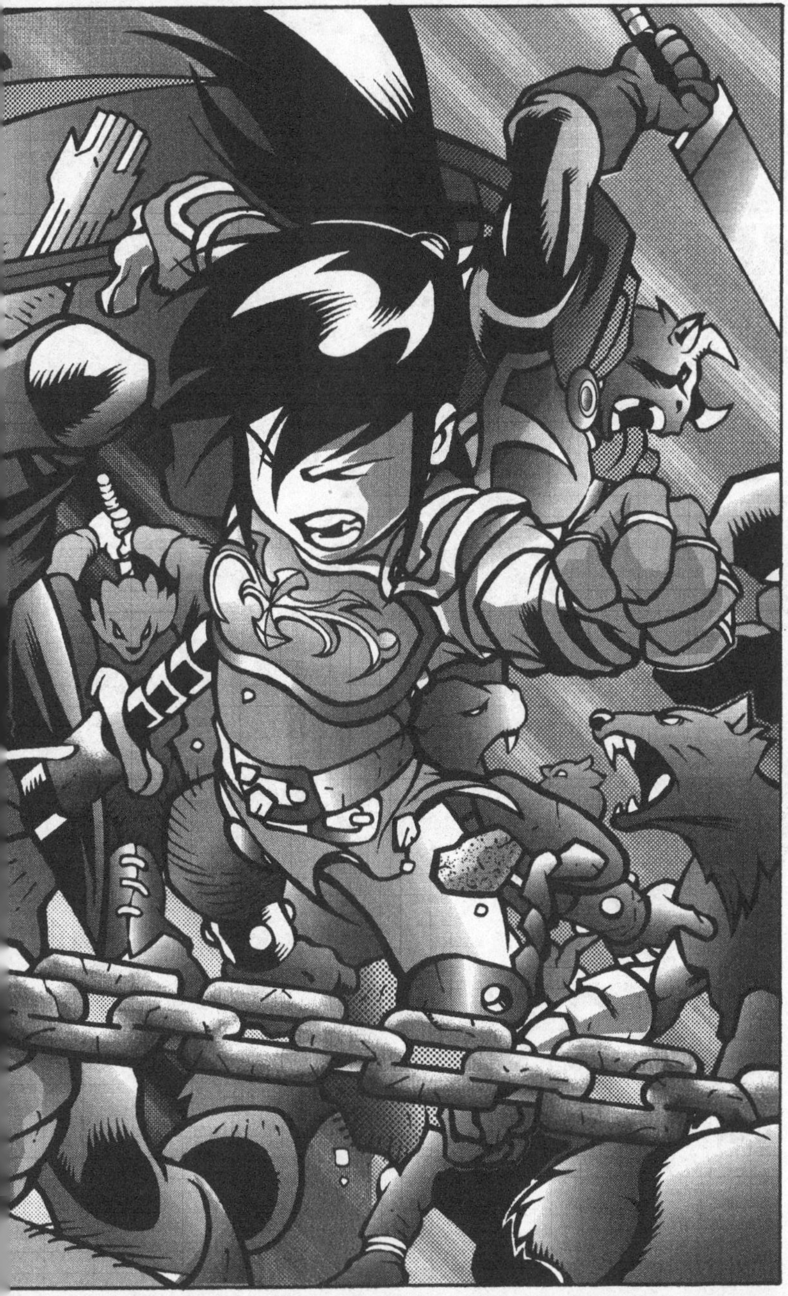

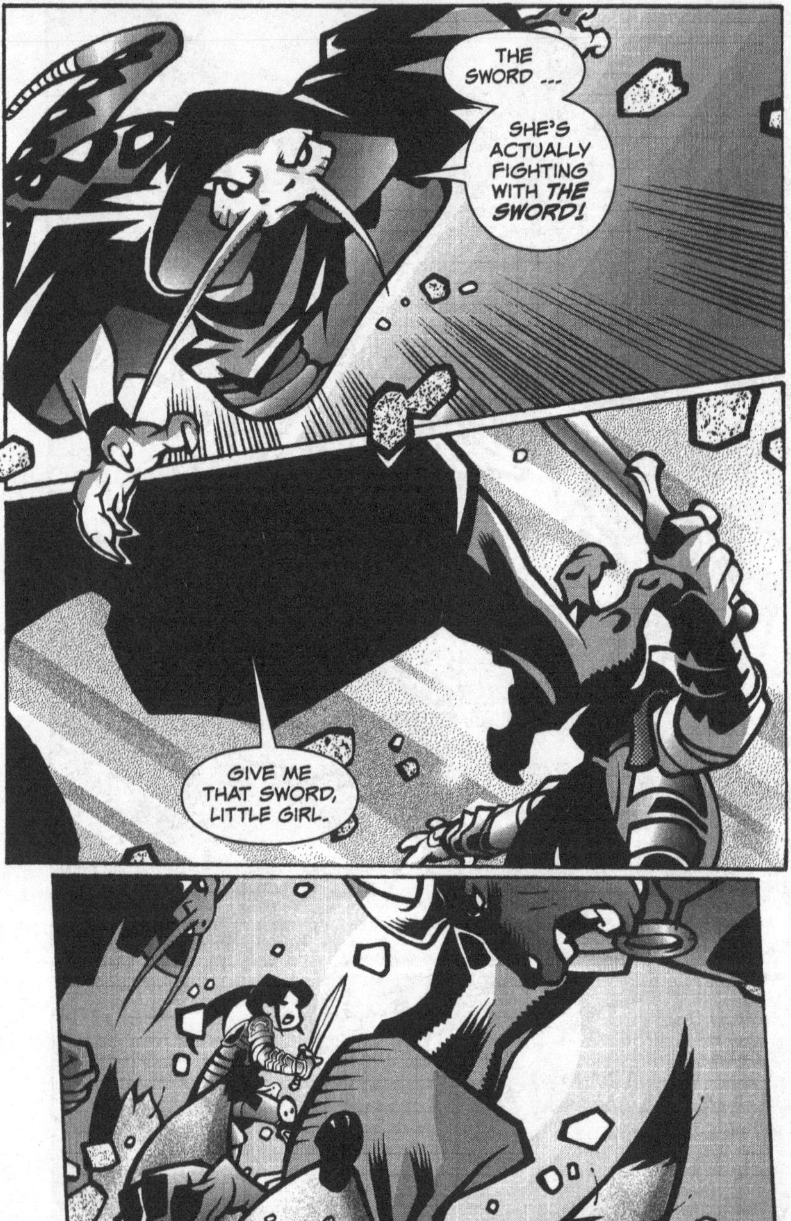

THE SWORD ...
SHE'S ACTUALLY FIGHTING WITH *THE SWORD!*
GIVE ME THAT SWORD, LITTLE GIRL.

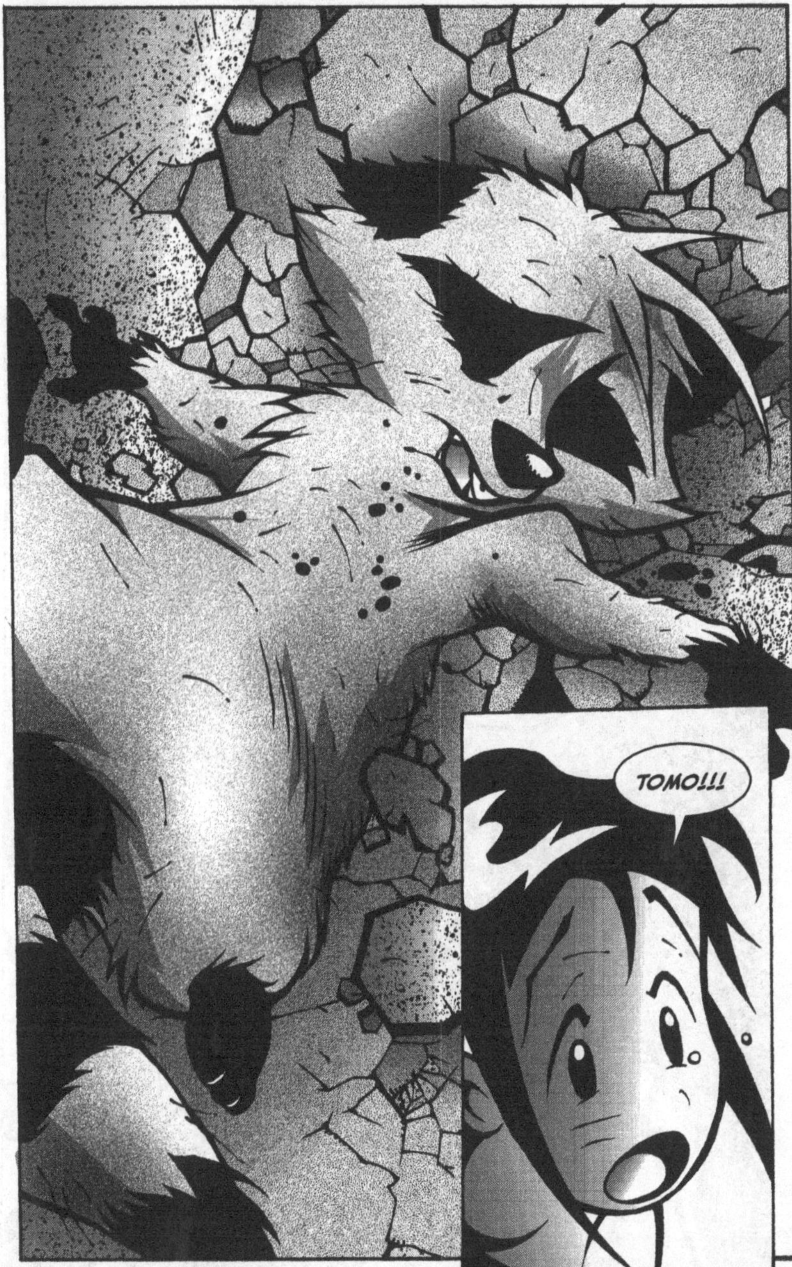
TOMO!!!

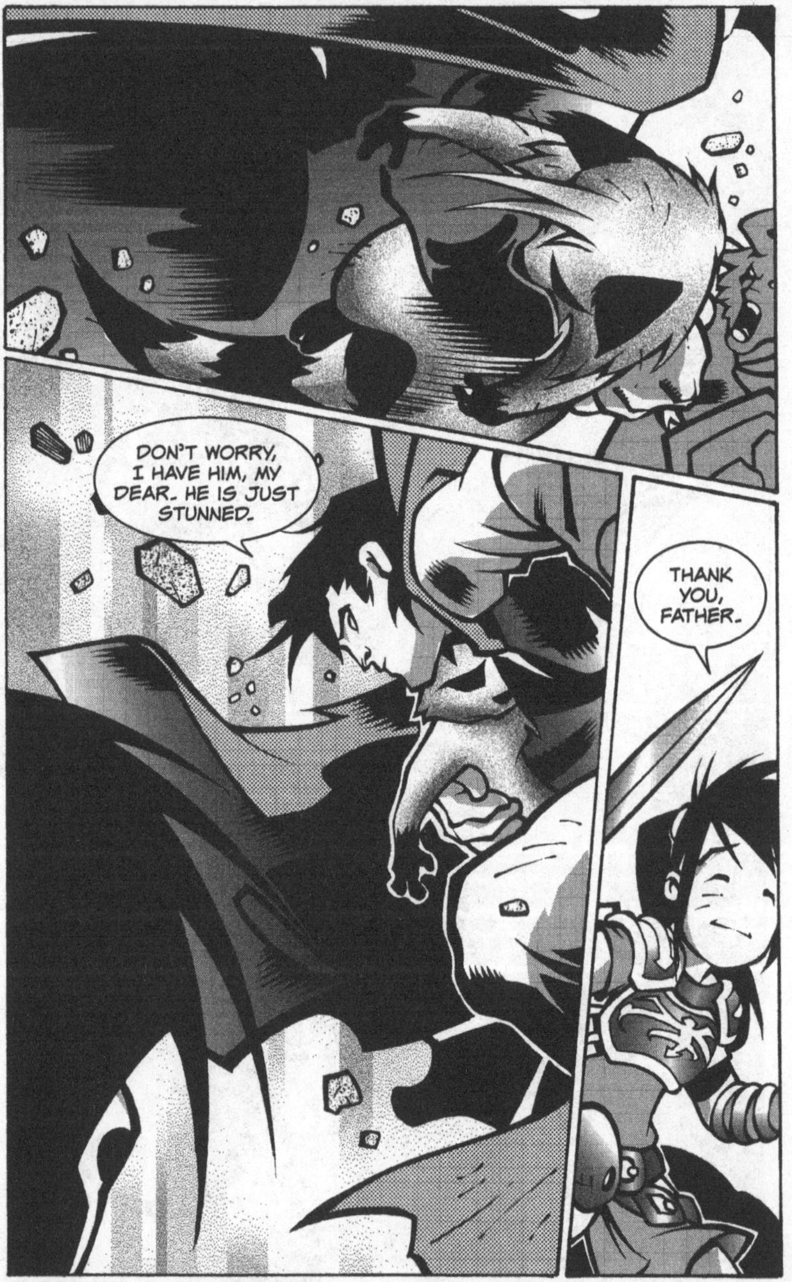
DON'T WORRY, I HAVE HIM, MY DEAR. HE IS JUST STUNNED.
THANK YOU, FATHER.

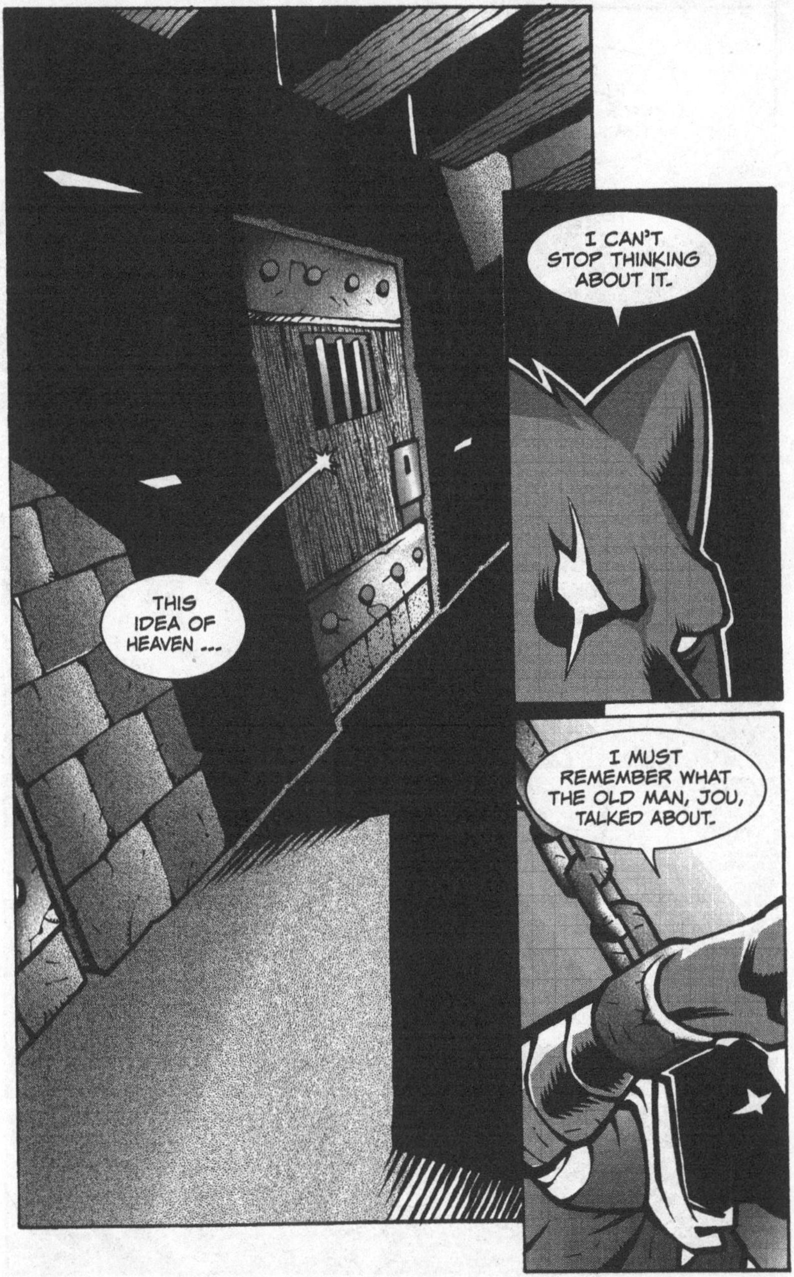
THIS IDEA OF HEAVEN ...
I CAN'T STOP THINKING ABOUT IT.
I MUST REMEMBER WHAT THE OLD MAN, JOU, TALKED ABOUT.

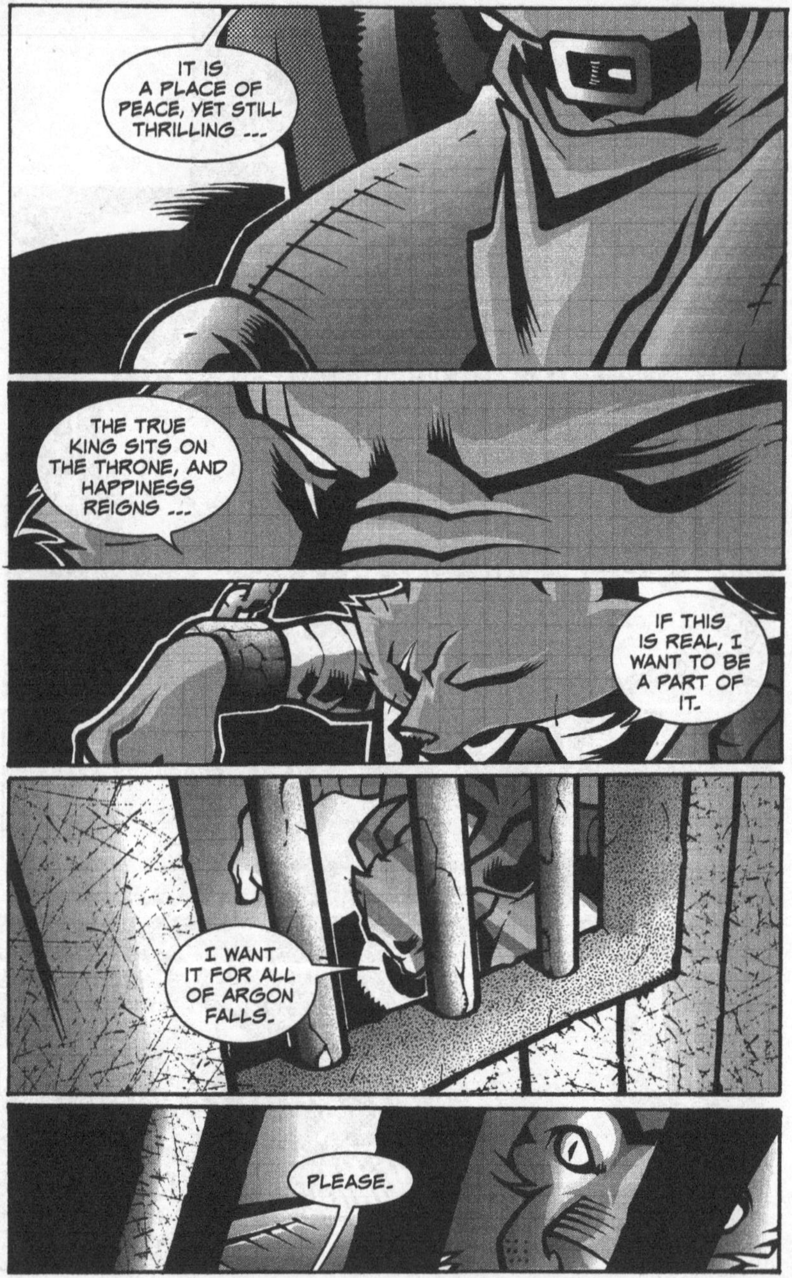
IT IS A PLACE OF PEACE, YET STILL THRILLING ...
THE TRUE KING SITS ON THE THRONE, AND HAPPINESS REIGNS ...
IF THIS IS REAL, I WANT TO BE A PART OF IT.
I WANT IT FOR ALL OF ARGON FALLS.
PLEASE.

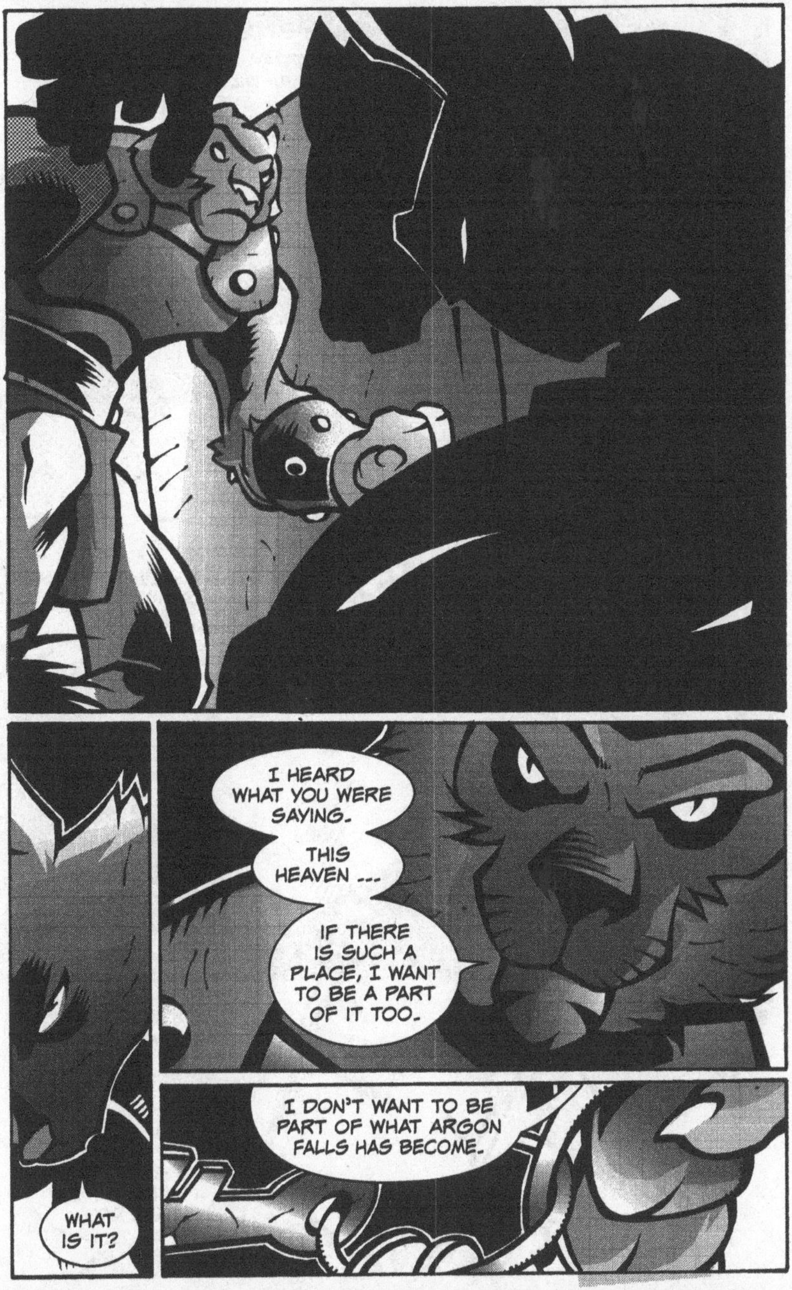
I HEARD WHAT YOU WERE SAYING.
THIS HEAVEN ...
IF THERE IS SUCH A PLACE, I WANT TO BE A PART OF IT TOO.
I DON'T WANT TO BE PART OF WHAT ARGON FALLS HAS BECOME.
WHAT IS IT?

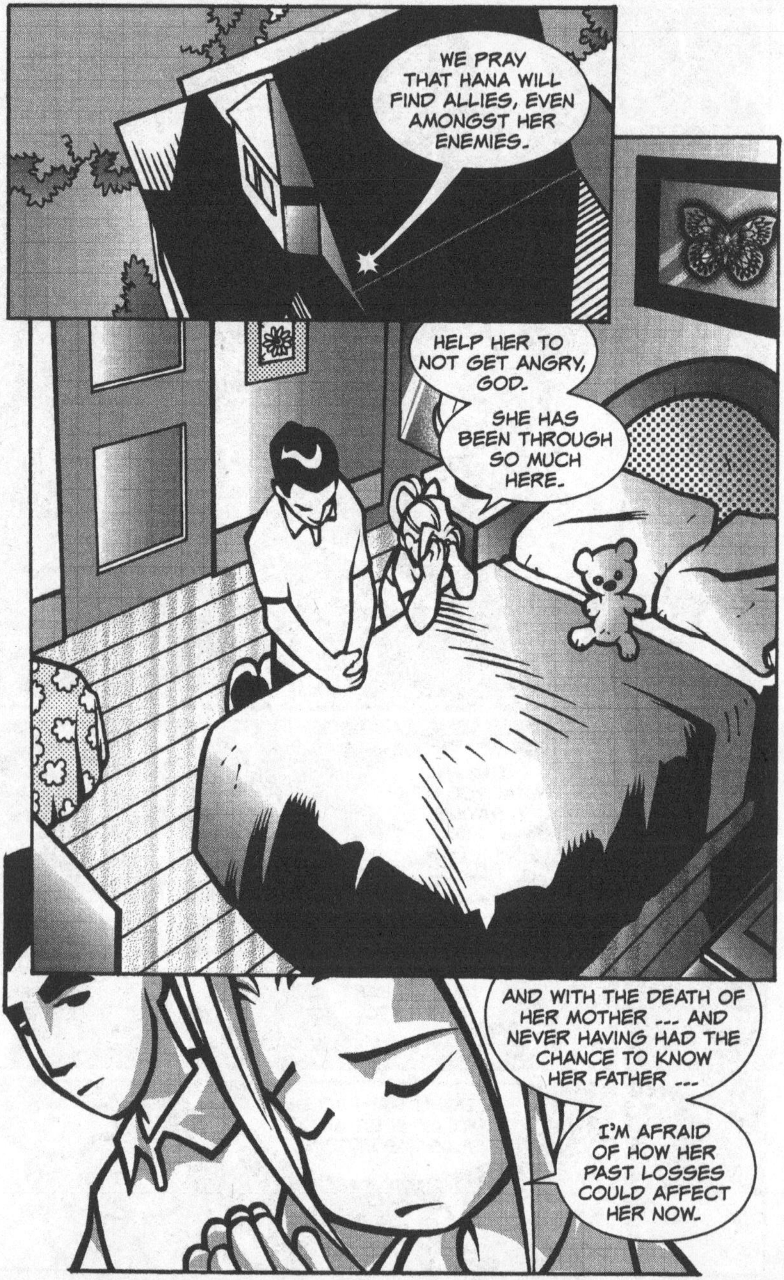
WE PRAY THAT HANA WILL FIND ALLIES, EVEN AMONGST HER ENEMIES.
HELP HER TO NOT GET ANGRY, GOD.
SHE HAS BEEN THROUGH SO MUCH HERE.
AND WITH THE DEATH OF HER MOTHER ... AND NEVER HAVING HAD THE CHANCE TO KNOW HER FATHER ...
I'M AFRAID OF HOW HER PAST LOSSES COULD AFFECT HER NOW.

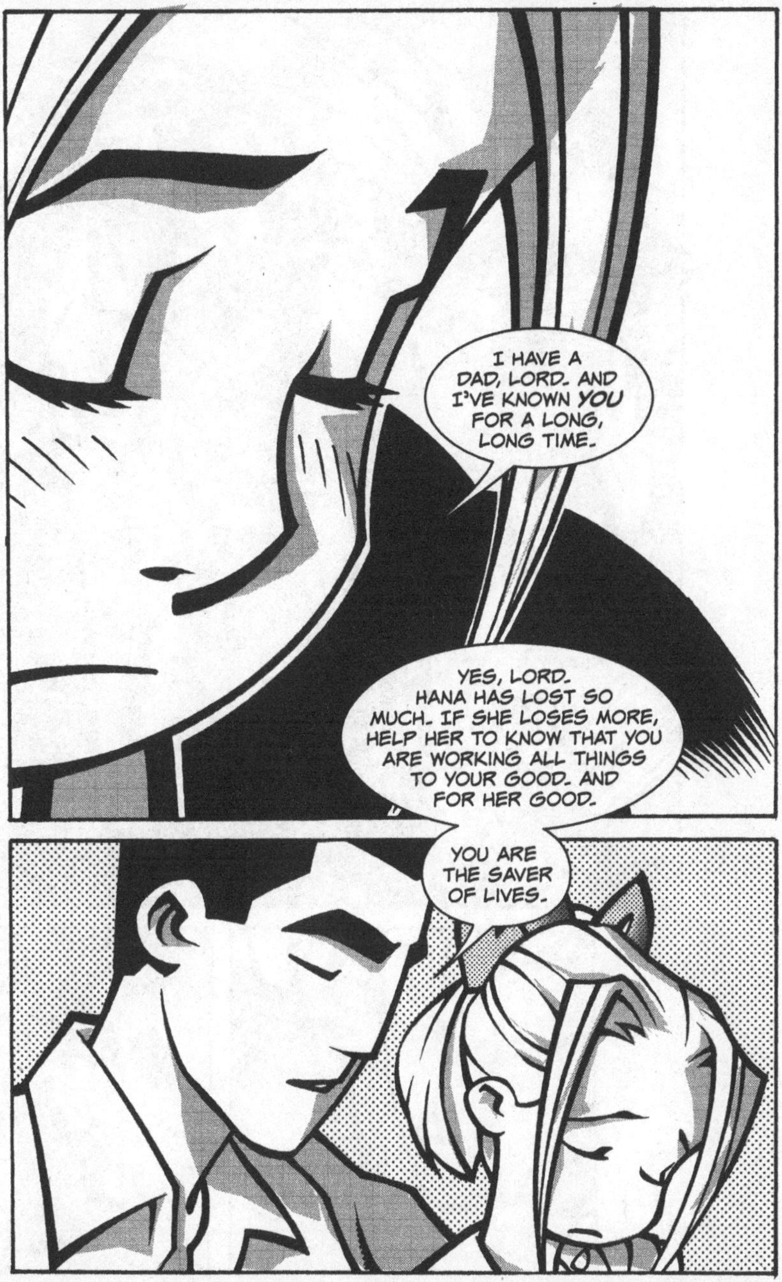
I HAVE A DAD, LORD. AND I'VE KNOWN YOU FOR A LONG, LONG TIME.
YES, LORD. HANA HAS LOST SO MUCH. IF SHE LOSES MORE, HELP HER TO KNOW THAT YOU ARE WORKING ALL THINGS TO YOUR GOOD. AND FOR HER GOOD.
YOU ARE THE SAVER OF LIVES.

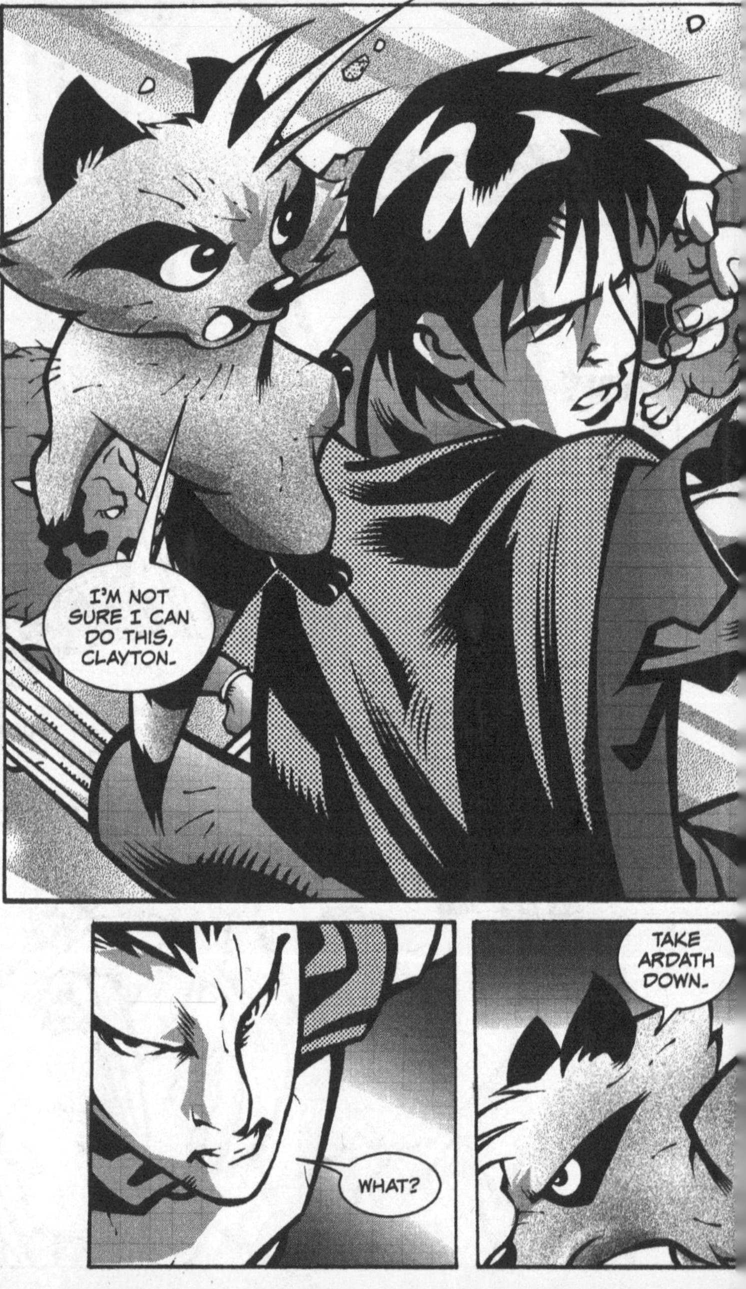
I'M NOT SURE I CAN DO THIS, CLAYTON.
WHAT?
TAKE ARDATH DOWN.

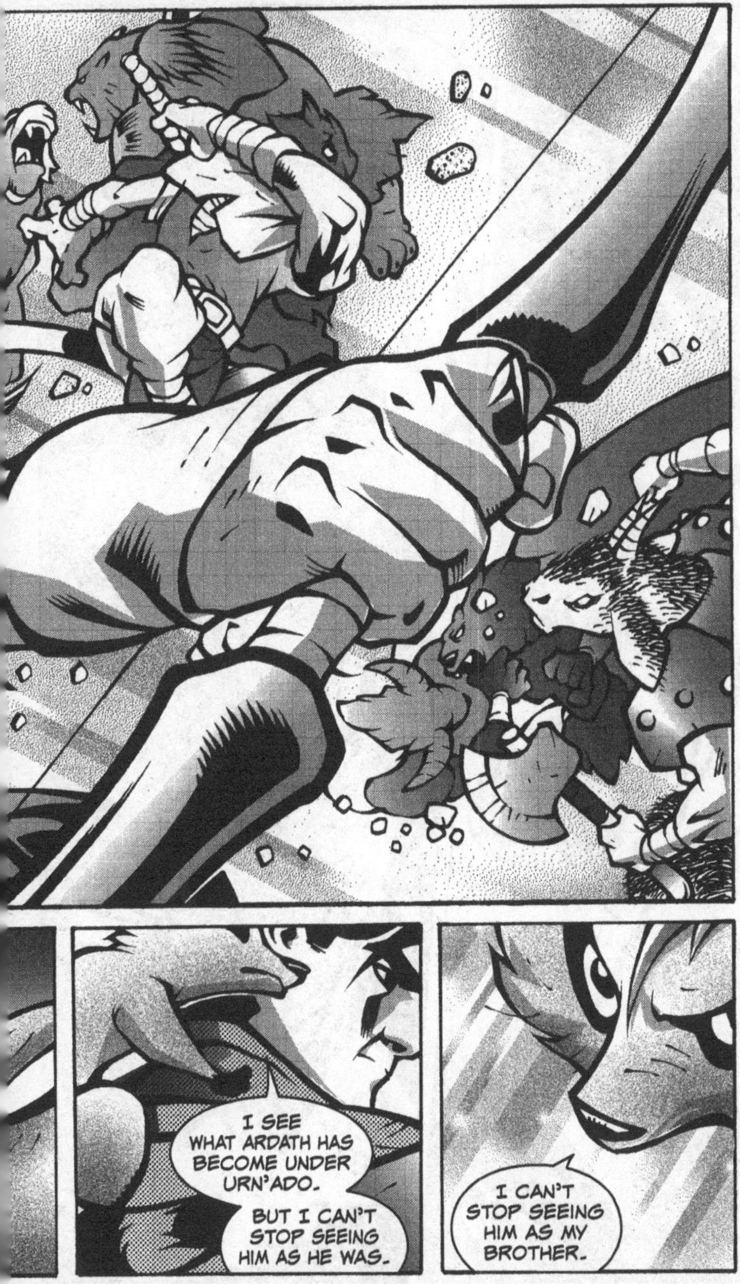
I SEE WHAT ARDATH HAS BECOME UNDER URN'ADO.
BUT I CAN'T STOP SEEING HIM AS HE WAS.
I CAN'T STOP SEEING HIM AS MY BROTHER.

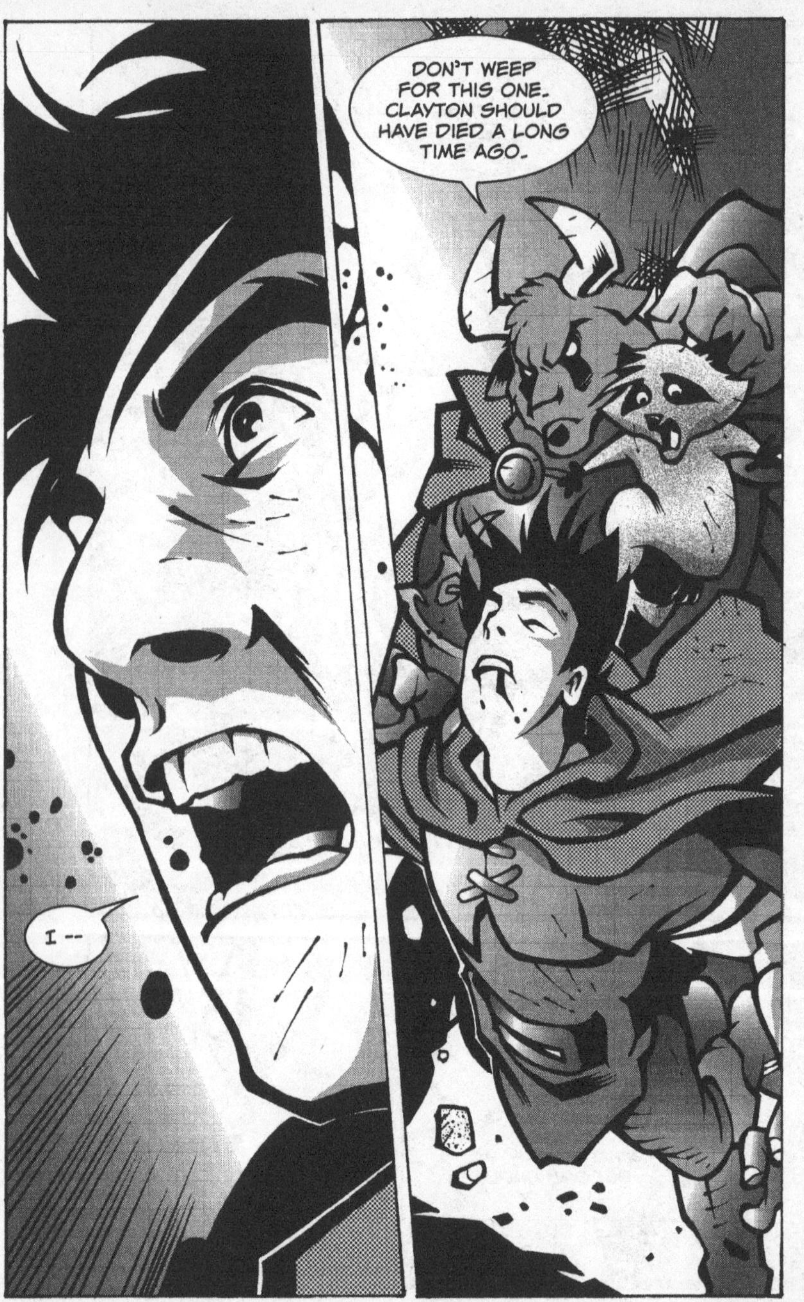
DON'T WEEP FOR THIS ONE. CLAYTON SHOULD HAVE DIED A LONG TIME AGO.
I --

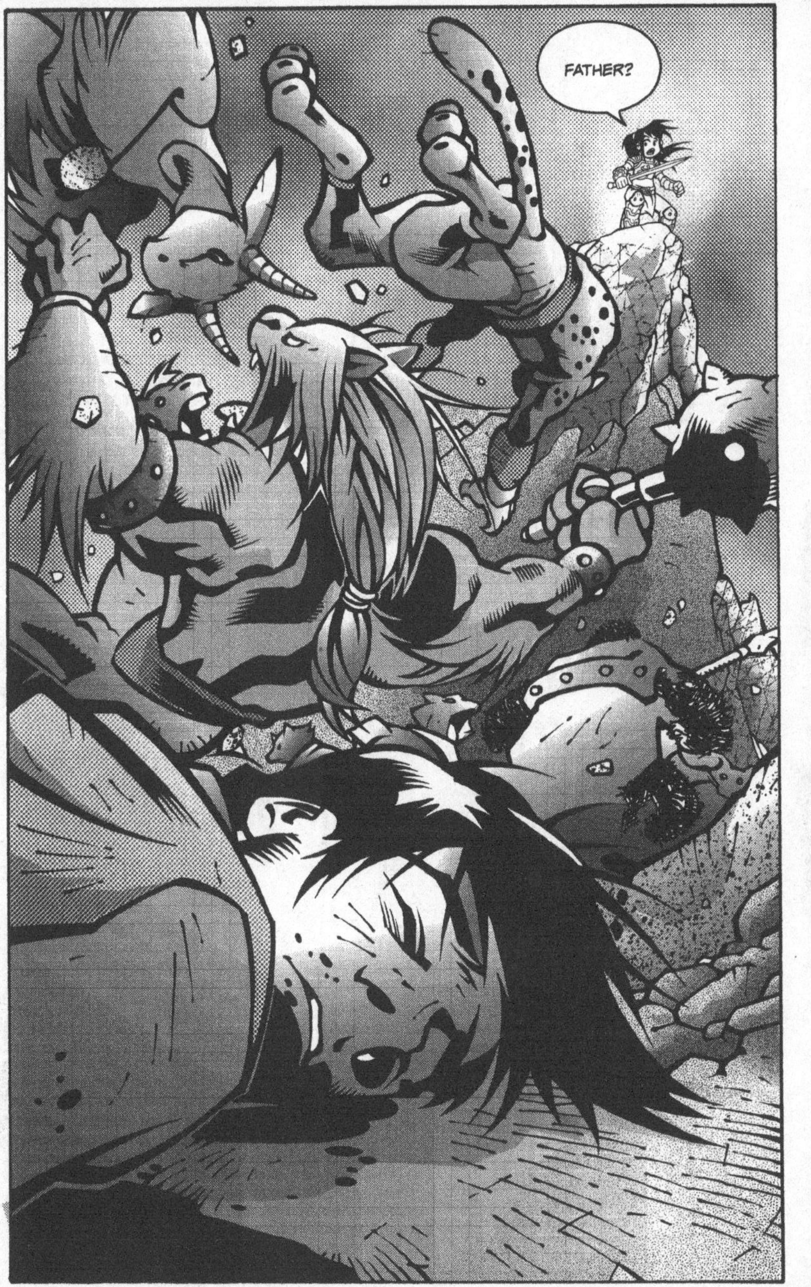
FATHER?

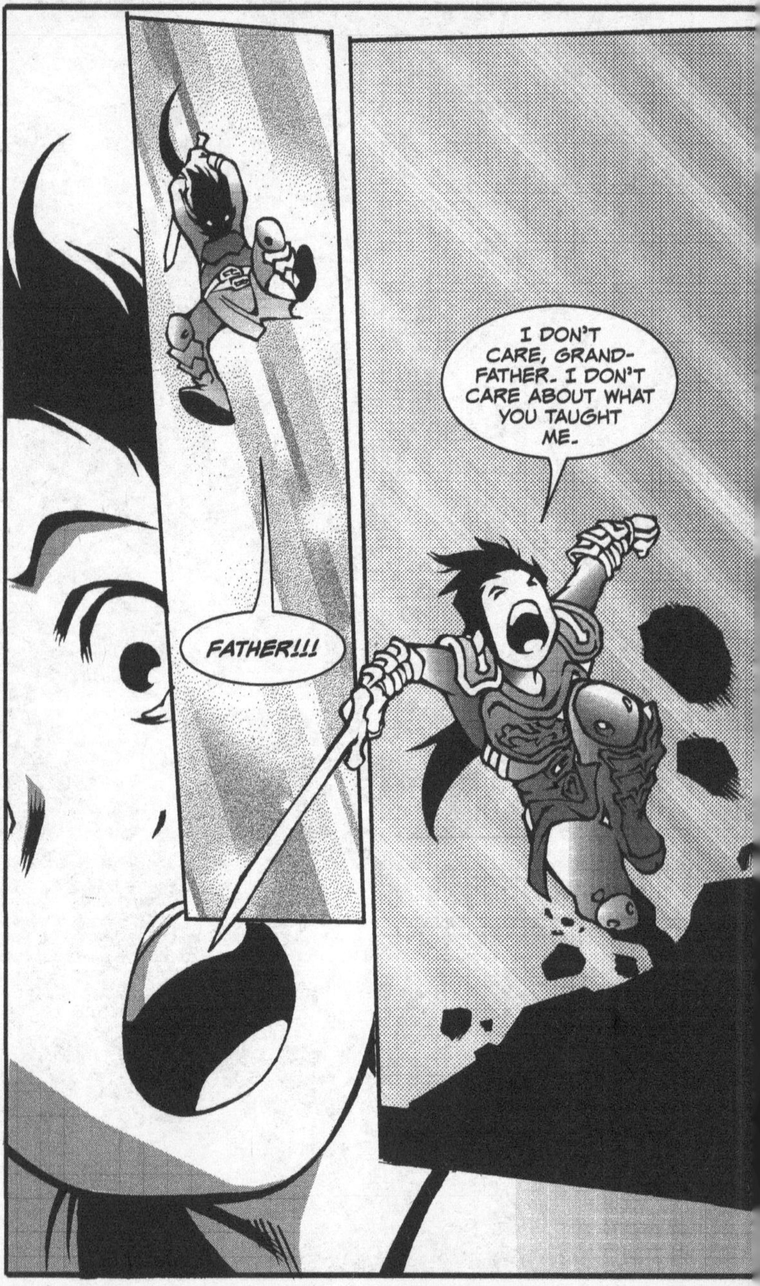
I DON'T CARE, GRAND-FATHER. I DON'T CARE ABOUT WHAT YOU TAUGHT ME.
FATHER!!!

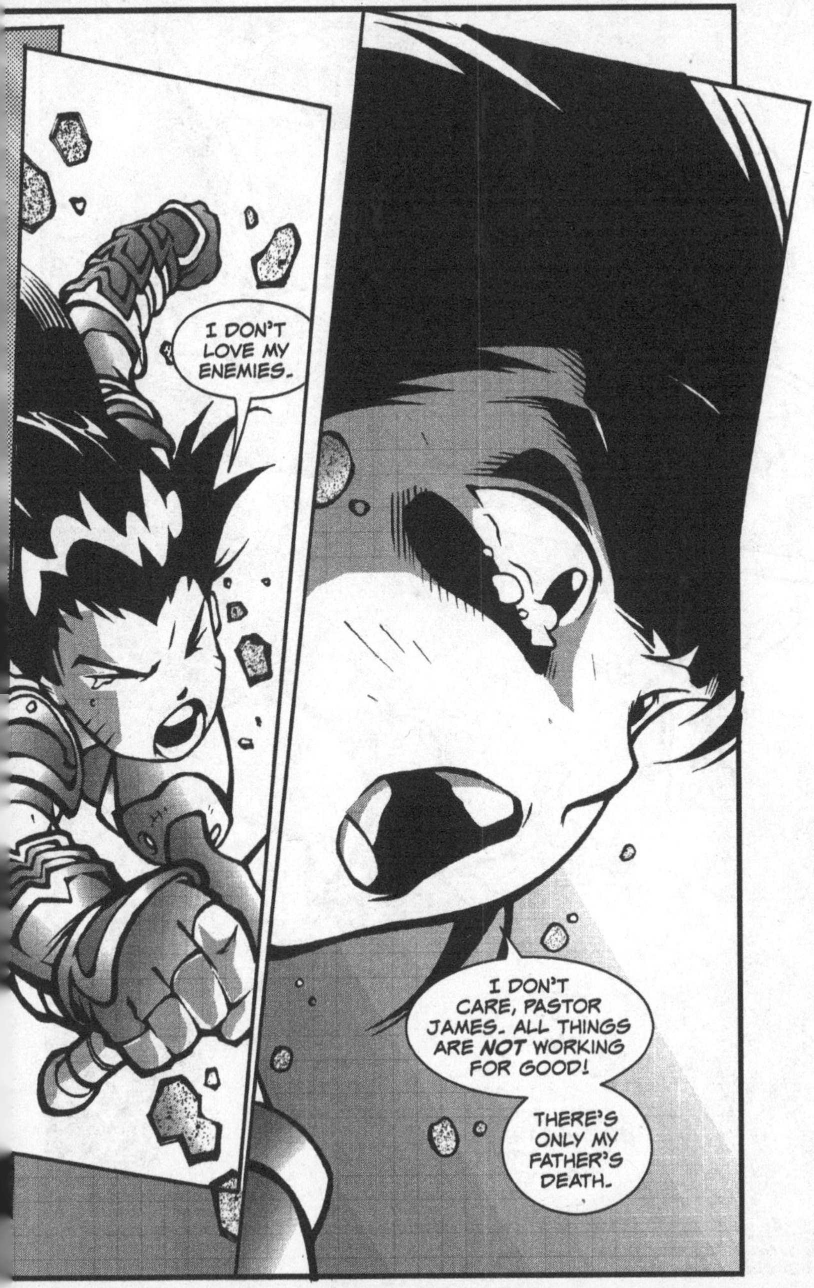
I DON'T LOVE MY ENEMIES...
I DON'T CARE, PASTOR JAMES... ALL THINGS ARE *NOT* WORKING FOR GOOD!
THERE'S ONLY MY FATHER'S DEATH...

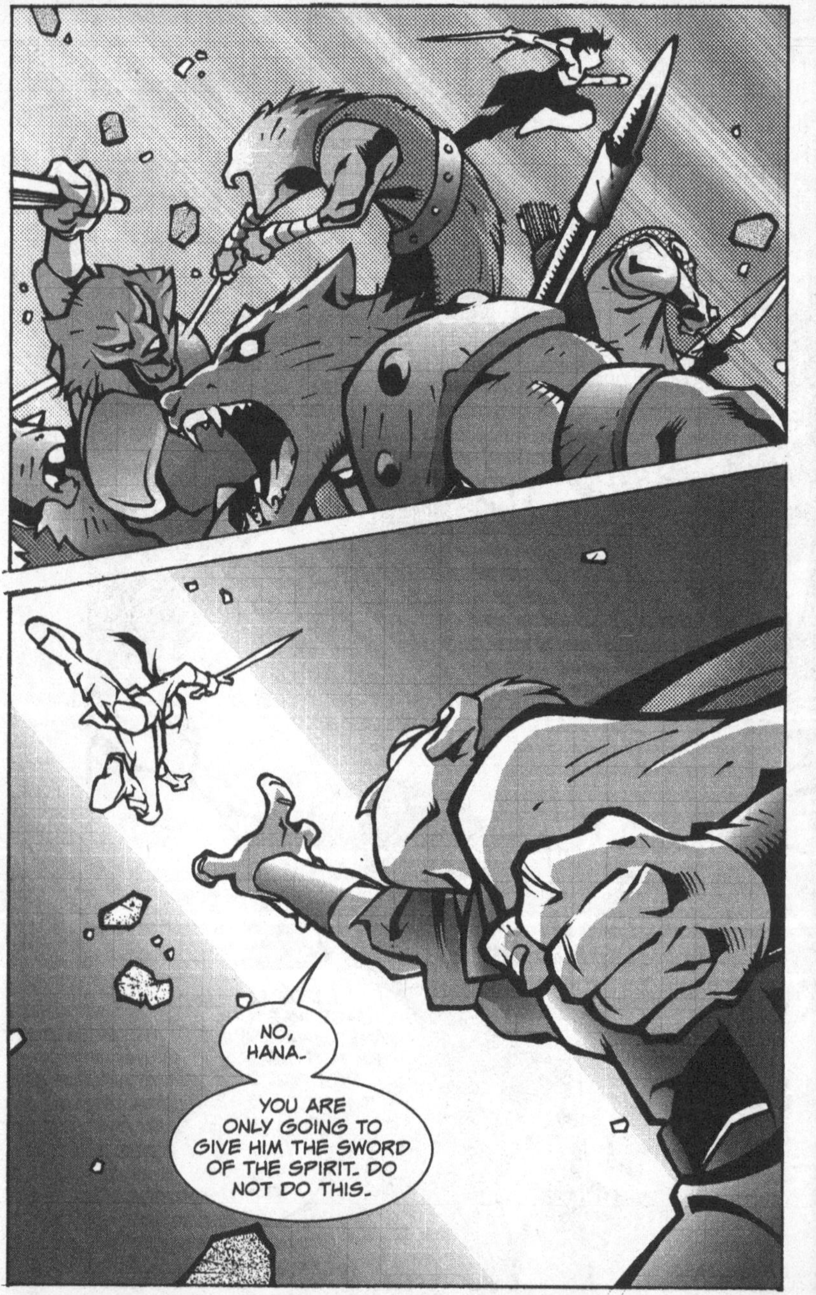
NO, HANA.
YOU ARE ONLY GOING TO GIVE HIM THE SWORD OF THE SPIRIT. DO NOT DO THIS.

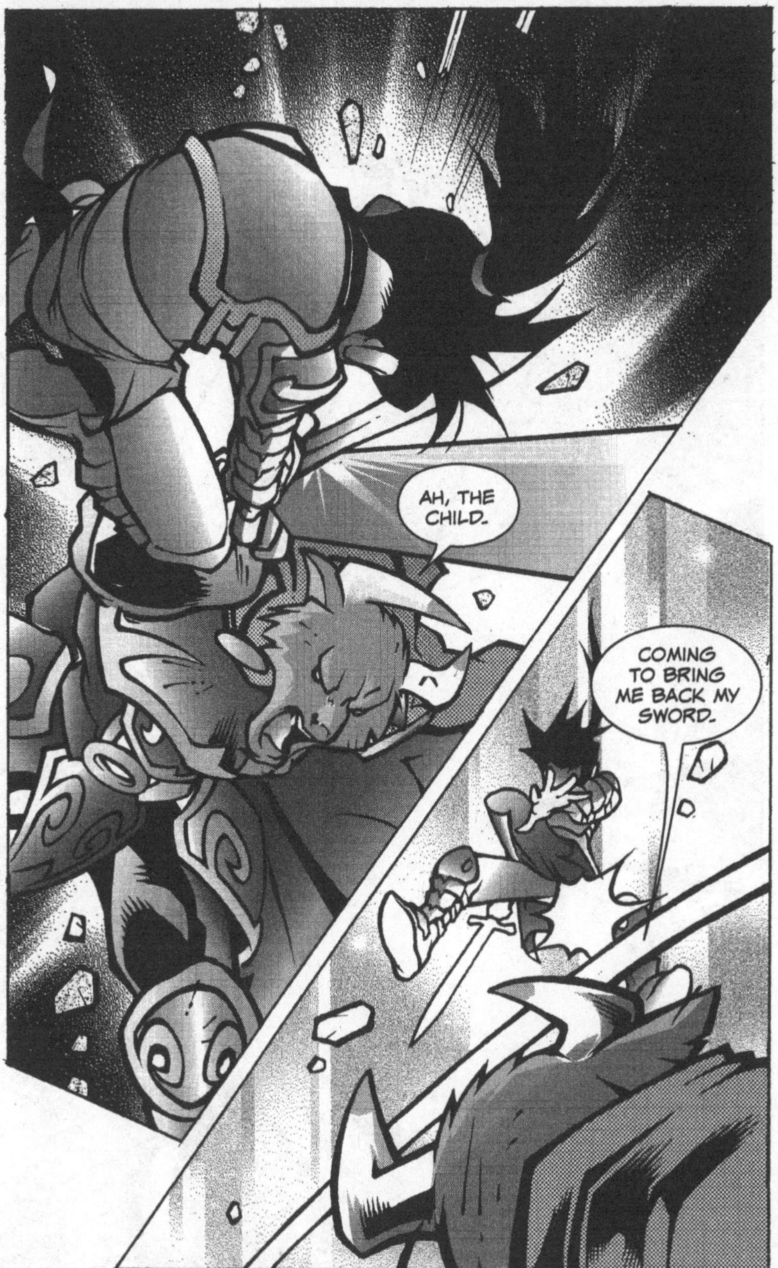
AH, THE CHILD.
COMING TO BRING ME BACK MY SWORD.

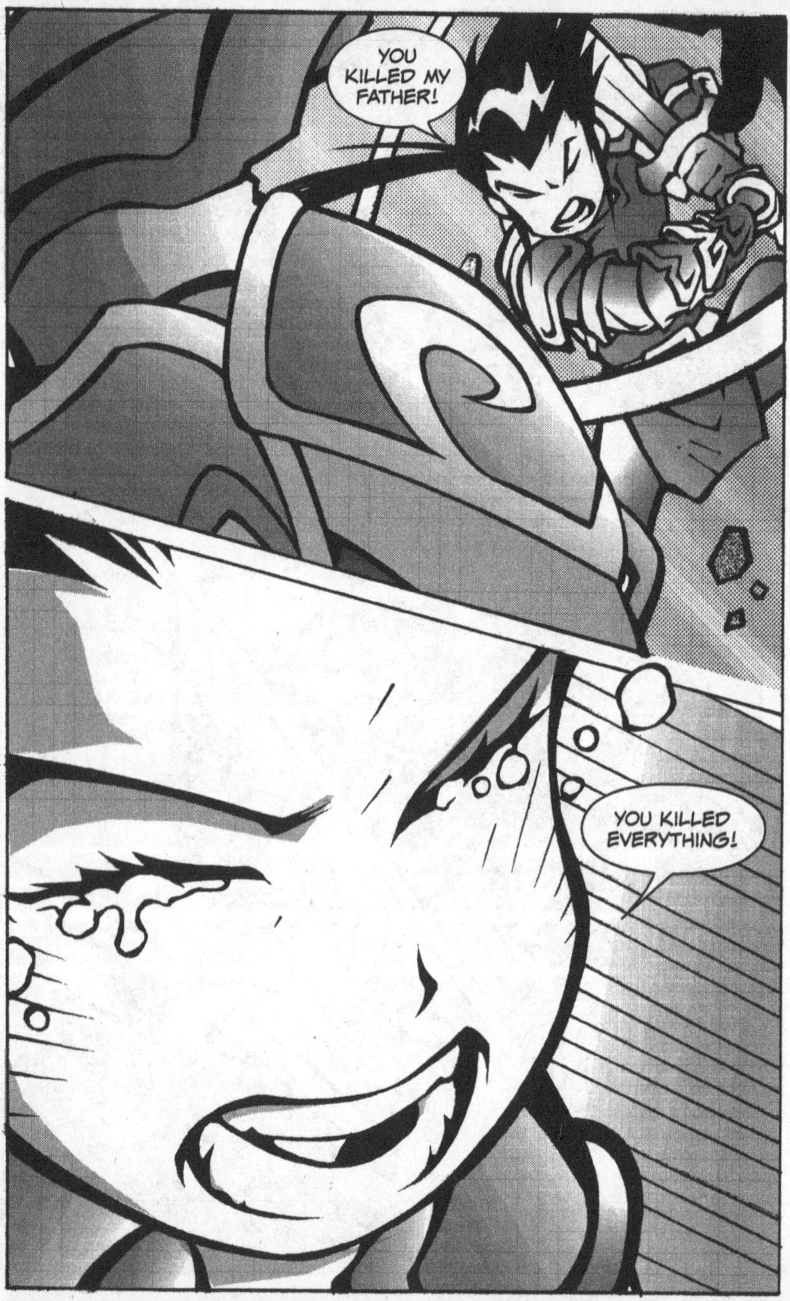
YOU KILLED MY FATHER!
YOU KILLED EVERYTHING!

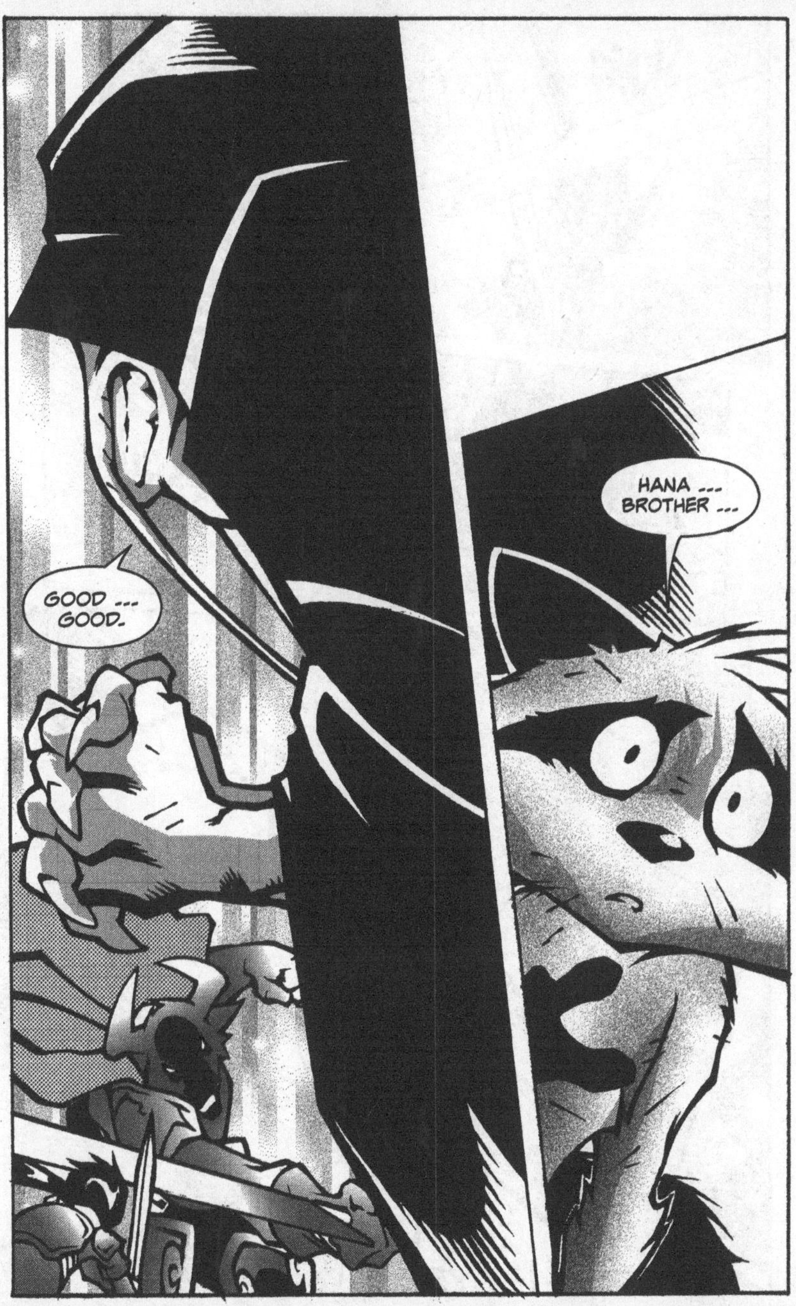
HANA ...
BROTHER ...
GOOD ...
GOOD.

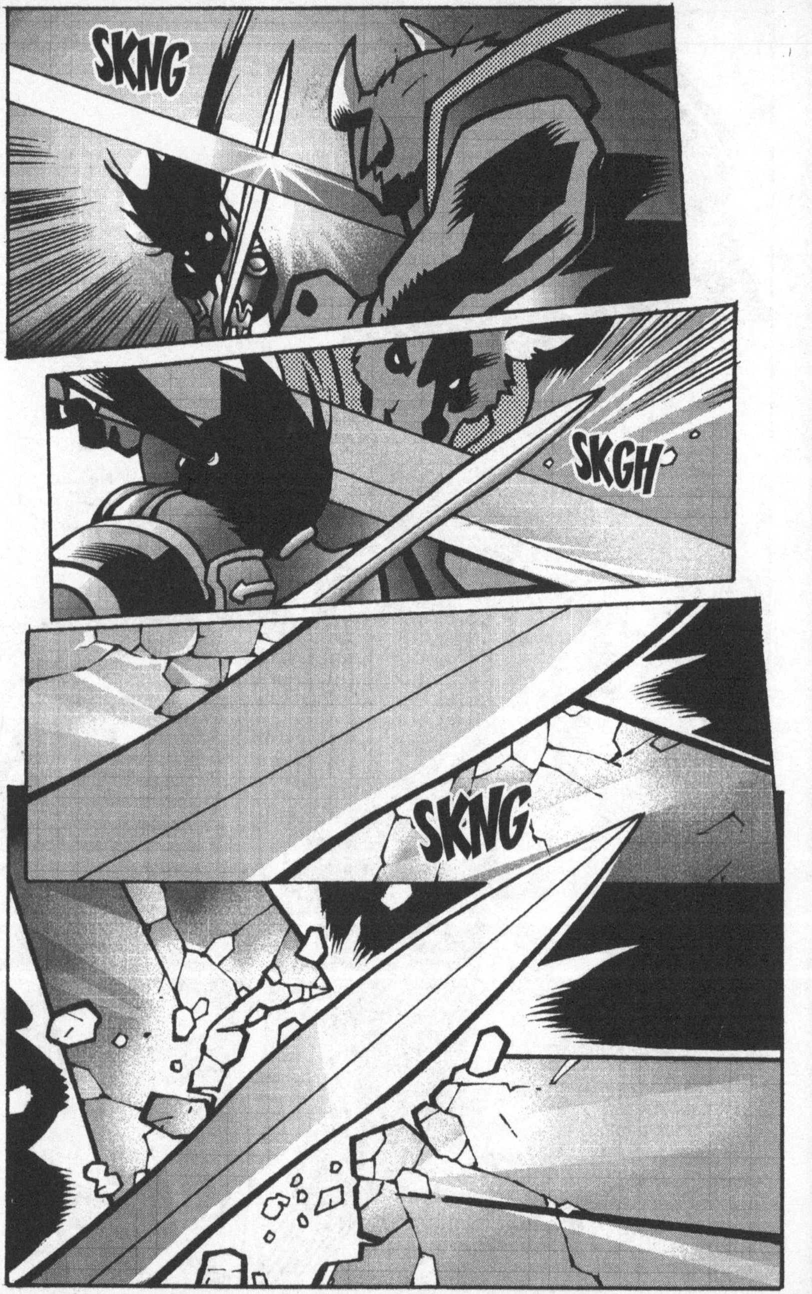
SKNG
SKGH
SKNG

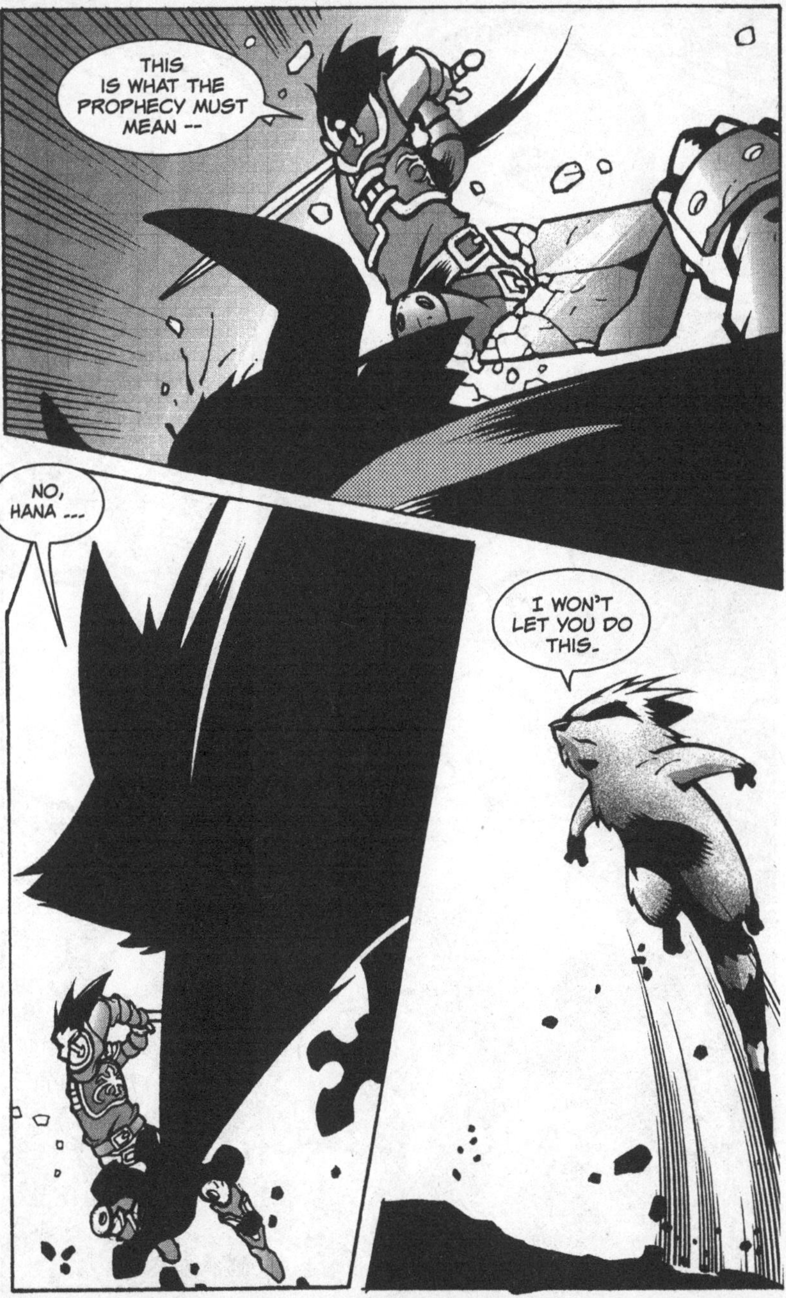
THIS IS WHAT THE PROPHECY MUST MEAN --
NO, HANA ...
I WON'T LET YOU DO THIS.

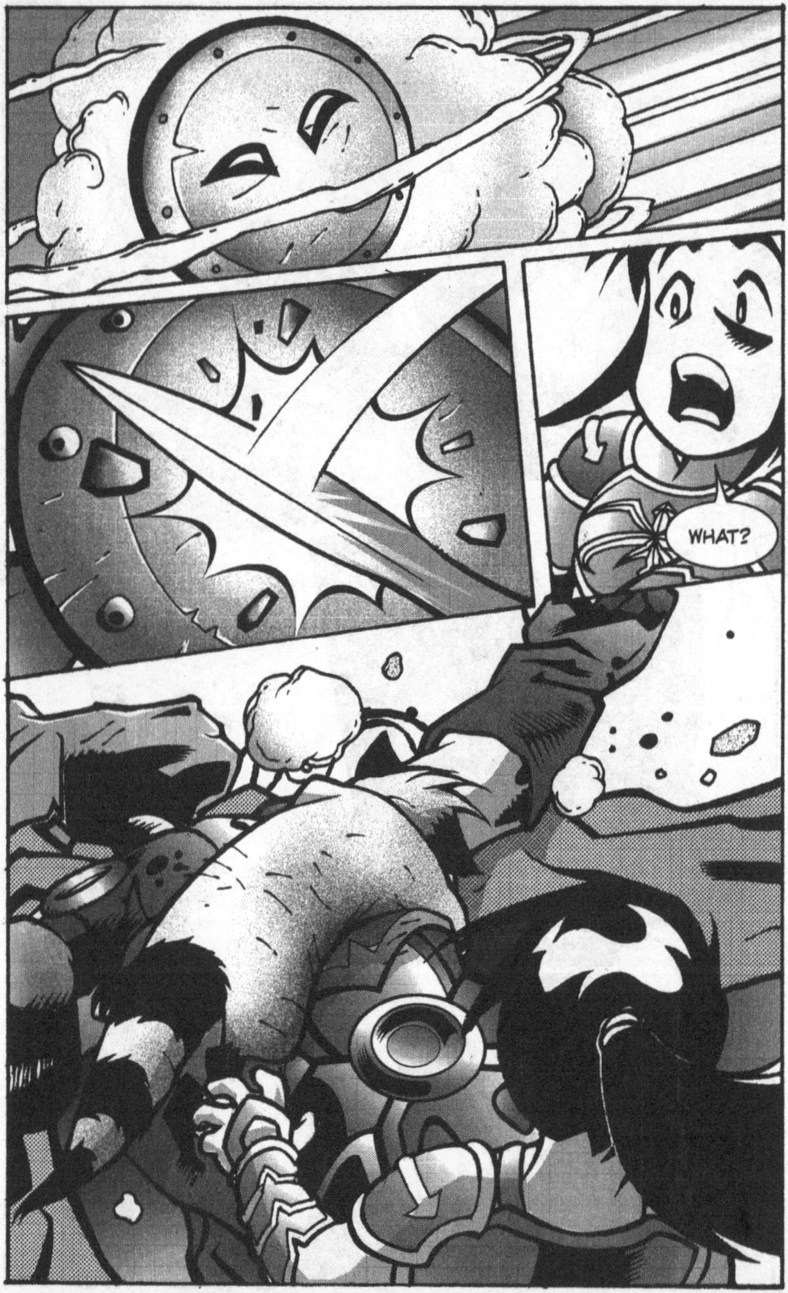
WHAT?

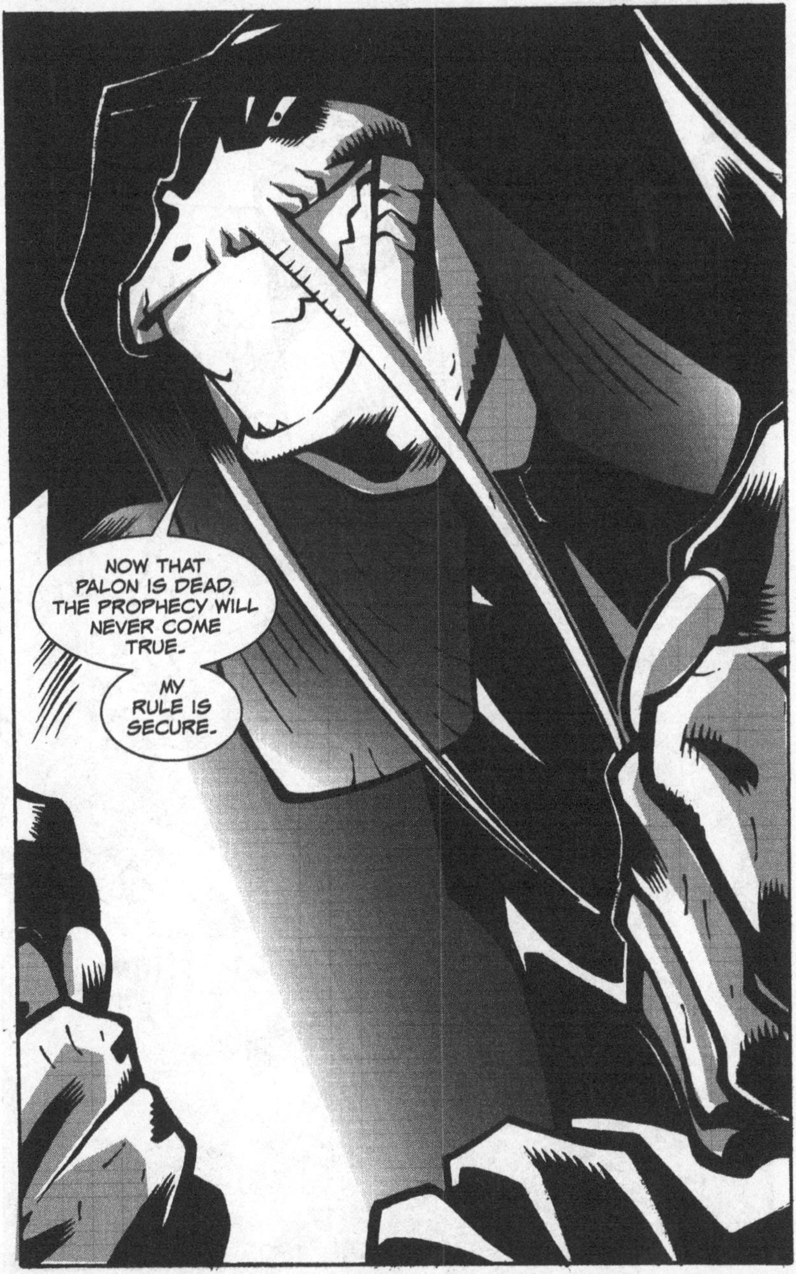
NOW THAT PALON IS DEAD, THE PROPHECY WILL NEVER COME TRUE.
MY RULE IS SECURE.

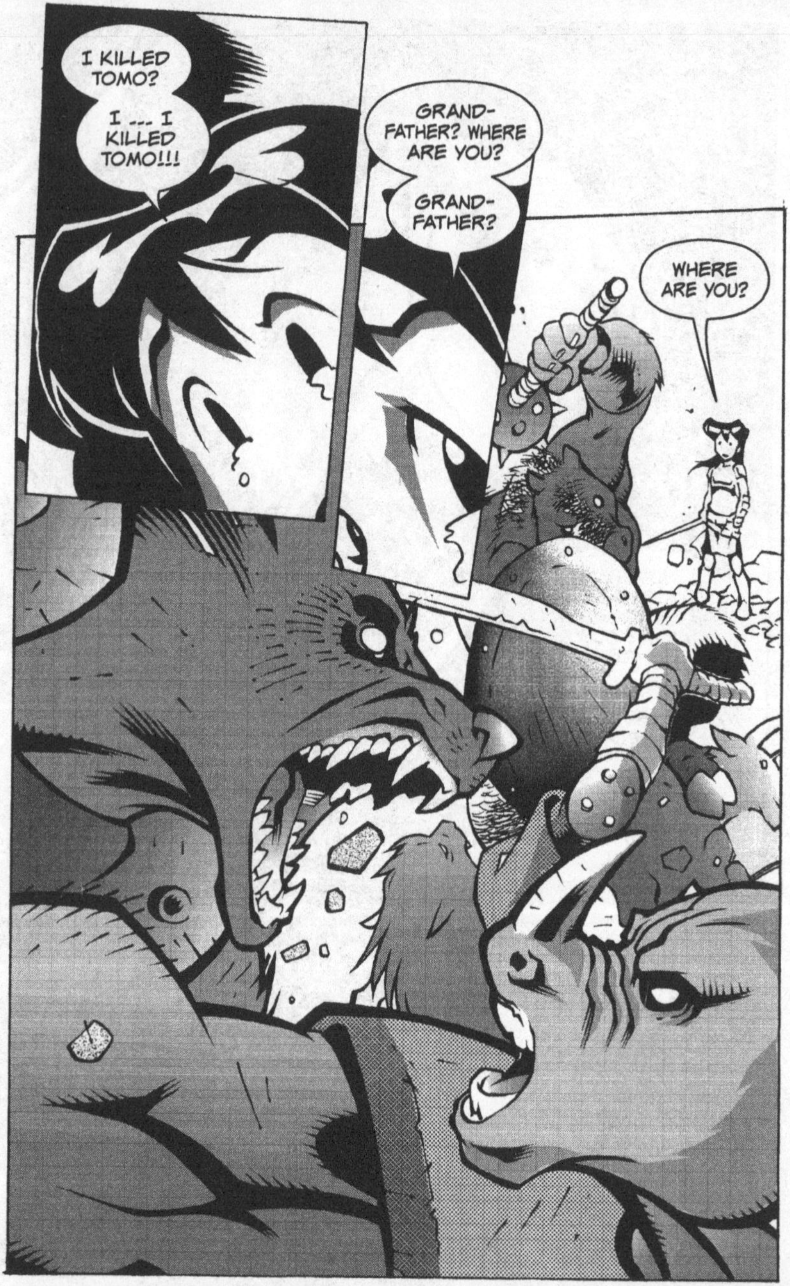
I KILLED TOMO?
I --- I KILLED TOMO!!!
GRAND-FATHER? WHERE ARE YOU?
GRAND-FATHER?
WHERE ARE YOU?

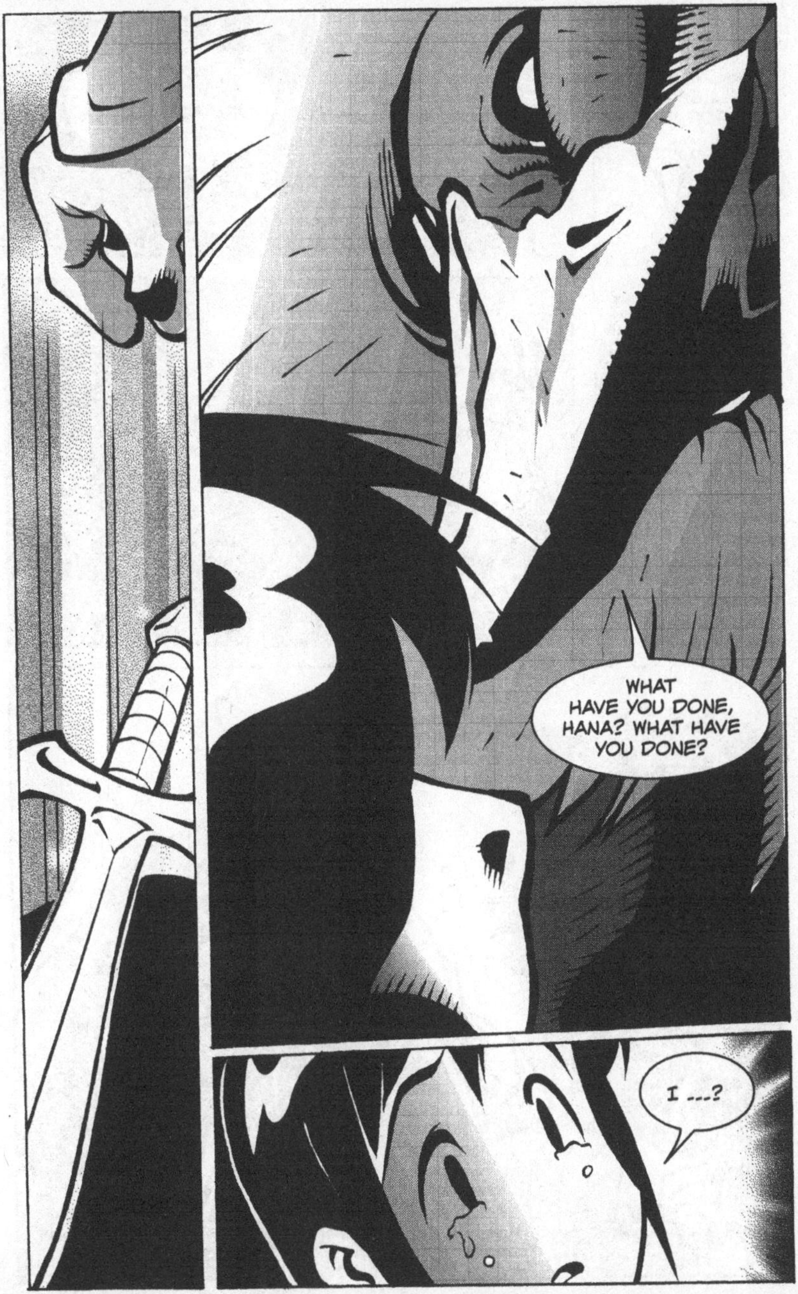
WHAT HAVE YOU DONE, HANA? WHAT HAVE YOU DONE?
I ---?

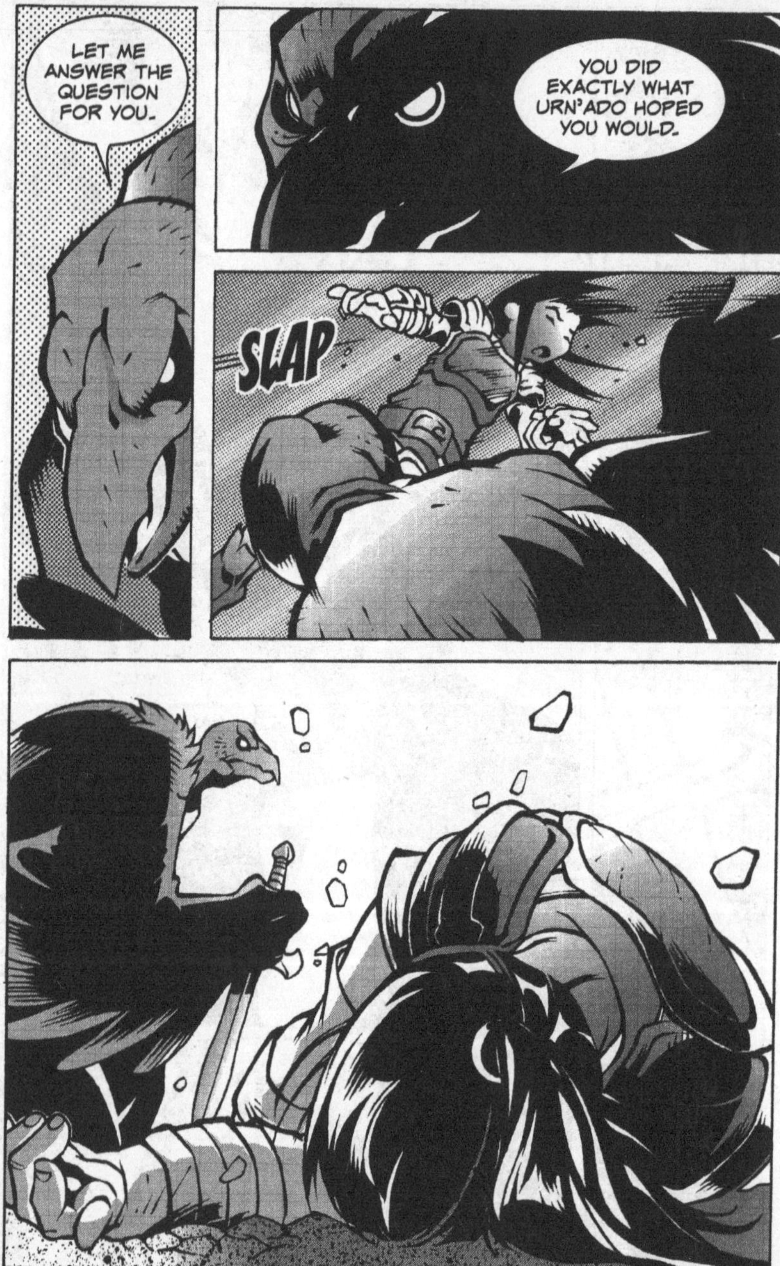
LET ME ANSWER THE QUESTION FOR YOU.
YOU DID EXACTLY WHAT URN'ADO HOPED YOU WOULD.
SLAP

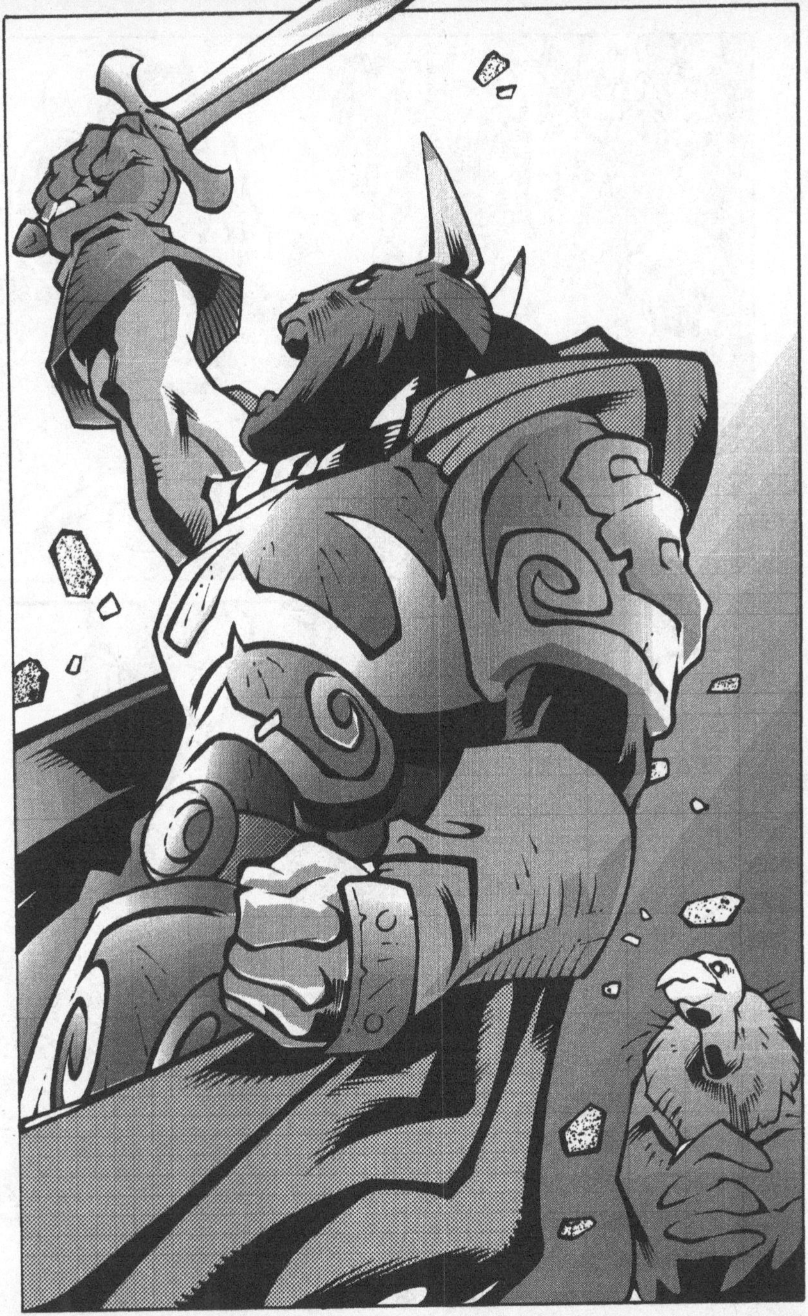

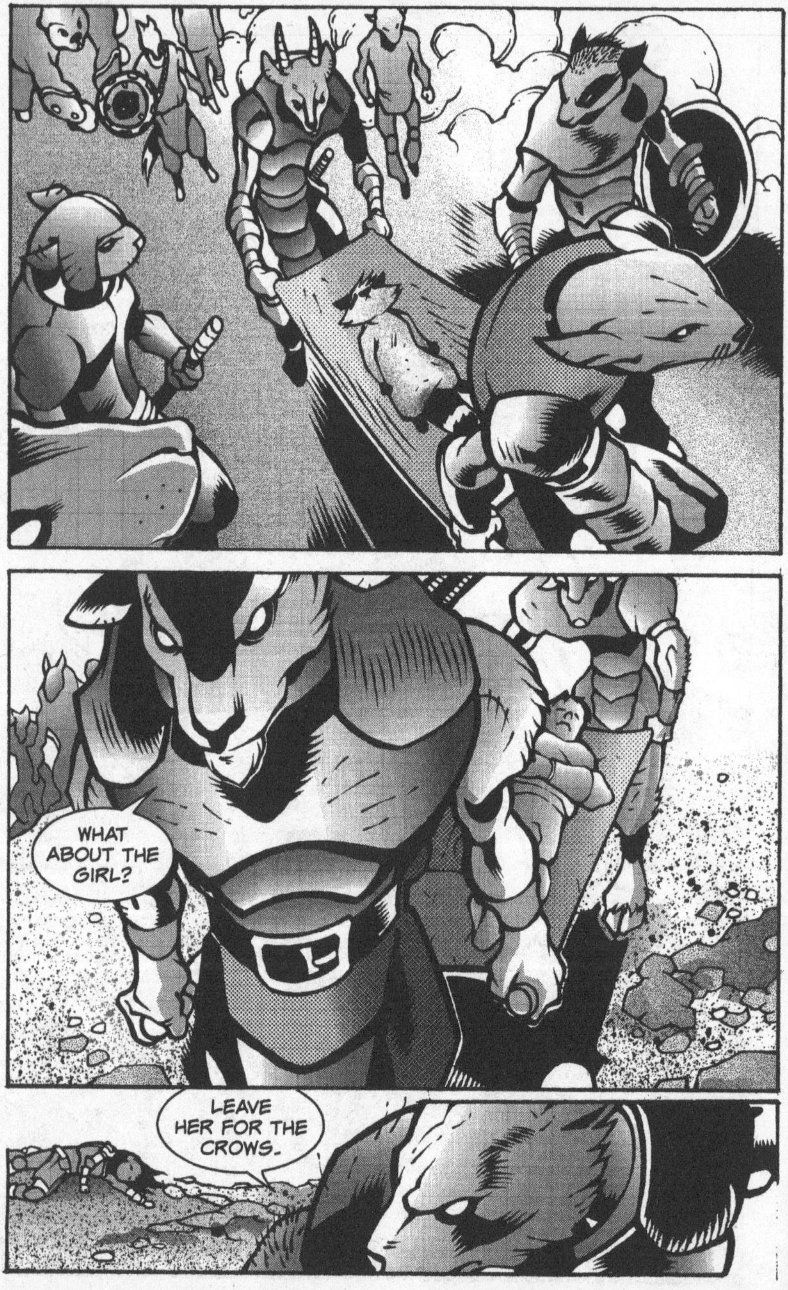
WHAT ABOUT THE GIRL?
LEAVE HER FOR THE CROWS.

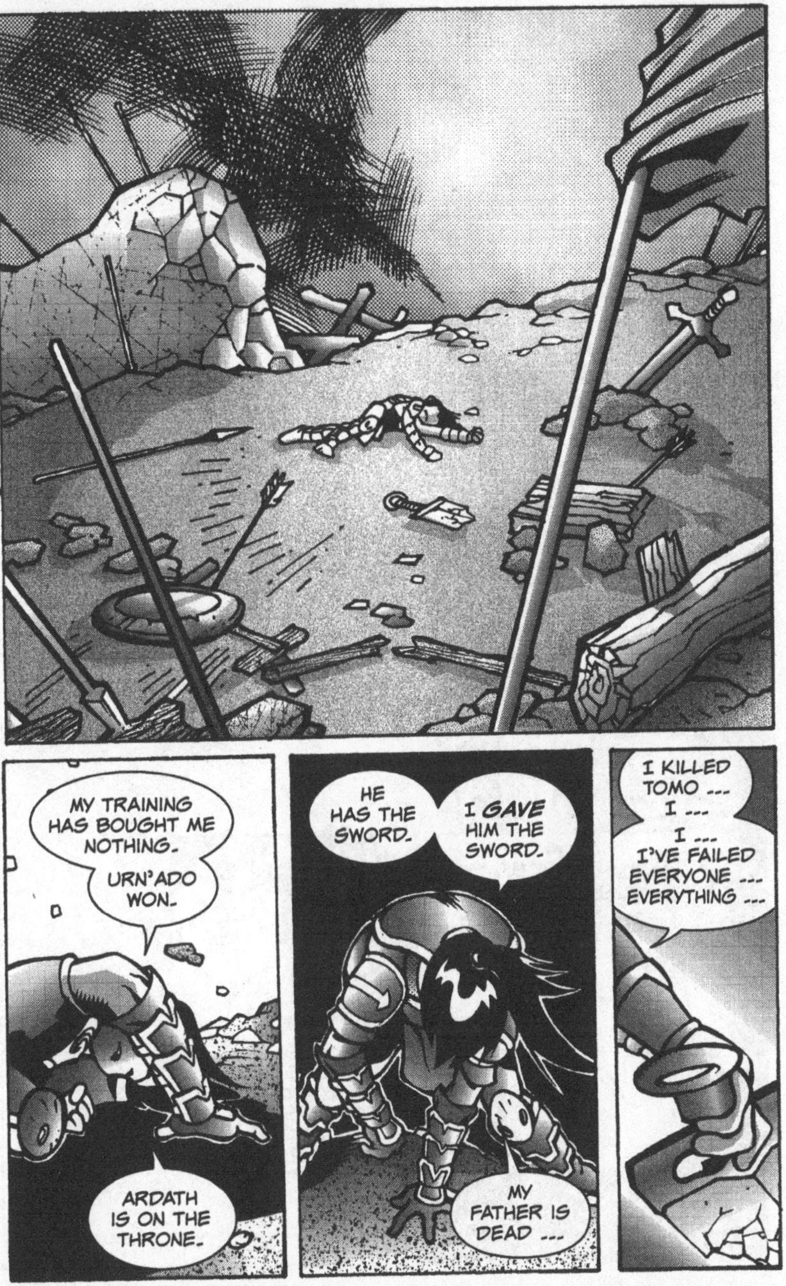
MY TRAINING HAS BOUGHT ME NOTHING.
URN'ADO WON.
ARDATH IS ON THE THRONE.
HE HAS THE SWORD.
I GAVE HIM THE SWORD.
MY FATHER IS DEAD ...
I KILLED TOMO ... I ...
I ... I'VE FAILED EVERYONE ... EVERYTHING ...

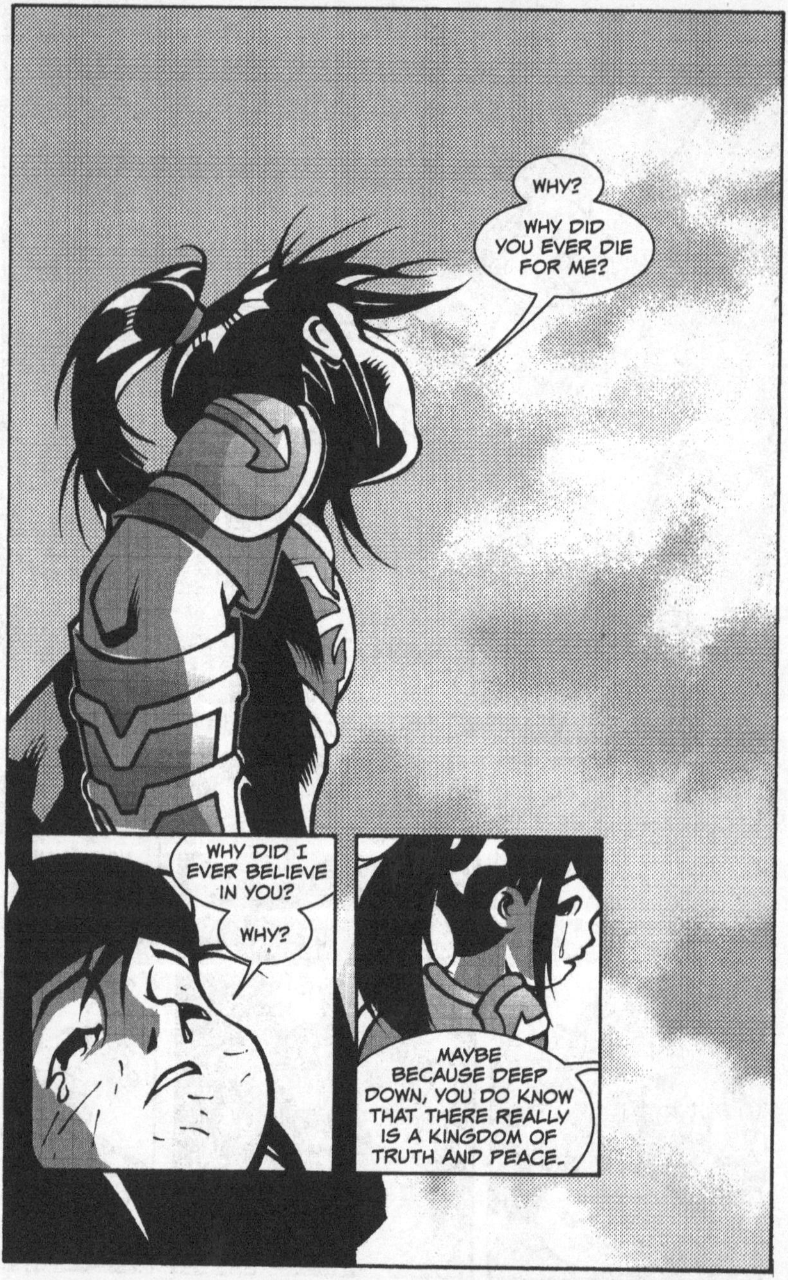
WHY?
WHY DID YOU EVER DIE FOR ME?
WHY DID I EVER BELIEVE IN YOU?
WHY?
MAYBE BECAUSE DEEP DOWN, YOU DO KNOW THAT THERE REALLY IS A KINGDOM OF TRUTH AND PEACE.

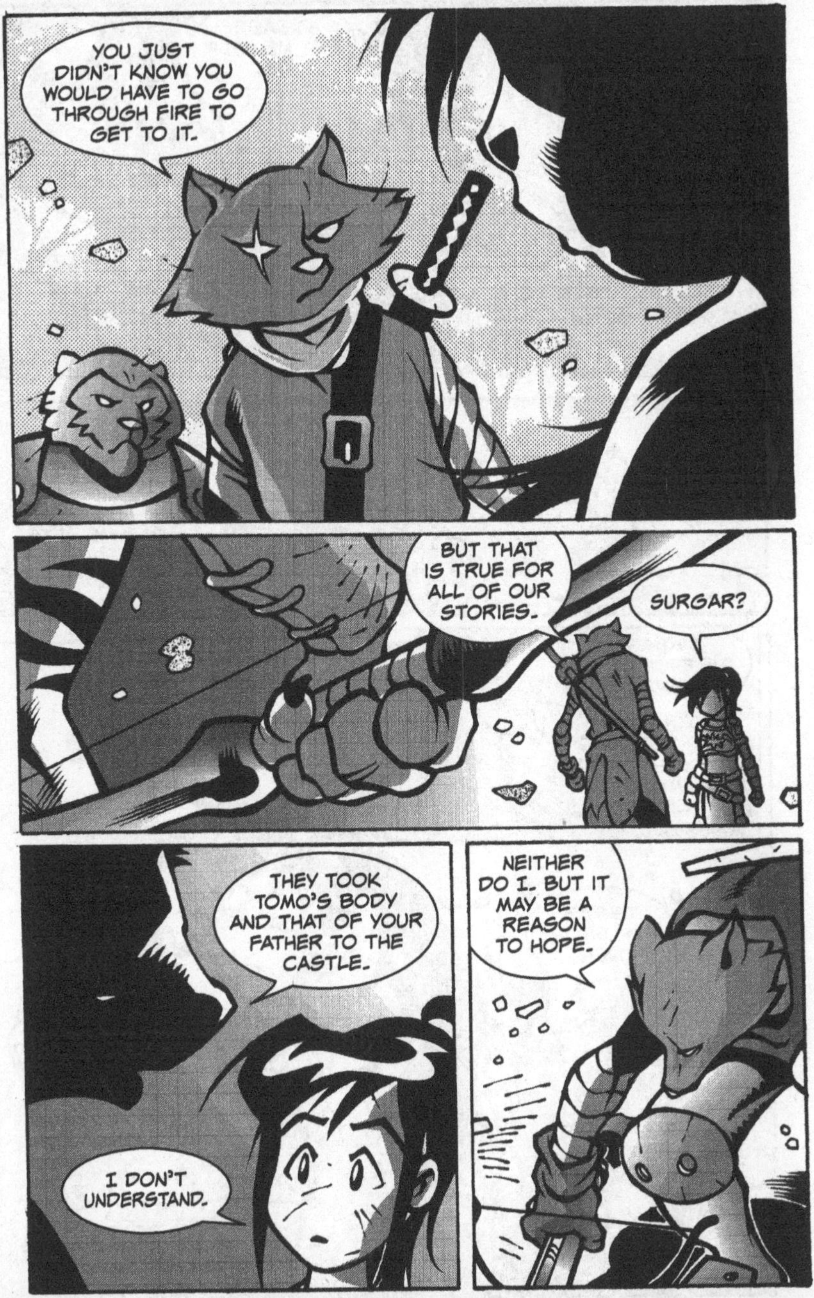
YOU JUST DIDN'T KNOW YOU WOULD HAVE TO GO THROUGH FIRE TO GET TO IT.
BUT THAT IS TRUE FOR ALL OF OUR STORIES.
SURGAR?
THEY TOOK TOMO'S BODY AND THAT OF YOUR FATHER TO THE CASTLE.
I DON'T UNDERSTAND.
NEITHER DO I. BUT IT MAY BE A REASON TO HOPE.

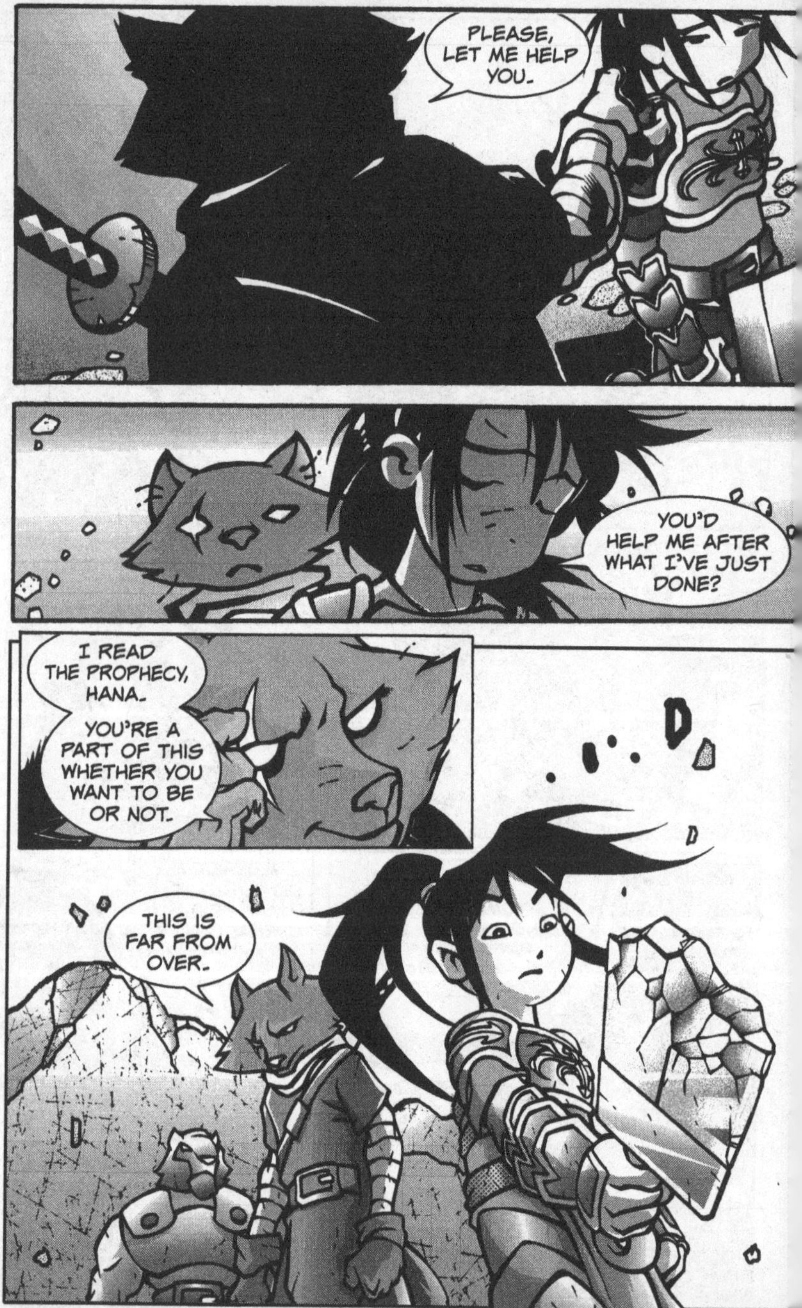
PLEASE, LET ME HELP YOU.
YOU'D HELP ME AFTER WHAT I'VE JUST DONE?
I READ THE PROPHECY, HANA.
YOU'RE A PART OF THIS WHETHER YOU WANT TO BE OR NOT.
THIS IS FAR FROM OVER.

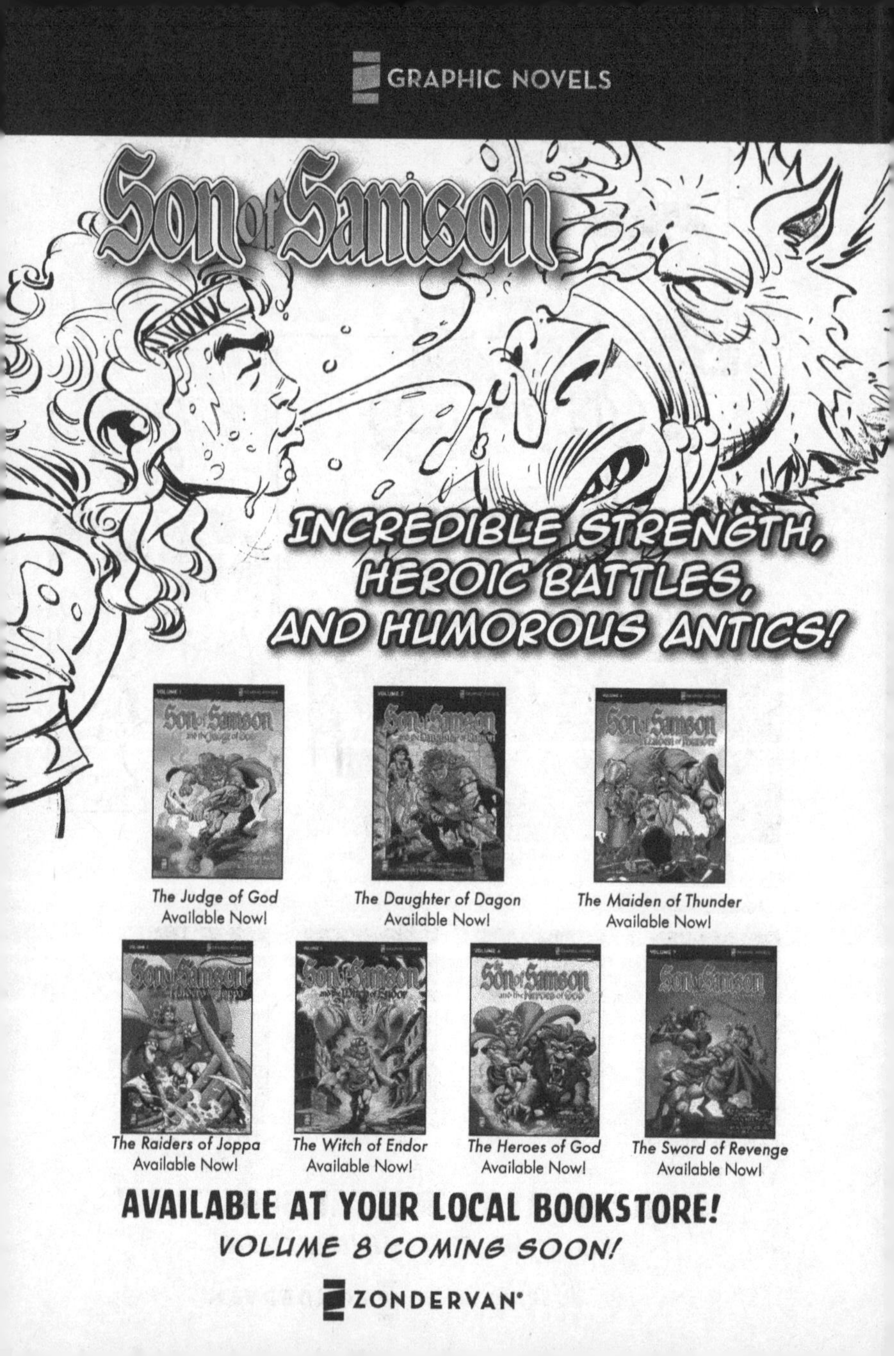
GRAPHIC NOVELS
Son of Samson
INCREDIBLE STRENGTH, HEROIC BATTLES, AND HUMOROUS ANTICS!
The Judge of God
Available Now!
The Daughter of Dagon
Available Now!
The Maiden of Thunder
Available Now!
The Raiders of Joppa
Available Now!
The Witch of Endor
Available Now!
The Heroes of God
Available Now!
The Sword of Revenge
Available Now!
AVAILABLE AT YOUR LOCAL BOOKSTORE!
VOLUME 8 COMING SOON!
ZONDERVAN®

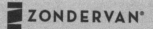